IN THE HEART OF TEXAS

The sheriff sighed with awe. "You know Texans say that on the eighth day, God created Texas, and that was the best of his work."

Lark laughed. "That might be sacrilegious."

"You wouldn't get a Texan to think that." He seemed so earnest and sincere as he looked down at her. They were standing close, too close. For a long moment, they looked into each other's eyes, and she felt his big hands tighten gently on her arms. She had the feeling that he was going to kiss her, and she wanted him to. She stood on her tiptoes and turned her face up to him, closing her eyes.

She heard him take a deep breath, then he cleared his throat and stepped away from her. She blinked and opened her eyes. He looked uncertain. "I wouldn't want you to get the wrong impression of me, ma'am. I ain't one to be forward with a lady."

Damn him, he was a perfect gentleman. Too bad at this moment he wasn't more like his rascal brother. She had a terrible need to be gathered into his strong embrace and kissed and kissed some more. . . .

GEORGINA GENTRY

To Tease A Texan

ZEBRA BOOKS
Kensington Publishing Corp.
www.kensingtonbooks.com

*This story is dedicated
with warmth and affection
to the true Texans among you,
the wannabe Texans,
and in memory of my Texas grandmother,
Sarah Jane Crooks Rushing.*

Chapter One

Last Chance Saloon, Oklahoma Territory
Early April 1890

They were cheating the cowboy at the poker table tonight. *He must be blind or very drunk not to see Snake Hudson dealing from the bottom.* Lark felt almost naked in her skimpy sky blue dress as she paused by the table, tray in hand. Dixie, one of the other saloon girls, stood behind the cowboy, and she was giving slight signals as she watched the cowboy's hand and nodded to her latest lover, Snake.

Lark hesitated. It wasn't really any of her business. After all, the big, black-haired cowboy was a grown man, and she needed this job.

"Hey you, girlie," Snake snarled. "You ever gonna serve them drinks afore we all die of thirst?"

"Right away." Lark began serving drinks around the table as the big cowboy grinned at her a little cross-eyed.

"Left-handed," he drawled, "just like me."

"I'm a Texan, too," she said. His accent told her he was a Texan. Land's sake, he was a grown man and ought to know better than to sit down at a poker table with a crooked bunch like this.

Snake sipped his whiskey and rubbed the whiplike scar on his forehead. Then he smirked. "Full house. Sorry, cowboy, reckon you lose again." He reached out and began to rake in the pot. "How 'bout another hand, Larado? You might be luckier this time."

Lark continued to serve around the table. The noise and the smoke made her head ache, along with the off-key music.

"Dunno, Snake," Larado said, chewing his lip. "You 'bout cleaned me out."

"Just one more hand," Snake urged. "Maybe this hand will win everything back."

The cowboy hesitated and Lark held her breath. "All I got left is my horse and saddle and my gold watch, and I set a heap of store by it." He pulled the watch out of his leather vest and stared at it as if trying to make a choice.

"Take a chance," Snake urged.

"Yeah, take a chance, cowboy," Dixie urged. She smiled with lips as bright red as her dress, the cigar smoke swirling around her blond hair.

He hesitated again. "Don't know if I ought to." He squinted thoughtfully at the gold pocket watch, his face furrowed in concentration.

Oh, no, I can't let him lose that too. Without giving it a second thought, Lark dropped a glass of beer in the cowboy's lap. "Oh, I'm so sorry!"

He stumbled to his feet, wiping at his pants. "Reckon I'm through for the night, then." He stuck the gold watch back in his pocket and left, weaving in a crooked line toward the swinging doors.

"Damn it," Snake roared, "I oughta get you fired for that, girlie."

"I—it was an accident." Lark put down her tray and followed the staggering cowboy out onto the wooden sidewalk. The night air was fresh and cool but noisy. In this wide-open town, there were a dozen saloons in a two-block area and not much else. Pianos blared a mix of Stephen Foster songs. Drunken trail hands galloped up and down the dirt street, shooting into the air and shouting.

The cowboy staggered down the sidewalk, whistling: *. . . as I walked out on the streets of Laredo, as I walked out in Laredo one day, I spied a young cowboy all wrapped in white linen, all wrapped in white linen and cold as the clay . . . .*

Her blue dress felt thin and skimpy. She wrapped her arms around herself to keep from shivering. "Hey, you!" she yelled at the tall Texan. "You need to stay out of places like the Last Chance."

"Well, now, sweetie"—he stopped, turned, and grinned down at her, a charming, crooked grin—"I reckon if you're gonna pour beer on me every time I come in, maybe I'd better."

"I was trying to keep you out of trouble."

He leaned against a porch railing and hiccoughed. "I reckon I can handle my own self, sweetie." He reached out and slapped her familiarly across the bottom.

"Don't do that. And don't call me 'sweetie,' you saddle tramp!"

"Okay, I'm agreeable. You got a name? I reckon we ain't howdied yet. I'm Larado."

"Larado what?"

"Sweetie"—he grinned, pushing his Stetson back—"since you're a Texan, you should know it ain't polite to ask a stranger too many questions. What's your handle?"

"I'm Lark, er, Lark Smith." She held out her hand awkwardly. Since she was a runaway, it wouldn't be too smart to give him her full name.

"Well, Lark, sweetie"—his big hand engulfed hers and he hung on—"I like tall, pretty brunettes. Any more like you at home?"

"I'm a mirror twin," she said before she thought.

"A what?"

"You know, I've got a dimple on the left side, she's got one on the right. I'm left-handed—"

"She's right-handed. Now I get it." He nodded. "Well, how about let's goin' up to your room?"

"I only wait tables here, nothing else." She tried to pull out of his grasp and kept her tone cold.

He swayed a little on his feet, and she could smell the whiskey. "I got no money anyway. Maybe you'd take a gold watch?"

"You want to get another beer poured on you?" She jerked out of his hand. "Now, go sleep it off somewhere."

"I reckon maybe I have had a little too much red-eye."

"A little?" She snorted. "Why, I'll bet you couldn't hit the ground with your hat in three tries. You had to be blind not to see the marked cards in that game."

He stumbled and sat down heavily on the edge of the wooden sidewalk. "Now, that Snake fella seemed like a right friendly *hombre.*"

Lark snorted again. "Why, he'd steal the butter off a sick beggar's biscuit. Cowboy, you'd better report back to your outfit and stay out of dives like this one."

He shook his head and rolled a cigarette with unsteady hands, looking up at her. "Came up with a trail herd a few days ago, but now they're sold, and I ain't found another job. Thought I might win enough to ship me and my horse back to Texas."

"Land's sake, partner," she warned, "you won't ever win playing at the Last Chance. I've only worked here a few months but I spotted the cardsharps right off."

He smoked with unsteady hands and seemed to be thinking it over. "Maybe I should go back in there and demand my money."

She shook her head. "I wouldn't do that if I were you. You don't know how tough the boys in the Last Chance can be."

"I can handle myself, sweetie." He tried to stand up, stumbled, reached out and caught her arm to steady himself. He was a big one, all right, taller even than her uncle

Trace or her cousin Ace. He stood swaying and staring down at her, and she was tall for a woman. "You cold?"

"Of course I am!" she snapped and pulled away from him. "This skimpy outfit they make me wear hasn't got enough fabric to cover a broom handle."

"Looks good to me." He grinned at her.

"Get out of here and go sleep it off," she snapped. "Now I got to go, they're yelling for me inside."

"Lark," he murmured, "can you sing?"

"Not very well. Now vamoose, *pronto*. Maybe tomorrow, you can get on with some outfit."

He shook his head. "Done tried. Nobody around here needs a wanderin' saddle tramp. Reckon I'll go back to Texas."

"Good idea. And a word of advice. Stay away from poker tables when you're blind drunk." She turned and went back into the saloon.

Larado squinted in the darkness and looked after her. He was drunk all right, but not as drunk as she thought. She was purty, a tall dark-haired girl in a gaudy blue dress. Like him, she looked like she had some Injun blood. His manhood stirred as he remembered the feel of her and the scent of her perfume. What the hell was he thinking? Girls like that one came high, and he hadn't a nickel to his name. He'd have to sleep out on the prairie tonight with his horse, and maybe tomorrow his luck would change. His pants were wet with beer and he was getting cold in the night wind. He pulled his coat collar up around his ears and stumbled away.

Lark scurried back into the smoky, noisy saloon. Joe, the short owner, stood scowling by the poker table with a cigar between his teeth. "Lark, where the hell you been?"

"Uh, just out."

"Snake here tells me you caused him to lose a sucker he was about to finish off."

"I accidentally spilled a drink in the cowboy's lap." She needed this job.

"Aww, don't believe her," said the blond whore Dixie, perching her rear on the poker table. "That was a pretty good gold watch. Besides, that broke up the whole game."

"Lark," Joe said, "you're a lousy waitress. Any more trouble outta you and you're fired."

"But, Joe—"

"You heard me." He walked away from the table.

Lark looked helplessly at the crowd around the poker table.

Snake frowned and shrugged. "You heard him. Next time I got a sucker on the hook, stay out of it. Now, Dixie, get that talented fanny of yours off the table."

The men all laughed. Dixie laughed too and started to saunter away. Lark caught up with her. "You were helping Snake cheat that cowboy."

"So what?" Dixie sneered. "Besides, that Texan's a grown man. He must have been blind not to see Snake dealin' them cards off the bottom. Anyway, what business is it of yours?"

Lark caught her arm. "I ought to slap you, Dixie."

"You do, and I'll pull out some of them beautiful black curls. Did I ever tell you I once got into a fight with your sister?"

Everything else was forgotten. "You know my sister?"

"Yeah."

"I don't think I believe you."

"Don't give a damn whether you do or not. Her name's Lacey and she's prissy and straitlaced. She wouldn't be caught dead workin' in a saloon."

That was her twin, all right. "Where'd—?"

"I don't wanta talk to you no more," Dixie drawled and started to saunter away, the red satin on her hips swaying as she walked.

"Dixie, tell me where you saw her." Lark ran after her and caught her arm.

"Let go of me, you bitch." Dixie swung at her and Lark stepped away, but Dixie came at her again. Lark was a Texas girl, and she could give as good as she got. She buried her fingers in the whore's bleached hair and gave it a good yank.

Dixie howled like a stepped-on cat and came at her, scratching and shrieking.

"You Southern-fried tramp!" Lark said, and they went down in a mix of short skirts, lace underwear, and tangled long legs.

"Fight! Fight!" The shout went through the crowded saloon and all the men came running to watch. The only thing a bunch of cowboys liked better than a good fistfight was two girls going at it.

Lark wasn't going to let the slut get away with this. She forgot she needed a job, she forgot everything but slapping Dixie silly. They crashed first into the piano, sending the player falling to the floor, then into a pool table, sending cowboys scrambling. Now other girls and male customers gathered around to watch the latest entertainment in the crowded saloon.

Nate, the big bartender, came running. "All right, break it up, you'll have the boss out here." He tried to pull the girls apart, but Lark poked him in the eye as she drew back on Dixie again. Oh, her sister Lacey would be mortified if she could see her tomboy sister in such an unladylike battle—but then, her twin was always so correct and Lark could never do anything right.

"Here comes the boss!" Someone yelled a warning, but Lark was on top, yanking the tart's yellow hair.

Joe strode up, grabbed both girls by the arms, and hauled them to their feet. "What's goin' on out here?"

"She started it," Dixie wailed.

"I was just giving as good as I got!"

"She was, too," the crowd assured him.

Joe took the cigar out of his mouth and frowned. "Lark, damn it, I warned you."

"I know you did, but I'm a Texan and that poor Texas cowboy was being cheated—"

"So what?" Joe shrugged. "If he ain't a big boy, he don't belong in a tough town like Buck Shot."

"But he was almost broke," Lark protested.

He looked at her and sighed as if speaking to a small child. "That's what we do here at the Last Chance, we take their money. Now, Texas, I warned you, so you're fired. Be out of here by morning." He turned on his heel and stalked back toward his office.

Land's sake, what had she done? Got herself fired over a drunken, penniless cowboy. Chin still high and defiant, Lark headed up to her cramped room to pack. What was she going to do now?

She'd gotten some satisfaction out of giving Dixie's yellow hair a good yank, but that wouldn't pay the bills. She could always wire home to Uncle Trace for money, but she was too proud to do that. Besides, Aunt Cimarron would come after her and take her back to the ranch. They had raised her ever since her parents had been killed and her rich grandfather had decided he couldn't deal with the twins. She'd just be on the run again as she had been for the last couple of years. She wondered where Dixie had run across Lacey. Last she had heard, Lacey was scheduled to marry that perfect paragon of virtue, Homer Something-or-other. By now, Lacey probably had a perfect baby while her twin made a mess of her life. Well, Lark would just drift on like she always did. It was easier than facing up to her own imperfections.

She sat down on her bed and listened to the music and laughter from downstairs. Where was she going to go now? Her prominent ranching family would be upset if they knew she was working in a saloon. Of course, ever since she'd dropped out of Miss Priddy's fancy academy in Boston while Lacey graduated with honors, they'd been upset with her. They said they weren't, but Lark knew better. If she ever did anything to make them proud, she'd contact them, but it was tough being the twin who always messed up.

She thought of the Texan. The nerve of him slapping her on the bottom so familiarly! And to think he'd wanted to buy a night in her bed with a gold watch. No man had ever bedded her, and a penniless, drunken cowpoke wasn't going to be the first. Oh my, what did she expect him to think? He wouldn't have believed the truth, that the niece of one of the biggest ranchers in Texas would be slinging drinks in a wild whiskey town along the border between Oklahoma and Indian Territories. The whiskey towns were the roughest in the West, existing to sell liquor and other brands of sin to the Indians and outlaws who hid out in Indian Territory, where whiskey was forbidden.

Lark blew out her lamp and went to bed with a defeated sigh. Tomorrow, she'd drift on. She was homesick but she couldn't go home. Lark was certain her relatives felt sorry for her because she couldn't seem to measure up. It was easier to run. As she drifted off to sleep, she wondered what had happened to the drunken cowboy. Damn him, he'd gotten her into a mess.

Larado stumbled out to a tree on a prairie where he'd left his horse and bedroll. "Hey, hoss, you doin' okay?" The bay stallion raised his head and nickered as Larado scratched his neck, then returned to grazing on the dried grass. "Maybe you are, but I ain't." Larado shivered in the raw wind, squinted, and looked back toward the long, muddy street of saloons. He could hear the off-key music and the laughter from here. Had the other man been cheating? Should he have called him out?

"Now, pard, that would have been a damn fool thing to do, and you know why," he muttered to himself as he spread his blankets and lay down. "You ain't that good a shot without . . . Well, you ain't no gunfighter."

It was a raw night for early April, and he shivered and pulled his blanket closer, thinking about the girl in the blue skimpy dress. She'd have been warm, all right, and he wished he had her in his blankets with him. What was her name? Lark. Like the bird. He remembered the feel of her as he'd pulled her toward him. He didn't have any money to spend on her, and she must have known it, but she'd come out anyway. He hadn't been nearly as drunk as she thought he was, it was only . . . Well, that didn't make no never mind.

Working at the Last Chance, she had to be experienced and really know how to please men. In his mind, he imagined pulling her close and feeling that curvy body all the way down his. Her legs under the short, skimpy blue dress had looked long enough to go all the way to her neck. "Oh, sweetie," he groaned, trying to get comfortable as his manhood stirred. "If I win a couple of hands next time, I'm gonna see how much you cost. The first night I spent a dollar on that Dixie, and she was okay, but I'll wager you're better."

Money. He was flat broke. The ranches around here all seemed to have plenty of cowboys. Larado had been trying to win enough to grubstake supplies to get back to Texas. Just what the hell was he gonna do now?

At daylight the next morning Larado sat before a small campfire, sipping the last of his little stash of coffee and nursing a hangover. He'd drift south now and maybe find a temporary job punching cattle somewhere where it was warm. What he really dreamed of was owning his own spread, but he couldn't see any way he could ever do that.

A sound. He turned his head and squinted. In the early dawn light, he wasn't sure for a moment who the rider was, then he recognized Snake.

"Kin I get down?" Snake yelled.

"Sure." Larado nodded. He had a bad headache from last night, and he felt as low-down as a rattlesnake's belly, but a Texan was always hospitable. He stood up. "Want some coffee?"

"You got an extra cup?"

He nodded, pouring the man a cup. Snake sat down on a rock, taking the tin cup in both hands.

"Damn, that hot coffee feels good on a cold morning." Snake took a sip and shuddered. "Don't you Texans make coffee any way but strong?"

Larado laughed. "If it won't float a horseshoe, we throw it out and make another pot." He studied the other man's ugly face with its jagged red scar on the forehead.

Snake touched the scar. "You're wondering how I got this, right?"

Larado felt his face burn. "Naw, I wasn't."

"I don't mind." The other man sipped his coffee. "Looks like a snake, don't it? A long time ago, I got into a whip fight with another fella. Since then, I've learned to use a pistol—safer for me."

Larado laughed but the other man didn't.

"Listen." Snake took another sip of coffee. "I felt bad about last night, realizin' you was pretty broke when you left the table."

"That happens when you play poker." Larado rolled a cigarette and shrugged. "I don't begrudge you the money."

"Maybe I could stake you a little," Snake offered. "I got something workin' and I might cut you in on it, being as how my last partner got kilt in a knife fight."

"Oh?" Larado felt a rush of warning. "I don't think—"

"Hear me out," Snake interrupted. "There's a fat bank in this town, almost as fat as the owner. You can't believe how much money goes in there from all these saloons."

"Uh-uh." Larado shook his head. "That dog won't hunt."

"Huh?"

"It's what Texans say when it's no-go. I ain't never done nothin' crooked much. I ain't hankerin' for no prison cell."

"You got any money to get back to Texas?"

"No. I'm flat busted except for my watch and my horse," Larado admitted as he stuck the smoke in his mouth and reached for a burning twig from the campfire.

"Look"—Snake leaned closer—"this bank would be a pushover. It just opened up and is bustin' with deposits. The sheriff's out of town, and it's too early for the bank to be open."

"Then how would you get in? You gonna blow it?" Larado asked.

Snake spat into the fire. "That'd draw too much attention. I been watchin' and I seen that fat little banker work on his books with his teller early in the mornin' before the bank opens."

Larado shook his head and blew smoke. "I ain't no robber, and I'd like to live a little longer."

"I never heard of no Texan being a coward," Snake said.

"When you say that, mister, you'd better smile. Our motto is 'Remember the Alamo.' Texans go down fightin'."

"I meant no offense." Snake tossed the last of his coffee in the fire where it sizzled and went up in steam. "You could just mosey in there with me and look around, see if you think it's doable."

"Do I look like my mama raised a fool?" Larado shook his head. "I ain't no bank robber, and to be mighty honest, I ain't too good with a gun."

"Hell, I am," Snake said. "I ain't askin' you to shoot somebody, just help me carry all those sacks of money out—they'd be mighty heavy."

"Mighty heavy," Larado repeated wistfully.

"Just come along with me and walk through the bank so I can look it over," Snake urged. "Maybe you can give me some leads on what I ought to do when I do get a partner. You seem like a smart *hombre.*"

Larado felt himself redden. "Don't have much book learnin', although my mama did teach me to read. I reckon I'm smart as the next fella, if only . . ."

"I reckon I know a smart *hombre* when I see one." Snake grinned, showing yellow teeth. "That's why I want your advice. It'd be worth a gold eagle to find out what you think."

Larado smoked and stared into the fire. A twenty dollar gold piece was a lot of money to a busted cowboy. "All I got to do is look over the bank and give you an opinion?"

The tough gunman nodded.

"Okay, here's my opinion," Larado said. "A man can get kilt robbin' banks. Don't do it."

"Hell, I take back my apology. I reckon what they say about Texans is true." Snake stood up slowly. "Folks say they're all gurgle and no guts."

Larado leaped up and grabbed him by the jacket sleeve. "You callin' me yellow?"

"Easy, cowboy, easy." Snake made a soothing gesture. "I wasn't askin' you to rob the bank, just help me look it over."

"I ain't seen the color of your money."

"Fair enough. You're a smart *hombre*, Larado." Snake nodded, reached into his coat, and tossed a coin.

Larado caught it and stared at it. "Ain't you afraid I'll take your money and skedaddle?"

"You strike me as a purty honest man," Snake said. "They say Texans got a sense of honor."

"Reckon that's true." Larado nodded. He didn't like the feel of this whole thing, but he needed the money—Lord, how he needed the money. Chico could use some oats, and he damned sure needed a new sack of Arbuckles', a hunk of bacon, and a little cornmeal to get back to the Lone Star State. "Well, I'll go along and look over this here bank, but I ain't gonna rob it with you."

"Sure, sure. Let's go now while it's still early and there's almost nobody on the street."

Larado put the gold coin in his vest, tossed his cigarette into the campfire, and stood. "I'll saddle up."

Snake followed him to saddle Chico. "I believe you're the most honest galoot I ever met. Anybody else would jump at the chance to cut himself in on a fat job like this."

"My mama would roll over in her grave if she thought she'd raised a son who would take another man's money," Larado said. "I don't know what she would say about just lookin' it over."

"Aww, that fat banker has plenty, and you know how bankers is. He probably took half of it from some old folks he foreclosed on or cheated some poor widow out of."

Larado gave that some thought as he saddled up and mounted. He began to whistle his favorite song: . . . *as I walked out on the streets of Laredo, as I walked out in Laredo one day . . .*

"I hate that song," Snake grumbled.

Larado stopped whistling. "I was wishin' last night I had a twenty dollar gold piece. I reckon that's what it would take to buy that gal."

"Dixie?" Snake laughed as he swung into the saddle. "Hell, she's my gal. She's meetin' me at my camp later this morning. I tell you what, I'll give you a few minutes on a blanket with her."

"I didn't mean her, I meant that tall one with the black hair." Silently, he wondered what kind of a man would offer the use of his woman to another man like he was offering to share some pecan pie. Maybe he didn't know Larado had had the blonde the first night in town. She was pretty good for a dollar.

"Oh, Lark?" Snake snorted as they rode out. "Don't know much about her 'cept she's a Texan too. She'll tease you, but that's all. Waits tables, won't work the cribs with the other whores."

"Oh?" Larado's interest heightened. "Damn, there was something about her got my blood runnin' hot."

"You ain't the only one," Snake laughed. "But she don't do nothin' but serve drinks—and not very well. You got your pants soaked with beer, so you know that."

Larado grinned, remembering the girl. "She can pour beer on me any time. She's purty as an ace-high straight."

"After you left, she and Dixie got into a fight and she yanked some of Dixie's hair out. Don't know what Dixie said to start it."

Larado pictured the scene, the luscious long legs, the tangle of dark hair, maybe a torn and revealing skimpy costume. "Texas gals ain't likely to let anyone give them lip. You can always tell a Texan, but you can't tell 'em much."

Snake yawned and shrugged. "Ain't that the Gawd's truth? A woman is a woman," Snake said, "they'll cheat you and trick you and they're all the same when the lights is turned out."

"I don't know about that," Larado drawled. "That one wasn't no coyote bait."

Snake scratched his crotch. "Weeks ago, I made a pass at her and got slapped for it. She acts like a lady, but no lady would work in a saloon."

"Reckon you got that right." She was mysterious and interesting. His head hurt, but he remembered the warm scent of perfume wafting up between her full breasts.

They rode away from the camp and into town. As Snake had said, the streets were almost deserted in the early dawn.

Snake said, "We'll tie up at the hitchin' post out front."

Larado looked toward the bank. "There ain't no hitchin' post."

"What? Oh, hell," Snake grumbled. "I forgot they took

'em down yesterday, doing something to widen the street
or some fool thing. Now what we gonna do?"

"Hey," Larado said with a grin, "look who's comin'."

Lark walked along the wooden sidewalk carrying her
small valise. She knew the stage stopped in front of the
butcher shop near the bank. She'd wait there for it.
Where she was going, she couldn't be sure. She ought to
yell "calf rope," which was Texan for admitting defeat,
and wire her uncle. He would be forgiving, but Lark was
not only defiant but proud. How could she go home, hat
in hand, where no doubt her twin sister, Lacey, the perfect example of young womanhood, was now planning
her perfect wedding to young Homer What's-his-name?

She heard the sound of horses and turned to see that
Texan from last night and the bad *hombre*, Snake, who
had been cheating him at cards. What was the Texan's
name? Oh, yes, Larado. He was either stupid, drunk, or
blind not to have seen what was going on at that poker
table, yet here he was riding into town with the bad
hombre.

She was almost abreast of the bank now, trying to
decide whether to acknowledge that rascal Snake and
the cowboy who had cost her her job.

She heard the two men dismount.

"Miss," Larado called.

She turned, not sure what to expect. The look in the
Texan's dark eyes told her what he'd like. Land's sake,
just because she worked in a saloon, did every man think
she'd fall on her back for a few coins? "Yes?"

The Texan touched the brim of his hat. "Mornin',
ma'am."

She almost wanted to scream at him: *You cost me my job,
you hare-brained idiot, and now you speak to me?* Instead, she
gritted her teeth and barely nodded to him.

Larado smiled that engaging, crooked grin. "You don't seem the type for a saloon, miss."

She felt herself color. "That's hardly your business," she snapped. "A girl's got to eat."

"You two stop all that jawin'," Snake griped. "We got things to do."

"Miss Lark." Larado took off his hat. "The hitchin' rail's down for the street repair. Maybe we could get you to hold our horses while we do a little business?"

"I reckon I can be obliging." She took a deep breath. The Texan was not only handsome with a lock of black hair hanging in his dark eyes—that grin would rock any woman back in her high-button shoes.

They handed over their reins.

Larado pushed his Stetson back. "We're much obliged. Won't be gone a minute."

She set her small valise down, took the reins from the pair, and watched them swagger into the bank. She didn't know what business they had in there. She figured the cowboy was broke after last night, and Snake was a ruffian, not the kind who put his money in banks. She fidgeted a long moment, wondering when the stage would arrive.

Abruptly, the early morning silence was shattered by the sound of gunshots from the bank.

The two horses reared and whinnied at the sudden noise, and she hung on to the reins for dear life. People hurried out of buildings, shouting and running. Lark fought to hang on to the rearing horses. *What in God's name is happening in the bank?*

Chapter Two

Larado was still feeling like the dogs had been dragging him around under the porch as he and Snake went into the bank.

"Damn, I'm cold," Snake muttered. He had his hat pulled low and his collar turned up.

Larado felt cold too, and his nose was dripping. As they approached the teller's cage, he pulled out his red bandana and brought it up to wipe his nose.

The little teller looked up as the two approached the counter. With alarm, he noted that they didn't look like anyone to fool with. What's more, one of them had his collar up as if to hide his identity, the other appeared to be holding a bandana over his face. Before either of the two could say anything, he yelled, "Mr. Barclay, come out here, we're being robbed!"

"What? Mister, you're makin' a big mistake—" Larado blinked as the fat owner came running out of the back room, waving a shotgun. From the corner of his eye, he saw Snake go for his Colt. Instinctively Larado grabbed for his too. His hand was still shaky from the booze, and he dropped it. When the Colt hit the floor it went off, and the bullet hit the big kerosene light fixture with a resounding roar, resulting in a shower of broken glass.

"Don't shoot!" the little teller begged. "We'll give you the money."

"Over my dead body!" the fat owner yelled.

Snake pointed his pistol at the bank official. "Mr. Barclay, I reckon that can be arranged."

"Snake, are you *loco*?" Larado said. "We ain't—"

"Shut up!" Snake snapped. "You! Open that damned safe!"

The fat man was shaking as he laid the shotgun on the counter and turned to open the door to the big black safe. He pulled out two leather sacks and tossed them across the counter. "Just don't kill us."

Snake grabbed both sacks as Larado, his vision blurred, leaned over and picked up his pistol. From outside, he heard the noise of shouting and running as people on the street must have figured out what was happening.

"Let's get out of here!" Snake commanded.

Larado needed no urging. How had he gotten mixed up in this anyhow? He saw the fat man reaching for the shotgun again and that put wings on his feet. As they ran out the front door, the shotgun roared and Snake screamed, "I'm hit!" followed by a string of oaths. Larado stopped to help him even as Snake stumbled and dropped one of the bank bags. Larado grabbed it up.

The fat banker ran out of the bank waving the shotgun and yelling, "Stop them two robbers! They've just killed my teller!" He aimed and fired again.

"Oh hell!" Snake swore. "He's reloaded. We may get the next one in the butt!"

That'd make for mighty sore riding. Larado ran even faster. Out on the wooden sidewalk, Lark hung on to the reins gamely although the scared horses reared and almost lifted her off the ground.

With a curse, Snake yanked his reins from the girl's hand and tried to mount. Around them, people were running and shouting for the sheriff.

"We got to get out of here!" Larado yelled and helped Snake mount up.

Lark's dark eyes were wide with surprise. "What are you two—?"

"Shut up!" Snake snarled.

"It ain't polite to tell a lady to shut up!" Larado scolded him.

"We got a town comin' to lynch us, a riled-up banker wavin' a shotgun, and you're worried about how to treat a lady?" Snake said.

"Well," Larado said, "after all, I am a Texan."

The banker fired again and Snake let loose with a string of oaths. "We'll meet at my camp on the bend of Rock Creek. You know the place?"

Larado nodded.

"Then let's get the hell out of here!"

The fat banker now stopped to reload his weapon as men ran out of businesses carrying rifles and shotguns.

They didn't look like a crowd who would listen to any explanation, Larado thought. He jerked his reins from Lark's hand and mounted up, leaving the astonished girl staring up at him as he galloped away. He wished he had time to explain to her that the whole thing was a big mistake, but there appeared to be a lynch party gathering up and he didn't intend to be the honoree. At the end of the street he and Snake split up, each heading a different direction. When he looked back, Lark still stood there with her pretty mouth open as if she were catching flies. Hell, he didn't want her to think badly of him, but it was too late to explain.

Chico was a fast horse, and Larado was a good rider, so he was soon out on the rolling prairie some miles from town. He reined in to rest his lathered mount. "Larado, you damn fool, how did you get yourself into this mess?"

Last night he had lost almost everything at cards when he never should have gone in there. He wasn't a very good poker player, but he'd been desperate. Today, he'd gone into a bank, blown his nose, and was suddenly in the midst of a bank robbery with people shooting at him. Then he discovered he was still holding on to the bank bag Snake had dropped in all the confusion. He hefted it in his hand. "Pretty lightweight, must be all bills."

Money. This morning he had been flat broke except for his gold watch and his horse and saddle. Now he held untold riches in his big fist. His first inclination was to turn around, go back to town, and turn it over to the bank. "Are you *loco*, Larado?" he muttered to himself. "They'd have you swingin' from a rafter of a barn before you could tell them it was all a big mistake—even if that fat banker didn't shoot you first."

Snake. That rascal had gotten him in a lot of trouble, but maybe Snake hadn't meant to—maybe he was just like Larado, always being misunderstood. Snake had taken some buckshot in the arm and might be bleeding to death somewhere. Even if he didn't much like the *hombre*, it wasn't like a Texan to abandon a man who was in a bad way.

Larado turned in his saddle and looked behind him, squinting in the early morning sun. He didn't see a posse coming yet, but it shouldn't take too long for one to form up and come looking for the two bank robbers. "I reckon I ought to light a shuck for Texas, bein' as how as I got all this money and that posse may be hot on my trail, but I can't leave Snake hurt and bleedin' somewhere."

The camp on the bend of Rock Creek. Yep, he knew where that was, and certainly Snake trusted him to meet him there. It didn't make good sense to alter his course, but then, Texans might be brave but they weren't always known for their good sense. Maybe he could convince Snake they'd be better off to explain to the law that it had all been a big mistake and return the money. He turned Chico to the east and headed for Rock Creek.

* * *

Lark had stood gaping in surprise as the two yanked the reins from her hands, mounted up, and put the spurs to their horses. "Land's sake, what—?"

She didn't get a chance to finish as the two galloped away. It was pretty obvious what had happened, with the fat banker waving his shotgun and men running from every direction. "Those two killers shot down my poor teller in cold blood!" he wailed. "And after I give them the money, too!"

"Lynch 'em!" the barber yelled, and the cry was taken up by the others. "Dirty robbers, we'll string 'em up. No need to wait for a trial."

Another man paused to stare at Lark. "Hey, that gal was in on it. She was holdin' their horses and bein' the lookout."

"No, you're mistaken." Lark drew herself up proudly. "I know nothing about this."

"We'll deal with her later," the blacksmith said. "Let's get saddled up and get them outlaws before the trail gets cold."

Men appeared from everywhere on horseback and in buckboards. "Come on, Mr. Barclay," one called to the banker. "We'll need you to identify them."

The fat man clambered up into the rig, still hanging on to his shotgun. "I'll give 'em a double load of buckshot for killin' my teller," he vowed.

"Shouldn't we wait to be deputized?" another man asked.

"Oh, hell no!" another swore. "We ain't gonna do nothin' official, just string up a couple of polecats."

The whole mob took off out of town in a cloud of dust and jingling spurs, leaving Lark and a curious hound dog staring after the posse.

"Oh my, now what am I supposed to do? They'll never believe I wasn't part of the plot. All I was trying to do was get the next stage." She looked up and down the street. A few curious women and some children were poking heads out of windows to see what the excitement was about. *The stage must be running late.* In a few minutes, some of the posse would surely be returning to arrest her.

"That damn Texan," she muttered. "If he hadn't had such a charming grin, I wouldn't have tried to help him last night and got myself fired. Now look at the mess he just got me into." In her mind, she imagined revenge, like maybe tying him down, Comanche style, on a bed of red ants. His charming, lopsided grin might fade then.

What was she going to do? By the time the stage got here, she'd be wearing handcuffs and locked up in the hoosegow. "Think, Lark, think. This mob isn't going to listen to your explanation. What would your smart sister do?"

Lacey wouldn't get herself into a mess like this in the first place, she decided, *not over some big, stupid cowboy.* For a moment, there didn't seem to be anyone on the streets. Picking up her small valise, she hurried down the nearest alley to get out of sight. Maybe she could hide there until the stage came though. Land's sake, that wouldn't work—they'd stop the stage and check it first thing, or at least go on to the next town, knowing she might get off there. Damn that Texan. That grinning cowboy had gotten her into more trouble in half a day than she could get out of in a week of Sundays.

Behind the barber shop, an old gray horse stood dozing, hitched to a wagonload of manure. "Well, any transportation beats nothing." At least this was one way she bested Lacey. Lark had always been a tomboy and could ride and rope and shoot like a man. She'd been happiest on her uncle Trace's ranch, but she'd been sent off to school with her smart, perfect sister to Miss Priddy's Female Academy in Boston in an attempt to turn Lark into a lady. It hadn't worked.

Lark considered taking the wagon, then decided a woman driving a wagonload of manure would attract too much attention. Instead, she unhitched the old horse and took his harness off. Hiking her dark blue skirts, she swung up on the bony back, balancing her small valise before her. She slapped the old horse on the neck and he started off at a slow walk.

"If I ever get my hands on that cowboy, I'll wring his neck!" she vowed. "He's cost me my job, got me tangled up in a bank robbery, and now I'm a horse thief on the run—riding a fugitive from the glue factory."

Which way to go? If she went due south along the stage route, that might be the first place a posse might look. Maybe if she rode to some settlement off the beaten path, she could get a job, or at least stay out of jail until she could decide what to do next.

The old gray horse had a backbone like a razor that cut into her bottom. If she were a real lady, she would only ride sidesaddle. "Who are you kidding?" she said. "Ladies don't steal horses, especially not a nag tied to a manure wagon. Your prissy sister would have an attack of the vapors if she knew what her twin was doing."

That made her smile to picture it. However, there was nothing funny about her predicament, Lark thought as she rode. She wondered if the posse had caught the pair. Funny, she might have expected something like this from the ugly, scar-faced one, but she'd thought Larado was just a Texas cowboy dealing with some bad luck. He didn't seem like a bank robber. "Now, Lark," she lectured herself, "how would you know what a bank robber was like—have you ever met one before?"

Of course not. She'd lived a sheltered life on her uncle's big ranch until she'd been sent away to school, failed there, came home, felt she had to compete with her twin, and run away. It was just so much easier to flee than compete.

As the day passed, she rode to the outskirts of a small town and drew in. "Whoa, old horse. This place looks pretty isolated. Maybe I can hide out here until things blow over."

She dismounted, turned the old horse back the way

they had come, and slapped it on the rear. It broke into a dead walk and started up the road toward Buck Shot. "At least they won't get me for horse stealing."

She watched the gray nag until it disappeared over the horizon, knowing it would return to its own stable. She smiled as she pictured the puzzled owner trying to figure out how that old horse had gotten out of its harness and unhitched itself from that wagon.

With any luck, she'd find a job and start fresh—a respectable job. She hadn't been cut out to be a saloon girl. If that damned Texan should ever show up here, she'd make him wish he'd let the posse get him. The posse. Even now, the two might be dangling from a cottonwood tree. "That would wipe the grin off that devilish face," she said to herself. Still, the thought bothered her. He'd been too charming for any woman not to care what happened.

Her bottom was so sore, she could hardly walk and her blue dress was covered with dust. As she limped down Main Street of this settlement, she made up an excuse about how a passing wagon had given her a lift. Damn that Texan, anyhow.

Larado galloped into the Rock Creek camp and dismounted. Dixie waited there on this cool morning. She wore a tight red dress, and there was a rented buggy tied to a nearby tree.

"You seen anything of Snake?" he asked.

"No." Her painted face seemed guarded.

"Well, he told me to meet him here. We're in a real mess, Dixie. With that buckshot he took in the arm, I was afraid he might not make it."

She didn't seem too concerned about her lover's health. "Looks like you got all the money."

He shrugged. "Reckon I got some."

"Hell, to tell the truth, cowboy, he's already been here and gone. You and me ought to skedaddle together."

Larado swore under his breath and shook his head. "I didn't reckon he'd double-cross me. What'd he say?"

"Not much. Gone off to find a doctor, I reckon. Told me to tell you he hadn't showed up, and he'd meet up with me later."

Larado tied his horse to a tree, took the bank bag, and tossed it onto the ground by the fire. "Hell, I never meant to get mixed up in no bank robbery. It just happened. Now we got a posse after us."

Her blue eyes gleamed as she picked up the bank bag. "Kinda light—you get away with much?"

"Reckon it's all bills." Larado sighed as he knelt by the fire and poured himself a cup of coffee from the big tin pot. "I don't aim to keep it. I was gonna talk to Snake about straightenin' this out by returnin' it."

"You must be *loco*," she sneered. "You get away with bank cash and you want to turn it back? Think of what this could buy, Larado."

"But I ain't a crook," he said. "I don't think Snake intended for this to happen."

"You don't know Snake. He get much?"

"He got one bag, just like me. There's a posse maybe on my trail, Dixie, you should clear out."

"Go with me. Don't you want to know where Snake's gone?"

He shook his head. "Reckon if he'd double-cross me, it don't matter. I'm gonna figure out how to return this loot and head back to Texas."

She ran her tongue slowly over her lips. Her scarlet dress was so tight, it showed her voluptuous curves. "Take me with you, Larado."

"What? I thought you was Snake's gal."

She shrugged, coming over and to look up at him. "I liked what I got the other night. You and I could be a pair."

Before he could speak, she slipped her arms around his neck and kissed him—a long, lingering, sensual kiss that made him gasp in surprise and drop his coffee cup.

For a moment he wanted to grab her, throw her down on the blanket by the campfire, and take her right then, knowing how warm and ripe she would be. Then he saw the image in his mind of a tall brunette in a dark blue dress staring up at him as he took the horse and rode away. He reckon he owed that Lark girl an apology. Maybe when he went back to return the money, he'd hunt her down and explain how everything happened.

He reached up and untangled Dixie's arms from around his neck. "This ain't right, Dixie."

She laughed, a hard, brittle laugh. "Neither is robbin' a bank. You remind me of a gambler I used to know, Larado, a man I really cared about. Take me with you and I'll make you glad you did."

"Naw, can't do that." He pushed his Stetson back. "I'm broke and there's a posse lookin' for me. I ain't gonna add to my troubles by stealin' Snake's girl."

"Are you *loco*?" she demanded as she confronted him. "I told you he's already deserted you, probably figurin' the posse will find this camp soon enough."

"I'm a Texan, Dixie, I'm as good as my word."

She said something obscene, walked over, and picked up the bank bag. "Well, let's just see how much you got away with."

"Won't do you no good, I ain't keepin' it."

She ignored him and pulled the drawstring, shaking the bag. When she did, a bundle of cut newspaper fell out in a shower and fluttered to the ground. "What the—?"

Larado strode over and knelt by her side, picking up a fistful of paper. "This can't be. Why would a bank keep chopped paper in their safe?"

Dixie shrugged. "Well, I reckon the joke is on you, Larado. You didn't steal no money after all."

He wiped his face with his bandana. "Hell, that's a relief. Maybe when the banker tells them we didn't get no cash, it'll all be a big joke."

"I wouldn't count on it. You think Snake's bag has real money in it?"

"How would I know?" Larado shrugged. "Didn't he open it while he was here?"

"Uh, no, he was in too big a hurry."

"Then he's the one you'd better go with, Dixie. He may be a rich man."

She favored him with a smile. "It don't make no never mind, cowboy, I'd still rather go with you."

He shook his head again. "Sorry, sweetie, but one can travel faster than two, and I'm broke. Since I didn't steal no money, I reckon I'll ride on to Texas and lose myself down there. When you see Snake, tell him about the fake bills, will you? I wouldn't want him to think I tried to cheat him."

"Oh, you Texans. I don't know whether you're stupid or too principled to live." She gave him a beseeching look. "I ain't known many men with principles, Larado. Take me with you. I promise you won't regret it."

He was already striding to his horse. "There's a posse lookin' for me, so you don't need trouble like that. I'm givin' you some advice; clear out before that posse shows up. Go back to town and wait for Snake to find you. And when you see that tall Texas gal. . . ."

"Yes?"

He mounted up. "It don't make no never mind. I reckon she's mad as a rained-on hen for the trouble I caused her."

"You mean about losin' her job?"

He paused, pushed his hat back. "No, about this mornin'. What about her job?"

"Oh, you didn't know? Joe fired her last night."

"That's a damned shame. Why did he do that?"

She wasn't about to tell him about the cat fight. "For pourin' beer on you. She was a lousy barmaid. So long, Larado. If you ever change your mind, I'll probably be right here workin' at the Last Chance unless something better comes along."

He nodded to her, turned his horse, and loped away.

Dixie stood there watching him until he was a dot on the far horizon. She could have cared about the lanky cowboy—only the second man she'd cared about in a long string of men that began when she was a ragged girl in Atlanta. Dixie was the bastard child of a Yankee soldier and a desperate slut from a Georgia cotton patch. Dixie's whole life had been a battle to survive.

What to do? Snake hadn't showed up yet and might not if a posse was after him, or even if it wasn't. Larado said he'd been shot, but he had a bank bag. She'd be a sitting duck waiting for that posse if she got caught with this bank bag, even if there was no real money. Now she wondered how she could turn this mess to her advantage. After some thought, she gathered up the bank bag and the chopped newspaper and put them in the campfire. The flames leapt as the evidence burned. She took a stick and stirred the fire, then watched until everything was burned beyond recognition. What should she do now? There was always the chance that Snake's bank bag was full of cash, and Dixie was greedy. She intended to end up with whatever Snake had stolen.

In a few minutes, Snake rode into camp on a lathered bay. "Hallo the camp!"

"Come on in," she yelled. "I'm the only one here."

He rode in and dismounted, tossing the bank bag at her feet. "Here you go, baby."

"Oh, you're hurt." She feigned concern at the blood on his sleeve, but her gaze was on the bag.

He shrugged, looking at his bloody sleeve. "A few shotgun pellets from that damned banker. Not as bad as I first thought. There's probably a posse behind me, so we need to clear out. Larado show up?"

"Uh, no. Was he supposed to?" She was angry at Larado for spurning her.

Snake began to curse. "He seemed pretty honest or maybe just stupid. I dropped one of the bags when we ran out of the bank and Larado picked it up. We were lucky to get away. All we had was pistols and that banker had a double-barreled shotgun."

"Well, honey." She gave him a bewitching smile. "Let's see the loot."

Snake grabbed it up. "Heavy," he said and poured the contents out on the blanket, then began to curse again. "I'll be damned, mostly change, a couple of double eagles." He sorted through it. "I'll be double damned. Probably not more than fifty dollars total, and I almost got myself killed for this. I reckon that damned Texan got the big stuff, that double-crossin' sidewinder. I ought to hunt him down and kill him."

Dixie was still smarting from Larado's rejection. "Yeah, you should. He gets away with the big money and you get nothin' much. You deserve better, honey."

"I was gonna buy you some presents," he grumbled.

"Maybe next time. Can I have the double eagles?"

"Naw," he snapped. "You greedy little bitch. Gimme the double eagles. You can have the small change. Too bad I grabbed the wrong bag. Now that Texan's gonna be rich and comfortable."

Somewhere in the distance, they heard gunshots, and on the far ridge, she saw the posse strung out in a long line. "I reckon they're signalin' each other. You better clear out of here, Snake."

"You too."

She shook her head. "Naw, they won't do anything to me because they won't connect me to the robbery. Besides, half them respectable men is my customers when their wives ain't lookin'. They wouldn't want me tattlin' on them. You just clear on out, and I'll delay them while you get away."

"You're one in a million, Dixie. I'll hide out and maybe come back for you sometime."

"Don't worry about me. I'll survive—I always do. Now get out of here." She picked up the empty bank bag and tossed it into the fire. "Now there's nothin' to connect this camp to any bank robbery."

"You're smart for a woman, Dixie. I won't forget you."

"Sure, sure." She didn't care about Snake. He didn't have any money, and she wanted a man who could give her nice things, a fancy carriage and a big house. "Get!"

Snake swung into the saddle, nodded to her, and rode out. She watched him go until he was only a speck on the horizon. He was heading in a different direction than Larado, so he wouldn't meet up with him and learn Dixie had lied. Anyway, Snake would never believe Larado's bank bag had been full of paper. He'd go looking for Larado for betraying him. For a split second, her conscience bothered her, because she knew what a good shot Snake was. Still, she was mad at the Texan for spurning her. And worse than that, he seemed attracted to that tall brunette at the Last Chance. That annoyed Dixie. She turned and watched the posse coming over the hill. The Texan deserved whatever he got—and that pretty Lark too. It was ironic, maybe. Lark's twin sister Lacey had stolen the other man that Dixie had cared for.

The posse rode into camp and dismounted.

"Hi, boys, out for a picnic on this spring day?"

The deputy pulled at his gray mustache and frowned at her. "What you doin' out here by yourself?"

"Waitin' for you boys to show up," she drawled. She had put the change down the front of her corset cover, and she could feel it, cold, but comforting there.

"You wouldn't be waitin' for anyone, would you?" The men dismounted and looked around the site.

"I told you I was waitin' for you," she pouted.

"Don't play with us, Dixie," the deputy snapped. "There's been a bank robbery in town and the teller was shot in the back. We're lookin' for two dirty yellow killers."

She tried to keep her lip from trembling. Neither Larado nor Snake had said anything about killing a man. That made this much more serious. If the posse got either of them, they'd hang them on the spot. "You gonna take me in?"

"You know anything about this?" one of the deputies asked.

"No, and that's the God's truth."

The deputy glanced skyward. "Be careful, girl, a lightning bolt might come out of the sky and hit you."

"Well, you can take me in, boys, if you want, but I might start tellin' all the wives in town what some of you boys are actually doin' when they think you're at a Civic Club meetin' or the church fundraiser committee."

A number of the men looked away, shuffled their boots, and cleared their throats.

The deputy said, "Well, it's plain she don't know anything—she's just a common whore. Let's ride on."

"How dare you, Cliff Rainey?" she snapped. "I'm the best ride you ever had. You don't think I'm so common when you're sneakin' up to my room while your wife's off visitin' her sister."

His face turned brick red and the other men laughed. "She's right," the barber said. "Taking her in will only get us in trouble with our women. Let's ride on."

The others seemed to suddenly remember that they'd spent a little time up in Dixie's room too. The deputy cleared his throat. "Reckon you're right, Jim. Let's get back on the trail. Miss Dixie, you'd better head back to town."

"Well, I will, unless some of you got time for a quickie."

"Don't mind if I do!" A couple of men stepped forward. The deputy roared, "What in tarnation you fellas thinkin' of? We ain't got time for women now. We're on a manhunt. Now get ridin'."

Reluctantly, the men headed to their horses. She'd bedded most of them at one time or another, but how many more years before she'd be too old for men to want her? "Bye, boys, see you back in town."

They mounted up, tipped their hats, and rode out. The wind had picked up, blowing dust across horse tracks, so she knew it would be difficult to follow either Larado or Snake. She watched the posse leave, heading in the wrong direction. If the deputy had offered a little reward, she would have told him everything she knew, because she didn't give a damn about Snake and Larado didn't give a damn about her.

Somewhere, there was a man who would buy her fine clothes and a fancy house. She watched until the posse had ridden away and sighed. One more night ahead of her, flat on her back for a dollar, under any drunk who wanted her for a few minutes. Abruptly she was sick of all that, sick of being a common whore. What she needed to escape this life was money, plenty of money.

Dixie stared into the dwindling campfire a moment before kicking dirt over it to put it out. Her mind was busy. Now, if Larado didn't have the bank money and Snake didn't have the bank money, who did? She thought about it a long time as she gathered up her things. Then the sudden knowledge popped into her mind like someone lighting a lamp. She grinned. *Of course!* Why hadn't she thought of that? Humming happily to herself, she hitched up her rented buggy and rode toward town. She'd get those fine clothes and glittering jewelry after all.

Chapter Three

Lark walked into town and found the weather-beaten old hotel. She didn't have much money, and she'd have to find a job fast. The frail, elderly man at the desk seemed curious. A stranger, particularly an unescorted woman, was a novelty in any area of the West.

"How's the job opportunities around here?"

His gold-rimmed glasses slid down his thin nose. "For a lady?"

She didn't want to lie, but she surely didn't want anyone tracking her back to Buck Shot and the bank robbery. "You see, I was a mail-order bride for a rancher in the next county and when I got here, he didn't want me, drove me to the nearest crossroads. I managed to catch a ride on a wagon, and now I'm pretty much stranded here."

"What kind of a low-down polecat would do that to a lady?" His voice was sympathetic.

She thought about Larado, that rascal. "Reckon I'm not a very good judge of men. Anyway, thought I might be able to get a job, earn enough for a train ticket back to Texas."

He scratched his white head. "Café might could use a new cook."

Lark sighed. She was a terrible cook, unlike her perfect sister, Lacey. "I'm a pretty good cowboy, really good with horses. I can rope and shoot better than most men."

The old man laughed. "Sorry, miss, you know most ranchers aren't gonna hire a female as a ranch hand."

His condescending attitude made her want to reach across the counter and smack him.

"Besides," he said, "even if a rancher was to hire you, where would you sleep? You wouldn't want to share a bunkhouse with a bunch of wranglers."

Now that was the truth. She pictured being surrounded by snoring, dirty cowboys scratching and breaking wind. "Well, I'll look around and see what's available in the morning. Is there a place to get a bite?"

"A café down the street, not too good. I told you they was needing a cook."

She turned to go. They'd think *not too good* if she was doing the cooking.

"Oh, and Mrs. Jones is looking for a housekeeper. She's got the biggest house in town, but she's real particular."

"Thanks." Lark wasn't much on housekeeping either. "Maybe I'll look into it."

The old man had known what he was talking about. She got herself a quick sandwich, which wasn't too good, then walked back to the small hotel. This was barely a town—few citizens, and not a lot of activity. It would be a perfect place to hide out until she could raise enough money to leave. She'd forgotten to even ask if a stage came through at all. It was obvious there was no train. Maybe it would take a while for word of the bank robbery to drift to this sleepy hamlet.

She counted her money and went to bed early. Tomorrow she would figure out what to do next. When she closed her eyes she saw Larado's rugged face and crooked grin, then cursed the night she had gotten involved with the saddle tramp.

The next morning, she began to look for a job. Already

word had spread about the newcomer in town, because a ranch wife stopped her to offer her a job as a bunkhouse cook. Lark sighed. She was desperate, but not that desperate. Besides, after they tasted her cooking she'd be fired right off.

She found some ranchers having coffee at the local cafe and tried to hire on as a ranch hand. One old geezer laughed so hard, he almost swallowed his false teeth. Lark managed not to whack him in the eye. The others seemed to think she was joking. Discouraged, she went out on the wooden sidewalk and looked up and down. What to do?

There was a saloon on the street, but she'd already decided she'd never work in a saloon again, no matter how desperate she got.

She tried the general store, but the short, bald owner said he and his wife could handle the business and suggested that if she needed a job she should get married. Lark had a terrible urge to push him into the pickle barrel, but managed to restrain herself.

It was still early. She returned to the hotel lobby, wondering if there was a local paper. The old man at the desk told her there was a weekly and handed her a copy. There were no job listings, but a mail-order bride column. Ha! She wasn't that desperate yet.

Abut that time, an elegant man came down the stairs carrying a black-and-white cat. "Ah, a damsel in distress? May I be of assistance, *mademoiselle*?"

"Meow," said the cat.

Lark looked at the man. He was about fifty, maybe, finely dressed, with a small mustache and goatee. His accent was foreign.

"How do you do?"

He stopped and bowed low, took her hand, and kissed the back of it. "I am very well. And you, miss?"

She pulled her hand away. "I'm new in town," she said. "I don't suppose you know of any jobs?"

"Hmm." He pulled at his goatee. "Come along with me and Miss Mew Mew to my shop, and we'll talk. At the very least, yes, I can offer you a cup of tea."

"That would be very nice. It's cool out there this morning."

He transferred the cat to the other arm. "I am Pierre. I own a millinery shop down the street. A beautiful woman like you, you wear fine hats, yes?"

"Sometimes." Actually, she wore a Stetson more often than anything, but she was flustered at the compliment. "And I am . . . Lacey, Lacey Van Schuyler." She decided to use her sister's name in case the law was looking for Lark.

"A beautiful woman always has lots of hats, *oui*." He escorted her out on the wooden sidewalk and down to a tiny shop at the end of the street. "Here I make the beautiful *chapeaus* for the lovely ladies." He opened the door and escorted Lark inside, where he put Miss Mew Mew in the shop window. The big cat promptly curled up to doze in the sun while he stirred up the tiny parlor stove and put on a kettle of water.

Lark looked around. It was a small shop with a display of fine ladies' hats in the window. "Oh my, these are beautiful."

He smiled at her. "I have talent, yes, and I eke out a living here, but sometime I will move on."

Lark walked around, admiring the hats. "You seem so out of place in this town. I'd expect you'd be more at home in some big city like New York or Chicago."

Pierre frowned as if his head hurt. "I was previously in San Francisco, and before that Cincinnati, but unfortunately, rich widows seemed to think my interest was more than professional and . . ." He shrugged and didn't finish.

So this is what a gigolo looks like, she thought.

He made the tea and poured it into dainty cups, gesturing her to a chair. "Ah, this is more like it. Perhaps business will be slow today."

"You actually make a living selling hats in this village?"

"Let us say, I have been the beneficiary of some very generous older ladies. I keep thinking I'll find another, perhaps one who has inherited a rich ranch or something." He gave her a charming smile.

"Ah." She nodded as the realization struck her. "And you meet these ladies because they come into your shop?"

"*Oui*, I fulfill their, ah, most wonderful dreams."

She looked around at the hats. "You have a lot of real talent," she said.

He smiled again. "That's exactly what the ladies said. Oh, you mean in the millinery business, yes?" He took a crisp linen napkin and wiped his penciled mustache. "But enough about me. How have you landed in this pitiful little town?"

She paused and looked away, thinking about that damned rascal of a cowboy. She hoped he was rotting in jail by now. "Let us just say that I had to leave the last town rather . . . well, unexpectedly."

"Ah, me too!"

She didn't have anyone else to trust, and now she admitted, "I'm looking for a job, and not having much luck because I'm not too good at housekeeping or cooking." She sipped the hot tea and savored it. "I'll only be able to stay at the hotel another day or two, and then if I don't find a job, I'm not sure what I'll do."

"Tsk, tsk." He made a clicking sound and gave her a sympathetic look. "I have a back room where I store supplies. You might manage to sleep there, *oui*?"

She was immediately on guard. "I'm not sure—"

"No obligation." He shook his head. "Unless you know an older rich lady, maybe a widow?" He looked hopeful.

"Sorry, I'm not from around here. I don't know anyone."

"Oh," he sighed. "Well, you could model the hats for the old bats—I mean, the lovely ladies who come in. If they think they would look like you in my creations, they will buy. Besides, it might amuse me to teach you the millinery business. Of course, the salary would be quite small."

"Almost anything would be acceptable," she blurted. "Until I figure out what I'm going to do next."

Pierre gave her a searching look. "I think we both may be in the same boat, maybe misunderstood by the law, no?"

She started to deny it, thinking of that damned cowboy and the mess he'd gotten her into. Then she sighed. "Misunderstood by the law, yes. Pierre, if you're offering me a job, I'll take it, but I have to warn you I know nothing about sewing or ladies' accessories to speak of."

"Ah, but *mademoiselle* looks talented." He set his cup down, went over to a shelf, and began to dig through boxes. "Look, you take a felt form like this." He pulled a black, large-brimmed hat from a box. "You pull up one side with a pretty jeweled pin, like so." He demonstrated. "Then you add a veil, and ooh la la, a magnificent *chapeau*."

"Why, it is beautiful!" Lark set her cup down. "Pierre, you are an artist."

He shrugged. "It is nothing. I know what the ladies like." He smiled modestly as he walked over and put the hat in the window. "Now get your things, my dear. My back room isn't much, but it will do."

In less than a month, Lark became quite successful at modeling hats for ladies who came in to shop. Men began to come in to buy gifts for their wives and to ogle the new girl in town. Lark was smart and more talented than she had realized. Pierre soon taught her to take a basic hat, add veils and flowers or plumes, and turn it into a thing of beauty. Business began to pick up as the weather warmed.

Several young cowboys tried to court Lark, but she

made it clear she wasn't interested. Somehow, none of them seemed as charming as the big Texan. Once Pierre mentioned that he might be moving on to a larger town, suggesting Lark might want to buy him out. Frankly, Lark told him, she couldn't see herself in a lady's hat shop the rest of her life—and besides, she didn't have any money except the small salary he'd been paying her. Uncle Trace would certainly have loaned her the down payment, but Lark was still too proud and stubborn to ask her wealthy in-laws for help.

One day at the café, she picked up a Texas newspaper that a traveler on the weekly stage had apparently left behind. Out of idle curiosity, she began to look through it. Someone had a black horse for sale. Someone else had some house furnishings, some cattle. Maybe there were some job listings. Then she spotted the matrimony ads. *Middle-aged lady who is a good cook, looking for widower with a nice ranch. Young lady looking for a young man of good family who is interested in matrimony.* She started to put the paper on the table, then an ad caught her eye: *Sheriff in up-and-coming west Texas town, former Texas Ranger, would like to meet respectable young lady. Object: Matrimony.*

A sheriff. If the law was looking for her, what better protection could she have than being married to a sheriff? Lark wasn't interested, of course, but she took the paper back to the shop with her, thinking about the ad. A sheriff. In west Texas, far, far from here. In fact, west Texas was far, far from everything. She commented on the ad to Pierre.

He sat in a chair with Miss Mew Mew in his lap and now he got the slightly pained expression of one with a headache. "A bumpkin? A sheriff? Surely you jest, my dear Lacey?"

"Of course." She shrugged and began to empty boxes of new merchandise. "Although, sooner or later, I would like to return to Texas."

"Texas!" Pierre sniffed. "What was it General Sherman

said? 'If I owned both hell and Texas, I'd live in hell and rent out Texas.'"

"But true Texans are never really happy anyplace else." She blinked back tears.

Pierre took the paper from her hand as he stroked Miss Mew Mew's fur. "Hmm. Any rich widows in here?"

"I haven't the vaguest idea." She began dusting display cabinets. "You know, a sheriff's home would be the safest place in the world for me."

"Hmm," Pierre sighed. "And he's young, perhaps handsome. You're pretty, my dear, I suppose you should marry."

"I can't cook or keep house. Why would any man want me?"

"*Mademoiselle*, you are so naive, you give me a headache. Are you going to correspond with this hayseed of a lawman?"

She shook her head. "I reckon not. It was just a thought, after all."

"Nothing ventured, nothing gained. Besides," he smiled, "he might have a rich old lady in the family."

"I doubt that. Lawmen are usually poor. Of course, that doesn't matter if you're in love."

"My dear, you are more naive than I thought."

"I'll admit it." She paused and looked out the window, her thoughts dreamy. "I want a big, handsome Texan who will sweep me off my feet and we'll live happily ever after."

Pierre made a moue. "Even if he's a poor sheriff?"

She shrugged. "Forget the sheriff. I already have."

Lark forgot about the conversation until a few days later, when Pierre brought her a letter from the post office. "Look here, my dear, he's answered. Open it so we can see what he says."

"What are you talking about?" Lark took the envelope, puzzled. She certainly wasn't expecting any mail. Besides, it was addressed to her sister. She almost said so and then she remembered that she was passing herself off as Lacey Van Schuyler.

Pierre stroked his tiny mustache, looked very pleased with himself. "I was trying to help you get back to Texas, yes?"

She had a sudden feeling of disaster. "What have you done?"

"Written a sweet letter to the young Texas hayseed who is looking for a mail-order bride. Now open it, my dear, and see what he's got to say."

Lark gasped in horror. "You sent my name to that sheriff without even telling me about it?"

"Well, why not?" he defended himself. "I believe in *amour*, in love. Besides, he might have a rich old lady in the family."

"How could you?" For a moment, Lark had visions of the law coming to arrest her for using her sister's name or tracking her down as an accessory to a bank robbery.

Pierre smiled. "Nothing ventured, nothing gained. Now let's see if the sheriff liked what I wrote."

"You have a lot of nerve. And I have no intention of getting myself mixed up in a mail-order marriage."

"Suppose," Pierre said, "he is the man of your dreams, the big Texan of romantic novels?"

"I think I ought to throw it away," Lark said.

"Ah, and disappoint that nice young sheriff?"

"How do you know he's either nice or young?" Lark demanded. "He's probably some old geezer, old enough to be my father."

"Aren't you the least bit curious?" He stroked the sleepy cat.

Lark shrugged and opened the envelope. The handwriting was big and awkward, as if the author was not good with the written word. "'Dear Miss Van Schuyler: I am glad you answered my advertisement and might be looking for a husband.'"

"Me? How dare he think I would do that?" She was outraged. "I could certainly get a husband if I wanted one."

Pierre shrugged and took the letter from her hand, then read aloud. "'I am tall and dark-haired.' Ah, very good. I told him you were tall and pretty."

"I'm not interested." At that point, Lark tore the letter in two, marched to the trash, and threw it away.

"You're not even going to see if he's old?" Pierre looked crestfallen.

"I don't care how old he is." Lark began applying a veil to a new spring straw hat.

"I hate to think I wasted my time, *oui*?" Pierre retrieved the letter from the trash and pieced it together, reading aloud. "'My name is Lawrence Witherspoon. I have a good job as the new sheriff of Rusty Spur here in west Texas.'"

"Lawrence Witherspoon? Sounds prissy. Besides, I've heard of Rusty Spur," Lark snorted. "Wildest, most lawless town—and so remote, they almost have to ship daylight to it."

Pierre shrugged and read some more. "'I am considered good-looking by the ladies . . .'"

"Oh, what a vain man."

The Frenchman's gaze swept over the page. "Hmm, he's almost thirty. He says he hopes to save enough to buy a ranch someday. That sounds like your kind of man, my dear."

She wouldn't admit it, but it did. Lark sighed. A ranch sounded good to her. She was suddenly very homesick for Texas and the cowboy life she loved.

"At least you're not older than he is. In the West, you might be getting a little long in the tooth."

"I beg your pardon, I am only twenty-five," Lark said.

"Way past marrying age in Texas."

"I am very picky."

"If you're looking for the perfect man, he doesn't exist, my dear. You just find one you love and marry him, warts and all."

"Humph. Men," she snorted. "They're only looking

for someone to clean, cook, and pick up after them. Our lovesick sheriff can just find himself another girl."

"Well, all right." Pierre patted his cat. "I'm becoming an old meddler."

Lark patted him on the shoulder. "It's all right, no harm done." For the second time, she tossed the letter in the trash.

However, late that night, lying sleepless in her little room at the back of the shop, Lark kept thinking about the letter. She pictured some earnest young sheriff checking the post office every day for the letter that was never going to come. Lark had a tender heart. The least she could do was answer and explain that she hadn't written in the first place and had no interest in matrimony.

She got out of bed and lit the lamp. Then she dug the letter out of the trash, reread it, and sat at the little desk to pen a reply.

> *Dear Mr. Witherspoon:*
> *I received your letter and enjoyed reading it.*

Now she paused. It would be humiliating to him to say that she wasn't interested and that her employer had sent the letter without Lark's knowledge. Maybe he would think something he had said in his letter would have changed her mind.

> *To be honest, I don't think you would be interested in me. My womanly skills aren't too good. I'd rather ride horses and go hunting than clean house. I'm a terrible cook but I can handle a rope better than most cowboys. Now that you know this, you probably won't want to write me anymore, and I'll understand. However, I am a Texan too, and really love the Lone Star State. Remember the Alamo!*
>
> *Most sincerely,*
> *Lacey Van Schuyler.*

She addressed the envelope to Sheriff Lawrence Witherspoon, General Delivery, Rusty Spur, Texas, and the next morning, put it in the mail. There, that took care of it. She would lose her correspondent without hurting his feelings. She returned to work in the millinery shop and for the next several days, thought nothing more about it. After all, with the business doing as well as it was, she was busy—and she had that bank robbery accomplice thing hanging over her head to worry about.

Then one day, Pierre rushed in, all excited, waving an envelope. "Look, dear, you've heard from your sheriff again."

"He is not *my* sheriff," Lark reminded him. "And it's probably a note thanking me for answering and saying he hopes I'll understand if he looks elsewhere."

The Frenchman's eyes lit up. "You answered his letter?"

Lark hated to admit it. "I wrote him and told him what a bad housekeeper and cook I was. You know, that's what most men are looking for."

He winked at her. "Obviously, my dear, you are naive."

"Pierre!" Lark was almost speechless.

"Well, open it and let's see what he says," Pierre suggested.

Lark took the letter from his hand and opened it. "'Dear Miss Van Schuyler,'" she read. "'You are being very modest about your assets. Every woman is born knowing how to cook and clean.'"

"That's what he thinks," Lark said, outraged. "I can see he is one of those who think women should shut up and stay obedient and in the kitchen." She read some more of the large, painful handwriting. "'I do like a woman who likes horses and ranch life. Did you say you were pretty?'"

Lark snorted, and Pierre nodded. "That's number one with most men. And you are pretty, child."

"I don't think so," Lark countered. "I'm too tall for a

girl, and I've got some Cheyenne blood. Some Texans wouldn't be interested in a woman who is part Indian."

"Well, maybe the sheriff's different."

"I'm not going to answer this letter," Lark said. "I can't imagine being stuck with some hick sheriff who's looking for a pretty girl who's a perfect housewife."

"He didn't say that's what he wanted," Pierre defended him.

"How do you know? You never met him," Lark snorted.

"He just sounds like a nice man, that's all. Lawmen are usually upstanding citizens."

And it would be a safe haven for a girl on the run from the law, Lark thought. She tried to imagine Lawrence Witherspoon. He might be tall and red-faced with buck teeth. He might be short and balding and burp a lot.

"I just think this has gone far enough," she said. "I regret the impulse to write him. I won't write again."

"Oh, by the way, I got a letter too." Pierre waved the envelope. "A rich old lady I've corresponded with in the past has invited me to come to New York."

Lark felt her mood fall. "I never thought you'd be going away. I'm so fond of you."

"And me you, and so is Miss Mew Mew, aren't you, kitty?"

The black-and-white cat blinked and swished her tail.

"Anyway," Pierre said, "life moves on. I've already found a buyer for the shop since you aren't interested. Perhaps the new owner will keep you on, although she has two daughters."

Lark went to the window and looked out. Dusty Plains was a very small town. Although business had increased, it wouldn't support four women and she knew it. "I'd been thinking about moving on anyway."

Pierre stroked his mustache. "Ah, to go meet that young sheriff?"

"Land's sake, no. You're an incurable romantic. Suppose I went clear out there and hated him on sight.

Suppose he was disappointed that I really can't cook and I'm not a clingy little blond doll?"

"You have to take a chance on love or you'll never have it. And believe me, dear, love is worth the gamble, if it's the real thing." He sighed as if remembering.

"I'll be moving on as soon as I make some decisions." With that, she put up the "closed" sign and began dusting the display cases.

That night, she lay awake for a long time. What was she to do? She might get along fine with the new owner, but Lark's heart wasn't in the millinery shop anyway. She longed for the sunny plains of Texas, but she couldn't go home until she'd made a success of her life. After all, Lacey was probably doing very well now with a picture-perfect life, and Lark had surely annoyed Uncle Trace by running away from that fancy finishing school.

What happened the next morning helped make her decision. Lark had been to pick up the mail and passed the sheriff's office. The early May weather was warm, and the door was open. A pile of wanted posters lay in disarray on the floor by the desk, and on the top was a fair likeness of Lark with the caption: *$500.00 reward. Accessory in Buck Shot bank robbery.*

She grabbed up the posters. Underneath was another with a sketch of Snake and Larado. *$1000.00 Reward. Bank robbers and killers. Teller shot in the back. Contact Buck Shot law enforcement.*

Oh my God. She hadn't thought Larado would shoot a man in the back. Since there was a poster out on her, it wouldn't be but a little while before someone around here recognized her. Very quietly, she clutched the posters, glancing around. She could hear the elderly sheriff talking to an inmate in a cell in the back. So far, so good. Lark went out the door, made sure no one saw her, and tore the posters to shreds. She was too close to the town of Buck Shot and she sure didn't want to end up in prison. Damn that Larado for getting her into this mess. She'd like to slap that handsome, grinning face into next week.

Late that afternoon, she told Pierre she would be leaving the next morning.

"So soon? But Miss Mew Mew and I don't want you to go until we're ready to leave town."

"I'll miss you, but I've got some prospects."

"Ah, the young sheriff?"

"Who?" Lark hadn't given another thought to Lawrence Witherspoon since she'd mailed the letter a few days ago.

"You wrote him again, didn't you?"

"I don't think it was meant to be."

"I'm sure you two will be very happy."

Lark laughed. "You're getting ahead of the story."

"I started the correspondence, so I'm responsible for this love match."

"I may not even go to Rusty Spur. West Texas is tough country, even for Texans. Now I've got some packing to do. You ought to be gathering up things too, if you're leaving for New York."

They ate supper together one last time. Afterwards Pierre tried to give Lark a little extra money, which she refused. The next morning, with much tears and hugs, Lark caught a stage. Except she really didn't know where to go from here. She'd at least try to get farther away from the scene of the bank robbery. Later, she took a train and rode that farther south. When she crossed the Red River, she knew she was back in Texas, God's country. She was homesick for her uncle's ranch and too pigheaded stubborn to go home defeated. She decided she couldn't face "I told you so." But in the meantime, what to do? Where to go?

Rusty Spur. The words popped into her head. She'd heard it was an isolated, tiny town way out in west Texas. West Texas was a vast, empty, flat prairie. The chances that anyone would find her there were pretty small. She wouldn't have to marry the sheriff—she'd go out there, get herself a job, and make her decision later. If she didn't like the town, she could always leave and go someplace else. "Everyone says that's the trouble with you, Lark," she muttered. "You never face up to anything. When the going gets tough, you run."

This was the most *loco* thing she'd done in her life—except for running away and then getting mixed up with Larado, that drunken saddle tramp.

In Dallas, she sent a wire to the sheriff in Rusty Spur:

Dear Sheriff Witherspoon. Stop. Coming to visit your town. Stop. You are not obligated in any way. Stop. I intend to get a job and just need a friend. Stop. Most sincerely, Lacey Van Schuyler.

After she'd sent the wire and gotten back on another train headed west, she had grave misgivings. Land's sake, what kind of fool thing had she done? Well, she needed a place to hide out until this whole thing blew over and no more wanted posters got sent out. The Territory might not send posters to Texas anyway. The farther away she got from the scene of the crime, the better off she was.

The train only went within ten miles of the town, although it was building that direction, the conductor told her. Then she had to take another stagecoach. She almost lost her nerve and got back on the train. After all, running away when faced with trouble was the thing she did best. Just as she was making that decision, the train slowed to a stop, and the conductor put her valise out on the crossroads. There was nothing visible for miles.

"You'll like the town," the conductor assured her. "Tough new sheriff turned it from a wild, wide-open place to a quiet place to live."

"Oh?" She was intrigued. Lawrence Witherspoon

didn't sound like a gun-totin', two-fisted lawman. But how could she tell? "I—I'm not sure I want to go—"

"But of course you do, ma'am." The conductor took her elbow and helped her off the train even as she was protesting. "Town needs strong young women to make it grow. You got folks there?"

"Uh, no, thinking of opening a business."

"A woman running a business?" His craggy face was nothing short of incredulous. "No wonder you're hesitating, lady. Women wasn't meant to run businesses."

That was like waving a red flag at a bull.

"I beg your pardon, I'm a very good businesswoman." She marched off the train and stood there with her valise as the train switched to another track and pulled out.

What had she done? She stared after the departing train, wishing she were on it. There was no place on earth as flat and desolate as west Texas. In the distance, she saw a cloud of dust on the horizon, and then a stage-coach loomed into view. After a few minutes, it pulled up near her in a rattle of harness and a cloud of dust.

"You for the stage, ma'am?" A lanky young boy stared at her with open curiosity. "We don't get many people on the weekly stage, especially not purty women."

She decided to ignore that remark as he hopped down, threw her valise up on top, and helped her into the stage. There was nobody else aboard.

Good, Rusty Spur really was a sleepy town with only a weekly stage. Chances were her wanted posters might not be arriving out there. She knew enough to open her own millinery shop . . . if she could get financing from the local bank. That would buy her some time, and then she could decide what to do next. Maybe when she had her own successful store, she'd be willing to let her family know where she was.

It was a long, dusty ride in the rattling coach out to Rusty Spur. There was a crowd gathered on the street as the dusty stagecoach rolled down Main Street. What was this all about? Then she saw the banner hanging over the middle of the street. WELCOME LACEY VAN SCHUYLER.

Oh dear, she hadn't expected this kind of attention.

The stage drew up before the two-story hotel and the crowd gathered around. As she stepped out, shaking the dust from her dark blue skirt, a man limped forward. "Miss Van Schuyler?"

He wasn't young at all, he was old and missing a front tooth. Her heart plunged. She had a terrible urge to say, *No, I'm Jane Smith. Miss Van Schuyler got off at the last stop.* Except out here in west Texas, Rusty Spur was the last stop, and she seemed to be out of money and out of alternatives. "Uh, yes, I'm Lacey Van Schuyler."

He grinned and nodded. "Lawrence is gonna be mad at me for writin' you and signin' his name, but once he sees you, it won't make no never mind."

"You're—you're not Sheriff Witherspoon?"

He shook his head. "I'm just Bill, his friend who works at the post office and telegraph office. Here he comes now."

Everyone turned to look at the man elbowing his way through the crowd. "Hey, Sheriff," everyone greeted him. "Good to see you, Sheriff."

She turned to get back on the stage and flee, but the stage was already pulling out, leaving her stranded on the wooden sidewalk and surrounded by a friendly crowd with her fate pushing through the crowd toward her. The crowd parted, and she heard a deep voice say, "What's all the excitement?"

The crowd parted to let him through even as she recognized the voice. It couldn't be, but it was. Just before she fainted dead away, Lark recognized that rascal. There was no mistake. It was Larado.

Chapter Four

Lark was aware that the big Texan scooped her up as she fell. Closing her eyes, she wished hard to die on the spot as she heard concerned voices around her.

"What happened to the lady?"

"Maybe her corset's too tight."

"It might be the heat."

A deep male voice she recognized said, "Maybe the lady was just swept away at meeting the sheriff."

The sheriff? She opened one eye and thought about slamming her fist into his nose. No, that wouldn't be smart, he'd probably bleed all over the front of her dress. As far as a corset, she wasn't even wearing one. That, of course, would scandalize her more ladylike sister.

Still, Larado appeared genuinely concerned as he carried her into the hotel, the whole crowd following along behind. Evidently, this was such a sleepy town, even a woman fainting was big excitement.

His chest felt hard and warm against her face. His shirt smelled like tobacco, sunlight, and man smell. She wanted to snuggle even closer in those big arms.

Lark Durango, are you loco? she thought. *This is the same rascal who fled like a scalded cat from the bank holdup and left you to take the blame.*

She felt him place her on a piece of furniture and she opened her eyes. She half reclined on an ornate scarlet horsehair settee in the hotel lobby. Curious faces gathered around.

The big man stared down at her, almost seeming to be concerned. "Somebody get the lady a glass of water," he ordered, "and maybe I'd better loosen her stays."

That brought her sitting up straight with a start. "I'm just fine now." How like that scoundrel to want to molest her. Lark wasn't sure whether she was worried about him putting his big hands on her body, or exposing to the world that she wore no corset. She took a deep breath, getting ready to shout to the world that this was a wanted man, not a lawman. Why, he was so rotten, he'd steal the milk out of a baby calf's bucket.

"Are you all right, *señorita*?" A young Mexican man with a bright smile handed Larado a tin cup of water, thrusting it at her awkwardly.

Puzzled, Lark took the cup. Funny, Larado didn't appear to recognize her. Had she made so little an impression, then? That infuriated her. Then she remembered that she was masquerading as her twin sister. "I'm fine—just the heat. Allow me to introduce myself. I'm Lacey Van Schuyler."

"Lacey?" he asked. "That's a nice name."

I'm Lark, you Stetson-wearing idiot! Remember leaving me hanging on to a pair of rearing horses while you and your low-down buddy robbed the bank? But of course she didn't say that. "Yes, my name is Lacey, and I've got a twin sister named Lark."

She waited for him to react, but he only nodded as he knelt beside the settee. "Funny, I'm one of twins too. Course, we don't claim the family black sheep. He's kind of a rascal."

Kind of? That was an understatement of the year. Lawrence? Larado? Could there possibly be two Texans this good-looking? *Lark, are you out of your mind? You know who this scoundrel is.* There might be a lot of rascals in Texas, but surely there couldn't be two like this one.

The Mexican grinned and nodded toward his buddy. "Oh, this is the sheriff, the one Bill wrote you about. Sheriff Witherspoon, didn't you say howdy to the lady?"

"Bill did what?" Lawrence? Larado? took off his hat and wiped his forehead with a red bandana.

The young man shuffled his boots. "Uh, maybe you'd better ask him about that, *sí*?"

The old man with the missing tooth limped forward. "We was planning you a surprise, Larry."

The tall man scowled. "That do seem like a bit more than a surprise. Paco, you in on this?"

The young Mexican nodded. "*Sí*, so is half the town. There's no young women here and we wanted you to be happy and stay."

The sheriff's face turned as white as a catfish's belly.

"So you had no idea about the advertisement?" Lark asked.

"Advertisement?" Larado—or Lawrence—or whatever the hell his name was, blinked. His rugged face stayed white under the shock of black hair as if he'd been bitten by a rattlesnake. "What advertisement?"

"Uh," mumbled young Paco, "I think the sheriff ought to take the lady up to her room and we'll talk about all this later."

"You're damned right we will, deputy," the sheriff growled. Then he blushed and seemed flustered. "Excuse me, ladies, for cussin' in front of you."

Lark blinked. This almost bashful man was a long way from the irrepressible rascal who slapped women on the bottom and called them "sweetie." Could there really be a twin brother after all? It didn't seem likely, but on the other hand, she wasn't sure the saddle bum was smart enough to pull the same kind of trick she was pulling.

In the silence, Paco made a sweeping bow. "In case nobody's said it, welcome to Rusty Spur, *señorita*."

"Thank you." She didn't feel very welcome. All the other faces were smiling at her, but the sheriff didn't smile. He looked like he had just put his boot in a bear trap and didn't know how to get out. Was getting married to her that horrifying to him? Was this the unmitigated rascal who had left her holding his horse while he robbed a bank?

So the sheriff hadn't sent for her. And by the look of his stricken face, he had no intention of getting married. How humiliating.

"I—I just came to get acquainted." She gulped.

The crowd around them buzzed like flies on a sugar bun.

"Well, now, Larry." Bill took out a bandana and wiped his wrinkled face. "We was all in on it. It was just a little ad in the mail-order bride section."

"What?" Larado croaked. "Miss," he turned to Lark, "I reckon you've been brought here under false pretenses."

"Obviously." Lark resisted the urge to pour the rest of the cup of water on him. She gave Larado a steely glaze. "You look vaguely familiar to me, Sheriff."

He shook his head as the color began to return to his rugged face. "I don't reckon we've ever met, ma'am. I know I'd remember such a purty girl. Now, I've got a twin brother who's kind of a rascal—Larado. Maybe you crossed his path?"

Could it be? Well, anything was possible. "Isn't that a coincidence?" She gulped. "I too have a twin. Her name is Lark."

Larado? Lawrence? still stared into her face. Was this not the rascal who had left her to deal with the law while he fled the robbery?

A motherly, plump lady of maybe fifty pushed through the crowd. "For heaven's sake, everyone should stop gawkin' like they never seen a lady before." She paused, wiping her hands on her apron. "I'm Mildred Bottoms, proprietor of this, the best hotel in Rusty Spur."

"It's the *only* hotel in Rusty Spur," a small, thin boy said.

"Hush, up, Jimmy." The gray-haired woman patted him on the head.

"Pleased to meet you," Lark said. "I'm Lacey Van Schuyler."

The older woman looked sympathetic. "Reckon the boys have made a joke, but they meant well. Now let's get you up to your room and give you a chance to rest and clean up."

She'd vote for that. It would give her a chance to figure all these unexpected surprises out. "I really would like to rest a little."

"We don't get many young ladies out here." The plump woman pushed a wisp of gray hair back in her bun. "I think in honor of your arrival, Miss Van Schuyler, we'll arrange a barn dance tonight."

A chorus of agreement ran through the crowd.

Lark started to get to her feet, but the sheriff protested. "You may be a little dizzy yet, miss. I'll carry you up to your room."

"You needn't bother—" she began. "I think my legs still work." She stood up, a little dizzy, and took an uncertain step.

"I reckon you need some help, miss." Lawrence? Larado? scooped her up in his big arms and started toward the stairs with long strides, followed by the crowd.

"Really, I think I can manage fine," she protested, but the big man kept walking. He made her feel tiny in his embrace.

"Don't want anything to happen to you, Miss Van Schuyler," he said in a resolute voice. "You might fall down the stairs or something."

"What?"

"You heard me, ma'am." He kept walking with the crowd following along behind.

Was that a threat? If he was Larado, she seemed to be the only one who knew his secret. He might do her in just to keep her quiet. But he had such a handsome face, and she fit into his big arms like she belonged there. He kicked open the door of a room and carried her in, dumping her on the bed. "There you are, ma'am."

The crowd had followed along behind and were gathered around, staring in open curiosity.

"Heavens," scolded Mrs. Bottoms. "Everybody clear out and let the lady rest up some. Lawrence, you'll come pick up the lady for the barn dance tonight?"

He hesitated, fidgeting like he had ants down his long handles. "Well, somebody's got to patrol the town. Maybe Paco could pick her up. There's lots of fellas that'll be willin' to dance with her."

"Hear! Hear!" yelled several of the men in the crowd.

The young Mexican grinned. "I'd be *mucho* pleased to, *señorita*."

Well, maybe the sheriff wasn't Larado. She couldn't imagine the man she'd known passing up a chance at dancing and some fun. This one was worried about patrolling the town. He looked as serious as a hanging judge.

"That will be fine," Lark said and breathed easier. "What time will the dance start?"

"Eight o'clock," Mrs. Bottoms announced. "That gives the ladies time to whip up some refreshments. Now everyone clear out."

Larado? Lawrence? touched the brim of his hat with two fingers. "Good day to you, Miss Lacey. Hope you enjoy your visit to Rusty Spur." He seemed sincere enough.

The whole crowd left slowly and reluctantly, but Larado or Lawrence or whoever he was cleared out like his pants were on fire. Lark was left sitting on the bed in disarray trying to figure this mess out. If this sheriff was Larado, he certainly didn't have the easy charm that she remembered. This man acted almost awkward around women. Could Larado really have a twin brother?

She groaned aloud. What kind of mess had she made? True, she was in a sleepy, remote settlement where she might be safe enough, but now she was going to have to continue to masquerade as her sister, Lacey—that perfect and prissy lady. Lark wasn't sure she could do that, but until she could figure out what to do next, she'd have to keep up the masquerade. She didn't even have enough money to catch the weekly stage.

Lark got up, went to the window, and stared out. She saw the sheriff crossing the street with long strides, maybe heading to his office. My! He had wide shoulders. *Don't even think about him, Lark. He surely isn't interested in you.* That hurt her pride a little. The street below her was dusty and quiet. A lone bay horse stood tied to a hitching rail down by the general store and a hound dog lay asleep in the middle of the dirt street. This really was an isolated place, Lark thought as she leaned out for a better look. A feed store, a church, a blacksmith shop, four saloons, but three of them looked to be boarded up. Why, there didn't even appear to be a bank in Rusty Spur.

She had an urge to grab her bag, slip out the back door, and leave. *Leave, how?* The stage was gone. Yet she had always run when faced with an bad situation, and she didn't see why she should change now. Well, land's sake, she was stuck in Rusty Spur for at least a week. Lark wondered if the upright Lawrence had any idea his brother was an outlaw and a bank robber. Maybe that was what had driven him into law enforcement, trying to clean up the family name from the shame his rascal brother had heaped on it.

The little boy called Jimmy brought her a pitcher of water. He was a thin child with big, dark eyes. "Have you ridden a train? I like trains."

"Yes, I have." She smiled at him.

"Mrs. Bottoms said this was so you could wash up."

Lark loved children. "Are you Mrs. Bottoms's grandson?"

He shook his head. "Nope. My folks died of the typhoid last year. She took me in." He looked up at her curiously. "You gonna marry our sheriff?"

She felt herself flush and shook her head. "I don't think so, it's all just been a big mistake."

"Oh." He looked disappointed. "We all like the sheriff. I thought if he got married, he'd adopt me."

"I'm sure he'd be pleased to have a fine son like you, Jimmy, but maybe not yet." She patted his shoulder. "Now you'd better run along and help Mrs. Bottoms get ready."

He looked at her gravely, nodded, and left.

Such a sweet little boy. Someday she hoped to have one just like him. Lark filled her washbowl and rinsed off the west Texas dust. So the sheriff wasn't even going to bother coming to the barn dance? If he'd been Larado, no doubt he'd have wanted a chance to talk to her and beg her not to tell what she knew, but he hadn't bothered. Maybe he was indeed a straight-shooting, honest lawman. Lark sighed. Somehow, she had preferred the charming rascal.

"Lark, you ought to be ashamed of yourself for even thinking that," she scolded herself aloud. What was it women found so intriguing about bad boys? She reminded herself again that Larado had gotten her in big trouble and then run like a jackrabbit. If she ever saw him again, she intended to see if she could get him thrown so far back in jail, the deputy would have to ship daylight to him.

She didn't really want to go to the barn dance and face all the curious stares. Word had probably already spread about what the sheriff's pals had done, and everyone would feel sorry for her—the jilted mail-order bride. That smarted and hurt her pride a little. Okay, she'd go anyway and hold her head high. Maybe everyone would think she'd turned him down.

She tried to decide what to wear. She really only owned two good dresses besides the severe dark blue traveling outfit she wore—she preferred men's pants and cowboy boots. She laid out the yellow dress and then smoothed out her blue and white checked gingham with the lace around the low-cut neck. It showed the curves of her breasts. She'd wear that one. She combed her long dark hair and pulled it back with a blue ribbon. Looking in the mirror, she pinched her cheeks and sucked her lips until they were red. Finally she stuck a lilac sachet between her breasts. She was as ready as she'd ever be.

Outside, the sun was setting, red as blood, and a workman was going down the street, lighting the few oil street lamps. With the window open, she heard laughter and an off-key piano drifting from the one saloon. Yes, indeed, it was a sleepy town. That suited her just fine. She was safe from being arrested here.

A knock at the door. "Dear?" Mrs. Bottoms's voice. "You about ready? Paco's here."

"Ready as I'll ever be." She grabbed a blue shawl from her valise and went out into the hall.

"My, don't you look purty?" the old lady said. "You're gonna turn a few heads tonight. You know, we don't really have any young single women in these parts. After seein' you, honey, I reckon some more of those cowboys will be puttin' ads in mail-order bride papers."

Lark felt her face burn. "It wasn't as if I didn't have other offers," she apologized.

"I don't doubt that, honey, but a man with a badge and a gun sure can take a lady's eye. I know. My Sam was a marshal over in Abilene. I came here for peace and quiet after he was killed."

"I'm sorry to hear that." They went down the stairs.

"I'm okay with it now, but I've got my memories. That's why I think so much of our new sheriff. Lawrence Witherspoon is cut from the same cloth as my Sam."

"You think so?"

"I'm a pretty good judge of people," the plump woman said. "You know, you wouldn't believe it now, but until Lawrence came in and put on that badge, this was a wild, wide-open town."

"Rusty Spur? I heard that, but I didn't believe it."

"Heavens, yes." Mrs. Bottoms nodded. "Robbers came through here headed for Mexico to hide out—rustlers stealin' herds off some of these isolated ranches. Our sheriff don't use his gun, but folks respect him. And I can tell you, I think he could outdraw some of these thugs if he had to. They say he used to be a Texas Ranger."

Well, the man must be Larado's twin brother, because she couldn't imagine Larado doing anything except hanging out in saloons, slapping women on the bottom, and inviting himself up to their beds. "How long's he been here?"

"Lawrence? Just a little while. Hear he came from El Paso, and you know how tough El Paso is," Mrs. Bottoms said.

"He ever say anything before about a twin brother?" Lark asked.

The old lady's brow furrowed. "I'm not sure. Maybe. Yes, I think so."

Lark drew a sigh of relief. Maybe she could stop worrying about the scoundrel of a brother.

Paco stood at the bottom of the stairs, looking all clean with his hair wet from combing. He wore a deputy's badge on his western shirt. Paco held his hat in his hand and looked uneasy, standing on one foot and then the other. Now his dark eyes lit up as he saw her. "Very beautiful. *Sí, señorita.* I'm honored to drive you to the barn dance."

"And me too, and Jimmy," the older lady reminded him.

He bowed low. "Of course, *señora,* you too. I do hope you bring those *muy bueno* sand plum cobblers you make?"

She laughed. "Of course. Get the basket out of the kitchen. Did the men get that beef on the spit?"

He nodded. "*Sí, señora.* Even now, it is being barbecued to a crisp brown." He went into the back and returned with a basket. "Oh, we didn't give the *señorita* a chance to shine with her cooking."

"Uh, maybe next time." Lark gulped. Her aunt

Cimarron said Lark couldn't cook even a biscuit so a dog would eat it. Well, she wouldn't stay long, so no one here would ever know that. As soon as she felt the trail had grown cold, Lark would leave. Where she would go next, she couldn't be sure. Tears came to her eyes as she walked out to the buckboard. She had a sudden wave of homesickness. At least she was in Texas. You could take a gal out of Texas, but you couldn't take Texas out of the girl.

Paco helped everyone up in into the buckboard, Lark seated next to him, then climbed up and snapped the reins at the bay horse. "Did you like our sheriff?"

Lark sputtered with embarrassment. "I—I don't know—I just barely met him."

"Paco," Mrs. Bottoms scolded, "what a question! You're embarrassin' the lady."

Jimmy piped up. "I think he liked her. Are they gonna get married?"

"Jimmy!" the old lady scolded.

Lark felt the blood rush to her face, but she had to ask. "Why—what makes you think he liked me?"

Paco chuckled. "Sheriff Witherspoon don't say much, but he was smiling when he left the hotel. He's a good sheriff, no, *Señora* Bottoms?"

"One of the best," the lady declared as they rode along. "Varmints sure back down from him when he gives them that squinty-eyed glare and almost whispers for them to throw down their guns."

"Hmm." Lark was impressed.

"Besides, *señorita*," Paco said, "everyone says that he used to be a Texas Ranger down around El Paso."

Lark blinked. "Then what's he doing out in a sleepy place like Rusty Spur?"

Paco lowered his voice. "They say he killed a man by mistake and it got to him. Besides, he's got a brother that brought shame to to the family."

"You can say that again," Lark said.

"What?" asked Mrs. Bottoms.

"Nothing," said Lark. A mysterious ex–Texas Ranger. It was romantic and thrilling. Maybe Lawrence Witherspoon could be as interesting as his saddle-tramp brother. "I notice the town has no bank?"

"Well," Mrs. Bottoms said somewhat defensively, "ours closed 'cause it had been robbed so much. But with the new sheriff and the railroad comin' in sometime this summer, the town'll grow, and I reckon we'll get one. They won't be afraid to open up here with a tough sheriff like we got to protect the money."

He's sure different from his brother, Lark thought. Larado would rob the bank, but Lawrence would protect it. She began to like Lawrence, even if he wasn't as charming.

When the buckboard pulled up in front of the big red barn, it looked like most of the county must have heard about the dance. There were horses, wagons, and buggies everywhere, and the barn glowed with lantern light. From inside, Lark heard fiddle music drifting on the warm May air.

Paco assisted Lark from the buggy.

"Heavens," declared the hotel owner as Paco helped her down, "looks like half the county has come to our wingding."

The more people, the better chance someone might have seen a wanted poster, Lark thought, but she'd just have to take that chance. After all, this was a very isolated area.

Cowboys rushed forward to meet her, stumbling over their feet in embarrassment, pulling off their Stetsons. "Howdy, ma'am, so you're the mail-order-bride lady."

"That's my fault and Bill's, *señores.*" Paco looked embarrassed. "The sheriff didn't even know she was coming."

She blushed furiously as the cowboys gathered around. "Then that means she ain't really spoke fer. I'd be much obliged if you'd save me a dance, miss."

She had never felt so popular. "Of course I'll try to save each and every one of you a dance," she said graciously.

They all beamed, and one of them took the basket from Mrs. Bottoms. "What you got in here, ma'am?"

"Pies and such."

Even in the moonlight, Lark could see the faces light up. "Mm. It's been a while since we've eat anything good. I'll bet the young lady is a good cook too."

"Actually, I'm a terrible cook," Lark answered.

"And she's modest, too," said one of the cowboys. The others nodded. "That's a good trait in a woman."

She had spoken the truth, and they didn't believe her. Well, her conscience was clear, in case the cowboys ever ate any of her cooking. She didn't say that she could hold her own in any type of riding, shooting, or ranch work. Those were not things cowboys liked to be outdone in.

The ranch hands trailed the ladies like hungry pups as they walked toward the barn.

One of them whispered, "She's real purty, ain't she? You reckon any *hombres* got a chance?"

"The sheriff must be *loco* if he don't grab this bit of calico up."

Lark didn't know whether to be relieved or disappointed that the sheriff was going to be patrolling the town rather than coming to the dance. The inside of the big barn was aglow with lanterns. It smelled of fresh hay and roasting beef that turned on a spit outside. Bales of straw were scattered about so people could sit down. Over to one side, a small band of settlers sawed away on fiddles or plucked guitar strings. . . . *Chicken in the bread pan, chicken in the dough, swing your partners and do-si-do . . . .*

Ladies gathered in groups to visit while the men traded stories, slapping their knees when someone told a good joke. Children ran through the crowd, yelling and playing. The whole scene made Lark homesick for her uncle Trace Durango's ranch, the Triple D.

The music stopped suddenly, and an old rancher climbed up on a box. "All right, folks, choose your partners for the Virginia reel, and don't mob that new young lady. Since there ain't enough ladies to go around, some of you will have to be heifers."

A groan went up from the young cowboys, but half a dozen men stood patiently while someone tied a red bandana around their arms to signify they would dance the lady's part for a while. In the meantime, Lark was surrounded by a crowd of bashful young cowboys. "Miss, will you be my partner?"

"Wait your turn, Jethro," another scolded.

"What do you mean, Al? I saw her first."

"No, you didn't. I saw her the minute she stepped off the stage."

There was lots of pushing and shoving, vying for her attention. "Me, Miss Van Schuyler."

"No, me. I asked her when she got out of the buggy."

"Gentlemen, gentlemen." She raised her voice and made a soothing gesture. "I'll dance with all of you, just wait your turn."

Mildred Bottoms, at her elbow, said in an undertone, "Are you sure you want to do that, my dear? There must be a couple of dozen of them green young fellas."

"If I don't, there may be a riot," Lark said.

"Ain't it nice to be so popular, though?" Mrs. Bottoms smiled.

Except with the sheriff, Lark thought. He didn't seem even interested in her at all. That annoyed her no end. His rascal of a brother would have slapped her on the bottom and called her "sweetie."

It seemed the cowboys were drawing straws. One let out a yell. "I got it! I get to dance with her first!" He pushed forward, grinning. His face was shiny with scrubbing, and his longish hair was slicked down with water.

"Allow me, ma'am." He bowed to her and offered her his arm.

She took it with a smile. "I'd be pleased to, cowboy."

"You kin call me Buck, miss."

Buck danced with more enthusiasm than skill, but she managed to keep her small slippers out from under his cowboy boots. When they finished that dance, another cowboy—this one smelling of rose water hair tonic—grabbed her and whirled her out on the rough board floor. After that, there was another and another.

Paco finally asked her to dance, and she accepted gratefully. "I swear I'm going to regret promising to dance with them all, but I'll do my best."

The young Mexican deputy grinned at her. "Now you can see why I sent for you. Everyone's afraid that if the sheriff don't find a woman, he won't stay here, and the town needs him."

"Doesn't appear to me he's much interested," Lark said as they moved to line up for the next square dance.

"Oh, he's just shy and takes his job serious, *sí*?"

"Well, he does seem conscientious," she admitted grudgingly. There was a strength and integrity about him that Lark liked.

After an hour, someone yelled that the meat was ready, and the little band quit playing. The ladies began serving out of big pans of cornbread, beans, and cole slaw. There were pies, cakes, cookies, and more barbecued beef than the whole town could eat. Lark hadn't realized she was so hungry. The friendly ranchers' wives kept refilling her plate and her lemonade cup over her halfhearted protests.

They were just finishing up, and the band had taken their positions to play again, when there was a commotion at the door. Everyone craned their necks to see what was happening. People began to step away as a motley group of *hombres* came through the door. They were a rough-looking bunch, Lark thought with alarm.

Mrs. Bottoms nudged her. "Heavens, some of that saloon crowd and railroad workers."

The leader needed a shave and a bath, Lark thought as he swaggered across the floor, followed by his friends.

Paco took a deep breath. "Holy mother of God, I better go get the sheriff." With that, he slipped out a side door.

The bad *hombre* strolled across the floor and stopped in front of Lark. He had an iron railroad spike stuck in his belt. The long heavy spike would make a good weapon. "So you're the new pretty they're gossipin' about in town? I'm Otto. Come on, honey, let's have us a dance."

Lark hesitated. *Oh my, what am I going to do now?*

Chapter Five

Lark took a deep breath as the varmint glared down at her. All the intruders were armed, but none of the respectable men were.

"Come on, honey," Otto demanded, "let's have us a dance. My friends want to dance too. Choose a woman, fellas." He turned and shouted at the little band. "Give us some music!"

The elderly men in the band looked at each other uncertainly as the rough *hombres* each grabbed a woman. Then they began an off-key version of "The Eyes of Texas."

The villain holding Lark scowled. "Don't want none of that slow stuff," he shouted at the band. "Don't you know 'Little Brown Jug' or 'Camptown Races'?"

The little band began to play "Yellow Rose of Texas," loudly if not well. They looked as frightened as the citizens standing around the barn. The intruders dragged their partners out onto the barn floor. Otto pulled Lark out and held her too closely. "All right, girlie, let's dance some."

She tried to pull away from him, but he kept a tight grip. His clothes looked dirty, and she could smell him. "I don't want to dance with you." She jerked out of his grasp and gave him a hard smack up the side of his head.

He looked stunned and shocked. "No woman is gonna—"

He came at her, and she grabbed a pitchfork and waved it dangerously. The little band stopped playing, and the villain's partners paused in middle step with their unwilling partners. "Come one step closer," Lark said, "and I put this through the part of your body you cherish most."

"Now, honey"—he grinned at her, gesturing for her to lower her weapon—"you just put that thing down before you hurt yourself, and we'll finish our little dance."

"I believe my dance card is all filled up," Lark said and then she kicked him between the thighs. When he doubled up with a groan, she whacked him on top of the head with the pitchfork. He stumbled and fell. The crowd began to laugh. Even his own men were guffawing.

"All right," Lark yelled, "the party's over. Now you rascals take your boss and get out of here before I put this pitchfork through his fat you-know-what."

Even though the intruders were all armed, nobody moved toward her. They looked at their boss and then at each other uncertainly. Probably they had never had a girl show such spunkiness before. Otto stumbled to his feet and backed away, wobbling in his boots. "You ain't seen the last of us, you spunky little tart."

Lark ran at him with the pitchfork. "Get out, I said!"

Otto turned and fled, his men following in confused disarray. An excited buzz ran through the crowd and then the people began to applaud.

"What a girl!" some man shouted.

"Did you ever see such spunk?"

"That's the girl for our sheriff, all right!"

They all gathered around to cheer her. Most of the men appeared to be a little embarrassed that they hadn't spoken up.

Lark suddenly felt shaky herself. She couldn't believe

she had stood up to the thug. She had done it instinctively. In the past, she had always run from trouble.

"Heavens," sighed Mildred Bottoms. "I reckon the dance can start again."

Now men lined up to dance with Lark. "If'n you should decide the sheriff ain't the man for you," one said, "I'd be right proud to get hitched to you."

"Miss Van Schuyler, if you decide you don't want to marry the sheriff, I'd sure like to court you."

The sheriff. She had forgotten about Larado or Lawrence or whatever the hell his name was. She still hadn't solved that problem.

About that time, the sheriff strode into the barn. "I just passed all those railroad workers outside leavin' like their coattails was on fire. What happened here?"

Immediately, the tall, lanky Texan was surrounded by people wanting to tell him about the incident and how the "spunky little filly" had saved the day.

He pushed through the crowd to Lark. "Are you all right, Miss Van Schuyler?"

Now that it was over, she was shaking at her own impertinence. She who always ran had stood her ground. She'd probably never do it again. "I'm fine, really I am."

"In that case, ma'am, would you care to dance?" He took off his Stetson and bowed low, a little shy and almost courtly with his manners.

Larado would have been winking and slapping all the girls on the bottom, she thought. "Why, yes, Lawrence, I think I'd like that."

The band began to play a soft, sweet tune, popular in the days of the Civil War: "Lorena." Lark felt everyone's gaze upon her as he led her out on the barn floor and took her in his arms. She hadn't realized how big and wide shouldered he was. She felt protected in his embrace as they danced. The warmth and the strength of the man made her take a deep breath. He smelled of soap, sun, and a rose water hair tonic. He danced well, and she relaxed against him, wherein he pulled back and put space between them. "I'm sorry, ma'am, I didn't mean to be so fresh and improper. I wouldn't want to offend a lady."

She had never felt so protected and feminine—she, who was the family tomboy. She smiled up at him. "The lady is not offended."

Maybe Fate had had a hand in bringing her to Rusty Spur to meet this virile knight of the west Texas plains.

"Everybody's lookin' at us," he gulped, turning red. "Would you like to go outside in the cool air for a moment?"

"Of course." They slipped out the back door and stood looking over the landscape. She shivered and pulled her shawl closer.

"Oh, Miss Van Schuyler, are you cold? It's a mite cool for May. Maybe I shouldn't have brought you out in the night air—"

"I'm fine," she said, not wanting to admit that just being close to this courtly gentleman was making her shudder with excitement. They looked over a scenic valley, shadowed now except for the full moon.

"Ain't it purty?" the sheriff said with a sigh of awe. "You know Texans say that on the eighth day, God created Texas, and that was the best of his work."

Lark laughed. "That might be sacrilegious."

"You wouldn't get a Texan to think that." He seemed so earnest and sincere as he looked down at her. They were standing close, too close. For a long moment, they looked into each other's eyes, and she felt his big hands tighten gently on her arms. She had the feeling that he was going to kiss her, and she wanted him to. She stood on her tiptoes and turned her face up to him, closing her eyes.

She heard him take a deep breath, then he cleared his throat and stepped away from her. She blinked and opened her eyes. He looked uncertain. "I wouldn't want you to get the wrong impression of me, ma'am. I ain't one to be forward with a lady."

Damn him, he was a perfect gentleman. Too bad at this moment he wasn't more like his rascal brother. She had a terrible need to be gathered into his strong embrace and kissed and kissed some more.

To break the awkward silence, she turned and looked out over the distant prairie. "Yes, this is beautiful out here."

"Ain't it, though? Some of them Yankee girls might not appreciate the big ocean of plains we got here, but a Texas girl does."

"I like it—I like it a lot." She wished he'd reconsider and kiss her, but she didn't think he could be pushed into doing that by the threat of Apache torture. What would he think if she grabbed him and kissed him? She quickly vetoed that idea, since no doubt he would be shocked out of his boots.

Lawrence sighed. "I been savin' my money, but a lawman don't make much. That valley's for sale, and I'd like to buy it and start ranchin'. Even though it's cheap, it's a little out of my reach."

She stared out at the valley in the moonlight. "How come it's cheap, with the railroad coming in and all?"

He shrugged. "Well, the land's so poor, it'd take three people to raise a fuss on it. Then, too, some of it has that dirty old oil seepin' up and ruining the land for grazin'. It wouldn't be good for nothin'."

"I know what you mean." She nodded sympathetically. "My uncle has some land with the same problem. He's tried to sell it, but nobody wants oily land you can't graze cattle on."

"You ready to go in, ma'am? We stay out here much longer, folks will talk."

"Yes." She wished he'd done something worth gossiping about. She took his arm. It was muscular and warm. She felt it tense when she took it. She could swear he was trembling. She heard him gulp awkwardly. Why, the poor shy thing. She'd have to be gentle with him or he'd never get around to kissing her. She was falling in love with him already.

"Yep." He turned and looked toward the barn. "I reckon we'd better go. Wouldn't want to besmirch your reputation by keepin' you out here too long."

She looked around at the cactus and sand burrs. Did he really think anyone would think they were lying on the ground making passionate love? Why, there were probably scorpions and maybe a tarantula or two. She looked up at him and batted her eyelashes slowly, licking her lips. Maybe she could get him to try to steal one little kiss. "I'm sure you're right, Sheriff."

She heard his sharp intake of breath and saw sweat break out on his forehead. She felt almost as if she were attempting to seduce the tall, courtly lawman. They started walking back toward the barn.

"Maybe—I mean, do you think I could take you for a buggy ride sometime?"

"Certainly. I'd love that." A few hours ago, she'd been ready to clear out of this sleepy town first chance she got, and now. . . .

From inside, the music drifted. She recognized the tune: "Red River Valley." ". . . from this valley they say you are going," she sang softly, "we'll miss your bright eyes and sweet smile . . ."

"Miss Van Schuyler, I reckon you don't mind me sayin' you got a purty voice—sound good as a bobwhite quail."

They paused outside the barn door.

"Why, thank you, Lawrence." She smiled at him, touched by his humble sincerity. *What a fine man. He'd make some girl a good husband. Husband? Are you loco, Lark? You're on the run, accused of being an accessory to a bank robbery, and you're thinking how it would be to marry a sheriff? What do you think he'd say if he found out and had to lock you up in the hoosegow? On the other hand, what* better place for a wanted felon to hide than in the house of the local sheriff?

Lark said, "I've got to be able to support myself. Do you suppose there's any jobs available for a woman in Rusty Spur?"

"A job?" He blinked. "Why, Miss Lacey, women don't work much here except those at the Cross-eyed Bull Saloon, and the kind of work they do . . ." His voice trailed off and she actually saw his face turn scarlet. "Never mind, ma'am, a lady wouldn't know about such goings-on."

Lawrence Witherspoon would faint if he knew she used to serve drinks at the Last Chance, one of the toughest dives in Oklahoma Territory. She wondered if she could keep him from ever finding out about that. Somehow, this shy sheriff's opinion meant a great deal to her. "I was raised on a ranch," she said. "I can rope and ride and shoot."

He laughed. "That'd be right handy on your own place," he said. "Help a husband out if he couldn't afford hired hands at first, but no Texan is gonna give a lady a job as a cowhand."

She had a terrible urge to kick him in the shins for his male superiority. No, someplace higher up. "Do you suppose the general store would be needing a clerk?"

He stopped and seemed to think it over. "Mr. Snootley might like that fine, but his wife wouldn't. 'Course, she ain't here half the time—always running off to Abilene to visit her sister or to buy pretties like dresses and hats."

An idea came to her. "You know, I used to work in a millinery shop. Do you think there'd be a need for that here?"

His rugged face brightened. "Well, now, there might be, Miss Lacey, what with the train comin' soon and more people movin' to town. Mrs. Snootley is always complainin' that she has to go off to shop 'cause her husband won't carry much in the way of pretties for ladies. He says there ain't enough call for it."

"Land's sake, there might be, once the train gets here with new settlers." Abruptly, she thought of something and wilted. "Oh, I just remembered, I don't have any capital to start up a shop. Maybe the bank—"

"Oh, we ain't got a bank," he told her. "Folks around now just tuck their savings under their mattresses. But we're bound to grow. The mayor is talkin' about advertisin' in some big-city papers to see if we can get a banker interested in movin' here."

Lark considered for a long moment. She could certainly borrow the money from Uncle Trace. After all, the Durango spread was one of the biggest in Texas. However, she was too proud to ask, and she didn't intend to come out of hiding until she could be as admired as her twin sister. If she had a successful shop and a handsome husband, she'd be proud to return home in triumph. Of course, there was still the little matter of the bank robbery. . . .

"Are you worried, Miss Lacey?" The big man took both of her small hands in his large ones gently but awkwardly. "I reckon you'd be too proud to ask, but I got a few dollars put aside for that ranch." He lowered his voice. "I'd be right proud to help you out some."

"I couldn't take your money, Lawrence. You hardly know me."

He grinned and looked bashful, scuffing the toe of his boot in the dust. "I reckon I know all I need to know. You're a fine, honest, upstanding person, Miss Lacey. I'd trust you with my money."

Oh, if this sweet, gentle man only knew. She winced at how innocent he was and then loved him for it. "Oh, I don't think I could—"

"Don't make a decision right now, ma'am," he urged. "Think on it some."

"But it's your ranch money," she said, aghast, "and the shop might not make it."

He looked deep into her eyes. "Ma'am," he drawled, "that don't make me no never mind. I just know I can trust you. Some folks just have an honest look about them, and I know you're that kind."

At that moment, she wished she were everything this wonderful man thought she was. This was a real man—the kind of man she'd been looking for all her life. How ironic that he was a twin to the biggest rascal who ever sat at a poker table. She blinked back tears as she reached up and touched his handsome, rugged face. "Lawrence, I'll think about it, all right? There's a lot to consider."

He grinned at her in the moonlight. In that moment, he looked exactly like his brother, but of course he had so much more character. "I—I like you a lot, Miss Lacey. I'm glad now my friends put that ad in the paper."

"I think I am too. Now let's go in and dance, Lawrence, then I'll let you drive me back to the hotel. It's been a long, long day."

"Yes, ma'am." He smiled and took her into the barn, where they danced a waltz. He felt rigid as a spring against her, but she felt safe and protected in his embrace. She would be safe with Lawrence Witherspoon, forever safe in his arms. She allowed herself to be swept away by the music as they danced, even though she knew that townspeople smiled and nodded and whispered. *Let them,* she thought. *After all, I may just be staying in this isolated town.*

When the dance ended, Lawrence tied his horse behind the buggy, put Paco, little Jimmy, and Mrs. Bottoms in the backseat, then offered a sweaty hand to Lark, as if he thought she were going to bite him. She put her small hand in his and lifted her skirt with her other hand, making ready to step up into the buggy. At that point, she caught her foot in the hem of her dress and almost fell. The sheriff caught her and lifted her up into the seat. "Are you hurt?" His rugged face was gentle with earnest concern.

"I'm fine."

My, what a far cry from his dastardly brother, who had fled the bank robbery in a most ungentlemanly fashion, leaving her to deal with the law.

She smiled at him. He was almost too good, too noble to be true. He got up on the seat beside her, staying way to his side as he cracked the little whip. The buggy started off at a fast clip. She almost wished he would slow the horse down. Besides enjoying the pleasant, start-studded night, she was enjoying riding next to him, and she really didn't want the evening to end.

"Well, heavens," said Mrs. Bottoms from the back. "That was a real wingding."

"Yep," Paco agreed, "we really cut the wolf loose. That was *mucho* party. Did you enjoy it, *señorita*?"

"Very much so." She glanced sideways at the strong profile beside here, remembering standing out by the barn in the darkness and how Lawrence had almost kissed her. She wondered if he might someday get up the nerve to try again. As bashful as he was, she might have to take the bull by the horns and kiss him. He'd probably be so shocked, he'd faint and fall out of his boots.

"Miss Lacey is thinkin' about stayin'," the sheriff said, sounding pleased.

"By the saints, then, you are not angry with me no more, *sí*?" Paco sounded anxious.

The sheriff laughed and glanced over at Lark. "Paco, I'm not mad at you no more. I'm much pleased."

The way he looked at her sent a shiver over Lark. She looked away, flattered by the sheriff's expression and comment.

"Matter of fact," she said, "I'm thinking about opening a millinery shop."

Mrs. Bottoms in the back made a sound of pleasure. "Oh, won't the ladies be pleased. We're all wearing old, battered hats. It's a trip, I'll tell you, to drive clear over to Abilene."

"Soon," Paco said, "the train will connect our town with all the others, and we'll grow big as the capital."

"I hope not," Lawrence said. "I like a small town where everyone can get to know each other." He glanced sideways at Lark again, and his knee brushed against hers, sending a thrill through her. It must have been an accident, she thought, because the man was too shy to make such a bold move deliberately.

Mrs. Bottoms and Paco began chatting about the dance and the rough railroad crowd from the Cross-eyed Bull that had tried to disrupt the party.

"I'll be glad when they finish construction," the sheriff said. "I'd hate to have to kill one of them."

Paco said, "*Sí*, they don't know they're messing with an ex–Texas ranger."

A Texas Ranger. Of course. Lawrence Witherspoon was everything a ranger should be—tall, virile, a bull among steers.

"Otto had better watch out," Lawrence said, frowning. "I heard what happened, Miss Van Schuyler. You can rest assured if Otto steps out of line again, I'll hunt him down and beat him like cornbread batter. Nobody mauls a lady when I'm the law here."

Be still my heart. Like a knight in shining armor he was, riding gallantly to her rescue. "I managed all right," she answered modestly.

"Oh?"

Paco chuckled. "*Sí*, you should have seen her, Sheriff. She kicked him in the—well, you know, and then she took after him with a pitchfork."

Lawrence glanced over at her with admiration. "Nobody expects that from a lady."

Oh, he must never, never know about her past as a waitress slopping beer at the Last Chance. Sir Lancelot must surely want his lady to be Guinevere, pale and chaste and retiring. She almost snorted at the thought. She was a Texas gal, and she could look out for herself—independent, sassy, and sometimes bold as brass. But now when Lawrence looked at her, she felt all clingy and feminine. Why, she'd almost give up bull riding for him. Her tomboy ways might shock him.

Mrs. Bottoms said, "Tell us about the shop, Lacey. I've got a little money I can loan you."

"Oh, I couldn't take your money," Lark protested.

"Well, heavens, I don't know why. Seems like a good investment to me."

"There's an empty building down and across from the hotel that's probably *muy* cheap," Paco suggested.

"That's right," Lawrence said, "It's been empty a long time."

Little Jimmy piped up. "I'd help you clean it up, ma'am."

"Thanks, everyone. I'll look into this in the morning." Lark felt happier than she had in a long time. Maybe she could still straighten out her mess of a life.

In the quiet night, a distant sound echoed suddenly through the darkness.

Lark started. "Land's sake, what was that? It sounded like someone being tortured."

Lawrence laughed. "A prospector's donkey, I reckon," he said. "They roam wild all over the prairie."

"Prospectors?" Lark asked.

"Yes," Mildred Bottoms said. "Was kind of a treasure craze farther out west. It's pretty much died down, but we still have an occasional one come through—or discouraged, head back the other way. They just toss their gear away and turn their donkeys out to go wild. There ain't no sound like it, is there?"

Lark felt relief. "I've never been around a donkey before. On our ranch, we raise good quarter horses."

"You got family in Texas?" Lawrence asked.

She must not say anything that he might use to find out the truth. "Ah, Colorado, actually."

He looked sideways at her a long moment. "Colorado? Then you certainly should know what a donkey sounds like with all that gold prospectin' up there."

How could she have been so stupid? Of course a gold-mining state would have prospectors and donkeys. "Uh, I reckon I forgot what they sound like."

Paco laughed. "How could anyone forget that sound, *señorita*? It sounds like a guitar being smashed while a coyote chokes. I like the sound."

"Surprisingly, I do too," the sheriff chuckled. "They're headstrong, stubborn little creatures, not unlike some women."

Lark managed to resist the urge to take off her high-button shoe and hit the superior male in the head with it. He might be wonderful, but he still had some of the flaws of most men. The sound echoed through the prairie again. The little donkey sounded lonely and lost.

Lark sighed. "I just hope a coyote doesn't get the poor thing."

The sheriff said, "Are you jokin'? Unless they gang up on it, the coyote that attacks one of them little Mexican burros better bring his lunch, because he may be there awhile, right, Paco?"

Paco laughed. "*Sí.* I've seen burros chase a coyote and kick it. It fled yelping and running. Donkeys is stubborn."

Like some women, Lark thought. She still wasn't quite sure what to make of the gallant sheriff, but one thing was sure—she was intrigued enough to stick around awhile and find out. What if a wanted poster got sent from the Territory and the sheriff found out the truth about her? She'd just have to take that chance. In the meantime, he might know where his rascal of a brother was hiding out and just be too loyal to turn him in.

Just then, Sheriff Witherspoon reined in the buggy in front of the hotel, jumped down, and came around. She started to get out, but he caught her waist in his two big hands and lifted her down. For a split second, she seemed to hang in midair as if he were loath to let her go, then he set her on the wooden sidewalk as carefully as if he thought she was a delicate china doll. A girl could get used to being treated like that—even a Texas girl who could ride and rope and shoot as well as any man.

Chapter Six

Mrs. Bottoms, Jimmy, and Paco took the picnic baskets and went in, leaving the two alone out by the buckboard.

Lark said good night, and the shy sheriff shook her hand awkwardly. "Well, good night, Miss Lacey. I hope you had a wonderful time at our dance, despite them railroad rowdies."

His hand was so big, it engulfed hers. She wished he would kiss her, but of course, shaking her hand was about as bold as this brave man could get.

Lark, what are you thinking? You're not supposed to kiss a man until you're engaged to him. That rough Larado might grab a girl and kiss her, but of course, he was no gentleman. Not by a long shot.

"I had a wonderful time." She smiled up at him.

He fumbled with the star on his vest. "Me too."

There was a long, strained silence.

He cleared his throat. "Then I'll see you tomorrow, maybe."

Lark nodded. "Mrs. Bottoms said she'll take me around to all the merchants in town and see if she can find several who might want to invest in my millinery shop."

"Miss Lacey." He hesitated. "I—I told you I got a few dollars. Maybe I could lend you some for your little store."

She was touched and told him so. "But I couldn't do that, Mr. Witherspoon. Land's sake, it isn't proper, and——"

"It would be if we was . . . Oh, never mind." He stubbed the toe of his boot against the ground.

"Besides, now that I know about that little ranch you're saving for, I just couldn't. The shop might fail."

He grinned at her and shook his head. "Not with you runnin' it. I got faith in you."

She put her hand on his arm, so touched she could hardly speak. "Thank you, Mr. Witherspoon."

"I wish you'd call me Lawrence—that is, if you don't think it's too soon."

"And you may call me L-Lacey." She'd almost forgotten her masquerade.

"Oh no, ma'am, I just couldn't. I wouldn't want to appear too forward."

Lark sighed. At this rate, the woman he married would have to live with him a dozen years before he'd ever get up the nerve . . . maybe not even then. What a waste of a handsome hunk that would be. She shocked herself. "Well, then, good night, Lawrence."

"Sleep tight," he said, "and don't let the bedbugs bite."

He was just so naive and childlike. She nodded and ran inside the hotel and upstairs. Once in bed, she couldn't sleep. She liked this little town, and she really liked the sheriff. Maybe her luck might turn after all.

The next day, Mildred Bottoms took Lark around to meet some of the other businesspeople. First she took her to meet the blacksmith who owned the empty store. "Mike, you met this young lady last night."

He was muscular and smeared with soot from his fire. "I sure did." He nodded with a grin. "She has grit—she's spunky. I like that in a woman."

Mrs. Bottoms said, "Lacey, Mr. Dillard is also our mayor."

To the blacksmith, she said, "Lacey plans to open a millinery shop."

He scratched his gray beard. "What is that?"

"You know," Lark put in, "I'll make and sell ladies' hats. With the railroad coming in, there'll be a market."

He groaned aloud. "Don't tell my wife. She spends too much money now."

"Mike," Mrs. Bottoms said, "I want you to let her have that empty store free for two months. If she makes it, you can start charging her rent."

He leaned against his forge and crossed his arms. "Now why would I want to do that?"

Lark said, "Well, it's not bringing in anything right now, is it? With me, you've at least got a chance at a return on your investment."

He grinned. "The little lady is not just a pretty face. She's got savvy. Okay, I'm in." He held out a big, dirty hand and Lark shook it.

"Thanks, Mr. Dillard."

"When you opening?"

Mrs. Bottoms said, "I got to find her some customers first."

"Try the lumberyard, the feed store, and the post office. I don't know if you'll get much interest from old Abner Snootley at the general store."

They nodded and walked out of the blacksmith shop.

They hit the places he mentioned and some others. The men weren't that interested, but their wives were. Lark left most places with no money but promises of customers.

"Let's try the general store anyway," Mrs. Bottoms said.

Abner Snootley was a dour, sour man with one long lock of hair carefully combed over his bald dome. He reeked of peppermint. "I already heard the gossip up and down the street," he grumbled, popping a striped candy into his mouth. "And you can forget it, Mildred. My wife spends too much money on clothes and hats now."

Lark stepped in. "Look at it this way, Mr. Snootley, your

wife wouldn't be gone all the time on the weekly stage to Abilene if she could buy her pretties here in town."

He frowned even more. "Is that supposed to be a selling point? The only peace I get from Bertha's nagging is when she's gone. Otherwise, she spends every dime the store makes."

Mrs. Bottoms smiled. "All right, Abner, but you're missing a real business opportunity to invest. When they get the railroad here in a few weeks, there'll be settlers pouring in, and all those ladies will want hats."

"Humph. If I had money to invest, I'd pay off some of the bills my wife has run up. Now good day to you." He dismissed them with a curt nod.

"Don't say you didn't get the chance," Lark said, and they left. Just outside the door, they bumped into the portly and very fashionably dressed wife. Mrs. Bottoms introduced Lark and told Mrs. Snootley about the shop.

The lady stuck her nose in the air and looked down at them disdainfully. "I'm sure anything this—this girl came up with wouldn't equal the fine things I buy in Abilene."

"On the contrary," Lark said, "I've worked with a superb designer named Pierre, and he taught me the business. I'll turn out some very fashionable hats. All the ladies in town will be wearing them."

Mrs. Snootley sniffed as if she smelled something bad. "If all these bumpkins buy your hats, I probably wouldn't care for them."

Lark took a deep breath to control her temper. "When I get the French Chapeau open, please come in and look over my merchandise. I'd like the opinion of a person with such discerning taste."

The uppity lady seemed slightly mollified. "Well, perhaps I might. Good day to you."

The three parted company and Lark and Mrs. Bottoms walked back to the hotel.

"Dearie, you wouldn't want Bertha as a customer anyway."

"Why not?" Lark asked.

"Well"—the pleasant woman lowered her voice—"they do say she wears something a couple of times and then returns it. That way, she always has nice clothes."

Lark was aghast. "That seems tacky."

"Tacky? Yes. Cheap? Yes. Just don't say you weren't warned about Bertha Snootley. You'd think she came from high society, but I happen to know her father was a butcher back in Cleveland."

Lark sighed. "I really hate borrowing money. If we had a bank in this town, maybe I could get a loan."

Mrs. Bottoms smiled. "The town council is looking for someone to open a bank by running ads in big-city newspapers. Maybe one will turn up."

"Lawrence offered to lend me some, but I hesitated."

Mrs. Bottoms smiled. "Heavens, that means he's serious about you, young lady. You need it, you borrow it. He'll get his money back when you're a big success. Now, what's the next thing we need to do?"

Lark chewed her lip, thinking. "I need to make a list of supplies and get them ordered. Then I need to clean up that shop and get it ready for customers."

"We'll get Jimmy and some of my hotel maids to help. I'm real excited about this."

"Why? You're a businesswoman yourself."

"Honestly, I inherited this hotel from my dad, and at first—after my husband died—I wasn't sure I could run it alone. But I've done all right."

Lark smiled. "I'll bet you've done more than just all right. Why, I bet you could open a second hotel in some other town if you could find someone to run it for you."

The older lady shook her head. "Heavens, I'd have to think about that. Anyway, that's not today's problem. Let's get started on opening your shop." She led Lark into the kitchen and got down the cookie jar, bringing out almost fifty dollars in soiled old bills.

Lark gasped. "Oh, I couldn't take your hard-earned money. You've done so much for me all ready."

The lady shook her head as she pressed the bills into Lark's hand. "I'm a good judge of people, young lady, and I think you'll be a big success. I was right about hiring the new sheriff, and I know I'm right about you. Both of you are loaded with character—you're both true Texans."

Lark's conscience hurt her. She looked away. "Land's sake, I wouldn't go that far, but I'll try not to lose your money for you."

"Now, you get your order ready and take it down to old Bill at the telegraph office down at the end of the street where they're building the new depot. Then we'll start on cleaning up that old building."

In an hour, Lark had her list ready, and the two ladies went down to the telegraph office. On the way back, they crossed the street purposefully and walked past the sheriff's office.

The door was open on this warm day, and the sheriff sat at a cluttered desk with his chair tilted back and his boots up on the desk. He was leafing through wanted posters, squinting and frowning in the bright sun.

For a moment, Lark held her breath. Suppose she was among those posters? That would ruin her chance to straighten out her life—and besides, she didn't want this gallant knight of the Lone Star State to be shocked and disappointed in her. "Why, hello, Sheriff Witherspoon, what a surprise to run across you."

"Howdy, Miss Van Schuyler, Mrs. Bottoms." He clambered to his feet and touched his fingers to the brim of his hat in greeting. "Nice day, ain't it?"

"It certainly is," Lark gushed. "Everyone's being so nice about helping me."

"Now I told you I'd like to put what little I got into your enterprise," Lawrence Witherspoon said.

"Oh, I couldn't—" Lark began.

"Miss, I wouldn't want you to think I was tryin' to put you in a compromisin' position, you know, acceptin' money from a man you ain't married to."

Be still my heart. He was so proper—such a gentleman— a true Texan. "It isn't that." She hesitated. There was just no way to tell him she already cared enough about him that she didn't want to endanger his dream.

"Miss Van Schuyler, I insist. When your hat shop is a big hit, I'd like to get in on it." He gave her that wonderful, crooked grin.

She looked up at him, feeling giddy. "I—I don't know what to think—"

"I insist," he said.

"All right."

Mrs. Bottoms beamed at him. "If I had a son, I'd wish he was just like you."

The sheriff blushed and kicked at the worn wood floor. "You're too good to me, ma'am. I'm just doin' my job."

Modest, too, Lark thought and felt even better about the man. How could this fine paragon of virtue, this towering pillar of strength be related to that swaggering, rowdy rascal, Larado?

"We're headed down to the old building to see how much cleaning it needs," Lark said.

He grinned at her and her heart fluttered. My, he was handsome.

"Well, now, I might just mosey along with you and carry any heavy stuff you got, miss. I need to make my rounds now anyway and see if there's any lawbreakers about."

Lark looked out. That didn't seem too likely. The only thing on the street besides them was the hound dog asleep over in the doorway of the feed store and two horses tied up in front of the saloon, switching flies and stamping their hooves. He was looking for an excuse to walk with them, Lark thought, and she was glad.

They started to walk along the sidewalk, and abruptly,

they heard the most gosh-awful noise—a cross between a cat fight and a dying coyote.

"What on earth?" Lark started.

The sheriff grinned. "Sounds like there's a burro around somewhere."

Mrs. Bottoms frowned. "I don't think anyone in town owns a donkey. Once you got one, you end up with more."

The sheriff nodded. "They're kind of a pest. Don't know why anyone would want one—nobody would pay much for one—so I reckon if a prospector left the area, he'd just abandon it."

"That's sad," Lark said. "Could it be the one we heard last night?"

"Could be," said the sheriff. "It might have followed some wagon into town, knowin' where there was people and horses, there'd be hay and oats."

The braying sounded again, and this time it was closer. "It's coming from down the street," Lark said.

Sure enough, ambling up the street was a small gray donkey. It was thin and frail, with the biggest softest eyes and the longest ears Lark had ever seen. Its tail was straggly, its legs spindly, and its back swayed.

Mrs. Bottoms shook her head. "That is the ugliest, most useless critter I've ever seen."

"Poor thing," Lark cried, and she went out to meet it. It stopped, looked her over, and then walked right up to her. "Why, look how thin it is. I reckon it's hungry."

"Oh, a burro can eat anything," Mrs. Bottoms said. "Cactus, any dry old grass, your vegetable garden, the flowers out of your flowerpots. They're nuisances."

"Here, girl," Lark crooned, stroking its matted hide.

For a moment it looked like it might run, but maybe it didn't have the strength to leave. Lark kept talking to it as she stroked it. The runty burro raised its long ears, studying her.

"Oh, look at her big sad eyes," Lark said as she began to scratch its ears. The little burro sighed and stood there, then began to nuzzle through Lark's pockets. She turned to the others. "Can we find her something to eat?"

Mrs. Bottoms said, "You feed her, you got her, and a burro isn't good for much except as a kid's pet or carryin' prospectors' gear. They're too little to ride and too stubborn to deal with anyway."

Lark stroked the velvety nose. "I don't reckon she would eat much—she's so little." She turned an appealing gaze to the sheriff.

He smiled. "I reckon I could scare up a bucket of oats and a bale of hay."

"Oh, could you? You're so kind." The donkey nuzzled Lark's hand and began to nibble on her dress.

"First thing you know," Mrs. Bottoms said by way of warning, "she'll have a foal, and then another, and then the babies will have colts. What are you gonna do with a whole herd of donkeys?"

"I'll worry about that later," Lark said, looking into the big, brown eyes. "She looks like the heroine in a novel about the Civil War I once read. Magnolia, that's what her name is, Magnolia."

Magnolia promptly brayed that earsplitting noise. A horse trotting down the street reared and whinnied, running away with its rider.

"See?" said Mrs. Bottoms. "Nothing but trouble."

"I don't care. I love her." Lark played with the donkey's ragged mane. "Where can I keep her?"

The sheriff laughed. "I think there's a little stable behind that old store. It'd be about right for Magnolia."

"She's so tame," Lark said. "She'll make a great pet."

"A pest, you mean," Mrs. Bottoms snorted. "You just can't keep a donkey up—they're too smart. They learn to open latches, and then she'll be into everything."

"Maybe not," Lark protested, still stroking the beast.

The sheriff laughed again. "Miss, you don't know much about burros. You just walk her on down to the old store and I'll go get you some feed." He turned and sauntered away.

"What a man!" Lark said, looking after him.

The other lady nodded. "Isn't he, though? Why, every day I pinch myself about how lucky our town is to have him upholding the law. Why, he's almost too good to be true."

The burro seemed eager to follow the ladies as they walked down the street. Magnolia was as tame as a puppy. They led her around to the stable out back. "Here you are, Magnolia," Lark said. "This is your new home."

Magnolia brayed as if she agreed.

The sheriff came around the corner with a bale of hay on one big shoulder, a bale of straw on the other. He tossed them into the stall. "Here you go, Magnolia. I'll go get a bucket of water."

"You're being awfully nice," Lark gushed as the burro spotted the hay, rushed over, and began to eat.

He flushed red. "For a lady, nothin' is too good. You're as kind as you are pretty, ma'am." Then he left to get the water.

"Heavens," Mildred Bottoms said, "you've sure made an impression. I believe that young man is courting you."

"By getting a bucket of water?"

The lady pursed her lips. "You know what I mean. He's too bashful to ask to call on you, I think. He's just doing it his way."

Lark stared down the street after the man. "Well, I like him a lot too." All her life she had waited for a man like this one—and why, oh why did he have to be a sheriff when she was on the run from the law? She wouldn't think ahead. Maybe the wanted posters would never make it this far south.

He brought back a bucket of water, and the little donkey drank and drank.

"Poor thing," Lark said, "she was near done in when she wandered into town."

The sheriff leaned over and stroked the donkey. "She'll be all right now, miss. However, I don't know if this pen will hold her. Donkeys is hard to keep up because they're smart. They can get under fences and learn to open gates."

"Oh, you're just saying that."

He smiled, the most charming crooked smile she'd seen since . . . but of course, they were brothers. When she knew him better, maybe he would talk about the scoundrel in the family.

"You just watch what a nuisance this little rascal will become."

"Land's sake, how can you say that? Magnolia's adorable, aren't you, girl?"

She knelt and put her arms around the burro's neck. It nuzzled her hair.

"Looks like you got a donkey whether you want one or not," the sheriff laughed. "Don't say we didn't warn you."

The little animal settled down on the new straw with a tired sigh as if she knew she'd found a home.

Lark looked up at the rugged sheriff and sighed herself. Maybe she had found a home too.

"Heavens," said Mrs. Bottoms briskly. "Now we've got to get this building cleaned up."

"I'll do it," Lark said. "I just need a broom, a mop, and a bucket."

The sheriff pushed his hat back. "A little slip of a thing like you doin' heavy work like that? Not while there's a man around, Miss Lacey. It's a slow afternoon—I'll help."

She was impressed. "You're not afraid to have some of the men seeing you doing women's work?"

His rugged face turned stern. Yes, she could imagine that this big man used to be a Texas Ranger. "Miss, there ain't an *hombre* in the county would dare make fun of me, and I ain't afraid of nothin'."

Lark sighed. She had never felt so small, fragile, and feminine. What a man!

"He ain't afraid of nothin'," Mrs. Bottoms agreed with

a nod. "Why, only last week, there was a fight out in front of the saloon and someone drew on him. Lawrence here didn't kill him. He just whopped the drunk up the side of the head with his pistol, picked him up, and threw him in jail."

The sheriff looked at the ground and kicked at the dirt, awkward under the praise. "Don't hardly ever use my gun," he said. "No point in killin' a man just 'cause he's got a little red-eye in him. Whompin' him in the head with my pistol seemed to do the job. Mostly, I just give 'em a stern glare, and they back down."

At least he wasn't a cold executioner like Wyatt Earp and some of those others were said to be.

Lark said, "I'm surprised you allow the saloon to stay open, sheriff."

He shrugged. "The Cross-eyed Bull? Men are entitled to a little fun and a drink now and then, Miss Lacey. The town council allows it because it brings in money from trail hands and the railroad workers. So as long as the boys behave themselves, I pretty much leave it alone. The Cross-eyed Bull ain't too bad a place. It don't have many of those hussies, those wicked women workin' there, fillin' men with whiskey and charmin' them outta their pay."

Those hussies, those wicked women. If this upright man only knew that Lark used to serve drinks in a place about like the Cross-eyed Bull, he'd be so shocked, maybe he'd never speak to her again. If he'd seen the tight, skimpy costume she wore, he'd probably keel over like he'd been hit between the eyes. No, he wouldn't understand. She hoped devoutly that he never found out.

She didn't want to think about the past, only the future as she looked up at him. "I reckon I need to see the inside and figure out where to place shelves and counters."

"I'll go get Jimmy and some of my maids," Mrs. Bottoms said. "Sheriff, you'll bring us some water?"

He nodded. "Anything to help out this lovely lady."

Mrs. Bottoms turned and left.

The two of them went inside and stood in the dim light, looking around at the dusty shelves and dirty windows. A tumbleweed blew across the wood floor, and the door hung at an awkward angle, almost off its hinges.

"There's an awful lot of work here for a real lady to do," he said.

"I was raised on a ranch," Lark said, putting her hands on her hips. "I can handle it."

"You got spunk," he said softly, "I like that."

Now it was her turn to flush. "Everyone in town's been awfully nice to me."

"It's a good town," he murmured. "They been good to me too. I see a great future for Rusty Spur, especially when we're gettin' new citizens like you."

There was a long, awkward silence.

"Oh," he said, reaching into his jeans, "here's what little money I got to invest."

"I hate to take it, knowing you're saving for a ranch."

He put the crumpled bills in her hand and closed his big hand over hers.

There was another awkward moment as they looked into each other's eyes. Finally she forced herself to pull away, when it was the last thing she wanted to do. "I'm much obliged for all your help, Sheriff," she said.

"I'm glad to do it," he stammered, swallowing as if he weren't quite sure what to say. They were alone in the dim store, and for a moment she wondered if he was trying to get up the nerve to kiss her. She wanted him to kiss her very much. A moment passed. He was standing so close, she could feel the heat of his big, virile body. She wanted him to grab her, sweep her up in his arms, and kiss her like she had only dreamed of being kissed. Her pulse quickened as she looked up at him.

"Well." He cleared his throat. "I reckon I better get

you that bucket of water." He turned and strode away, his long legs making big strides.

Damn. She sighed, watching him go. What would it be like to be Mrs. Lawrence Witherspoon? She'd come here because of his friends' meddling, and she certainly hadn't intended to stay. Yet here she was, thinking about how it would be if he kissed her until she was breathless and then kissed her some more.

Mrs. Lawrence Witherspoon. They wouldn't have much money, but there were things more important than money. Her mind went to how it would be at night in his arms. She really didn't know much about that part of marriage, but she'd be willing to let that big man teach her. He'd be honorable too, and not want to take her virtue unless he married her. Not like that rascal of a brother who surely never passed up a chance to get a girl's drawers off. She frowned just thinking of Larado. She'd wager his stalwart brother could be as good a lover with a little practice.

Mrs. Bottoms returned with two Mexican girls and Jimmy, all carrying soap and mops and brooms. Then the sheriff brought a brimming bucket of water in each hand. They made sort of a party of scrubbing the place down, and finally, it was almost finished.

Mrs. Bottoms wiped her sweating face. "I reckon that about does it. Me and the girls got to get supper ready at the hotel. Come on, Jimmy."

He looked from Lark to the sheriff, grinning. "I want to stay with them."

"Come on, boy, you can peel potatoes. I reckon these two can finish up alone."

"Sure we can, run on." The sheriff pushed his hat back and leaned against a counter.

Lark sighed and wiped her wet hands on her apron. "We'll be there after a while. I'm getting hungry."

The others left, although Jimmy kept looking back over his shoulder.

The pair stared after them in the growing dusk.

"That's a nice boy," the sheriff said. "If I were a family man, I'd adopt him."

"You're very sweet," Lark said. "Maybe we could take him for a train ride when it finally gets here. I hear he's *loco* about trains. By the way, I'm much obliged for your help."

"For you, Miss Lacey, anything." His voice was low as he looked down at her.

She knew he was trying to get up the nerve to kiss her and she wanted him to, badly. Would he think she was too forward if she kissed him instead?

He just kept looking at her. "You—you got a smudge on your face," he said. He pulled his bandana from his hip pocket, reached out, and wiped her cheek slowly. His fingers were soft against her cheek.

"Thank you," she said. "I must look a mess." She tried to brush her untidy hair back and laughed.

"I think you're as purty as a speckled pup in a red wagon," he said, his expression serious. "I'm awful glad you came to town, Miss Lacey."

"I am too." She felt like the worst kind of person, deceiving a fine, upright man like this one.

"Can I—can I ask you a question?" he stammered.

Was he going to ask permission to kiss her? *Yes*, she shouted in her mind, *hell, yes!* She nodded with enthusiasm.

"I was wonderin' if I could walk you home after church tomorrow?"

"What?"

He shuffled his feet some more. "I know there'll be lots of fellas wantin' to court you, but after all, Bill and Paco did write you on my behalf."

"Are you—are you asking to court me?"

"Don't say no yet, Miss Lacey," he begged. "I ain't got much yet, but maybe if someday I can raise the down payment on that ranch. . . ."

Don't say no? Was he *loco?* At that moment Lark wanted nothing more than to grab him and kiss him until he was breathless, but of course, this Texas gentleman would be horrified at that forward behavior. She had to remember to act like her demure twin. "I'd be right proud to have you walk me home after church, Lawrence. We're having apple pie."

He grinned. "My favorite. Made with your two little hands, I'll wager."

"Uh, not quite. Mrs. Bottoms has had me doing other things." Actually, Lark couldn't cook an egg so a dog would eat it—no, not even a starving hound.

At that point she wished devoutly that she knew how to cook. In her mind, she pictured herself in a dainty apron, placing a well-cooked meal with lots of apple pie in front of this wonderful man. He would catch her hand and kiss her fingertips while he declared it was the best he'd ever eaten. Who was she kidding? A coyote wouldn't eat Lark's cooking. Uncle Trace said her cooking would poison a billy goat that was used to eating cans.

It was getting dark outside. She imagined him finally getting up the nerve to kiss her when the room was shadowed in darkness.

"Uh," said the sheriff, "I'd better walk you back to the hotel, Miss Van Schuyler. I wouldn't want to compromise your reputation by keeping you out after dark without a chaperone."

Oh, please compromise my reputation, Lark thought with hope. *Take me out back to that stall full of straw and tumble me around until I look like the dogs have had me under the porch.* "I—of course." Damn him, why hadn't he just kissed her without worrying about her reputation?

"We'll stop and see about your new pet afore we leave," he said. They went out back to where Magnolia stood hip deep in good hay, chewing contentedly. The donkey looked up and brayed when she saw Lark. "Looks like you've made a friend for life," the sheriff said. "That's what I like about you, miss, you're so kindhearted. I hope, as we get to know each other better, you'll feel kindhearted to me."

She was feeling kindhearted enough to back him against the wall and kiss him and tousle his black shock of hair, but of course she did not. "I really like you, Mr. Witherspoon."

"I wish you would call me Lawrence."

She was already thinking, Mrs. Lawrence Witherspoon. Yes, that would look good embroidered on her linens. "I'd be happy to . . . Lawrence, and you must call me . . . Lacey."

Land's sake, what a tangled web she'd woven. How could she get away with him calling her by her sister's name the rest of her life?

The rest of your life? Lark, are you out of your mind? You're only staying until you feel safe enough to stop hiding from the law. When you do, you'll just flee this town.

"Oh, Miss Lacey"—he fumbled with his cowboy hat— "I couldn't presume to be that forward with a real lady, especially one I ain't got to know well yet."

She took his arm, and they started toward the door and out onto the wooden sidewalk. "Lawrence, I believe I'd like to get to know you a lot better."

And she meant every word of it.

Chapter Seven

That night, Lark dreamed that the sheriff took her in his arms. "You're prettier than a speckled pup," he whispered, and then he kissed her. The kiss was as wonderful as she had imagined in all those romantic novels she'd hidden under her bed back at Miss Priddy's Female Academy.

"Make me the happiest sheriff in the whole Lone Star State," he said, kissing her again and again. "Miss Lacey, will you do me the honor of marryin' up with me?"

Miss Lacey? Uh-oh. Lark awoke with a start. Now there was a mess she hadn't considered. If she married that handsome hunk of a man under her sister's name, would it be a legal union? Would their children be . . . oh my God, bastards? On the other hand, for kisses like the ones Lawrence Witherspoon would offer, she might be willing to live a lie the rest of her life.

She hardly slept the rest of the night. The church bells tolling on the warm May morning woke her as the tiny church alerted everyone within a mile (which was the whole town, really) that services would soon begin.

Hurriedly, Lark dressed in her blue gingham with the pert bustle. Putting on a big white hat with flowers on the brim, she grabbed her lace parasol, ate a quick bite in the kitchen, and ran out to climb in Mrs. Bottoms's buggy. Paco helped her in back. Jimmy sat up next to him as they started for church.

Jimmy grinned at her. "You're beautiful. When I grow up, can I marry you?"

"Jimmy!" said Mrs. Bottoms.

Lark leaned over and kissed his cheek. "I'm old enough to be your mother, Jimmy. When you're grown, you'll think I'm an old lady."

He grinned. "The sheriff thinks you're beautiful too."

"Oh?"

Paco was driving. "Jimmy," he said, "don't tell everything you know."

Lark smiled to herself. "Does the sheriff always come to services?" she asked as they drove down the dusty street.

"Heavens, child, you're really taken with him, aren't you? I never thought these mail-order-bride things worked out."

"Remember"—Paco looked over his shoulder—"Bill and me get to be best men."

"You're getting a little ahead of yourselves." Lark felt herself flush as they reined in before the little white church.

Mrs. Bottoms said, "The sheriff is usually too busy patrolling the town to attend, but I have a feeling he'll be there today."

They entered and found a pew. It was a beautiful little church with stained-glass windows. Lark reached for a hymn book and looked around. No Lawrence. Oh well.

Then just as the congregation stood to sing the first hymn, Lawrence came down the aisle and slipped in the pew next to her. When he grinned and she scooted over to make room for him, her heart almost skipped at beat. His handsome face was tanned from the west Texas sun, he smelled of bay rum hair tonic, and his dark hair was slicked back. They shared a hymn book, and she wasn't sure if he had deliberately touched her hand or if it was accidental.

He had a good, strong voice, she thought with admiration as they began to sing: "There's a church in the valley by the wildwood, no lovelier place in the dale . . . no spot is so dear to my childhood as the little brown church in the vale. . . ."

After services, he offered to walk her back to the hotel.

"I don't know. I came with Mrs. Bottoms," Lark said. She didn't want to seem too eager, as shy as he was.

"Oh." He looked disappointed and fumbled with the brim of his Stetson hat. "Well, then—"

"But I offered old Miss Wiggly a ride," Mrs. Bottoms interrupted. "So I reckon Miss Van Schuyler will have to walk."

"In that case," the sheriff grinned, "I'd be right proud to walk you back, ma'am."

"Of course." She opened her parasol against the warm sun.

"Oh, young man," Mrs. Bottoms called after him. "Do stay for dinner. We've got pot roast and apple pie today in the hotel dining room."

"Hmm," the sheriff said. "And is there some good cornbread to go with that?"

Lark laughed. "You know there is. Come on."

Mrs. Bottoms's buggy left with Jimmy hanging over the backseat, grinning at them. The pair strolled leisurely away from the church.

"You know," Lark said, glancing sideways at him, "I think you must be identical twins. You look exactly like your brother."

He paused, his face grim. "You know my brother?"

Land's sake, what had she done?

"Uh, no, but I thought you said you were an identical twin."

He frowned, his face dark as a thunderstorm. "Miss Lacey, if you don't mind, I'd rather not discuss my brother. We ain't seen each other in a while, and we didn't part on good terms."

"Well, my sister and I had a little rivalry going too. It does get old having to deal with someone who looks like you."

"It's more than that." He seemed reluctant to talk about it. They resumed walking. For a long moment she did not think he would say anything else, and she scolded herself for mentioning Larado.

"I'm sorry I brought it up," she apologized.

He looked sideways at her. "Well, you don't know— nobody around here does—but my brother is a rascal of the worst sort."

And a real lady-killer, Lark thought. "No! Really?"

"Yes ma'am," he nodded. "He—he's just a saddle tramp, really, not makin' much of hisself, chasin' women, drinkin', and gamblin'. He ain't got a serious bone in his body, and he don't act very gentlemanly to ladies. Why, if he got the chance, he'd pull your drawers off—pardon me for sayin' that, but it's the truth."

You can say that again, Lark thought.

"Matter of fact, ma'am, I been tryin' to live Larado down all my life. He's a devil with the ladies too. Why, if he were here, you'd be so smitten with him, you wouldn't give me a second look."

Lark snorted. "I don't know about that. He sounds pretty shallow and uninteresting to me. And he probably thinks he's more a devil with the ladies than he really is. I doubt if he's all that charming." She thought of Larado's crooked grin, his swaggering walk, and the way he just melted her when he gave her that look.

Oh please, God, don't strike me with lightning for lying. She looked up at the sky anxiously, but it remained clear and blue.

Lawrence gave her a searching look. "You—you don't think you'd prefer him to me?"

"Oh, my, no." She paused and looked up at him. "Why, every woman wants a serious, no-nonsense man she can depend on—one who's home every night at six, doesn't drink, chase women, or gamble."

"You think?"

She gave him an encouraging nod, and they began to stroll again.

"And what's your twin like, ma'am?"

She didn't really want to talk about Lacey, afraid she'd reveal too much and trip herself up. "Well, let's just say she's really different from me. Lark's a tomboy who likes to ride, and rope, and shoot—not ladylike at all."

"Sounds like a challenge to any man," he said. Somehow, that annoyed her. Larado might prefer the real Lark, but she'd expect Lawrence to choose the staid Lacey.

They walked to the hotel and sat down at a table in a big, sunny window of the dining room. It seemed the hotel was famous for its Sunday dinner, and rightly so. There were heaping platters of fried chicken and pot roast. There were steaming bowls of vegetables from Mrs. Bottoms's garden. There were hot rolls and cornbread in heaping piles, with fresh butter from the local cows.

She noticed Jimmy shoveling in the food and then helping Paco carry empty plates back to the kitchen.

"Ah, iced tea," smiled Lawrence with satisfaction as the waitresses hurried to their table. "The mother's milk of the South."

He could eat like a real man, Lark noted as he plowed into his platter while she tried to eat daintily. Finally there was bread pudding, chocolate cake, and apple pie with homemade ice cream to finish dinner off.

"Mrs. Bottoms," Lawrence said as they finished and the lady stopped by the table, "I believe if you was a little younger, I'd marry you."

The lady chuckled. "And if you were about twenty years older, I might take you up on it. I'm sure Miss Van

Schuyler is a great cook, we just haven't let her show her talent yet."

"Uh," Lark stammered. She didn't want to be put to the test. She looked toward the window. "Land's sake."

The others turned to look. Magnolia grazed in the flower box in front of the hotel window. When she looked up, pink petunias hung from both sides of her mouth.

"Magnolia, stop that!" Lark called, scrambling to her feet. Magnolia surveyed her and then calmly returned to eating the flowers. Everyone in the dining room laughed.

"I told you what burros are like," Lawrence said, getting up. "I fed and watered that little rascal before I came to church. You'll have a tough time keepin' that donkey penned up."

They both went outside and confronted the donkey.

"Oh, Magnolia," Lark said, "you must not get in people's gardens. You must stay in your pen."

Magnolia gave her a big-eyed look, then she gravely flicked her long ears and returned to eating petunias.

"You're wasting your breath." The sheriff smiled. "Besides that, they're pretty worthless except for prospectors."

"Let's go put her back in her pen," Lark said.

"All right," the sheriff shrugged, "but I reckon she's learned to open the gate, and from now on she'll keep gettin' out."

"Can't we just change the latch?"

"Sure, but she'll figure it out. Burros are smart and stubborn, and they have a mind of their own. Just like some women."

"I beg your pardon?"

"I—I mean, some women, but not you, Miss Lacey," he stammered and shuffled his boots. "You're a genteel lady."

"Of course." No, her sister was a genteel lady. Lark had always thought Lacey dull and prissy. "Let's take Magnolia back."

They started walking down the street, the little donkey

following along happily. When they got to the stable behind the shop, she walked right into her pen and got a drink of water from the bucket.

"Now, Magnolia, you must stay here and not go wandering up and down Main Street."

Magnolia raised her velvet little muzzle and looked at Lark. Then she snorted and began to eat the corn in her feed bucket.

The sheriff laughed. "I don't think Magnolia gives no never mind about rules and regulations. You just figure she'll be a nuisance from now on." He leaned against the fence and smiled at her. "You get your stuff ordered for the shop?"

She nodded. "Ought to have it up and running in a few days."

"Good. The railroad should be buildin' into Rusty Spur in a couple more weeks. There'll be settlers arrivin' and the ladies will be wantin' gewgaws and pretties. If you run short on money, remember—I might could get an advance against my salary from the town council."

She shook her head. "I'd hate to take any more of your money, knowing you're saving for that ranch you want."

"Would you like to ride out and see it?" He sounded like a small boy with a new toy.

"Of course." What she really wanted was to spend more time with him.

"I'll go down to the livery stable and get a rig." He sounded eager. "Now you wait right here, Miss Lacey."

She nodded and he strode away. She looked after him, wishing she knew how to straighten out this mess she had made of her life. Well, if things got too serious with Lawrence Witherspoon where it looked like it might lead to complications, she could do what she had always done—run.

In a few minutes, here came the sheriff with a horse and buggy. "I was hopin' you'd like to see the place," he said, jumping down. He came around to help her up into the rig. His hands were big and strong, almost encircling her small waist as he lifted her to the seat. For just a moment he hesitated as he lifted her, and she thought he might kiss her. She took a deep breath, wanting him—no, willing him to kiss her. Instead, he sat her up on the seat and came around to climb up himself. They started down Main Street at a leisurely pace, nodding to people they saw sitting on porches or standing in groups and visiting.

"A right friendly place to live," said Lawrence.

"It sure is," Lark agreed.

"Good place to spend the rest of your life, maybe settle down," he said.

"Hmm," Lark said, not certain what to say. She couldn't stay the rest of her life here, not while she was using her sister's name and had that bank robbery thing to worry about. She was already homesick for her family, and she couldn't imagine never again having contact with any of them.

They drove in a pleasant silence, listening to the sound of bobwhite quail in the grass. Longhorns grazed in pastures as the couple passed.

She heard a sound and looked back. "Oh, my."

Magnolia was galloping after them as fast as her spindly little legs could carry her. "Eee haw, eee hawww."

It was a horrible sound that made Lark wince and the buggy horse snort.

Lawrence looked back and chuckled. "I told you it was nigh impossible to keep a burro penned up. Next thing you know, someone will bring you another, and then you'll have two donkeys. Then Magnolia will have a foal, and you'll have three. You could end up with a pasture full, and burros live a long time."

"Oh well." Lark shrugged and decided there was no point in getting upset about it. As soon as Magnolia caught up with the buggy, she walked along behind it as if she too had been invited to come along for the fun.

They drove up on the crest of a small rise, and the

sheriff reined in. "This is where I plan to build my house. Look at the view."

"It's breathtaking!" Lark exclaimed. "Why, I bet you can see all the way to New Mexico Territory from here."

"Not quite, but far enough." He came around and helped her down. This time as he lifted her she put her hands on those wide shoulders, and for a moment, they stood looking at each other. He was so close she could see the slight shadow where he was already needing a shave, and the curve of his sensual mouth. Under her hands, his shoulders were muscular and seemed taut.

He kept looking at her. "Miss Lacey," he gulped. "Oh, Miss Lacey."

"Yes?"

"Uh," he pulled away. Abruptly, there was sweat on that rugged face. "Let's walk around some."

He wasn't going to kiss her. He was simply too shy, she thought. Well, sooner or later. . . .

"It's beautiful land," she said, looking out across the valley.

"Ain't it, though?" He beamed at her. "It does have some worthless acres that ain't good for nothin' cause of that oil seepin' up, but a man could run a few cows, raise some good horses, start a family. That is," he stammered, "if he could find the right woman."

"I reckon he could," Lark agreed. Was he hinting that she was that woman? Could she possibly marry him without him ever finding out she had known his brother? She sighed.

Now the handsome face saddened. "'Course, it's just a dream, 'cause it would take a miracle to get this much money. I'll never earn that much as a sheriff."

She took his hand. "Well, maybe if my shop does well, I can not only pay you back, but lend you some money to help buy this place."

"Oh, I couldn't let you do that, ma'am, well, not unless we was married. Then I reckon it would be all right."

She wanted to get away from all this talk about marriage when her common sense told her it could never be. Magnolia stopped grazing and came over, chewing at the edge of Lark's lace parasol. "My! I reckon we ought to get back to town"—she pulled away—"before this furry little rascal chews up my parasol completely."

When she reached out to pet Magnolia, the little animal set up an ungodly braying. Both of them started and then laughed.

"I swear," Lawrence said. "Anybody never heard a donkey would sure be startled out of his boots by that racket, wouldn't he?"

"It is sort of a horrible sound," Lark admitted. "And very loud for such a small animal. Well, let's get back to town."

He helped her back up into the buggy. "Thanks for coming out for a look, Miss Van Schuyler. I ain't showed this place to anybody but little Jimmy and Paco. Paco would like to own the land next door, but he's got no money, either."

"Well, maybe if you ever get rich, you can loan him some."

He slapped the horse with the reins and they started off. "Reckon there's no chance of that unless I marry a rich woman or rob a bank somewhere." He laughed, but Lark didn't. Oh, if this innocent and naive man ever found out about what Larado had done, he'd probably die of shame. So what would he think of Lark if he knew that she'd been involved too? She didn't want him to think badly of her.

"Come on, Magnolia," she called to the burro. "We're going back to town now."

"You think she understands English?" The sheriff grinned.

"I reckon she does, she's following the buggy."

And indeed she was, contented as a hound dog, trotting back to town.

* * *

The railroad was coming. Excitement built in the town as the tracks moved closer and the June weather grew warmer. Men were already arriving to build new businesses, anticipating the settlers who would rush in with the train. New buildings were going up, and there was talk of paving Main Street. The supplies for Lark's new store arrived, and in just a few days, business was booming among the ladies of Rusty Spur. There was going to be a big celebration the day the first train pulled in, and all the ladies wanted to look their best.

Lark wondered if the sheriff was avoiding her, or maybe he was just busy. With the sudden growth of the town, he seemed busier than usual, keeping the place peaceful.

He had been right about Magnolia; there was no way to keep her penned up. Today, Lark looked out the window of her shop and saw the little donkey pulling hay off the back of a wagon parked in front of the general store. Oh, Abner Snootley would have a fit about that if he saw it. Bertha Snootley had come in several times, but she was not one of Lark's favorite customers. She was too demanding and arrogant.

Jimmy was just passing by.

"Hey, dear," she called. "Would you put Magnolia back in her pen?"

"Won't do no good, miss," the boy smiled. "She'll just get out again."

About that time, there seemed to be a disturbance down at the saloon. Lark took a deep breath. Uh-oh. Something for the sheriff to deal with. She stepped out on the sidewalk, looking that direction. Other people were coming out of stores or pausing on the sidewalk to look.

Jimmy frowned. "I better get the sheriff. He's the only one who can keep law and order around here." He took off running down the street.

Lark waited, as did everyone else. In seconds, she saw the sheriff's lanky form come out of his office and stride toward the noise. By now there were two drunks falling out through the swinging doors of the the Cross-eyed Bull and fighting in the street, rolling under the hooves of two bay horses tied at the hitching post. The horses whinnied and tried to rear. The men rolled over and over as they fought in the dirt.

"Hey," someone yelled, "you better scat, here comes the sheriff."

One of the drunks stumbled to his feet. "I ain't afraid of no stinkin' lawman. I kilt one or two in my life."

He was fumbling for his pistol as Lawrence walked up. "Don't do it, *hombre*," he whispered.

"Watch out, Sheriff, he's a gunfighter," someone warned.

"Uh-huh," Lawrence said coolly. "I said, keep that gun in its holster, mister."

"You better do as he says, Jack," someone yelled. "That sheriff used to be a Texas Ranger!"

The man was going for his pistol anyway. In that split second, Lark held her breath as the sheriff pulled his own Colt. No doubt, Lawrence was a dead shot. She held her breath, waiting. Instead, Lawrence whacked the drunk up the side of the head with the barrel of his pistol. The drunk collapsed like a tornado had hit him.

The crowd cheered.

"Bravest thing I ever saw!" someone yelled.

"What do you expect from a ex-Ranger?" someone else said.

Lawrence shrugged. "No use killin' him just to show off my fast draw. Some of you fellas drag him down to the jail and we'll let him sober up some."

Lark heaved a sigh of relief and ran down the street to him. "Oh, Lawrence, I was so afraid for you."

He holstered his pistol. "All in a day's work," he said. "Never had to kill one yet."

Paco looked up at him, his dark eyes big with admiration. "You must be the fastest gun in the West, Sheriff, *sí*?"

"Yes," said Jimmy, "the fastest!"

Lawrence shrugged. "Bein' fast don't matter none, Paco—havin' a cool head and thinkin' fast is better. You remember that now, hear?"

The blacksmith stepped out into the street. "Three cheers for the best, the toughest sheriff in all Texas! Hip hip hooray! Hip hip hooray! Hip hip hooray!" The crowd joined in the cheering.

Lawrence only looked embarrassed. "I ain't tryin' to build no big reputation, but I hope every *hombre* who saw this just now will pass the word that the sheriff of Rusty Spur is a true Texan and ain't gonna allow no hard cases to shoot up our town."

The crowd murmured agreement as they began to scatter. "He's a tough one, all right, toughest sheriff in Texas."

Lark took his arm. "You know that your reputation is liable to draw gunslingers to this town?"

He patted her hand and they started to walk back toward her shop. "If we get any would-be Billy the Kids, I'll show them just how well I can shoot, but I won't kill them if I don't have to."

"You're a brave man," Lark gushed as they walked. "We're gonna need you even more as the town grows."

He shook his head. "Once word gets around that the sheriff's tough, gunslingers will avoid this town. Then maybe I can resign, turn the office over to Paco, and just do a little ranchin'."

She heard a sound and looked back. Magnolia was following along behind her like a dog.

Lawrence laughed. "I warned you about that little critter. There ain't a flowerbed or a vegetable garden safe from a donkey. I saw Mrs. Snootley shooing her out of her yard just yesterday."

"I hope they understand that I try to keep her penned up, I really do," Lark said. "The only one who really complains is Bertha Snootley. But then, she complains about everything. She's been wanting to know if I'm ever going to get hats from Paris."

"Paris, Texas?"

"No, silly, Paris, France."

"They named a town in some foreign country after ours?"

"You know, Lawrence, Texans might think this blasphemous, but Texas is not the center of the universe."

"But of course it is. Don't the Good Book say that on the eighth day, God made Texas?"

"I'm not sure that's the way the scripture reads."

"If it doesn't, it should," he said with confidence. "Oh, speak of the devil, and here she comes now," Lawrence warned.

"Oh no." Lark paused in the doorway of her little shop. The big woman was heading toward her, head high and nose in the air. "You'd think she was royalty, the way she acts—and worse yet, she wears the hats, then returns them and says they weren't satisfactory."

"I don't mind a gunfight," Lawrence said, "but I don't want to get in the middle of a tiff with ladies." He turned to go. "Afternoon, Mrs. Snootley." He tipped his big Stetson and kept walking.

"Well," said Mrs. Snootley by way of greeting, "I see that dirty little beast is out again, doing her business on the street."

"I try to keep her penned up," Lark apologized.

"You ought to just shoot her," the woman snapped as she glared at Magnolia. Magnolia brayed so loudly, both women jumped.

"Well, I think she's offering an opinion." Lark smiled. "Now, what can I help you with today?"

"I saw a new hat in your window."

"All right, let's go in."

They went inside, and the pompous woman went to check the merchandise. "There'll be a big party to welcome the arrival of the first train and I want to look nice. Besides, I've heard gossip we'll be getting a new resident, a banker and his wife from back East."

"Oh, really?"

The lady looked down her nose at Lark. "As a social leader of Rusty Spur, I intend to show them this isn't just some jerkwater hick town. Why, we might end up as big as San Antonio or Austin. If I had more time, I'd go into Abilene to shop, but I don't have time—so I'll just have to buy whatever you've got in your tacky little shop."

Lark bit her tongue to hold back her retort. "I'm sure we'll find something to suit you." No doubt the cheap woman would certainly wear whatever she bought one time, then insist on returning it.

Mrs. Snootley picked up a pink straw hat with a wide brim. Lark had added a flowing pink veil, and the brim was a profusion of pink and burgundy flowers.

"That's quite expensive," Lark warned.

"Well, then," the snooty lady said, "I'm probably the only one in town who can afford it, aren't I?"

Lark wasn't sure what the proper response should be. "It's a lovely hat," she said.

Mrs. Snootley put the hat on and walked over to look at herself in the cheval mirror. Since she was a short woman, the hat's brim was much too wide for her. She looked as if she were standing under a giant pink toadstool. She walked up and down, admiring herself in the mirror. "What do you think?"

"It's a lovely hat," Lark said again.

"I don't know why I'm asking you, I doubt you've ever been to the capital or seen real fashion. I've been to Paris, you know."

"How nice." Lark doubted that.

Bertha Snootley surveyed her puffy face in the mirror. She adjusted the pink veil and sighed. "I'm just withering away from lack of social opportunities in this jerkwater little Texas town."

Lark smiled encouragingly. "Well, maybe as the town grows, you can be the social leader who starts some women's clubs."

"Hmm." That idea seemed to have some appeal at first, then the woman shook her head. "I don't know who I would invite. There's just no one of any consequence here."

Again Lark bit her tongue to hold back her retort. "Well, if we get a banker and some new business owners, there's bound to be someone who's worthy of your friendship."

The lady looked at her a long moment as if trying to decide if Lark was being sarcastic, seeming to decide the girl wasn't smart enough for that. "Perhaps you're right."

The lady paraded up and down in front of the mirror. "Yes, I like it. I'll take it."

"Are you going to pay for it?" Lark asked, although she knew better. If Mrs. Snootley paid for an article, it would be easier to refuse to let her return it.

"Of course not. Put it on my husband's bill."

Lark bit her lip, trying to be diplomatic. "Uh, you've already charged quite a bit, Mrs. Snootley. Your husband said—"

"I don't care what he said!" she snapped. "He's a nobody anyway who ought to feel lucky to have such a scion of Cleveland society for a wife. He misrepresented himself, you know. I thought he was rich when I married him. Turned out he was all hat and no cattle."

No one could insult a Texan more than to say he was a man of all mouth and no substance.

"And I'll wager he thought you were an angel," Lark said without thinking.

The former butcher's daughter didn't seem to realize she was being insulted. "I'm sure he did."

About that time, Magnolia stuck her head through the open front door and brayed loudly, causing Mrs. Snootley to jump. "Oh, my heart! That filthy little beast! We'll never become a thriving metropolis with donkeys wandering the streets."

"She's a very nice donkey." Lark went to the door and

shooed Magnolia out. "We've tried, but we can't seem to keep her penned up. She's learned to open the latch on the stall gate."

"I think the sheriff ought to shoot her," the lady said coldly. "She's just a dirty little good-for-nothing beast."

Lark managed to control her temper, but it was difficult. "Everyone else in town seems to like her."

"That's because people in this town have no class." She stuck her nose in the air and sailed out the front door wearing the big pink hat.

"What a day!" Lark watched her sail down the sidewalk like a big oceangoing boat with the pink veils flowing out behind her. Out the big front window she could see Magnolia eating the flowers out of the flowerbed in front of the local newspaper office.

The sheriff came in the back door just then. "What was that about?"

"Oh, Mrs. Snootley," Lark sighed. "I almost wished she wouldn't come in here. She wears what she buys once or twice, then returns it."

He leaned against the counter. "Why don't you say no?"

"I'm considering that, but I'm not sure it would work. I'm thinking of something more subtle. Oh, by the way, she wants you to shoot Magnolia."

"Why?"

"Because she leaves little calling cards on the sidewalk and eats everybody's flowers."

He grinned. "Miss Lacey, everyone but her likes the little donkey. I'm not gonna shoot her. Oh, by the way"—he fumbled with the brim of his hat—"there's a big hayrack ride next Sunday night. I was wonderin' . . . no, of course you've already been asked." He turned to leave.

Oh, how to deal with a bashful man. "I haven't been asked anywhere."

"No?" He turned around, his dark eyes hopeful. "Well, you see, there's a hayrack ride."

"You said that," she prompted.

"I—I was wonderin', if maybe you don't get a better offer . . ."

"Yes?"

"Well . . ."

"Would you like to take me?" Lark finally lost her patience.

His handsome face broke into a grin. "You must be a mind reader, Miss Lacey. I'd be right proud to carry you to the hayrack ride."

"What about patrolling the town?"

"Sundays is pretty quiet with the railroad workers and cowhands havin' to go to work on Monday."

"This sounds like fun," Lark said, and she began to make her plan. She cared more about Lawrence than she was willing to admit. As Texans would say, it was time to pee on the fire and call in the dogs—bring this matter to a close. If the bashful sheriff didn't kiss her on this hayrack ride, she was going to kiss him. What would happen after that was anyone's guess.

Chapter Eight

It was a dark, hot June night later in the week, and Lark was leaving the store. She'd been there checking inventory. She started down the sidewalk, her mind on the upcoming hayrack ride. More and more, she was feeling something for the shy sheriff. All week she'd seen little of him because he'd been helping the town council with security and the plans for a big ceremony and party when the first train finally pulled into Rusty Spur. Already, there was increased hustle and bustle on Main Street, and the sound of big hammers and men laying track could be heard when the wind blew just right.

As she passed the alley near the saloon, a big drunk stepped out of the darkness, blocking her path. He was unsteady on his feet, and she could smell the cheap whiskey on his dirty clothes. "Hey, there, girlie, how about goin' into the saloon and havin' a drink with me?"

Oh my, it was Otto. She could see the big iron railroad nail in his belt. She took a deep breath and squared her small shoulders. "Otto, ladies don't drink—now step out of my way."

He laughed. "Oh, it's you. Then it's time you learned, honey."

Before she realized his intention, he reached out and grabbed her, dragging her toward him.

"You pig!" Lark struggled and screamed, clawing at his bearded face.

"Why, you little—!" He slapped one dirty paw over her mouth and dragged her toward the darkness of the alley. "I'll teach you to insult me!"

Oh God, what's going to happen now? Lark fought and scratched. She tried to bite his hand so she could scream again, but he was too strong for her. The street was deserted with the night dark. She felt the sweat on her back beneath her yellow dress as she struggled. The drunk kept his dirty hand over her mouth as he dragged her into the darkness. She could not let him carry or drag her away from the main street where someone might hear the noise of the struggle and rescue her.

"Honey," his voice slurred, "when I get you out back, we're gonna have a little fun!"

The image he brought to mind terrified her, and she renewed her struggle.

Just then a big shadow loomed across both of them in the moonlight.

Oh my God. Lark froze, motionless. *He's got a partner.* But the drunk stopped in confusion, too.

"Let go of the lady and step away," a deep voice commanded.

Lawrence. Oh, thank you, God, it was the sheriff come to save her. Otto froze in position, his hand still clamped over her mouth.

Lark bit down hard on the dirty fingers. He let go of her and howled in protest, fumbling for that big iron spike. She screamed, "Look out, Sheriff!"

At that moment Lawrence Witherspoon took three long strides, coming straight at the big drunk as Lark rolled out of the way.

The moonlight gleamed on the iron spike as Otto swung it. "I'm gonna nail you to a wall!" he snarled.

The lawman dodged the deadly spike. Then he stepped close and caught the drunk across the temple with the barrel of his Colt. Otto collapsed like a mountain falling down.

"Oh, Lawrence!" she cried. "He was going to kill you!"

"Everything's all right now," he said confidently, pulling her to her feet. She ran sobbing into his big arms. "Everything's all right now."

She wept against his wide chest. "That was the bravest thing I ever saw!"

"A man's gotta do what a man's gotta do," he said, "leastways if he's a Texan." He held her close against him, stroking her hair.

People were running from all directions now, shouting and peering down the alley.

"What's going on?"

"Did I hear a scream?"

"Sheriff, what happened?"

"Nothin' much," Lawrence said modestly, his strong arm around her shoulders as they turned to face the curious crowd.

What a man. Her heart did flip-flops. "It was a big thing," she shouted to the growing crowd. "This drunk attacked me. Otto tried to stab the sheriff with that spike he carries, and the sheriff didn't even try to kill him—he coolly hit him in the head with his pistol."

"Well," Lawrence grinned, "I was afraid I'd hit the lady."

"So you risked your own life," she sobbed some more. "Bravest thing I ever saw!"

He took out his bandana and handed it to her. She blew her nose in a most unladylike manner.

Paco walked over and picked up the spike. "Uh-oh, Sheriff. It's got blood on it."

Lawrence frowned. "Well, it ain't mine. Somebody better go out to the railroad camp and see if he's killed someone. Paco, get some of the fellas to carry him over to the jail and lock him up. I reckon he's headed for the state prison at Huntsville."

The deputy grinned with admiration. "*Sí,* boss."

Four men grabbed the half-conscious thug and half carried, half dragged him down the street, following Paco to the jail.

Lark liked the feel of Lawrence's protective arm around her shoulders.

In the background she heard someone whisper, "I told you the sheriff was coolheaded. Not many lawmen would try to take that *hombre* alive instead of just shooting him."

Another answered, "What a man!"

Amen, Lark thought with a sigh.

"Now, folks"—the sheriff waved his hand in modest dismissal—"don't make more of this than it was. I've faced down death before."

"Of course," someone murmured. "What else can you expect from a Texan except bravery?"

"Remember the Alamo!" someone shouted, and they all cheered. Lark couldn't see that the Alamo had anything to do with this situation, but of course it would be sacrilegious to say so. The crowd began to disperse.

"I—I reckon I'll walk you home if you don't mind." He took his arm away and looked down at Lark.

Mind? How naive can he be? She managed not to cheer and jump up and down. "I'd feel so much more safe." Lark kept her tone demure and took his arm. They walked along toward the hotel in the moonlight. The tiny hamlet was once again quiet. "I'm so lucky you came along," she said.

"Yep. If I hadn't heard you scream as I was makin' my rounds . . ." His voice trailed off, and he shrugged.

"That was very brave, to hit him in the head rather just shoot him."

"Couldn't endanger a lady, that's a Texan's code. Besides, as well as I shoot, he wouldn't have had a chance against me."

"Land's sake, everyone in town knows that. Have you ever had to kill anyone?"

They paused in front of the hotel and he squinted down at her, his face shadowed. "If you don't mind, Miss Lacey, I—I'd just as soon not talk about that."

"Oh. Of course." This sensitive man had probably killed a bunch of outlaws, and it haunted him even though the villains had deserved it. "I'm sorry I mentioned it. The memories must be terrible for you."

He sighed. "I try not to think about it." He kept looking down at her. "Miss Lacey," he said finally, "can—can I ask you something?"

Her prissy sister would have corrected his grammar. *May* I ask you something?

"Surely."

"Would I be too bold . . . I mean, would you be offended if I wanted, well . . ." He took a deep breath.

Would he never finish?

"Would you mind if I kissed you? I mean, if you're offended—"

"Say no more. Yes." She closed her eyes and tilted her face up to his. His big hands holding hers were sweaty and his fingers trembled. She waited, eyes shut with breathless anticipation.

At this point, he leaned over and planted a slight peck on her cheek. She heard his deep intake of breath at his own daring as she slowly opened her eyes.

That's all? she thought. *That's what he calls a kiss?* She wanted to grab him and kiss him until he was breathless, but he'd probably think she was a fast woman—a tart—if she did. "That was lovely," she said.

"Oh, Miss Lacey," he sighed and gulped, stepping back awkwardly. "Well, I reckon I'd better mosey along now. We still goin' to the hayrack ride?"

"Of course." Lark had come to a decision. If he didn't kiss her, *really* kiss her at the hayrack ride, she was going to kiss him—and it wouldn't be some mild little peck on the cheek, either. She watched him amble away, and then she went inside for supper.

Everyone in town seemed to be making plans for the hayrack ride. All week, ladies coming in and out of her shop talked about what they would wear and who was going. One said she'd been to Abilene over the past week and had seen Mrs. Snootley there. "Bertha was wearing that lovely pink hat you used to have in your store window," one of them said.

Lark breathed a sigh of relief. "Well, at least, she decided she really liked it," Lark answered.

However, the next day Mrs. Snootley was back in the shop with the fluffy pink straw hat in her hand. "I'm returning this. I've decided I don't like it."

"Don't like it?" This time, Lark was really caught by surprise. "But you've worn it any number of times. It's now used merchandise."

The big woman drew herself up and sniffed disdainfully as she pointed to the sign on the wall. "It says satisfaction guaranteed. I've decided I'm not satisfied."

"Are you ever?" Lark said.

"What?"

She must not lose her temper. Everyone in town would hear about it. "Nothing. Mrs. Snootley, you've worn this hat a lot. I can't take it back."

"Whoever said that lied," the woman snapped. "You will take it back, or I won't shop here anymore."

That would probably be a relief, but there was nothing Lark could do. "All right, I'll let you return it, but please stop doing this. I can't resell this hat now that it's used."

"I told you I never wore it," the lady lied. Tossing it on the counter, she sailed out of the shop.

Lark sighed. What she had really wanted to do was throw the pink flowered hat in the snooty matron's face, but of course she couldn't do that. What could she do to stop this woman from continually returning merchandise, and what could she do with the hat, now that it was used? Lark tried it on in front of the cheval mirror and shook her head. It was much too prissy for her. It was the kind of hat her sister would have favored, but it looked ridiculous on a tomboy.

Magnolia was out of her pen again. The little burro stuck her head in the open front door. "You rascal," Lark laughed. "It's hot outside—you'll get sunstroke if you don't stay in the shade."

The burro let loose with an earsplitting bray that startled a paint horse tied at the feed store across the street. The horse reared, broke loose, and galloped off down the road. The owner ran out of the feed store, shouting curses at the stupid horse and shaking his fist.

"Oh, my! Magnolia, you're going to get me in trouble yet."

Lark took off the pink straw hat and looked at it again, wondering what to do with it. Now that everyone in town had seen Mrs. Snootley wearing it, no one else would buy it.

She stared at the hot little donkey wiggling its long ears in the summer heat. Now she had an idea. Taking a pair of scissors, she carefully cut two holes in the hat and carried it over to Magnolia. She pulled the burro's long ears through the holes and tied the pink veil under the donkey's chin. "My," she laughed, "have I told you how much you look like Bertha Snootley? Come to think of it, it looks a lot better on you than it did on that old cow."

Magnolia seemed proud of herself and very pleased to be wearing the big pink hat. Maybe she realized that she was the only donkey in the state with a pretty *chapeau*.

"At least it will keep you cool," Lark said.

The little donkey snorted and then ambled off down the street, stopping to nibble on a sack of vegetables that had been left out in front of the general store.

Lark heard some passing cowboys laugh. "Don't that

beat all? That hat looks a lot better on the little burro than it did on Mrs. Snootley."

"Ain't that the truth?"

Down the street, she heard someone yell, "Hey, Joe, you got to see this. That little donkey is wearing Mrs. Snootley's fancy hat!"

"She'll be furious!"

"Let's hope so!"

All up and down the street, people were coming outside to see the proud little donkey in her big pink hat.

That night, everyone at the dining room of the hotel was laughing when Lark entered. Mrs. Bottoms met her with a big smile. "Heavens, child, that was a stroke of genius. Everyone's saying the hat looks better on the donkey than it ever did on Bertha. They say she's so humiliated, she may never return anything again."

Lark shrugged. "She's probably so mad, she'll never come back in my shop. I don't know how that long-suffering husband of hers puts up with her. It's a wonder to me that he doesn't run off and leave her."

Later in the parlor, while the Mexican girls cleaned up the kitchen, Lark sat with Mrs. Bottoms as she sewed.

"Why so thoughtful?" Mrs. Bottoms paused with her needle in midair.

Lark sighed. "I know this is a *loco* question, but do you think it's possible to be in love with two men at the same time?"

She thought the old lady might laugh, but instead she seemed to be rolling the question over in her mind. "Well, I reckon it is, my dear. I've never told a soul this, but I was also in love with my Sam's best friend."

"No! What did you do?"

Mrs. Bottoms shrugged and returned to her sewing. "Well, I knew his friend was sort of a charming rascal, while Sam was steady and dependable. Women always love the rascal, but of course, sometimes better sense prevails and they marry the dependable one."

Lark pictured Larado in her mind. Yes, he was a worthless rascal, while his brother was so responsible. "Too bad you can't have both in one man. Aren't you going to ask more?"

The old lady looked at her a long moment and shook her head. "I don't know who the other one was, my dear, but the sheriff is a real catch. If we had any young women in town, someone would already have her brand on him."

"You're probably right," Lark said. Of course there were all these complications about the bank robbery and her being wanted by the law, but maybe she could put all that behind her. It seemed impossible, but maybe she could spend the rest of her life in this tiny town, happily married to the sheriff and living under her sister's name. Why, the dangerous way that drifting saddle tramp lived, he might be dead by now.

"You got it all settled in your mind?" asked Mrs. Bottoms as she sewed.

Lark nodded. "I—I think so. Maybe the dependable can be changed some."

Mrs. Bottoms laughed. "I wouldn't count on that, my dear. Women marry men hoping to change them, and that becomes a disaster."

Lark tried to imagine teaching the staid sheriff to be more like his charming brother. It did seem impossible. "I believe I'll go to bed now."

She went up the stairs to bed, but she couldn't sleep. The two brothers looked so much alike, she could marry Lawrence and pretend he was Larado. She felt guilty at the thought, but at least the upright Lawrence need never know of her fantasies.

The rest of the week passed quietly. Otto was found to have stabbed a fellow worker, but not fatally. He was sent to the county seat for trial, and he was probably headed for the state prison at Huntsville. The railroad construction came even closer. One could stand out at the end of Main Street and see the gangs working, hear the big hammers hitting the spikes that anchored the tracks. It would only be a few more days before the track and the new depot were finished.

Magnolia still wore her big pink hat and kept the town laughing. Even sour old Abner Snootley told Mrs. Bottoms privately that his wife deserved it.

Finally, Sunday night came. The hayrack wagon stopped along Main Street to pick up all its passengers.

Lawrence Witherspoon came to escort Lark to the wagon. "My goodness' sakes alive," he breathed. "You do look pretty as a songbird in an apple tree."

"You think so?" She blushed at his awkward compliment. She wore a pink checked gingham dress and little high-button shoes. Lark took his arm, attempting to match his long strides as they walked over to the big wagon. Paco and little Jimmy got to sit up on the seat with the driver. People were laughing and scrambling aboard.

Lawrence put his big hands on her small waist, lifting her up into the straw. "Miss Lacey, you don't weigh as much as my Stetson."

"Well, I weigh a little more than that." She found herself giggling like a schoolgirl as the wagon pulled away.

People began to laugh and point back down the road behind them.

"Oh dear, not again," Lark sighed.

Magnolia was out of her pen and ambling along behind the wagon as if she too, were going on the hay ride.

"Oh, let her be," said the sheriff. "She looks cute as a bug in that pink hat, and she ain't botherin' nobody."

So Magnolia trotted along behind the wagon as it wound its way through the countryside under the big summer moon. The crowd on the wagon sang an old song: ". . . He floats through the air with the greatest of ease, a daring young man on the flying trapeze, his movements were graceful, all the girls he did please . . . ."

The night turned cooler. Lark used this as an excuse to snuggle closer against Lawrence's big chest.

"You cold, Miss Lacey?"

"A little."

"I might could borrow a horse blanket off the driver."

Lark sighed. "Never mind." If he was too naive to cuddle her, she reckoned she could forget about getting a real kiss. There were some things the sheriff needed to learn from his rascal of a brother.

The wagon finally reached a spot under some cottonwood trees, near the big barn where the dance had been held. Someone built a roaring fire and put on a pot of real Texas chili to cook, while tin cups of strong coffee and hot cider were passed around. The crowd laughed, and joked, and sang more songs. Of course Magnolia had a lovely time, because she went around the circle begging bits of bread.

The sheriff laughed. "I think she's becomin' the town mascot."

"Humph!" snapped Mrs. Snootley. "How can we turn this town into a sophisticated metropolis with a stupid donkey roaming the streets, scaring the daylights out of folks when she opens her mouth?"

"She's just mad the burro looks better in that pink hat than she does," someone called.

"Who said that?" Mrs. Snootley said, looking around.

"Oh, Bertha," Abner sighed. "Get over it."

"But I was insulted—didn't you hear that?"

"You brought it on yourself," he chided.

"How could I have married such a country bumpkin?" she snorted as she went to sit on the wagon by herself.

That ended the awkwardness, and the crowd began to sing again. It must have been almost midnight when the driver sent Paco to gather up the crowd for the ride back.

Little Jimmy had gone to sleep in the hay. The moon had gone behind a cloud, and the night seemed as black as the inside of a cow, Lark thought.

Lawrence lifted her up on the wagon. "I reckon I never had such a good time before, Miss Lacey."

She was determined he was going to kiss her—*really* kiss her—tonight. She snuggled up to him and lifted her face. She could smell the sweet bay rum hair tonic and the mannish scent of sun and tobacco. She looked up at him in the darkness, oblivious to the others around them who were now singing: ". . . In the evening by the moonlight, I could hear those banjos ringing. . . ."

"Miss Lacey," he whispered. "I—I wish, I mean, if you wouldn't think me too forward—"

"You aren't too forward, Lawrence," she said. She reached up, put her arms around his neck, pulled his rugged face to hers, and kissed him—*really* kissed him.

He stiffened, almost in shock, then hesitantly, his big arms went around her and he kissed her like she'd never been kissed in her whole life. Wow. Lawrence had some hidden talents after all. When they finally pulled away from the embrace, both were gasping.

Lark managed to stifle the urge to grab him and kiss him deeper still. She thought she might shock him.

"Miss Lacey," he gasped. "You—you didn't think me too forward?"

Hell, no! Of course she didn't say that. Instead she blinked innocently. "Why, of course not, Lawrence. After all, you have been calling on me, and I presume your intentions are honorable?"

"I'm not sure if this is the time or place," he stammered, "but I reckon it's good as any."

"For what, Lawrence?"

"Uh, Miss Lacey, I think you're a fine figure of a woman."

She waited and listened to the horses clopping along. "Yes?"

"Uh, I think you're nice and sweet."

"That's kind of you to think that." *If he only knew.*

"I reckon you probably got lots of homemakin' skills that would make a man real happy."

"Uh, maybe." Aunt Cimarron said her cooking would choke a billy goat, but of course Lawrence needn't know that. She wondered how fast she could learn to cook. Was she out of her mind? Had she let that blissful kiss make her forget she was on the run and in a mess that she wasn't certain how to get out of?

"Maybe this ain't the time and place," he said, retreating.

"Whatever you think, Lawrence." How could this ex–Texas Ranger be so timid in dealing with a woman?

"No, I ain't gonna back down now." She could see sweat on his face, and he was chewing his lip. She reckoned he'd faced down killers with less fear than he was showing at this moment. Her heart went out to this earnest, sincere, inept man.

He cleared his throat and swallowed hard. "Miss Lacey, would you consider—I mean, would you do me the honor of marryin' up with me?"

Her brain told her to be cautious, but her heart could only remember that kiss and how it had felt to be in his arms. Was she doing the right thing? *A woman's heart will always overrule her brain,* she thought. "I'd be honored, Sheriff."

"Yippee!" he shouted. Then he looked around, embarrassed. People stopped singing and craned their necks to look. "Excuse me, folks, but I have something to holler about. Miss Lacey just said she'd marry me!"

The crowd broke into a storm of congratulations—even Paco grinned and nodded. Men were reaching to pat Lawrence on the back, and the ladies were cooing and smiling at Lark.

Lark went suddenly numb. *Oh my God, what have I done?*

Chapter Nine

They were planning a June wedding. It would be a simple outdoor affair with the whole town invited to see the popular sheriff wed the new girl.

The first train was finally scheduled to arrive in Rusty Spur. The new depot with its telegraph office would be at the end of the street where the tracks ran through town. The local weekly newspaper, the *Rusty Spur Beacon*, proudly announced: RAILROAD TO ARRIVE IN TOWN. GROWTH AND EXCITEMENT EXPECTED.

Well, this was about as excited as the tiny town could get, Lark thought with a smile as she looked out on the main street. A dog slept out in the middle, and two horses flicked flies as they stood tied in front of the hotel. However, several new buildings were under construction, the first in many years. The biggest was to be a bank, down near the depot, several blocks down the street from Lark's shop. It was two story, too, with living quarters above. Until now, the only two-story building in town was Mrs. Bottom's hotel, across the street and down from the French Chapeau.

Like everyone else, Lark walked over to watch people hanging red, white, and blue bunting at the depot. One man shouted to the crowd, "First train arrives tomorrow at high noon, folks."

"We're ready," Mrs. Bottoms shouted back. "The Odd Fellows band will play, and the mayor will make a speech."

Little Jimmy jumped up and down with excitement. "I ain't never ridden on a train before."

"The sheriff and I will see that you get a ride," Lark promised. "Maybe after we're married, we'll take you on a little trip."

"I love trains!" he said.

New people were already streaming into town. The town council had been getting letters from interested settlers and businessmen. The hotel was filling up as the big day approached, but then, there were more lawbreakers for the sheriff to corral. The town council had finally been contacted by a rich banker. He and his wife were coming all the way from St. Louis soon. Yes sirree bob, Rusty Spur was about to be put on the map.

The following morning dawned bright and warm. The streets were full of good-natured people jostling each other and going into the stores. The hitching rails in front of every building were full. Toward noon, people began to close their businesses and gather at the depot for the festivities. The Odd Fellows's little band played loudly, if not too well. The mayor made a speech about progress that only used "Remember the Alamo" three times. Not that anyone listened much; they were too excited.

A pompous railroad official with a big mustache had arrived early on the stagecoach and was waiting on the platform for the train to arrive. He, too, made a speech, mentioning the Alamo four times—which, of course, the Texans considered a superior speech.

Lark had closed her shop early to help Mrs. Bottoms and some of the other ladies set up a bunting-covered tablecloth on the platform, complete with lemonade and delicious oatmeal cookies. Jimmy and several other boys set off a string of firecrackers, which caused all the horses to rear and whinny. One buggy ran away with a man, dumping him in the middle of the dusty street. Magnolia merely looked around calmly. She wandered up to the refreshment table, ate a cookie or two, and made her own deposit on the station platform before Mrs. Bottoms shooed her away by waving her apron.

Lawrence grinned at Lark as he ambled up. "Ain't it great? We're part of history today. No telling what kind of future awaits the city of Rusty Spur."

She tried to smile back, but all she could think of was how many more people would be passing through the town now. The more people, the bigger the chances of her secret getting out.

As noon approached on the hot summer day, the crowd grew, as did their excitement. In the distance, the distinct whistle of a train echoed across the prairie. Everyone cheered. After a moment, they could hear the chugging of the engine and see the smoke rising from the big black engine as it approached the town. It whistled again, and the scent of burning wood from the engine floated on the warm air. The little band struck up "For He's a Jolly Good Fellow" as the engine chugged into the depot, blowing its whistle and causing more horses to rear and run away. Dogs barked, and men shouted and cheered as the engine slowed with a great grinding of brakes, pulling into the depot. The engine flew both an American and a Texas flag. Red, white, and blue banners hung on the cars, and dignitaries waved from inside.

Finally it stopped in the depot, blowing steam like an angry dragon while the people of the town pressed closer for a good look. The band played on, festively.

The conductor swung down from a car, shouting, "Rusty Spur! All off for Rusty Spur!"

The first passengers began to alight from the train.

"Welcome to Rusty Spur," the mayor shouted. "Hope you folks is comin' to stay. This town is gonna grow."

Mrs. Snootley carried her valise and was already stepping aboard. "Bertha, where you going?" her husband demanded.

"I'm going shopping in Abilene," she shouted back. "I'll be going a lot more often now that the train comes through."

"I can't afford for you to do any more shopping!"

"Oh, hush," she dismissed him with a disdainful sniff. "You don't think I can dress fashionably in a town whose only shop caters to donkeys, do you?"

Maybe the word "donkey" set Magnolia off. She set up a discordant braying in protest. Of course that made a bunch of stray dogs start barking. The noise so startled the visiting railroad executive that he dropped the metal key to the city on his foot and hopped about, whimpering in pain.

Lark hurried to grab Magnolia. The railroad man pulled at his big mustache and stared at the little beast. "Is that a lady's hat that animal is wearing?"

"That's a long story," Lark said, leading Magnolia away as the town roared with laughter.

The next few days made Lark aware of how much the arrival of a train was going to change the town. It arrived every Saturday at high noon, and there were always children waiting at the depot just to gawk at it. More people began to arrive in town. Some of them were settlers, looking for good farm or ranch land, and some were businesspeople looking for opportunities. A new school was now under construction, and there were new houses being built. Tiny Rusty Spur, which had been isolated except for an occasional freight wagon or stage, was growing faster than anyone had thought possible. Of course among the arrivals were a few saddle bums and ne'er-do-wells, but for the most part, the town stayed quiet and orderly.

As one ribbon drummer told Lark, the legend of the tough, silent sheriff who wasn't a man to be trifled with had spread throughout Texas. Outlaws and troublemakers wanted to avoid Rusty Spur rather than tangle with the deadeye lawman.

Lark had gotten over her original doubts and was busy planning her wedding with Mrs. Bottoms. The hotel owner would be Lark's matron of honor, and Paco would be Lawrence's best man. Jimmy was pressed into service as the ring bearer, although he complained about having to wear a suit. The whole town was invited, as the ceremony would be held in the small church with an outdoor reception to follow.

Mrs. Bottoms helped Lark make her dress, since Lark had admitted she didn't sew well enough to do it herself. She also acknowledged that she couldn't cook, either.

"Well, I reckon that won't matter at first," the older lady said with a grin. "At first, the groom is interested in only one thing, and it ain't cookin', honey."

Lark felt herself blush to the roots of her hair. "Mrs. Bottoms, I'm surprised at you."

"Well, it's true. I've seen the way that sheriff looks at you, and I don't think he's dreamin' about biscuits."

Biscuits. Her uncle Trace said Lark's biscuits could be substituted for cannonballs. Actually, what he had said was, "If the defenders of the Alamo had had a supply of Lark's biscuits, they might have wiped out Santa Anna."

Okay, so for her dear Lawrence, she would learn to cook.

Mrs. Bottoms adjusted the veil as Lark tried it on. Lark took a look at herself and took a deep breath. "Oh my, I really do look like a bride, don't I?"

"Sure do." She had a mouthful of pins. "You don't have any kin to come to this, child?"

Lark hesitated and tears came to her eyes. She blinked them away. Oh, how she missed her family. With her parents dead, her aunt and uncle and their clan were all the relatives Lark had. Still, considering the circumstances, she could hardly contact the Durango ranch and let them know she was getting married. The law was looking for her. Maybe someday, all this would fade away so she could go home and introduce her new husband. She had to hope Larado never showed up and spilled the beans about her past, working in the saloon and being part of the bank robbery. Lawrence—that pillar of virtue—would never understand.

It was a beautiful late June evening for the wedding, with flowers everywhere in the church. Of course there was a problem finding enough flowers because Magnolia had eaten most of the flower gardens in town. She had a particular taste for daisies and petunias. Some of the roses were spared because of the thorns, so Lark carried a bouquet of white old-fashioned rosebuds, which created a perfume that scented the whole church. Old Bill—the telegraph operator who had been part of the mail-order-bride conspiracy—would give the bride away.

The elderly maiden organist played the wheezy old organ as the pair made ready to come down the aisle. The church was full to overflowing. The elderly minister stepped to the pulpit, holding his Bible and nodding to the crowd. Somewhere in the audience a baby whimpered, and the mother tried to shush it. The wheezy old organ played, and the warm night air drifted through the open windows while the old ladies fanned themselves with paper fans.

Old Miss Wiggly wore a dress as gray as her hair. She stood up solemnly and began her solo in a quavering voice that set a dog outside howling: "Oh, promise me that someday, you and I . . ."

Peeking from the back, Lark saw Lawrence and his best man step out of a back room and stand next to the pulpit. He looked nervous and sweaty palmed as he gazed up the aisle. Then his expression changed when he saw Lark, and his eyes lit up.

Mrs. Bottoms walked down the aisle in a no-nonsense blue dress that could be worn again later. Then Jimmy, his dark hair slicked back and his face shiny from scrubbing, solemnly went down the aisle, carrying a little pillow with the ring. It was a plain gold band from Snootley's General Store.

The pastor gestured the crowd to stand, and the organ played louder, if not better. Lark thought she had never been so happy as she was now, starting down the aisle. She was only sad that her family was not here to take part.

It seemed a long way down the aisle to her waiting groom, but she had eyes only for him.

They stood side by side. Lawrence looked so nervous, Lark was afraid he might faint. The organ wheezed to a halt, and the minister motioned for the crowd to sit. "Dearly beloved . . ." he began.

Lark barely heard him as she took Lawrence's hand. They looked into each other's eyes. He looked like he was about to break and run, but she held on to his big hand firmly. If the shy sheriff decided he couldn't go through with this, she wasn't going to allow him to escape up the aisle and humiliate her.

He mouthed the words: *You look prettier than a speckled pup in a red wagon.*

Okay, so it wasn't very romantic, but after all, he was a Texan. He could have compared her to some longhorned heifer.

The minister said something about obeying. She nodded, although it rankled her. She should have had him take that part out.

"Lawrence Witherspoon, do you take this woman to be your lawfully wedded wife, in sickness and in health, until death do you part, as long as you both shall live?"

"I sure do, Reverend. Long as I got a biscuit, she gets half." A Texan couldn't make a deeper commitment than that.

"Lacey Van Schuyler, do you take this man do be your lawfully wedded husband, in sickness and in health, until death do you part, as long as you both shall live?"

For a moment, Lark hesitated. Land's sake, what was she doing? This wasn't going to be legal, getting married under her sister's name. What's more, prissy Lacey would have a hissy fit when she finally found out she was legally married to a sheriff she had never met. Besides, wasn't Lacey about to marry Homer What's-his-name?

The congregation stirred uneasily and a small buzz ran through the crowd.

"Uh, Miss Lacey?" said the minister.

"What?" She came to with a start. How in the hell had she gotten herself into this mess, getting married under her sister's name? Could they throw her in jail for that too?

The minister was looking at her strangely. Poor Lawrence looked stricken.

"I asked, Miss Lacey," the pastor asked patiently, "if you're willing to marry Lawrence here?"

"Uh, yes, of course. Long as I got a biscuit, he's got half."

The preacher and the whole congregation seemed to sigh with relief. "Is there a ring?"

Jimmy stepped up and handed Lawrence the pillow. His hands were shaking so badly, he dropped the ring, which rolled under the front pew. This set a bunch of people crawling around on their hands and knees looking for it. What if nobody found it? Lark thought, could they call off the wedding?

"Found it!" announced a little girl in the front row. She carried it up and handed it to the sheriff.

The audience sighed with relief, and a small boy asked, "Is it over yet?"

His mother shushed him.

Lawrence slipped the gold band on her finger. His hands were so sweaty and his face so strained, Lark thought he might faint on the spot. If he did, was she legally married?

The minister drew a great sigh of relief. "Now, by the power of God, this church, and the greatest state in the whole world—Texas, of course—I now pronounce you man and wife. You may kiss the bride."

He looked like he expected to be shot. "In front of all these people?"

The crowd roared with laughter as Lawrence leaned over and gave her a quick peck.

Oh my. Maybe she had made a mistake. It might not be a wedding night to remember, Lark thought with dismay. Well, it was too late now. She'd just have to make the best of it. The organist was just about to play the recessional when there came a terrible braying from the back of the church, causing everyone to jump. Magnolia had managed to get the church door open and stood there staring inside.

"There's your flower girl," someone laughed. The organ began to play as Lark and Lawrence ran up the aisle and outside into the warm summer darkness.

Once out on the grass, he picked her up and swung her around. "Honey, you gave me quite a scare in there. I thought you was about to back out on me."

She smiled up at him. "Funny, I thought the same thing."

"Who, me? Nope, but I'd rather face Billy the Kid than go through that again. I'd look like a damned fool in front of all these folks if you got cold feet on me."

"You'll find out about my cold feet this winter," Lark laughed with a wink. Then she wondered if she'd shocked him. Around them, people were crowding in to congratulate them. The empty lot next door was decorated with hanging kerosene lamps to light up the festivities and crepe paper streamers. The men had laid out a wooden dance floor up near the refreshments, and the Odd Fellows band was set to play. Mrs. Bottoms and the other ladies set up the wedding feast on tables under the giant cottonwood trees. Lark placed her bouquet on the table near the big fancy cake. When she looked again, the irrepressible Magnolia was calmly nibbling on the dainty white rosebuds.

It was a fabulous feast as only Texans could put on. A whole steer had been roasted on a spit, as well as a suckling pig. There were mounds of homemade rolls, salads, and homegrown vegetables, as well as corn on the cob and buckets of iced tea and lemonade. A whole table of desserts competed with the big wedding cake in the middle. Magnolia promptly started in on the roasting ears, and Paco had to catch the donkey and tie her up to keep her out of people's plates. Some of the men brought out a keg of beer, which the good reverend pretended not to see as the dancing began. Children ran in and out of the crowd, ignoring the halfhearted scolding of mothers who were having too good a time to pay much attention to them. The band began to play that old Texas favorite: "Put Your Little Foot."

Put your little foot, put your little foot, put your little foot right there. . . .

Lark wanted to dance with her new husband, but men were lining up to dance with her. She sighed as she glanced around for Lawrence and saw him standing over by the beer keg, laughing with some of the other men.

It was late when she finally got to dance with him. He'd been drinking. She could smell it, and he was a little unsteady on his feet. "Congratulations, Mrs. Witherspoon," he mumbled. "Do you reckon we could slip away soon?"

She blushed. "I know, I can hardly wait, either."

He looked abruptly green. "Then you're as sick as I am?" he mumbled, staggering off into the shadows. She could hear him throwing up in the bushes. Oh hell, so much for romance. Of course, being Texan, it was a wonder he wasn't drunker than he was. He came staggering back. "I reckon I need another drink."

"I think you've already had enough," Lark snapped. "Don't you think we ought to leave now?"

He looked at her cross-eyed, then he leaned closer as if not certain who she was. "And miss this good party?"

"Lawrence, if we don't leave soon, people will start whispering. They expect us to try to sneak off."

"They do? Okay." He put his arm around her and swayed. If he went down, as big as he was, she wasn't certain she could get him on his feet.

She was almost holding him up. "Look, here comes Paco with the buggy. See how it's all decorated up with flowers and dragging old shoes?"

Well, actually, since this was Texas, it wasn't dragging old shoes. It was dragging old boots.

"Where?" The sheriff looked around and swayed again.

The whole crowd had turned to watch. The men were nudging each other, and the ladies were giggling.

"Paco," she called, "I think I need some help here."

"*Sí, señorita*, I mean, *señora*." The young deputy jumped down from the buggy and ran to help her lead Lawrence across the grass.

"Three cheers for our sheriff and his new bride!" a man shouted. "Hip hip hooray!"

Others joined in, as did Magnolia with her ungodly braying. "Hip hip hooray! Hip hip hooray!"

"Thank you, one and all," Lark said with as much dignity as she could manage, considering the big lanky lawman was reeling as he leaned on her with one big boot tangled in her long veil. With Paco's help, she got Lawrence into the buggy, and Paco drove them away.

"To the sheriff's house, *sí*?" Paco asked.

"To the sheriff's house," Lark repeated. There was no time for a honeymoon—there really wasn't anyone to replace him except Paco, who was a bit young to take over corralling the whole town. The sheriff's tiny house was also on Main Street, right in the middle of town. They drove up in front, and Paco helped her get her drunken groom inside.

"Help me get him into the bedroom," she ordered. Her veil had come off, and her dress was askew. They half carried, half dragged the big Texan in and laid him across the bed. He lay there, spread out like a dead possum and snoring loudly.

Paco pulled off the sheriff's boots. "That was a great wedding," he said enthusiastically.

"Well, it was 'til toward the end. Will he be all right?"

"*Sí*, I reckon so. The sheriff don't drink much. Well, I'll be going, ma'am." He touched the brim of his hat with two fingers and started for the door. "I'll put away the buggy and Magnolia, *señora*. There's a stable out back of the house."

"*Gracias*, Paco." She watched him leave and turned to look at her groom. Lawrence was dead to the world, and his snoring sounded like Magnolia's braying. How romantic. Just what kind of a wedding night was this going to be?

As a matter of fact, not much at all. Lawrence never woke up all night. Lark didn't know whether to be sympathetic or mad. She'd heard of reluctant brides, but a groom?

She decided the next morning to pretend as if nothing had happened. She was in the kitchen cooking bacon and eggs when he stumbled out of the bedroom.

"My," she said, a little brighter than she felt, "are you doing okay this morning?"

He squinted at her a long moment as if trying to focus his eyes. "Uh," he groaned, putting his hand to his head. "I feel like I been rode hard and put away wet."

She could only wish about the hard ride, she thought.

"Is there some coffee?" He staggered across the kitchen.

"Sit down." She decided to be sympathetic. "I'll bring you a cup. Want anything in it?"

"Maybe a shot of whiskey," he groaned. "The hair of the dog that bit me, you know."

"I meant cream, or sugar." She tried not to let her voice be too icy. She brought a cup and set it before him. "How do you like your eggs?"

He groaned again and sipped the coffee, shuddering. Okay, so she didn't make good coffee, either—but in the state he was in, how could he tell the difference? "Don't even talk about food. What happened, anyway?"

"We got married," she said. Surely he was joking. "You don't remember that?"

"Uh, of course." He didn't look at her, and she wasn't sure whether he was telling the truth or not. "Reckon I celebrated a little too much. How was it . . . ?" He looked at her "I mean, you know."

He couldn't remember that either—or lack thereof. She stifled an urge to hit him in the head with the frying pan—but of course, with the eggs in it, it would make a mess she'd have to clean up. "I don't reckon the town will expect you to work today."

"Oh, I'll work." He gulped his coffee and stood up, looking a little green. "Somebody's got to protect the town."

As sick as he looked, she didn't figure he could unbutton his own pants if he had to pee, much less outdraw a lawbreaker, but she didn't say that. "No more than happens around Rusty Spur, I imagine Paco could handle it for the day."

He avoided her gaze. "Reckon you got things to do, cleanin' up and all. Oh, by the way, the town is givin' us a poundin' tonight."

"A pounding? I thought that was a custom for preachers."

"Mostly, it may be, but the ladies thought it was a nice idea to give us a good start. Mrs. Bottoms told me to remind you yesterday, but I forgot."

She looked around the untidy house with growing horror. "They're all coming here?"

"Well, Mrs. Bottoms and some of the other ladies'll bring the refreshments, I reckon."

"And you're going to run off and leave me with this

mess?" She looked around. The place looked like possums had been nesting in it.

"Well, after all, ain't you the wife?"

She would kill him. Yes, she would kill him. And then the best man from her wedding would arrest her, but the ladies would still gossip about how dirty her house was. She tried to tell herself she didn't care what they thought, but she did. "I can't get this—this stable cleaned up by tonight."

He grinned. "Sure you can, you just scrub hard all day, that's all. By the way, I could use some clean socks."

Yes, she would kill him. Washing his dirty socks was not what she had in mind for the morning after her wedding.

Before she could say anything else, he stumbled to the bedroom for his boots and hat and went out the door, squinting in the bright sunlight.

Lark took a deep breath. What kind of a mess had she gotten herself into? She was married—no, probably living in sin with a man who couldn't even remember last night. She went to the window and looked out. The sheriff limped along the street as if he didn't feel too well. And she, who was no great shakes as a housewife, had to clean up a pigsty of a home for dozens of townspeople to come calling tonight. She turned and surveyed the mess. If she had seen it before the wedding, she might have backed out on this deal. Dishes were stacked in the sink and on the cabinet. Lawrence had left a trail of clothes across the floor and hanging on doorknobs. Old newspapers and coffee cups were piled around on the living room furniture, and the floor could use a good scrubbing. Housekeeping was not an area that Lark shone.

"What have I gotten myself into?" Her first inclination was to go into the bedroom, pack her bag, and clear out. She'd never been good about facing trouble head-on. Yet her leaving might raise a lot of questions that she'd just as soon not answer.

Lawrence might be a totally wonderful man, but so far he hadn't shown her anything.

About that time, there was a knock at the door and she hurried to answer it. It was Mrs. Bottoms, accompanied by two of her maids.

"Hello, my dear, how is the old married woman this morning?"

The Mexican girls put their hands over their mouths and giggled.

"Feeling very old. Just look at this place. I don't think it's been cleaned up since Texas entered the Union."

She stepped back and ushered the trio in.

"That's a sore point with some folks, dear," the lady said. "I wouldn't mention it."

"What? The sheriff's dirty house?"

"No, Texas joining the Union. You know many Texans think we did better as our own nation. Besides, remember we teach our schoolchildren that the rest of the Union joined us."

"Oh, yes, I forgot. Can I get you some coffee?" She led the three into her kitchen and poured three cups. They all took sips and frowned.

"Uh, dear," Mrs. Bottoms said, "remind me to teach you how to make coffee. Now, girls, let's get to work."

The two maids started picking up and sweeping.

Mrs. Bottoms turned and smiled at Lark. "So, how was it?"

Lark felt herself flush. "If you don't mind, that part is not something I want to discuss." How could she admit nothing had happened in her marital bed?

"Heavens, he's more man than most, I reckon," the lady said with a wink. "I reckon all the ladies is curious."

The Mexican girls giggled and nudged each other.

Lark decided to change the subject. "I understand the town is giving us a pounding tonight. We're much obliged."

The other woman shrugged. "Sheriffs don't make money, so we thought maybe we'd give you a good start."

She paused and looked around. "I'd say you could use a little help. This place looks like a tavern on Sunday morning after a Saturday night fight."

"Exactly what I thought." Lark didn't want to admit she hadn't the slightest idea where to begin.

"We'll pitch in and slick it up," Mrs. Bottoms promised, "and the ladies will bring refreshments. It will be a lovely evening."

Frankly, Lark had been looking forward to getting her bashful groom alone and sober in the bedroom tonight. Well, that could wait. After all, she wasn't certain at that moment if she wanted this marriage consummated. She might still decide to flee the town. "I appreciate all the help I can get."

Mrs. Bottoms and her maids began to clean. Lark watched them, hoping to pick up a few pointers.

"You have any vinegar?" Mrs. Bottoms asked.

"I don't know." She looked under the cabinet and came up with a jug. "Yes."

"Good, we'll get those dirty windows sparkling. Lacey, why don't you take down the curtains and wash them while I do that?"

Wash the curtains. She wasn't very good with an iron, either. She began to pull down the short gingham curtains. There were cobwebs hanging across the room and in the corners. "We can't get it ready in time."

"But of course we can," Mrs. Bottoms said, her plump face shiny with exertion. "It's a small house, but with a little spit and polish, we can get it sparkling and homey."

"If you think so," Lark said. She got a bucket and went out in the backyard to the well. She carried in two buckets of water. One of the maids was already putting a kettle on to boil so they'd have hot water to wash the dishes. "Looking at this mess, I wondered if Lawrence didn't marry me so he could have a housekeeper."

The old lady looked up from her cleaning. "I doubt that,

honey. I've seen the way he looks at you, which makes me think he married you for a totally different reason."

The Mexican maids giggled again.

They cleaned all morning. When the three women left, Lark collapsed in a chair with a groan. Then she got up, set up the ironing board, and put the irons on the stove to heat. Housework was harder than branding and working cattle with the Triple D cowhands. About one o'clock, Lawrence came home, looking considerably better. "You got lunch ready?"

She stifled the urge to hit him in the head with an iron. "I'll rustle you up a sandwich."

He smiled and sat down at the kitchen table. "I think I'm gonna like bein' married."

I think I'm not, Lark thought, but she didn't say that. She sliced up cold roast beef, got out some stale bread, and put it before him.

"I hope you know how to make pickles," he said. "I dearly love homemade pickles and fresh tomatos."

"I'm sorry"—she gritted her teeth—"but I haven't had time to plant a garden yet, much less can pickles."

He seemed to miss the sarcasm. "Place looks good, Lacey. You better give yourself time to get cleaned up. You look like something Miss Wiggly's cat dragged in."

"Of course. I'll spend the whole afternoon in my bubble bath."

He went right ahead eating, seemingly unaware that she was being sarcastic. "Whatever you think."

He finished and wiped his face on his sleeve. "What are we havin' for supper?"

"How can a man just finish dinner and be thinking about supper?"

He grinned at her. "There's two things men think about a lot, and eatin's one of them." He winked. "Well, I got to get back to work. Don't you work too hard now."

Supper. She leaned against the cabinet and watched him leave. Maybe she could try broiling a steak and frying some potatoes.

Supper was none too good, but Lawrence put up a brave front as he sat down to lumpy potatoes and burnt steak. He looked across at Lark, and she couldn't hold the tears back. "I reckon now you know I can't cook."

"That's okay. I didn't marry you for your cookin'." He grinned at her. "Tonight I'll show you why I married you."

She had never heard him say something so bold. She felt her face go red. "Why, Lawrence."

"Reckon I overstepped myself. I'm sorry."

She stared at him in the awkward silence while he went brick red. "We've got to get ready, the whole town is coming. You must be the most popular sheriff ever."

"I reckon I'm the *only* one that ever lived long enough for them to get to know very well."

She smiled at him. "Everyone says this was a really tough town before you cleaned it up."

He ducked his head modestly. "A man's gotta do what a man's gotta do. It was my duty."

Could she expect anything less from a former Ranger?

He stood up. "Now I reckon we'd better get ready for our company." He hesitated. "Lacey, I reckon last night wasn't so good, and I'm sorry for it. Maybe tonight I can make it up to you."

"Oh, Lawrence." He was the thoughtful, wonderful man she'd thought he was. She went into his arms, and he kissed her—*really* kissed her.

She pulled away after a long moment. "Land's sake."

He grinned at her, and somehow, that crooked grin was so much like his black-sheep brother. "Just wait 'til later," he promised.

Her heart pounded with excitement. Later. Oh, she

was so glad she hadn't packed up and cleared out. "I'll get the table cleared. Folks should be here soon."

"I could lock the door and pull all the curtains," he said, kissing the tip of her nose.

"Lawrence!" she scolded. "What would everyone think?"

He grinned even bigger. "You know what they'd think."

She felt herself flush. "We'll talk about that later."

For the bashful sheriff, he certainly was getting more cocky and confident than before. Maybe that would translate into the bedroom. Well, in about three hours she intended to find out.

Chapter Ten

At about seven on that hot summer evening, the crowd began to arrive. Everyone, that is, but Mr. and Mrs. Snootley. She had sent word that she had a headache and her husband had to stay home to look after her, Mrs. Bottoms said. Everyone was laughing about the incident, though, knowing how she reacted to the pink hat and the little donkey. Speaking of which, Magnolia—who didn't seem to realize she wasn't invited—managed to get out of her stable and show up too. When Lark glanced out the window, the little burro was quietly munching the flowers out by the front door.

The crowd filled the little house to overflowing, and the gifts they had brought piled up deeper and deeper on the dining table.

"Land's sake." Tears came to Lark's eyes as she looked at the bounty. "I didn't realize he was so well liked."

"And you, too, my dear," said Mrs. Bottoms. The crowd applauded. "Now look at what the good people brought."

There was a pound of Arbuckles' coffee, and a pound of cornmeal. Someone else had brought a pound of flour and a pound of sugar. Another sack held a pound of salt, and here were a dozen eggs, and a gallon of milk. The pile got larger and larger as folks arrived.

"Why," Lark said, "there's enough supplies to keep us for weeks."

"We wanted to show how much we care about you two newlyweds," Paco said. "The ladies also brought a few dishes and a pan or two to help you get started."

Lawrence put his arm around Lark's shoulders. "We're much obliged, folks. Someday, I'm gonna build this lady a nice big house when I can afford a ranch, but 'til then, we're much obliged to you."

"We certainly are." Lark smiled. His muscular arm around her shoulders felt comforting. "This is a good place to live, and I'm proud to be a citizen of Rusty Spur."

The jovial crowd applauded.

"Now," said Mrs. Bottoms, "let's get down to the refreshments. We knew the new bride wouldn't have time to bake up a bunch of cakes, so some of the ladies brought a little something."

"Hooray!" Little Jimmy jumped up and down. The men also cheered. Lark thought she wouldn't have the least idea how to bake a cake, and a dog probably wouldn't eat it, anyway. Well, maybe she could learn. She looked fondly at her new husband as he shook hands good-naturedly. Men slapped him on the back and ladies handed him new babies to admire. Yes, Lawrence Witherspoon was a mighty popular sheriff.

The ladies began to serve the refreshments. There was plenty of iced tea served in pint jars, and fresh-ground coffee with thick cream and sugar for those who wanted it—made like Texans liked it, strong enough to float a horseshoe. There were blackberry and rhubarb pies, apple and peach cobblers, chocolate cake, and Lady Baltimore cake with creamy fruit filling, and even a tub of homemade ice cream. Everyone went back for seconds. Lark had never been so happy. She forgot all about her troubles with the law, exalting in her new husband and the love of this town. For once, she didn't feel inferior to her perfect sister.

Finally, people began to take their departure.

Lark and Lawrence stood arm in arm, seeing them off, thanking them again for the bounty they had brought. Magnolia was still out munching on the front flower bed.

Paco grinned. "Jimmy and I will put her back in her stall so you won't have to come out, Sheriff."

Lawrence nodded. "I'd be much obliged, Paco."

Finally, the house was empty. Lark sighed and closed the front door. "That was so generous of the town."

"I didn't think they'd ever leave." He grinned and held out his arms to her.

"That's not nice," she scolded as she went into his embrace.

"I reckon it isn't, but being as how we're newlyweds . . ."

She tilted up her face and he kissed her—*really* kissed her. It was so unexpected and so passionate that Lark was taken by surprise.

"Oh my," she whispered against his lips.

"If you'd just as soon I didn't—"

"I didn't say that," Lark said kissing him back.

"I think I owe you a wedding night, Mrs. Witherspoon," he murmured against her lips.

He was a lot more forward than she had expected from the shy sheriff, but that was okay. Maybe he always had to compete with his brother too. "I'm looking forward to it."

"I'm surprised at the fellas," he said as he nuzzled her neck. "Usually, when someone gets married, they got to put up with a shivaree. You know how Texans are."

"I certainly do," she laughed, remembering some of the shivarees she'd heard about around her hometown. A shivaree was a Southern custom mostly, but Texans liked it too.

Usually, about the time the couple was going to bed, a rowdy crowd of men would gather around the house, hooting and making noise, until the couple came to the door and rewarded them with refreshments. If they didn't, some of the ruffians had been known to kidnap the bride and keep her all night so her poor groom couldn't enjoy his marital rights.

"I reckon since we've been married one night, and we've already served refreshments, the boys won't bother with that," Lawrence murmured.

"Let's hope," Lark whispered, and she kissed him. The kiss deepened, and she forgot about the townsfolk—she forgot about everything but experiencing that kiss, longer and deeper until they were both gasping with excitement. She hadn't thought the bashful sheriff could be so skilled, but he certainly wasn't bashful now.

"I think I'd better turn off all the lamps," Lark murmured, pulling away from him reluctantly. "I'll join you in a minute." She walked through the small house, putting her hand behind the chimneys and gently blowing out the flames. After a moment, she was left standing in the moonlight that filtered through the windows. "Here I come, ready or not."

"Lady, I'm almost ready—I got my shirt off."

In the darkness, she could barely see his big silhouette. She returned to her husband, splaying her fingers across his bare chest. He swung her up in his arms. She could feel his heart pounding against her face as he ducked his head and kissed her again, eagerly, insistently. She let his mouth force open her lips, and his tongue explored along the curve of her mouth.

Oh my. This was going to be something worth remembering. Last night's fiasco didn't matter anymore. She returned his kiss eagerly as he stood her slowly on her feet by the bed. They clung together, exchanging eager kiss for eager kiss. His big hands went to cover her breasts, caressing there.

"I reckon, Mrs. Witherspoon, you need to put on your nightgown."

"Suppose I don't put on anything at all?"

"That would be even better." He pulled her to him again, kissing her face, the tip of her nose, and stroking her hair. His hands went down her back to cup her bottom, and he squeezed gently.

She clung to him, reveling in the deft touch of his hands as he caressed her. Lawrence was certainly a big surprise, but she was thrilled at his ardor.

He stepped away from her. "Reckon I'll take off my boots and pants."

She took a deep, shuddering breath. She wanted him to watch her undress. She'd do it very slowly and deliberately, so he could savor every move with anticipation.

He sat down on the edge of the bed, and she knelt and pulled off his boots. "You know," he said, "in the moonlight, with you bending over like that, I can see right down the front of your dress."

She laughed. "Now why do you think I did that?"

"You surprise me, lady, you're more forward than I'd expect."

"You don't like it?"

He laughed awkwardly. "No, ma'am, I didn't say I didn't like it." He stood up and pulled off his pants, then took off his long drawers. "Come here to me."

She went into his arms, putting her hands on his rear. His hips were small, and lean, and powerful. When he pulled her close, she was only too aware of his aroused manhood. "Now you," he commanded.

Lark started to unbutton the bodice of her gingham dress, fully aware that in the moonlight he could see every movement. Deliberately, she stretched it out, kicking off her slippers, taking the ribbon from her hair, and shaking her dark hair loose so that it fell in a black cascade over her shoulders.

"Quit stallin'," he said. He pulled her to him again, tangling his hands in her hair, breathing hard as he kissed her deeper still.

About that time outside, all hell broke loose. There

was shouting, and singing, and loud noise clattering around the house as if someone was banging on pans.

"What the—?" Lawrence stumbled away, and Lark was terrified. Then abruptly she realized what the racket was.

"It's the boys!" She raised her voice over the din of noise. "We're being shivareed."

"Oh, damn it," Lawrence said and reached for his pants. In the confusion, he couldn't seem to find them. "Ouch!" He stumped his bare foot against a bedpost and hopped around on one foot, swearing.

"Let's just keep quiet and ignore them," Lark suggested. "Maybe they'll go away."

"Texans give up? It ain't likely." She could hear him stumbling about the room, still looking for his pants.

About that time, the rowdies burst through the front door, laughing and singing. "Hey, Sheriff, we thought we'd have a little fun with your bride."

She protested, but already, Paco and Bill had her by the arms, leading her out the door with Lawrence calling after them. "Hey, bring her back! We was just about to—"

"We know!" The men laughed. "You'll have to find her!"

With Lark protesting, the good-natured crowd led her out and lifted her up into a wagon. Lawrence ran out into the yard in pursuit—but he must have stepped on a rock, for once again, he was hopping about and cursing.

"Hey, Sheriff," Paco yelled, "don't you know you can get arrested for going out in public naked?"

"I'll get you *hombres* for this!" The sheriff waved his fist at the crowd.

"You'll have to catch us first!" someone yelled. There was a snap of the reins, and the wagon pulled away.

"Lawrence!" Lark yelled. "Come save me!"

"I'll have to find my pants first!"

Magnolia must have gotten out of her pen again because

she suddenly joined the confusion. She brayed so loudly the horses snorted, and the wagon took off at a gallop.

It was all good fun, Lark thought with a sigh as she hung on for dear life, but she wished the rowdies had waited another hour. No, even half an hour would have been fine. As the wagon rolled along, she thought wistfully of her first night in Lawrence's arms and how these fun-loving rascals had ruined it. Well, there was always tomorrow night.

She had thought the jokesters would just take her out to the big barn where the square dance had been held, but of course that would be the first place Lawrence might have looked. They took her out on a hilltop, and Lark sat on a rock woebegone while the men sat around a campfire, laughing and drinking.

"Did you see the sheriff's face?"

"Oh, he was mad!"

"You ain't upset with us, is you, missus? We're just havin' a little fun."

"Oh, you're just being Texans," she sighed, remembering the urgent promise of that last kiss just before the rowdies had invaded the house.

After a couple of hours, a lookout rode up. "He's comin'! I reckon he's searched everywhere else."

All the men paused and looked at each other uncertainly. "I reckon we'd better clear out. The sheriff may not think this is as funny as we did."

"*Sí*, we'd all better clear out," Paco decided, discretion being the better part of valor. To Lark, he implored, "Tell the sheriff we was just funnin' around. We wouldn't want to have him on the prod after us."

"It'll be all right," she reassured them with a tired sigh. "Being a Texan himself, I'm sure he'll understand."

With that, the men ran to their horses and scattered

like quail before a running bird dog. Lark watched them leave, then stood and waited for Lawrence to arrive.

He rode up, looking anxious and upset. "You all right?"

She shrugged. "You know Texans, having a little fun."

"I ought to break their necks," he muttered as he dismounted.

She ran into his arms. "It's okay. They're really worried about you being mad at them. You have a tough reputation around these parts."

"That reputation cleaned up this town," he said, kissing her forehead.

The night had grown cool, and she shivered in his arms. He took off his shirt and put it around her shoulders. "You're liable to catch your death of cold," he said, pulling her against his big, warm body.

"I don't think so, at least not now," she whispered and snuggled closer still.

He squinted down at her. "I'm mighty glad to find you."

"Why don't we go home and finish what we were starting?"

"Mrs. Witherspoon, I reckon you've got a good idea."

He picked her up and carried her easily to his horse. He put her in the saddle and swung up behind her. His big arms went around her, pulling her up against his warmth, and he kissed the back of her neck.

The caress of his warm breath on her skin sent a shiver through her.

"You still cold?" He clucked to the horse, and it started away at a walk.

"No, I'm fine . . . now that you're here, dearest." She leaned back against him and he kissed the back of her neck again. They rode back to the little house in town. The whole village was still asleep, everything still.

"I reckon," the sheriff said as he helped her down and carried her into the house, "the rascals is all home sleepin' it off."

Once in the house, he carried her into the bedroom,

stood her on her feet, and blew out the lamp. "Now where were we?"

"I had just taken off your boots."

"Oh, yes." He smiled and sat down on the edge of the bed. "Go ahead, I like lookin' down your dress."

"And I thought you were bashful." She smiled and dropped to her knees. She took a long time taking off his boots, making sure he got a good look at the rise of her breasts. He reached down and caught her hand, pulling her to her feet as he stood up. He was so tall, she could lay her face against his big chest as he kissed her hair.

"I reckon I ought to take off my pants."

"You reckon the rowdies are liable to burst in again?"

"They wouldn't dare," he said firmly. "This time, I might shoot them."

He took off his pants and stood in the shadows. "You gonna undress?"

She had never felt so daring. "You want to undress me?"

"Best invite I reckon I ever had." He grinned and came to her. His dark eyes were hot with intense desire.

Lark closed her eyes and relished the feel of his big hands fumbling with her buttons. He got the front of her bodice undone, and then his hands went to cup her breasts. She took a deep, shuddering breath.

"I thought womenfolk always had corsets and all that stuff underneath?"

"My sister would, but then she's more ladylike—" She remembered in time and stopped.

His big hands caressed her breasts until she felt her nipples go erect and turgid. He pulled her hard against him, and she could feel his erection, big and urgent against her body. Before he kissed her again, his hands cupped her face and turned it up to his. She had no experience, but even then, she was surprised by his expertise. She hadn't thought Lawrence had any experience with women because he'd been so inept and shy.

"Oh," she whispered. "Ohhh."

He pulled her against him so hard, she could feel every inch of him up and down her slender frame. He was kissing her, kissing her, kissing her. . . .

Then he pulled her dress down so expertly that she was barely aware he did it, except that she heard it fall in soft folds around her ankles. She stepped out of it. Now he took both big hands and slid her drawers down slowly. As his hands brushed against her hips, she trembled at the sensation. Then her drawers fell about her ankles. She stepped out of her little slippers.

"You are really something," he gasped against her mouth. He swung her up in his arms, kissing her mouth, her face, her eyes, before bending his head to her breasts.

"Oh, Lawrence." She arched her back so that he could reach her breasts more easily with his hot mouth. She knew she was shaking all over, but she couldn't seem to stop herself as his kisses and caresses grew more urgent. Finally he laid her on the bed and stood, looking down at her a long moment. His face was shadowed, but she could hear his heavy breathing, see his muscular chest rise and fall as he stood there. "Do you—you like what you see?"

"Mrs. Witherspoon, I love what I see, and I've waited a long time for this moment." Saying that, he lay down next to her and pulled her against him, caressing her bare skin with his big hands.

She felt goosebumps rise as he touched her, and she pressed even closer to him, her hands tentatively running across his virile male body. His muscles were hard and knotted along his back, and his hips flexed like steel as she touched him there. Then very hesitantly, she touched his manhood and he gasped. "More," he gasped. "More!"

She felt aroused but uncertain as he kissed her face, her eyes, and down her throat in a feverish gesture.

Then he reached the feast of her breasts and nuzzled until she gasped and cried out.

Now swiftly, he separated her thighs and touched her mound. "You're ready," he whispered.

She was a little scared, but too excited not to want what he was about to do. "I'm ready," she assured him.

He came into her slowly, very slowly, and she wanted more of him. In a wild gesture of excitement, she cupped his hard hips and pulled him down into her, crying out as he broke through the thin skin of her virginity. He muffled her cry with his gentle kisses. Then he began to ride her in a slow, deep motion and excited her still more. She locked her long legs around his lean body, urging him to ride her harder and faster until the bed was rocking and they were both covered with a sheen of perspiration.

Now it was her turn to whisper—no—demand, "More! More!"

He complied, plunging deep into her very core until her excitement rose higher still. She was riding the crest of a wave that she didn't understand—and didn't know when it would come crashing down—but she didn't care, she only wanted more, and more, and more. . . .

Then the wave crested, and she was swept away in a wild, dark tumble of ecstasy that she had never known she could experience. The tumult seemed as dark and wild as was the man himself, and she was tumbling and disappearing into nothingness. She was only vaguely aware that suddenly, he too was gasping and crying out, holding her to him in a deathlike grip as his big body went rigid and shuddered. For a moment there were only the crashing waves and two spirits locked together, quivering and gasping, and then it ended. Lark realized dimly as she came out of the blackness that she was held tightly against his chest, protected there as if he would never, never let her leave the circle of his embrace.

They lay there a long time, both breathless and covered

with perspiration. Their bodies were still locked together, their passion spent, but both of them were unwilling to separate.

He made a tender gesture of brushing her dark hair away from her face and kissing her forehead. His face looked puzzled and surprised.

"Did I—did I do it wrong?" she asked.

He shook his head, almost as if he were too overcome to speak. "No, you did everything right—oh, so right!" And he kissed her again. He rolled over on his side, but he did not let go of her. He pulled her on top so that her hair hung around his face like a black veil, and he kissed her again.

She felt so tender toward him, and she touched his dear lips with the tip of her finger. "Can we do that again?"

He chuckled. "You'll have to give me a minute to rest—then I promise you, we'll do it again and again."

"I love you, Lawrence," she said.

All of a sudden, his mood changed. She could feel the sudden stiffness of his frame, the way he pulled away from her. "Did I say something wrong?" she asked.

He shook his head. "No, I reckon not."

Yet she could feel the coolness of his mood, and he did not tell her he loved her too.

"Whatever I said, I'm sorry." She came up on one elbow and stroked his rugged face.

"Forget it," he almost snapped at her. "There's only one thing that's important now—our wedding night." He pulled her down to him so that he could kiss her breasts. Then he began to make love to her again, but more roughly this time, as if he were punishing her for something. Still his expert touch excited her, and they rode the crest of passion together again, and yet a third time before he dozed off in her arms. For a long time she did not sleep, wondering about the mystery of this man and thinking how little she actually knew about him. But she loved him.

Finally she dropped off to sleep, her head cradled against his shoulder.

Lark came awake slowly. For a moment she couldn't figure out where she was, then remembered and smiled. Dawn was just breaking outside. Her husband lay sleeping against her. From somewhere, Magnolia brayed. Lark couldn't help but smile. The sound was ghastly—sort of a cross between someone being tortured and a saw being dragged back and forth on a rotten board.

He came awake and looked at her. He smiled and tousled her hair. "Well, that was some night. You surprise me."

"In a good way?" She gathered her rumpled nightdress around her and stood up.

"You'd better believe it." He didn't seem shy or hesitant at all. He stood up too. "You see my pants?"

"On the floor. How about some coffee?" she asked.

"Love some, sweetie." He reached out and whacked her across the bottom as she passed him.

"Sweetie?" She whirled and looked at him. "Did you call me 'sweetie'?"

He cocked his head and looked back, that lopsided grin so evident this morning. "Oh, come off it, Lark, you don't have to pretend not to know me any more."

"What?" She could only gulp in anger and surprise. How could she have been so stupid? That tone, that arrogant grin, the easy way he whacked a woman across the rear. There was no doubt it was Larado.

Chapter Eleven

For a moment she felt so confused, she could only stare and blink. Then reality dawned. "Why, you rascal—!"

"Oh, come on, Lark, sweetie, don't tell me you didn't guess?" He grinned at her.

"I—I'm not Lark, I'm—"

"And a liar, too." He laughed and pulled up his pants. "How stupid did you think I was, kid? I knew it was you from the start."

She was stammering in confusion. "How could you? I mean, I have a twin sister—"

He sat down on the bed and began pulling on his boots. "Yes, and you told me back in Buck Shot that you were mirror twins. Remember I noticed we were both left-handed? A mirror twin's sister would have to be right-handed."

She was so furious with him, she was shaking. "You bastard! You misled me—you made me think you were your law-abiding brother."

He pulled on his boots, stood up, virile and sexy with his bare chest. "You're more naive than I thought," he chuckled. "I reckon I figured you were just like me, pretendin' not to know."

"I think I'm gonna kill you!" she shrieked, running into the kitchen and looking for a butcher knife.

He followed her. "Why? For givin' you the time of your life in bed last night?"

She felt the blood rush to her face as she whirled on him. "A gentleman wouldn't mention that."

"Lark, I'm no gentleman, I'm a saddle tramp, remember? Now how about that coffee?"

She couldn't find a butcher knife. "How can you think about coffee at a time like this?" she shouted.

"I'm not just thinkin' about coffee," he grinned, "I'm thinkin' about bacon and biscuits, too."

"I'll give you coffee!" She threw the small pot at him. He ducked, and it crashed against the wall behind him.

"Oh come on, sweetie, don't be mad."

"Mad?" She was so angry, tears came to her eyes. "I'd like to kill you! I thought I was getting a law-abiding, sweet, gentle sheriff."

"You didn't see through that? You're more naive than I thought." He grinned and leaned against the door frame.

A thought suddenly came to her. "You're wanted for bank robbery. I'll turn you in for the reward."

"In case you've forgotten, you're also wanted."

"But I didn't do anything!" she shrieked. "I was just an innocent dupe—"

"So was I, sweetie. Snake got me into the bank, then something went terribly wrong."

"I'll say!" she confronted him. "A teller was killed, you—you murderer!"

He shook his head and his rugged face turned serious. "Lark, I swear I didn't do that. I dropped my gun, and it went off when it struck the floor."

"You shot a man in the back."

He put his hands up in a placating gesture. "I swear I didn't. With all the confusion, I'm not sure what—"

"How can you stand there and lie, you killer! I'm going to the telegraph office and wire the Texas Rangers—"

"I wouldn't do that if I were you, Lark." He caught her arm and whirled her around. "We'll both end up in the pokey, and Snake is the one really at fault."

She jerked out of his grasp. "I was only holding the horses."

He looked at her. "You think they'll believe that?"

"I'll explain. My testimony will send you to the gallows, you—you saddle tramp, you."

"Well, now, Lark, remember you're my wife, you can't testify against me."

Reality crashed down on her. "Oh!" she gasped. "That's why you did it. You married me to keep me quiet. Why, you rascal, I'll have it annulled."

He grinned. "You can't have it annulled, it's been consummated. Boy, has it been consummated!"

"You rotten scoundrel!" She swung at him. He ducked and grabbed her, hanging on as she tried to bite his hand.

"Ow, you little wildcat!" He held on to her while she kicked his shins.

"This isn't a legal marriage," she howled. "I married you under my sister's name, and I don't even know what the hell your legal name is."

"Tsk! Tsk! Ladies shouldn't swear!" He hung on to her while she struggled.

"They shouldn't get mixed up with rascals and bank robbers, either. Do you hear me? This marriage isn't legal. I'll testify against you."

He shrugged and grinned again. "Now, what will folks think? You sleepin' with a man you may not be legally married to?"

She was so furious, she was gasping for air. "Why, you bastard, you thought this all out. You seduced me, then charmed me into marriage so I couldn't testify against you."

"I reckon this is what Texans call a Mexican standoff— and don't tell me you took serious what I was pokin' at you in fun?"

"Oh you!" She broke away from him. Grabbing the

little sack of flour from the pounding, she threw it at him. It split when it hit him, like a snowy white bomb. Flour went everywhere, making his dark features ghostlike. "You don't expect me to stay in this marriage, do you? Why, I'll bet I'm not the only one under an illegal name, I'll wager you—"

"No, my name really is Lawrence Witherspoon," he coughed, brushing the flour off his face. "So you're the one who's broken the law by marryin' under your sister's name. I don't think the good folk of Rusty Spur will take kindly to the news that the outlaw lady has fooled their dear, sweet sheriff."

"I'll tell them their dear, sweet, beloved sheriff is an outlaw and a saddle bum," she seethed.

"Now, sweetie, do you think anyone will believe you?"

"I am not going to stay in the same house with you!" she shouted. "I'll move back to the hotel."

"Suit yourself." He grinned again. "Really will start tongues awaggin'. You want the ladies to gossip about you?"

She thought a long moment, and another thought hit her that was even more hurtful. "You knew from the first. You only married me to protect yourself from my testimony."

"Well, the benefits were good, too," he admitted. "I'll take some more of what I got last night."

"You rascal, you rotten sonovabitch!" Lark was boiling over, grabbing stuff off the kitchen counter to throw at him. "You took my innocence."

"Sweetie, I didn't *take* it, you were pushin' it at me as eagerly as some saloon whore—"

"And I reckon you'd know about saloon whores."

He grinned. "Reckon I do. Now let's be sensible and calm down."

"Calm down. Calm down?" Her voice rose to a high pitch. "Oh, I'll calm down, all right, you—you scoundrel. From now on, until I decide what to do, you sleep on the couch."

"But you enjoyed last night too," he reminded her. Her face felt hot as the blood rushed to it.

"No, I didn't," she lied. "And we're not legally married."

He grinned and winked. "That don't make me no never mind. You know in Texas, we got something called common law marriage. Reckon that's what we got."

"Not on your life!"

"If it really bothers you," he said, "we could go to another county and get married again."

"You don't understand!" she screamed. "I don't want to marry you again—I don't want to be married to you at all."

"Now, Lark, you don't mean that."

"Oh, but I do."

He ran his hand through his black, tousled hair. "You ain't too grateful for the pleasure I gave you last night."

She flushed again. "Will you stop about last night?"

"It was pretty damned good, you'll have to agree." He sighed as if remembering.

"I'll not agree to anything, you cheap, four-flushing thief. What did you do with all the money from the bank robbery? Gamble it away? Spend it on cheap whores and liquor?"

"Don't I wish?" He shrugged. "Actually, I didn't get a dime. I'm not quite sure what happened to the money."

"Don't give me that! I saw those bags you and that Snake Hudson were carrying as you ran out of the bank."

He shrugged again. "Snake must have gotten the money—I didn't get any. If I was rich, you think I'd be hidin' out here?"

"You're not only a thief, but a liar," Lark said. "I hate you for wrecking my life this way."

"Wreckin' your life?" He looked askance. "Must I remind you that you were slingin' drinks in a tough saloon when I met you? Figure for you, the only way was up."

"And this is it? A fake marriage to a fake sheriff? And last night, you took my innocence. How could you?"

He grinned. "Oh, sweetie, it was so easy, but enjoyable, too. Don't tell me you didn't enjoy it?"

"I didn't. I—I was faking it." She felt the blood rush to her face.

"Uh-huh."

"So what do we do now?" she snapped.

He grinned at her and held out his arms. "What say we kiss and make up? We got time for a quickie before I go patrol the town."

She exhaled in an angry rush. "You are joking, aren't you? Do you think I'd get in bed with you again?"

He grinned. "Well, there's no point lockin' the barn after the horse is gone."

"Could you be any more crude?"

"Oh, Lark, admit it, you loved every minute of it."

"I hate you," she said, keeping her voice cold, "and I do not intend to stay married to an outlaw."

"You just got through sayin' it wasn't legal." He grinned at her, his face covered with flour like a ghost.

She took a deep breath to get control of her temper.

"All right, here's what we'll do to keep the town from gossiping and wondering. We'll occupy the same house."

"And the same bed?" His voice was hopeful as he took out a bandana and wiped his face.

"Hell no. You will sleep on the sofa."

He shook his head. "I don't think so."

"Yes, you will sleep on the sofa. We will pretend to be a happily married couple when we are out in public. But in private—"

"Yes?"

"In private, I'll make you wish you'd never been born."

"Sounds like most marriages," he griped.

"Aren't you ever serious?" she snarled.

"Well, I'm pretty serious about bein' the sheriff. Matter of fact, I like it."

"And these poor, innocent citizens think they've got an ex–Texas Ranger—"

"I never said that."

"Then where did they get the idea?"

He scratched his head. "Well, I might have said something that—"

"Aha! An outlaw posing as a sheriff. How low-down can you get?"

"I've been a good sheriff," he defended himself. "This town was a lawless hellhole when I came here."

"You just waiting for a chance to rob the bank?"

"Lark, we don't have a bank." His voice was patient, as if he were dealing with an idiot.

"Well, we're supposed to be getting one soon. Then you can rob it."

"I wasn't plannin' on it, but if you think I should—"

"I didn't say that!" she screamed. "Isn't one bank enough, you—you saddle tramp?"

"Fine," he snapped. "I reckon I thought maybe you cared about me, even though I figured you knew who I was. Maybe you married me to keep me from testifyin' against you."

"Why, you." She turned away. "That never crossed my mind. I thought Lawrence Witherspoon was a thoughtful, sensitive—"

"I can be all that," Larado said.

"Ha—just trying to get in my drawers again."

"That's not a bad idea." He grinned at her. Lark picked up another bag of flour and hefted it in her hand.

He held one hand up for protection. "Lark, sweetie—"

"Don't call me 'sweetie.'"

"All right." Now he was no longer grinning. "We'll do it your way. We'll both live here and pretend to be a happy couple when we're out in public. The rest of the time, we'll just share the house until you decide what you're gonna do."

"Good." She crossed her arms. "I'm glad we agree."

"I didn't say I agreed," he snapped. He pulled out his gold pocket watch and looked at it. "Well, I can't stand and argue with you all morning, I got a town to patrol."

"Aren't you going to eat something?"

He turned. "Were you plannin' to cook breakfast?"

"Are you joking? For you?"

"Then why did you ask?" He shrugged. "I'll get a bite at the café."

"What will people think?"

"You expect me to go hungry?"

"I hope you starve to death."

He reached for his Stetson. "Thanks a bunch, Mrs. Witherspoon."

"I am *not* Mrs. Witherspoon—I think my poor sister is."

He winked at her. "She wasn't the one I screwed."

"Oh, you rotten—!" She let loose with a bag of flour. He ducked, and it hit the wall behind him. "You want breakfast? I'll give you breakfast!" She tossed an egg.

He threw up his arm to protect himself, but the egg caught him in the face and ran down his cheek in a glob of yellow. "I really prefer mine sunny side up," he said.

"Get out of here!"

He strode out the door and slammed it so hard, the whole house rattled.

Lark went into the parlor. Flopping down on the sofa, she began to sob. "What kind of a mess did I get myself into? I'm stuck with that rascal." She sat up straight. She could run. That's what she always did when she had to face something she couldn't or wouldn't deal with. No. She shook her head. Several citizens had advanced her money to open her shop, and she couldn't let them down.

She wiped her eyes. This was no way for a strong woman to behave. Was she upset because he wasn't who she thought he was, or because he had only married her to keep her from testifying against him?

She took a deep breath. Okay, so the rotten bastard didn't care about her—so what? She would pull herself together and make her plans. She'd tighten her budget so she could pay everyone back except Larado. She'd paid him back in bed like some cheap whore. Then when she'd made enough money from her millinery shop to buy a train ticket, she'd leave town. What would happen to Larado, she didn't know—and didn't care. He deserved whatever he got, the rogue.

Larado was still dusting flour from his shirt when he strode into his office. Paco looked up from his *Police Gazette* magazine. "Hey, boss, what happened to you? You look like you fell in a flour barrel." He laughed, but Larado didn't.

"Marriage," he snarled. "Now I know why they make so many jokes about it."

The younger man opened his mouth as if to ask, but Larado cut him off. "Haven't you got something to do? Go check on the prisoners or something."

"Boss, we got no prisoners."

"Then go arrest some, damn it!" Larado flopped down in his chair and put his boots up on his desk. The young Mexican grabbed his hat and fled.

Larado sighed. Things were a mess, all right. Here he'd thought he had a good place to hide out, even a job he really liked, and then she'd showed up. He couldn't risk that she'd tell what she knew, especially in this town that was giving him both affection and respect. He liked that. As an orphaned saddle tramp, he'd had little of either. Just when he'd thought he had a whole new life, Lark showed up, pretending she didn't know who he was and pretending she cared about him. He'd had to woo and marry her to keep her from spilling the beans, hadn't he? Yet after last night, he didn't know what to think. He'd never had loving like that before. A virgin saloon girl. That really surprised him.

"Lark Witherspoon, you are the fly in my buttermilk—

and have been since the first time I met you," he grumbled to himself. What was he to do? He couldn't move out of the house—it would cause too much gossip and too many questions from curious townspeople. Yet, living with the fiery Lark would be like sharing quarters with a bobcat. He could drift on, like he'd always done, rootless and alone. He'd taken this job to have a refuge after the bank robbery, but he was growing used to the homely little hamlet, and he liked the respect he got from the townspeople. He didn't want to leave. Damn Lark, anyhow. What was he going to do with her?

Through his dirty window, he saw someone walking along the wooden sidewalk on the other side. Larado leaned forward and squinted. It was Lark, walking toward her hat shop, followed by that ridiculous donkey with its big pink hat. So she was opening her shop today. Maybe she had cooled off. If not. . . He shuddered. What a hellhole married life with her was going to be. He smiled when he thought about last night, then he frowned. She'd made it clear there wasn't going to be any more fun and games in the bedroom. It wasn't even noon yet. Maybe by dark, she'd be cooled off enough that he could return home without being hit in the head with a coffeepot.

Lark walked down to her shop, followed by Magnolia. She'd almost given up trying to keep the little gray donkey in her pen. As she passed across the street from the sheriff's office, Lark turned her face toward it. Yes, she could see him sitting in there with his feet upon his desk. That rotten sidewinder. So he'd married her to keep her quiet. She had never felt such humiliation. She would make him pay for this—that is, if he ever came back to the house.

Business in her shop was slow that day. Lark had brought a sandwich for lunch, and she imagined Larado would eat at the corner café. She wouldn't have to face him until tonight, and then she was not sure what she would do. She opened her door to catch the breeze in the hot summer afternoon. Somewhere a dog barked, and a child laughed. A wagon with creaking wheels rolled down the dusty, dirt street. At least the town seemed more active and there were lots of new citizens since the railroad had gone through.

Paco came into the shop, removing his hat. "Hallo, missus, what's wrong with the boss?"

She pretended to be very busy sewing the veil on a big white hat. "I'm sure I don't know what you mean."

"He's meaner than a snakebit dog," Paco declared, "and he had groceries all over him."

She certainly didn't want to discuss this with the deputy. "Uh, I think he tripped and fell into the stuff the town brought to us."

"*Sí.*" The deputy nodded, but he didn't look as if he believed her. "You pleased to be married to the sheriff?"

"Of course," she said, but she didn't look at him. "Maybe he wasn't feeling well."

"Uh-huh. Well, reckon I'd better go." Paco gave her a long, searching look and left the store.

So the sheriff was upset. Good. He couldn't be any more upset than she was. In her mind, she imagined all the things she'd like to do to that scoundrel besides just hit him with a couple of eggs and a bag of flour. She went to the window and looked out. After a moment, she saw Larado saunter out of his office and start down the street toward the local café. He had his hat tipped back, and he was whistling "The Streets of Laredo."

She'd like to wrap him in white linen and lay him out, cold as the clay.

During a slow period that afternoon, she went over her books. Bertha Snootley had charged several things before the pink hat and had never paid for them. The bill was past due. Perhaps she should go down to the general store and pressure the stout lady for payment.

Taking the delinquent bill, she walked down to the store.

The place smelled of stale crackers and sour pickles. Mr. Snootley was behind the counter. The long hair he combed over his bald spot was in disarray, and he was sucking a peppermint. She could smell it. "Is your wife in?"

He shook his head. "At home. She don't really like to work in the store. What is it you want, ma'am?"

Lark didn't really want to get the lady in trouble with her husband. "It's a private matter."

He eyed the paper in her hand. "Bertha been buyin' stuff again? I declare, that woman is gonna bankrupt me."

Lark chewed her lip. "As a matter of fact, she hasn't shopped with me in a while."

He grinned, showing yellow teeth. "Heard about the pink straw hat. Can't say she didn't deserve that."

Lark shrugged. "I'm sorry it had to come to that, but she was taking advantage—wearing things and then wanting to return them soiled and worn."

"I know. Her clothes buying has kept me on the verge of going broke for years." He leaned on the counter and leered at her in a way that made Lark nervous. "Here, let me pay that. I'll even pay for the pink hat." His cash register opened with a clang.

"That's awfully nice of you." Lark smiled warmly at him. She handed over the bill, and he handed her a generous amount of cash. "Oh, but this is too much."

She tried to hand part of it back, but he reached out and closed his hand over hers. "Keep it. Are you sure that's what you really came in for?"

She pulled away. "I—I'm sure I don't understand—"

"You know Bertha is gone half the time to Abilene."

"So?"

"And your husband, as sheriff, has to work long hours."

"I don't understand—"

"I just thought, maybe—when we're both alone—we might, well, console each other."

Lark drew herself up proudly. "Mr. Snootley, I have

never given you any reason to think I would be interested in you. I should tell my husband."

"Oh, don't do that." He began to back away, shaking his balding head. "I wouldn't want to rile him none. I was just funning you, okay? I thought maybe . . . Well, I reckon I thought wrong."

"You certainly did." She turned on her heel and fled the general store. She ought to tell Larado. Then she paused. Maybe she'd misunderstood the man's intent. Besides, Larado didn't care anything about her. He'd probably laugh.

It was finally suppertime. Reluctantly, Lark closed her shop and walked back to the house, taking as long as possible to get there. If Larado thought she'd forgotten and forgiven everything, that he'd be welcome back in her bed—boy, was he in for a surprise!

Chapter Twelve

Larado sauntered along Main Street after dark, whistling his favorite tune: *. . . oh, as I walked out on the streets of Laredo, as I walked out in Laredo one day. . . .*

Mrs. Bottoms came out on the porch of her hotel and hailed as he passed. "Heavens, Sheriff, I'd thought you wouldn't be still workin'—what with a new bride and all."

He grinned at her. "Crime never sleeps, Mrs. Bottoms. A sheriff always has work to do. How's little Jimmy?"

She looked at him quizzically. "Jimmys fine. He's inside drawin' pictures of trains. I don't reckon little Rusty Spur has so much crime it would keep a man away from his new bride."

Oh, damn. He couldn't do anything that would arouse suspicion. "You are right, dear lady, sometimes a man gets so involved with his work, he forgets about the little lady."

She snorted. "I'd think it'd be hard to forget that one, pretty as she is."

"She is that. I reckon I'd better head home. She's probably got a larrupin' supper waitin' for me." *With rat poison in it,* he thought. He tipped his hat to the woman and started slowly toward his house. He knew Lark had closed the shop—he'd seen the lights go off. Yet knowing he was probably going to get a violent reaction, he'd put off heading home.

He could stall no longer without raising suspicion among the townspeople. It was a showdown at the OK Corral all over again. Of course, Wyatt Earp had only had to face a few angry cowboys. Larado was headed to face one angry woman. He'd have traded places with Wyatt in a heartbeat.

Lark had closed the shop and gone back to the house, not knowing what else to do. Still, she'd rather have been walking into a nest of rattlers than into his house, the scoundrel.

He wasn't home yet. She breathed a sigh of relief as she went about, lighting the oil lamps. The place was small, but still, it could be a cute and cozy love nest with a little work and elbow grease.

"Lark, are you out of your mind?" she asked herself aloud. "Why would you want to fix the place up and make it comfortable for him? After what he's done, you need to make him as miserable as possible—he deserves it."

On the bureau in the bedroom, she noticed for the first time a small daguerreotype of a pretty, dark, older woman. Lark studied it. The woman might have had some Indian blood. Against her photo frame rested a pair of gold-framed spectacles. *Hers,* Lark thought. She picked up the old photo and studied it. The woman looked like Larado, with the same dark eyes and crooked smile. So the rascal had a sister, or maybe a mother. Well, even Jesse James had a mother.

Lark went into the kitchen and looked around. She was hungry. Even if she refused to cook for him, she had to feed herself. At her best, she wasn't much of a cook. Her sister Lacey was a great cook, of course. Tomboys' talents weren't in the kitchen. Too bad she hadn't been a boy—Lark made a great cowhand. She looked around at the supplies from the pounding. There was some bacon, some eggs she hadn't thrown at Larado, and some flour. She reached for a big iron skillet.

She heard him come in the front door.

"Lark, sweetie, you home?" He sounded hesitant—as well he should be.

"Yes, I'm here," she snapped as he stuck his head around the door. She resisted the urge to throw the skillet at him.

"Are you still mad at me?" He gave her that charming, crooked grin.

"Now why would I be, after everything that's happened?" Ice frosted every word, but either he didn't hear her cold tone, or he chose to ignore it.

"Good, sweetie." He whacked her on the bottom as he came into the room. She whirled and swung the skillet at him, but he caught her arm and pulled her into his embrace, putting his face against her dark hair. "Now, Lark, we're in this together. We might as well make the most of it."

"You sonovabitch!" She tried to hit him in the head with the skillet, but he took it out of her hand.

"I didn't know you'd hold a grudge. And after all the fun we had last night."

"Don't you dare mention that." She looked toward the eggs on the shelf, but he stepped between her and the possible missiles. "Maybe it was fun for you, but I was just doing my wifely duty."

"You're not a good liar," he said, winking at her. "You enjoyed it, too. Boy, did you enjoy it!"

She felt her face flush brick red. She had never wanted to murder anyone as much as she did Larado at that moment. "Let's get one thing straight, cowboy. I truly thought I was marrying your upstanding, law-abiding brother."

He threw back his head and laughed. "I don't have a brother. What's for supper?"

"At a time like this, you expect me to cook for you?"

He shrugged. "Well, we both gotta eat."

"I got news for you, Larado," she snarled, "I'm not the housewife type. And I wouldn't cook for you anyway."

"You're good in bed, so I reckon that makes up for it."

"Will you shut up about last night?" Her voice rose both in humiliation and anger.

He paused and looked at her hopefully. "Now, sweetie, just 'cause we have this little disagreement, that doesn't mean we still couldn't have fun every night in the bedroom."

"Are you out of your mind? I'm not going to sleep with you—not tonight, not tomorrow night, not ever. I rue the day I let you charm me into your bed."

"Well, don't make a decision now. Give it some thought." He got himself a dipper of water out of the bucket on the cabinet.

"I've given it some thought," she said coldly. "We may have to share the house for appearances, but you aren't sleeping in my bed again tonight."

"May I remind you that it's *my* bed?" He grinned at her and looked around. "Can't we eat first and argue later?"

"I told you, I'm not cooking for you."

"Fine, I'll fix up something for both of us. See? I'm nicer than you are." He pushed her to one side and began digging through the pantry.

"Men!" she sniffed. "They only think of two things, their bellies and their—well, you know."

He grinned. "Yep."

"I'm sure you can't cook any better than I can." She stood glaring at him, arms crossed.

"Maybe not, but I'm willing to try. How about some fried potatoes and eggs?"

"I will not eat your cooking." She stuck her nose in the air, picked up the *Rusty Spur Beacon*, and went into the parlor.

She couldn't keep her mind on the newspaper. She kept listening to him banging around in the kitchen. After a few minutes, pleasing aromas began to drift from there.

"Hey, Lark, I've got it ready, you want some?"

"No." Her growling stomach was trying to make a liar out of her.

"Suit yourself."

From where she sat, she could see him taking a plate and sitting down at the small table in the kitchen. His smacking told her he was enjoying his meal. Or wanting her to think so. She got up, still carrying the paper, and went into the kitchen for a dipperful of water. She tossed the paper on the table. "Must you wipe your mouth on your sleeve?"

"Why, does it annoy you?" He grinned up at her.

"You scoundrel, you know it does."

"Good, then maybe I'll keep doin' it. Mmm." He returned to eating, smacking and wiping at his plate with a piece of bread. "Really good."

She paused in the middle of the kitchen and looked toward the stove. There were still fried potatoes, scrambled eggs, and bacon in the skillet. She licked her lips, but she didn't touch the food. She wouldn't give him that satisfaction. Behind her, she heard him pick up the newspaper.

She turned. He was squinting and staring at the page.

"What's the matter?" she asked. "Can't you read?"

He glanced up, looking embarrassed. "Uh, of course I can. I—I was just takin' my time, that's all."

She was almost ashamed of herself. Maybe he couldn't read. Lots of people couldn't. She had a feeling there were a lot of things about Larado she didn't know. He had duped her in the worst way, making her love him when it was only a farce. She wanted to scream at him, hit him, and throw things at him, but he didn't look up. He kept eating and staring at the paper. He looked tired and defeated, and she felt almost ashamed of herself. "You—you want I should read that to you?"

He looked up at her, squinting. "I said I could read, you don't need to bother."

She began to clean up the kitchen. He didn't say anything.

"I saw the picture in the bedroom," she said finally.

"What about it?" He was immediately defensive. "I don't want to talk about my mother."

"She's dead?"

He nodded. "Typhoid. I been on my own since I was a young kid."

She wanted to ask him why he'd kept her eyeglasses, and what had happened to his father, but she had a feeling there was a deeper part of himself he wasn't willing to discuss.

"I'm going to bed now," she said.

His head came up from the paper.

"I said *I* was going to bed. *Alone.* I'll throw out some blankets for you." She walked across the room.

"Aw, Lark, sweetie—"

"Don't 'sweetie' me, you cad." She went into the bedroom, threw some blankets and a pillow out the door, then closed and locked it.

She heard him get up and come to the door. The knob turned. "It's locked," she said.

From the other side of the door, she heard swearing.

"I can see that."

"Go away, you unchivalrous, low-down polecat."

"Aw, Lark, honey, you don't mean that. Is this the way it's gonna be?"

"It certainly is. At least until I get enough money made from my shop to leave town."

He rattled the doorknob again. "What will people think if you leave me?"

"Who cares? Maybe I'll whisper the word around to the ladies that you were a terrible lover."

"Well, now," he drawled, "that would be lyin', wouldn't it? You loved every minute of last night."

"I did not! I—I was pretending so you wouldn't be disappointed, that's all."

"If you was pretendin', you're the best damned actress I ever met."

"Now quit rattling my door. You'd better get used to sleeping on the sofa."

"That old horsehair settee is hard as a mother-in-law's heart. My back'll hurt so bad, I'll be cripplin' around in the morning."

"Good." She flounced over to the bed and reached to blow out the lamp.

"I reckon one of the girls at the Cross-eyed Bull would be willing to let me in her bed."

Lark paused in taking off her dress. "Don't you dare!"

"I reckon I'd tell her you were so cold, I couldn't stand to sleep with you. You'd like that to get around town?"

"And what would people think of the sheriff if he did that?" She continued to unbutton her dress and reached for a nightgown.

"The men would think I was a typical man—the ladies might gossip some."

"Go away, Larado. You're not getting in my bed. This is going to be a marriage in name only."

"I'd hate to think as good as that was last night, we'd never share it again."

Her curiosity got the better of her as she blew out the lamp and climbed into bed. "You—you thought it was good?"

"Best I ever had." He sounded woebegone and sincere. For a moment, her heart almost melted, then she remembered what a rascal she was dealing with.

"Go sleep on the couch!" she shouted.

With a sigh, he stomped away from the door. She lay awake a long time and wondered if he did too. Her stomach was growling again. She got up, pressed her ear to the door, and listened. His snoring sounded like a hive of bees.

She tiptoed out and paused to look into the parlor. Larado was lying all tangled in a quilt on the old horsehair settee.

He looked uncomfortable. Good. She hoped he got a back-
ache like a broken-down bronc. She tiptoed into the kitchen
and got a plate of cold leftovers. She was so hungry, she gobbled. Then she sneaked back to bed, making sure her door
was locked.

The next morning, she rose early and went into the
kitchen to make coffee. Larado still lay asleep on the
settee. She made sure she banged the coffeepot. Why
should he continue to sleep? She heard him groan aloud
as he woke up. He came stumbling into the kitchen in
his long handles.

"Good morning," she said brightly. "How did you sleep?"

"Damn it, you know how I slept. I trust you enjoyed my
bed?"

"Very much."

He sat down at the table with a groan.

She smiled at him. "Maybe I'll fix you some breakfast."

He sighed and scratched himself. "Is it gonna be
edible?"

She smiled. "Probably not."

"In that case, I think I'll catch a bite over at the café."
He got up and stumbled around, evidently looking for
his boots and clothes, which were strewn about the
parlor.

"Don't say I didn't offer. My, isn't married life wonderful? If I'd known I was gonna end up with you, I'd have
put poison in your coffee."

"And, sweetie, if I'd known what I was gettin' into, I'd
have gladly drunk it."

"Oh my! We both know where we stand then, don't we?"

He stared at her glumly as he put on his clothes and
reached for his Stetson. "Is this the way it's gonna be
from now on?"

She smiled back. "You can be sure of it."

"You're punishin' me." He limped over to the front door.

"Why would you think that? After everything you've done? Why, this is a marriage made in heaven."

He went out the front door and slammed it so hard, the house rattled.

Good, she had made him furious. Funny, she didn't feel much satisfaction. She only felt sad that he had betrayed her and had never really loved her.

Suddenly she didn't want any breakfast. She had a cup of coffee, tidied up the house, then dressed and walked to her little shop. It was a busy morning. With all the new settlers coming in on the weekly train, she had plenty of new customers. She might be able to pay back her investors sooner than she thought so she could leave town.

Several days passed. No, dragged by was a better description. She was busy with all the new business at her shop, but at night, she and Larado did not speak, and she made sure she locked her door at night, making him sleep in the parlor. Not that he tried to come into her room again. Most of the time, he ate at the café. Evenings were long with two people sharing a house but not speaking. Once or twice, she almost reached out to him, then stopped. He had not only lied, he was a killer and a thief. That was just too much.

Friday morning, she sold two bonnets and was sewing white flowers on a new one when Mrs. Bottoms came in. She was so glad to see a friendly face. "Hello, Mrs. Bottoms, I've missed you and little Jimmy."

"Heavens, I reckon I figured with a new husband, you wouldn't have much time for old friends for a while."

"Uh, yes." She didn't look up, she kept working on the hat.

"Folks is gossipin' about the sheriff eatin' at the café or the hotel dining room all the time."

"Folks ought to mind their own business." In spite of everything she could do, tears began to fill Lark's eyes.

"Heavens, child, what did I say wrong?"

"N—Nothing. It's just—it's just not going as well as I thought."

"Oh?"

"He—he—" She didn't dare tell this sweet lady the whole truth.

The old lady put her arm around Lark's shaking shoulders. "Tell me about it. Maybe I can help."

"It's just awful, not like I thought it would be."

"Oh, you can't cook, and that's the reason he ain't eatin' at home?"

Lark only wept.

"Well, honey, that can be taught."

"I was always a tomboy. I ride and rope and shoot much better than I bake biscuits."

"Then you just need a little help. Come by the hotel and I'll teach you."

Lark didn't dare tell her the whole story. "I'll—I'll try."

"Men are like dogs," Mrs. Bottoms said. "Give them something to eat and a comfortable place to sleep, and they'll stay happy and won't stray."

Lark pictured the hard settee. "I don't think he's too happy."

"Oh, of course he is. Now you just come over to the hotel sometime and I'll teach you a little about runnin' a home."

"Okay," Lark gulped. Oh, if it were only that easy.

"By the way," the lady said, "did you hear the news?"

Lark shook her head and wiped her eyes. "I reckon not."

"Well, that new banker and his wife are finally arriving tomorrow on the noon train. They got the new building ready, except the upstairs apartment ain't quite done."

"It's about time," Lark said. "It's been inconvenient not to have a real bank."

"The mayor's hopin' everyone will turn out to meet the train, show 'em some of that good Rusty Spur civic pride. Big ceremony."

"That's good." Lark nodded.

"By the way, I saw the sheriff limping this morning going down the sidewalk. He fall or something?"

"Uh, maybe so." Lark avoided her eyes. "I think it was the settee."

"He fell over the settee?"

"You might say that."

"Well, heavens. I thought maybe it might have got a little strenuous in the bedroom, you know." She winked at Lark.

Lark felt the blood rush to her face. "No, I swear, it's the settee."

"Reckon I'd better run. Got to get my best room fixed up. I reckon the new banker and his wife will be staying at the hotel for a few days 'til that apartment over the bank's finished. Oh, the mayor has requested that you pen Magnolia up. Some think it wouldn't do to have a burro roaming through the crowd—especially one in a big pink flowered hat."

"I'll do my best."

Business slowed the rest of the afternoon after Mrs. Bottoms left. Lark fed Magnolia and started home. She was both dreading and looking forward to seeing Larado. He was a heartbreaker and a rascal, but oh, he was charming. In the meantime, how did she get into this mess, and now how would she get out?

When she walked into the house, there was only silence.

"Larado? Are you here?"

"I'm in the kitchen."

She started into the kitchen. "If you think I'm going to cook—oh, my God."

She stopped, dumbfounded. Larado was just getting up from a washtub full of water by the stove. He was naked and wet as he turned and grinned at her. She had forgotten the look of that big, virile body with its slim hips and wide shoulders. Her gaze went lower, and then she realized she was staring and backed away, covering her eyes. "Have you no modesty?"

"Well, sweetie, you aren't seein' nothin' you haven't seen before. Toss me a towel, will you?"

It was difficult to locate the towel on the back of a kitchen chair when her eyes were closed. "You might have warned me." She felt indignant. She opened one eye.

He had the towel wrapped around his lean waist. "Oh, come now, let's not play games. You were tickled to get a peek."

"I was not!"

"Liar, of course you were." He gave that crooked, easy grin. He turned toward the stove. "I started some supper."

"Aren't you going to put some clothes on?"

He paused with a pan in his hands. "I'm wearin' a towel."

"Yes, but it doesn't look very secure. Suppose—?"

"You can only hope," he laughed.

"You are an unmitigated bastard," she snarled.

"I don't know the meanin' of the one word, but yes, I am a bastard." He wasn't smiling now. "My old man ran off and left without marryin' my mother."

"I—I'm sorry. I shouldn't have said that."

He shrugged without looking at her. "It's okay. I've had to deal with it my whole life."

He sounded so sad that she forgot about their quarrel. "I really am sorry. I reckon I know now why you kept her spectacles."

"Her spectacles?"

"Her eyeglasses."

For a minute, he tensed. She could see it in his wide

shoulders. "Don't touch those, and don't mention them to anyone," he snapped.

"Why? Lots of older ladies wear them—"

"You heard me."

She had not realized that the tough cowboy could be so sentimental. Having lost her own parents, she was suddenly sympathetic. "Here." Her voice softened. "I'll take over the cooking and you go get some clothes on." She shouldered him away from the stove and took the pan.

"Thanks, Lark." His voice softened to a whisper. "I'll admit I've been a rascal, but I've been on my own for a very long time. Maybe if there'd been a good woman in my life the last few years, I wouldn't be such a bum."

"It's okay, Larado. I didn't mean to hurt you. My parents are both dead too, so I know how you feel."

He paused and looked down at her. She was more than a little aware of his virile naked body and the thin towel between them, the water still shining on his wet body. If he took her in his muscular arms, she thought, she wasn't sure she could resist him.

"I'm sorry I've made such a mess of things," he said. "I reckon there's nothin' I could say now that would make you trust me."

"No." Just the way he was looking at her made her want to turn her face up to his and let him kiss her.

"In that case, I'd better shut up. Just to put you at your ease, I'll go put some clothes on."

Let's go into the bedroom and you make passionate love to me like you did that one night. She thought it, but of course she didn't say it. "I—I'll finish cooking supper."

He grinned at her. "I thought you said you can't cook?"

"Honestly, I can handle a gun, a horse, and a rope, but I'm not too good around a stove. I'll do the best I can."

"That's all anyone can ask, Lark." His voice was gentle. He gave her one last grin and disappeared into the bedroom.

When he came out, she had managed to fry a steak

and some potatoes and make a pan of cornbread. She slid it all onto a plate.

"Looks good." He gave her an encouraging smile as he cut into the meat. "Uh-oh."

She whirled away from the stove. "What's the matter?"

He was poking at the rare meat with a look of distaste. "Sweetie, I've seen steers hurt worse than this get well."

"That's the way I like it," she said.

He frowned at her. "I like mine well done, almost burnt, actually. You see, my old lady wasn't much of a cook either, so I feel right at home with you."

"That's not a respectful way to speak of the dead."

"Mom wouldn't mind." For a long moment he seemed to disappear inside himself. Then he looked up and seemed to see her searching look and shrugged. "Do you reckon you could put a little more fire under this meat?"

"And ruin a perfectly good steak?"

"Fine. I'll do it myself." He got up from the table, grabbed the plate, took it over, and put the steak in the skillet.

"You can see," she pointed out, "that we could never make it as a couple."

"Why, because we like our steak two different ways? The other night, we were in perfect harmony."

"You are a rotten cad to keep bringing that up."

"I thought we might make a fresh start." He busied himself at the stove.

She thought about it a minute. "With a bank robber? I don't think so."

"Well, actually"—he turned the steak over—"it was Snake Hudson's crime. I was just a stupid *hombre* who blundered into it."

"You expect me to believe that?" She sat down at the table and looked over the weekly paper.

"Didn't you blunder into it, too? If I could, you could, too."

"I didn't blunder into it," she said pointedly. "A certain someone tricked me into it. I was trying to be obliging by holding the horses."

He grinned at her. "A likely story, the jury would say." He brought the pan to the table and flipped the meat onto the plate. "So now I'm here, and I'm respectable, even if I'm not rich. Maybe if you'd be content to be my wife, I'd be content to be the sheriff here from now on."

"I don't believe that," she snapped. "You're just hiding out until the heat is off, then you'll be back to your old criminal ways. Good God." She glared down at the charred steak. "You've burnt it up."

He cut into it and put a bite in his mouth. "Yum, just the way I like it. You want a bite?"

"Of those ashes? You must be joking." She began to eat some of the fried potatoes. "Snake was no friend of yours."

"I reckon I know that now."

She looked at him wolfing down the charred steak. "You must have been really drunk that night in the poker game. Even a blind man could have seen he and the dealer were in cahoots. I spotted those marked cards a mile away."

"Hmm." He shrugged. "Well, I reckon I need to stay out of card games."

"Or keep your snoot out of the liquor bottle. By the way, Dixie was in on it. I think she gets part of the pot."

He winced, then grinned. "Ouch, that really hurts. I thought I'd given that girl such a good time, she wouldn't do that to me."

She threw down her fork. "Is there a woman anywhere you haven't been in the hay with?"

"It wasn't hay, sweetie, she had a perfectly good bed."

"You know what I mean, you—you libertine."

"Now, Lark, I ain't educated. You know I don't know what a big word like that means."

"It means you've got to act like a stallion around any mare in heat."

He finished his food and pushed his plate back with satisfaction. "Can I help it if ladies find me irresistible?"

"Here's one who doesn't, and I'm going to prove it to you." Lark got up and strode to the bedroom. When she closed the door, that's when she discovered the lock had been removed.

Chapter Thirteen

"Why, you!" She flung open the door and glared at him. "What?"

"You know damned well what. Well, it won't do you any good, mister. I'm putting a chair under the door."

He stood up. "Now, Lark, sweetie, do you really think that's necessary? If we'd just sit and talk this over—"

"No." She shook her head. "You charming rascal, you could talk a cow out of her calf, or a dog off a meat wagon. I'll not listen to anything you have to say. Go sleep on the couch." With that, she slammed the door shut.

"Hey," he yelled from the other side, "you didn't give me a blanket or a pillow."

"Make do without either!" she shouted, and then she put a stout chair under the doorknob.

She heard him get up and come to the bedroom door, sighing loud enough for her to hear. "I'll probably be shiverin' all night on that horsehair settee."

"Go sleep in the stable with Magnolia. She'd probably be glad to have another jackass for company."

He put his face against the door. "Aw, Lark, sweetie, please. I really do care about you."

"No, you don't. You're only trying to keep me from telling what I know."

"I've already admitted I'm a rascal, what more do you want?"

She ignored him and began her bedtime ritual. She put on her favorite old faded nightgown that was oversized, ragged, and comfortable. Then she tied up her hair all over in little rags so it would be wavy in the morning. Lastly, she began to cream her face with white hog lard.

"Lark?" Lavado called from the other side of the door. "You in bed yet?"

"No." She shouted back as she rubbed the lard liberally all over her face. "But I'm getting there."

"It's cruel of you to tease me like this. I can just imagine how you look, all soft and pretty, perfume and lace."

"Yep, that's exactly what I look like, all right. It would make you *loco* with desire to see me." She stared into the mirror over the bureau and blinked at the ghastly mess staring back at her. "Eat your heart out, cowboy, but you aren't gettin' any tonight."

"Aw, sweetie—"

"Don't you 'sweetie' me. Have you no shame? You've taken a position as a lawman in a tiny, trusting town. What are you waiting for, the new bank to get set up so you can rob it?"

"Reckon that might be a fine idea."

"Oh, land's sake, you're terrible." She double-checked to make sure the chair under the door was secure. "Go to bed, Larado. This door will not open until tomorrow."

"It ought to be against the law to tease a man— especially a Texan." He sounded as if his face was right against the door.

"You're a fine one to talk about the law," she snapped as she blew out the lamp. "I reckon I might wire the U.S. Marshal tomorrow and tell him where you are."

"You do that, you little wildcat. And while you're at it, remember they'll take you away too."

"It would almost be worth it to toss your butt in jail. Now shut up. You are not going to talk your way into my bed."

He banged on the door. "Your bed? Listen, you little vixen, that's my bed."

"It's mine now. Good night."

He put his ear against the door and heard the distinct sound of the springs creaking as she got into bed. In his mind, he saw her lying there in a sheer, pretty nightgown that begged him to rip it off. Her hair would be spread across the pillow like silken black gold, and she would smell of some faint flower scent. Just the image made him gasp for air. Tentatively, he tried the knob. The door didn't move.

From the other side of the door came vindictive laughter. "Did you think I was lying about the chair? Now yell 'calf rope,' you coyote, and go sleep on the couch."

"Calf rope" was the Texas version of giving up, which a real Texan would never do—but tonight, there didn't seem to be any alternatives. With a sigh, Larado blew out the lamp and retreated to the horsehair settee. It was as hard and unrelenting as an old maid's heart. By morning, he'd be so stove up, he'd be limping.

Sure enough, he was. He felt so stiff, he could barely get his boots on. He limped down to the corner café where some of the men were having coffee. They exchanged glances and winks as he joined them.

"Well, havin' a hard night, Sheriff?"

"Mattress none too good?"

"I don't want to talk about it," he snapped.

"Even if you're honeymooning," Paco said, "you shouldn't do it so much that you can't get out of bed in the morning."

The men at the table laughed and nudged each other.

Larado rolled his eyes. "If you only knew."

The men all gathered closer. "Yes?"

"A gentleman never tells. You *hombres* know that."

They all sighed and leaned back in their chairs.

Little Jimmy had just walked up. "Tell what?"

Larado frowned. "You'll find out when you're older." He turned back to the men "What you *hombres* been talkin' about?"

Old Bill ran his tongue across the opening in his gapped teeth. "Money. I been puttin' a little in telegraph stock and now I'm thinkin' about that new gadget, the telephone."

The blacksmith snorted. "Telephones! Dang-fool toy, if you ask me. I told Bill he was wasting his money—better put it in the new bank and save it."

"Hey," one of the men said. "I understand the new banker is arrivin' on the train from St. Louis today."

Larado sipped his coffee and nodded. "I heard that. He got a family?"

"Just a wife," Abner Snootley said. "She's said to be a real looker—lots of class."

Old Bill grinned. "And what would you expect from a banker? Boy howdy, finally having a bank in town will really help this town grow."

Paco looked toward Larado. "More work for the sheriff," he said, "having to worry about holdups."

"Aw, with our sheriff and his reputation across Texas, nobody would dare try to rob a bank in Rusty Spur," little Jimmy said.

The others agreed that this was true.

About that time, Magnolia came wandering down the street in her pink hat. When she saw Larado sitting in the café, she stopped, threw back her head, and brayed. It startled two men and caused them to spill their coffee.

"That is the damndest sound," the blacksmith complained. "Like a cross between a whore enjoyin' it and a cat bein' killed."

"Watch your mouth," Larado snapped. "There's a boy here."

Jimmy wandered over to the counter, out of earshot.

The scrawny feed store owner snorted at the blacksmith. "Don't kid nobody," he challenged. "You ain't heard a whore moan since before the War of Yankee Aggression."

"You mean the War of Southern Rebellion," corrected the blacksmith, who was from Maine. "Anyway—have too."

"Gentlemen," Larado soothed, "this ain't the time to refight the Civil War. We're all Texans now."

Every man took off his Stetson and held it over his heart.

"Ain't it the truth?" said old Bill reverently.

"Remember the Alamo!" they all shouted in unison.

Paco looked out the window. "Hey, lookee, Sheriff, there goes your bride, *sí.*"

All heads turned and watched wistfully as Lark minced along the street toward her millinery shop. She wore a bright yellow dress and her little bustle waggled enticingly.

Larado thought about what he was not getting and sighed.

All the men in the café sighed, too.

"Gosh," Bill said, "Sheriff, you're one lucky *hombre.*"

Larado stifled a groan when he moved and his sore back hurt. "You don't know the half of it."

The train bearing the new banker and his wife was to arrive at high noon. There was a lot of excitement around town with the mayor, the sheriff, and almost everyone else in town going to meet the train. The Odd Fellows' little band would be there to play, and the ladies of the town had planned to serve tea and cookies on the platform. The summer day was hot as hell with the lid off, as only it can be in Texas.

Larado would try again to reconcile with his bride. He stuck his head in the door of her shop. "Hey, Lark, the train's due in in fifteen minutes. It would look good if you was standin' by my side to welcome the new banker from St. Louie."

"I'm not too worried about your looking good." She kept her voice icy.

"Okay, but consider this. He's got a fancy wife, and I reckon she'll be buyin' lots of hats and other trinkets."

"In that case, you're right—I do need to show up and be part of the welcoming committee."

"Oh, by the way, I just locked Magnolia up. Old Abner Snootley and his wife think it don't make our town look too good to have a burro wearin' a hat, wanderin' the streets, and leavin' her, er, little callin' cards everywhere."

Lark sighed. "She's smart, and she's learned to open the gate with her teeth. I don't know what I'm going to do."

In the distance, the whistle of a train drifted across the Texas plains. Larado pulled out his gold pocket watch and checked it. "Sounds like she'll be right on time."

Lark looked out her front window. People were coming from all directions, gesturing and shouting to each other. This was indeed going to be an exciting day in the little town. She checked a mirror and pulled a wisp of dark hair back into her bun. "All right, I'm ready to go."

He tried to take her arm, but she pulled away from him. "Don't use this as a excuse to molest me," she snapped.

"I was tryin' to be a gentleman," Larado said.

"Ha! You don't know the meaning of the word."

"Whatever you say, sweetie." He followed her out the door. Little heat waves drifted up from the street as they walked down to the depot. A large crowd had gathered on the platform for the arrival of the train. Dogs barked and ran up and down, boys chased each other and yelled. The mayor attempted to look dignified, but it was difficult since sweat poured down his face, which already seemed scarlet from a too-tight collar. Lark took out a dainty hankie and wiped her damp face, remembering the old joke about the soldier who had spent years in west Texas. It was said that when he died and went to hell it was so cold by comparison, he sent back to earth for some blankets.

The big black engine blew smoke as it slowed, coming toward the station. Bertha Snootley held an armful of straggly wildflowers. When Lark gave her a questioning look, the lady sniffed disdainfully. "Can't find any nice flowers to present to the banker's wife with that dirty little beast eating every bloom in sight."

The train pulled into the station, blowing smoke and coal dust. The bandleader held up his baton and the crowd grew quiet with anticipation. The portly train conductor, full of his own importance, stepped off the train. "Rusty Spur!" he shouted. "All off for Rusty Spur!"

There was a moment of breathless silence, broken only by the hissing of steam from the locomotive. Then a well-dressed, balding, fat man stepped from the train. To Lark, he looked vaguely familiar. He turned to help his wife down, and Mrs. Snootley stepped forward and thrust the big bouquet of flowers into the lady's arm. It was so big, her face could not be seen. The Odd Fellows band struck up a chorus of "For He's a Jolly Good Fellow," playing loudly, if not too well. The banker's wife held the big bouquet of flowers close to her face and began to sneeze. She sneezed and sneezed as the mayor tried to say words of welcome to the arriving couple. At that moment, someone mercifully reached out and took the offending bouquet.

Lark gasped. She turned and looked at Larado, but his face had gone as white as fresh milk. There was no mistake. The newly arrived couple was the former banker from Buck Shot, and his wife was none other than Dixie.

For a moment Lark teetered, and Larado reached out and caught her arm to keep her from fainting.

Oh my God, Lark thought. *What are the chances of this happening? Will they recognize us?*

She only caught the end of the mayor's speech. " . . . and so we welcome you to our growing town."

At this, the band began to play so loudly that the mayor had to shout, "Allow me to introduce the town council—and oh, this is our sheriff and his lovely wife."

The crowd was pushing them forward. The banker's wife looked as ashen as Lark felt. However, Larado stepped forward, shaking the man's pudgy hand. "Welcome, Banker Barclay and your missus. This is my wife L—Lacey."

The fat banker shook hands with Larado silently, but his homely face furrowed as if trying to place him. The blonde, wearing a demure, dark blue dress, seemed to recover nicely as Lark took her hand. It was damp and trembling. "So good to meet you," she said.

"Uh, likewise, I'm sure." Lark's hand was trembling too, and she wasn't sure what to do. Certainly, Dixie recognized them both, but she gave no sign. On the other hand, the banker's plump face wrinkled in thought.

"Haven't we met someplace before?"

"Well, now," Larado shrugged, "I've got a brother that looks like me, but don't know if he's ever been to St. Louie."

The mayor signaled for the band to stop playing. "Banker Barclay, we're right proud to have you in our town. You come along now. We've got a suite for you at the best hotel in town—"

"The *only* hotel in town," Mrs. Bottoms corrected as she came forward.

"I'm sure," said the mayor, "that soon we'll have lots of hotels. We're a growing community, and with your new bank, things can only get better."

The banker smiled and nodded. "I'm sure all the cattlemen and farmers in the county have been looking for a safe place to keep their money, and that'll be my bank."

Dixie was looking about in distaste as if disappointed in the town. Maybe after St. Louis, Lark thought, Rusty Spur was too tame for the whore turned banker's bride.

Stout Bertha Snootley stepped up and said to Dixie, "Come along, my dear. I know it doesn't look like much, but there's a few genteel ladies about like myself who are trying to bring class to Texas. Anyone can see you're from the finest people, and I've been so short of women like you to converse with. I thought when you got your new home built, we might form a ladies' club for culture."

"Texas and culture?" some wag called. "Don't rightly seem to go together."

"Oh, shut up!" snapped the stout fashion leader, elbowing all the others aside. "Abner," she called to her husband, "let's escort these good folks to the hotel."

The Snootleys took the banker and his wife to their buggy and drove away toward the hotel. As the crowd drifted off the platform and toward the buggies tied near the platform, Lark drew a sigh of relief. As strange as it seemed, evidently the banker had not recognized the pair, and Dixie had decided to keep her mouth shut. This was going to be a three-way Mexican standoff. It would not be in Dixie's best interest to have the town discover she used to be a whore at the Last Chance Saloon in Oklahoma Territory.

Lark linked her arm in Larado's. "We need to talk," she said through clenched teeth. She continued to smile and wave as the important people exited.

"I thought you might." Larado smiled, nodding to the people who waved and spoke to him. Lark took his arm as any wife might do, and they walked back to her shop.

When they got inside, she closed the door and whirled on him. "Of all the dirty—!"

"Sweetie, I don't know what you're talkin' about." He leaned against a display counter and rolled a cigarette, but she noticed his big hands were shaking so badly that he kept losing tobacco. He seemed as nervous as a long-tailed cat in a room full of rocking chairs.

"Don't give me that. Somehow, you've contacted Dixie and she's come because you're here."

"No, you got that wrong." He shook his head. "I had no idea. But she's got as much to hide as we do. We need to be more afraid he'll recognize us."

"Land's sake," Lark sighed, "what are we going to do?"

Larado managed to finish rolling the cigarette. "Damned if I know. Wait and see if he finally puts two and two together, I reckon."

"And when he does?"

He stuck the smoke in his mouth and reached for a match. "Reckon it ain't smart to borrow trouble. Maybe he never will."

"And you'd have me believe it's just a coincidence the two of them came here to start a new bank? I saw the way Dixie winked at you as she left the platform."

"She probably had something in her eye. I swear—"

"I wouldn't believe you if you were standing on a stack of Bibles, and don't you dare light that smelly tobacco in my shop. Ladies don't like the smell."

He looked like he might argue but decided it wasn't worth it. "Look, Lark, I don't know nothin' about this, honest. She didn't come here for me. It's probably a co-incidence. And after all, she's got a soft spot there, bein' married to a rich banker who may not know her past. I don't reckon she's gonna rock the boat."

"Maybe you're right, but I won't draw an easy breath from now on until I find out what her game is." In the distance she heard the train whistling as it gained speed on its way out of town. She wished she'd emptied her cash register and run to get on it. But there wasn't that much money, and she couldn't do that to the people who had funded her. She was paying them back gradually, but it would be several weeks before her business was free and clear.

"You gonna be all right?" He looked at her anxiously.

"Oh, sure," she snapped. "Let's see, I'm married to a bank robber when I thought I was marrying his upstanding brother, and said robber involved me in his mess, and now two people who might tie us to the whole thing have just showed up in town. Of course I'm worried, you idiot!"

He made a soothing gesture. "I'll talk to Dixie—find out what the situation is."

"Oh, you'd like that, wouldn't you? Any excuse to cozy up to that whore."

"Well, somebody needs to. That settee is harder than a tax collector's heart."

"It's not as hard as mine," she snapped. "Get out of here. I've got some hats to decorate."

"Okay. Oh, did I tell you the town council has planned a big Fourth of July celebration, complete with a shooting match?"

"You going to enter?"

He squinted at her in the bright light. "Of course not. Why, as good a shot as I am, no one would enter if I did. It wouldn't be fair to the other men."

"I reckon that's true. You've got a real reputation with guns." She had a thought. "They let women enter?"

He stared at her. "You must be jokin'."

"I'll have you know, I'm a damned good shot."

He shrugged. "Okay, enter. And when you beat a bunch of Texas men, how many of them will let their wives buy hats in here anymore?"

She chewed her lip. "I reckon you've got a point."

"Glad you're willin' to admit I might be right now and then. See you at home tonight, sweetie." Before Lark realized his intent, he whacked her lightly across the bottom as he headed toward the front door.

"Don't you ever do that again!" she seethed. "Keep your hands to yourself from now on, you hear me?"

He grinned and winked. "But you've got such a nice bottom. It just seems to fit my hand."

"Do it again, and you'll draw back a nub."

"I can remember when you liked me puttin' my hand on your bottom."

She felt the blood rush to her face. "We will not discuss that. Now get out of here."

"I'm goin', I'm goin'." He backed out the door. "They're havin' a welcomin' thing at the hotel for the banker and his lady."

"Land's sake, I had forgotten about that."

"You comin'?"

"I don't think I can face that pair until I've had a chance to steel myself. Tell everyone I'm feeling poorly."

He paused. "That'll look suspicious."

"I'm not as good a liar as you are," she snapped. "I'm afraid I'll give myself away."

"Okay, whatever you say. You know, I'd forgotten how purty Dixie was until I saw her again today." He sauntered away whistling: . . . *as I walked out in the streets of Laredo, as I walked out in Laredo one day* . . . .

An emotion flickered through Lark, an unfamiliar emotion. Could it be jealousy? Naw, of course not. She went to the door and looked out, watching Larado cross the street toward the hotel.

Then Lark collapsed in a chair and shook a moment. This was her worst nightmare. She'd thought things couldn't get any worse when she'd ended up married to Larado rather than his nonexistent brother—and now two more people from the past had shown up. It was probably only a matter of time until she and Larado were both unmasked and arrested.

When Larado left the shop, he ambled over to the hotel, his emotions not nearly as relaxed as his expression. Sure enough, the reception continued with sherry being served to the ladies and the men going for stronger stuff. The mayor looked up. "Well, here's our brave sheriff. Where's the little lady this afternoon?"

"Uh, she was feeling poorly," Larado said.

Several people snickered. "She couldn't be, ah, in the family way, maybe?"

"Already?" Larado said.

"It doesn't take much time." Mrs. Bottoms smiled at him.

He thought about Lark having his baby. It wasn't a bad thought. However, unless she let him back into her bed, the chances were slim.

"Well, Sheriff," Dixie said and came forward and put her hand on his arm, "I don't believe I caught your name. I'm Mrs. Wilbur Barclay." Her hand was warm, and she squeezed his arm.

"Uh, Witherspoon. Lawrence Witherspoon."

"Well, Sheriff Witherspoon," she gave him a big smile, "I'm pleased to see our bank will be so well protected."

She was looking at him in a way that made him feel hot under his collar. He ran a finger around the collar that suddenly seemed to be choking him. "I do my best, ma'am."

The banker had wandered off to talk to Abner Snootley and some of the town council. No one seemed to be paying much attention to the sheriff and the banker's wife. Now she looked up at Larado and ran the tip of her tongue over her lips in a suggestive way that no one else seemed to see. "Have you and your wife been married long?"

All he could see was the tip of that pink tongue flicking in and out, and he imagined that moist ribbon caressing his body. Dixie knew how to please a man. However, it hadn't been as good as it had been with the innocent Lark—but Lark had made it clear that he would never be touching her again, and a man had needs.

"Sheriff?" she said.

"What?" He could see the swell of her full, creamy breasts in the neck of the blue dress.

"I asked about your wife?"

"Oh." Larado came back to reality. "We're newlyweds, actually. And you and your husband?"

"Last April." She smiled a little too sweetly. "Wilbur and I are looking forward to a very prosperous business here in Rusty Spur . . . That is, if we don't get robbed." She winked very slowly.

Larado looked around to make sure no one else was paying attention. "This is a very law-abidin' town, Mrs. Barclay. Your bank will be safe."

"That's so comforting," she almost purred, putting her hand on his arm again. Her fingers caressed ever so slightly there. "You live in town?"

He pulled his hand away, nodding. "Got a ranch picked out, but a sheriff don't make enough money to buy land."

"Maybe you'll come into some money," she said.

He shook his head. "Not likely."

She smiled. "You just never know what will happen."

"Dixie, dear," the fat banker called as he pushed his way through the crowd. "Oh, hello, Sheriff." He gave Larado another puzzled look.

"Hello. I was just assurin' your wife how safe your bank will be in this town."

The banker nodded and smiled. "Have to tell you, Sheriff, one of the reasons I picked this town—besides the fact it's got a bright future—was I heard about the legendary sheriff who protects it. I'd like to see you shoot sometime."

Larado shook his head. "I'm a peaceful man, sir. I kill as few men as possible. My reputation keeps trail scum outa this town."

"Good. Well, come along, Dixie, dear, I want you to meet some of the other important folks in this town."

They both nodded to Larado and walked away. As she left, Dixie turned ever so slightly and winked at Larado.

Oh hell, now what was he gonna do? He figured Dixie had some fun and games in mind, and he suddenly realized he didn't want to play unless his partner was Lark. He real-

ized at that moment that the truth was, he really cared for
Lark and he'd never had as much ecstasy as he'd experienced in her arms. Of course Lark would never believe that,
so it appeared hers was a bed he'd never share again.

In the meantime, Dixie had made it clear that she was
interested in renewing their old acquaintance. If he
didn't take the bait, would she act the spurned, jealous
woman, blowing the whistle on him for the Buck Shot
bank robbery? And what had happened to Snake
Hudson?

He excused himself and left the reception, returning
to his office to sort through the wanted posters and
think.

Paco came in. "Hey, boss, you're not at the reception?"

"I was. I reckon it's still goin' on."

"That bank gonna make a big difference in this
town?"

Larado nodded. "Reckon so."

"That banker's got a pretty wife." The young Mexican
sat down on the edge of Larado's desk.

"I didn't notice." Larado leafed through the posters.

Paco laughed. "Didn't notice? Boss, you must be
blind. She's a beaut. Blond as a palomino filly."

Larado shrugged. "Rich men can attract women like
that."

"She's not as pretty as your lady," Paco noted.

"No, she's not, is she?" He pictured Lark's face and
dark eyes. She had a mane of black hair that made a man
want to tangle his fingers in it. Tangle his fingers in it,
pull her to him, and kiss her and kiss her and . . .

"Someday, you gonna teach me to shoot, si? Remember, you said you would."

Oh damn, he'd forgotten about that. He didn't want
his worst secret uncovered. "Sure, maybe sometime
when things slow down around here."

"Boss, it couldn't get much slower. Here it is, almost
the beginning of July, and there's two dogs and a burro

asleep out on Main Street." He stepped to the window and looked out.

Larado groaned. "Magnolia out again?"

"*Sí.*"

"Bertha Snootley will be bellyachin' about that. I reckon I'd better go put the damned donkey up." He got up and went outside, squinting against the blinding sun. Texas at this time of year was hotter than the hubs of hell. Texans not only relished the heat, they bragged about it to Yankees who came in on the train.

He went and caught Magnolia, taking her back to her stable. He stuck his head in the hat shop. "You closin' any time soon?"

"Why would you care?" Lark snapped. "You tired of flirting with Dixie?"

He should have known this was coming. "I was just puttin' in an appearance. Everyone asked about you. I told them you're feeling poorly."

"Good." She turned her back and began to rearrange a display case.

"Some of them hinted they think you might be in the family way."

She whirled on him. "I hope you didn't encourage that thought."

He grinned. "Actually, maybe I did. I got to thinkin' how cute our kids would be—"

"I'm not having children sired by a bank robber." Her dark eyes widened with horror.

"You've made that clear enough."

"I can't close yet. I've sold several hats, and I might sell more. Ladies are all getting new hats for Sunday services so they can impress the new banker's wife."

Larado snorted. "If Dixie comes to church, the roof may fall in."

"Well, it didn't when you came to services, and she's no worse than you are."

"Point well taken." He moved closer. "Lark, do you reckon we could reach some kind of truce?"

"Why should we?" She turned on him.

"Because it would make it easier for both of us."

Her expression turned as hard as her biscuits.

"I'm perfectly satisfied with things the way they are." He had hurt her, and she was angry with him for it.

"But I'm not satisfied." He sounded serious for a change, and he reached out, putting his big hand over hers. He was standing so close, she could feel the heat of his big body and smell the scent of tobacco and sunshine and bay rum hair tonic.

She had forgotten how big and hard the palms of his hands were, and she remembered now as his hand covered hers. She hesitated a long moment, remembering his touch, the safety of the embrace of his strong arms. As she weakened, she reminded herself that he had married her only to keep her from testifying against him, and that knowledge stung her pride—no, it hurt her soul. She pulled away from him.

"Don't try to sway me, Larado. Now that your whore is in town, I'm sure she'll find a way to keep you from being lonely."

"You really think I sent for her, don't you?"

She looked up at him, wishing she didn't believe that. "Now what are the odds she and her banker would end up in this tiny, dusty town when there are a thousand more appealing ones across the West?"

"But most of them aren't in Texas," Larado pointed out. "And the worst town in Texas is better than the best one in the rest of the states. Any Texan will tell you that. Maybe it's just because there's a lot of money in this town now with the railroad here, and new settlers."

"Haven't you got work to do?" She kept her voice icy.

"I certainly have." And she began to bustle about, rearranging merchandise.

"Well, I reckon I'll see you at the house later."

She nodded and gestured him out the door. He left whistling his favorite song, but it had a *muy* slow, sad quality about it today. She had begun to care about the man, even though he had hurt her deeply. She would not forgive or forget that, and she could not—would not—trust him. She closed her eyes in mental anguish. Had Dixie come to town for Larado? And if so, did Lark even care? She wasn't sure of the answer to that question.

Chapter Fourteen

Between them, they managed to get supper cooked that night. After that, she watched Larado looking through the newspaper as he sat at the table. He appeared frustrated, squinting and leafing through the pages.

Oh my, he can't read, she thought. Well, that wasn't so unusual on the frontier; lots of people were illiterate. "Would you like me to read it to you?" she blurted without thinking.

"You think I can't?" He seemed angry and defensive.

"No, I merely thought that since I read pretty well, I'd be happy to—"

"I don't need you to do that," he snapped.

"Okay," she shrugged. "I think I'll go to bed."

"By the way, you don't need to put the chair under the door," Larado growled. "I won't try to come in without a personal invite."

"Don't hold your breath," she said. "I presume you and Dixie will be sneaking clandestine meetings in someone's barn?"

"You know I don't know the meanin' of big words like that. I never had much chance to get much schoolin' after my ma died."

Her heart softened as she thought of a motherless child

trying to make it in a hard world. She thought of him as uncaring, yet he had hung on to both his mother's photo and her gold-framed eyeglasses. "I just figured you and Dixie— oh, never mind, you'd just deny it anyway."

"Lark, I swear to you, I didn't know she was comin'."

"Uh-huh." She went into her room and closed the door. *How stupid of you,* she scolded herself. If she didn't care anything about the man, why should she care if he sneaked away for a romp in the hay with the whore? Because if they got caught and the secrets came out, Lark herself was in jeopardy. At least, that's what she told herself. She put the chair under the doorknob anyway.

The next morning was Sunday. When she got up, Larado was already frying eggs. "You want some?"

"You cook any better than I do?" she asked.

"Nope. Between us, we'd poison a hog." He grinned.

"Don't give me any ideas," she said. "I'm going to church this morning. You want to come?"

"The church might collapse if I occupied a pew more than two Sundays a month."

"You might chance it. Besides," she kept her voice icy, "I imagine Banker Barclay and his wife will be there. It's good for business, you know."

"Does it matter to you if I come or not?"

"As any Texan would say, it don't make me no never mind."

"Well, maybe I will, then. After all, we need to keep up appearances of a happily married couple."

She made a choking sound as she sipped her coffee.

"By the way, I got a good deal on a buggy and a gray horse. The livery stable is deliverin' it this afternoon."

"I didn't think we could afford a buggy."

He grinned at her. "He's so pleased I'm protectin' the town, he almost gave it to me."

"Huh, if he only knew."

They dressed and walked over for morning services. Lark wore a light green lawn dress and a big white straw hat with daisies on the brim.

He smiled. "You look purty as a fluffy kitten with a ribbon around its neck. Who you dressin' up for?"

"Not you," she snapped. Actually, she didn't intend to be outdone by that blonde. She noticed with a frown that the sheriff wore his badge and his gun belt. "Larado, is that really necessary?"

"Suppose there was some kind of trouble durin' services?" he asked. "People would expect the sheriff to be armed."

"The most exciting thing that might happen is if old Miss Wiggly dozes off and falls out of her chair in the choir section during the sermon."

He grinned. "Most of the congregation's asleep by then—they'd never know the difference."

The church was full this sultry summer morning, and when Lark looked around, she saw Dixie and the plump banker in a row across from them. She nodded to the woman politely, and Dixie grinned back—but she didn't seem to be looking at Lark. She was looking at Larado.

The preacher was on a roll today, banging his Bible on the pulpit. The louder he got, the more the paper fans advertising the local funeral home flapped as the congregation stirred the hot air. His sermon was about how much hotter hell was than Texas, and they should all give that some thought and mend their wicked ways.

Mrs. Bottoms and Jimmy were sitting behind them, and she heard Jimmy say proudly, "There ain't no place hotter than Texas."

People around him giggled, and the old lady shushed him. Citizens who had heard him were nodding with a smile. Everything about Texas was bigger and better. But then, the preacher was originally from Gainesville, which was north—almost to the Red River—which almost made him a Yankee. So what did he know about west Texas heat?

Lark thought about the bank robbery and silently agreed with the preacher about wicked ways. Finally the service was almost over, and they reached for the hymnbooks.

"Number three hundred," the minister announced. "'Praise God from Whom All Blessings Flow.'"

She shared the hymnal with Larado. When their fingers touched, she felt a charge of electricity. He looked down at her as if he had felt it, too. ". . . Praise God from whom all blessings flow, Praise God, all creatures here below . . ."

Lark noted that Larado lifted the songbook higher and seemed to be squinting at the words. He couldn't read, she thought, despite all his denials. She had to find a way to teach him without hurting his pride.

Then services were dismissed, and people stood about on the lawn talking of small things like the weather. Texans always talked about the weather, taking an almost perverse pride in how hot it got. There was also talk of the Fourth of July festivities planned for day after tomorrow.

The banker and his wife walked over and joined them. Dixie wore an expensive lavender silk dress and a hat with big ostrich plumes on it. "Well," she said, "so nice to see you again, Mrs. Witherspoon. I hear you have a lovely shop."

Lark smiled guardedly. "Some say it is. I hope you'll come in and look around."

The fat banker put his arm around the blonde's waist. He was too short to put it around her shoulders. "Honey, you go in there and just buy anything you want."

"You see?" Dixie said. "He just spoils me rotten."

The banker smiled and nodded. Sweat gleamed on his bald head in the heat. "Anything my darling wants, I'm gonna buy for her. Reckon we'll be building a fine new home, too."

"You movin' into the new bank buildin' apartment this week?" Larado asked.

Barclay smiled with satisfaction. "Yep. We open the new bank tomorrow, and word's spread. I reckon folks'll be bringing all that money out from under mattresses to put in my bank."

Mrs. Bottoms walked up just then. "Well, heavens, you won't ever have to worry about bein' robbed—not with our sheriff on guard."

Lark made a choking sound. When everyone turned to look at her she said, "I'm sorry, I must have swallowed a gnat."

The banker nodded toward Larado. "Why, one of the reasons I chose this town was that my darling Dixie here heard this town had a sheriff who kept things peaceful."

"He sure does," said Mrs. Bottoms. Then she wandered away looking for Jimmy.

Lark called after her, "Look down at the telegraph office at the depot. You know how he loves talking to old Bill about trains."

About that time, Magnolia came trotting down the street, mingling with the crowd. She began to bray.

The banker jumped. "What in the name of hell? Oh, I beg your pardon, ladies."

Larado laughed. "My wife has a pet donkey we can't seem to keep locked up."

"Yes." Lark smiled a little too sweetly. "We have several asses in the family."

"I beg your pardon?" said the banker.

"Never mind," Lark said. The man must be blind not to notice the way his wife was eyeing Larado, like a hungry Texan eyes a big, juicy steak. "Reckon we'd better go, honey. I left dinner cooking in the oven."

"Yep," Larado said. "My wife is such a great cook. We must have you two over for dinner sometime."

Lark made that choking sound again.

Dixie smiled. "I'm afraid my talents lie in other directions—

but of course, when we get our fine new home built, I'll have servants doin' the work."

"Well, darling," the banker looked at Dixie, licking his lips, "let's get back to the hotel, shall we? After dinner, I want to take a nice nap."

Larado's eyes gleamed and he looked at Lark. "Sounds good to me."

Lark glared back at him. "You don't need a nap," she said pointedly.

"Oh, yes, I do."

The four nodded their good-byes and joined the crowd scattering from the church.

"Well, as you could plainly see," Larado said, "Dixie's the one eyein' me like a coyote eyein' a lamb."

"Oh, my! You're just *so* innocent," Lark scoffed.

"Now I didn't say that, I just said I didn't start it."

"Yes, but you were returning that look she gave you."

"Maybe I was just thinkin' how nice a nap after dinner would be."

"You can have a nap," Lark told him. "You just can't have the dessert the banker is probably going to get."

"Oh. Well, you can't blame a man for tryin'. You think he knows about Dixie?"

Lark puzzled over that a moment as they walked, the donkey trailing along with them. "Hard to tell. Maybe he never visited the Last Chance Saloon. What worries me is if he finally figures out where he met us."

Lark managed to fry a chicken for dinner and chop a little salad. Larado gobbled it up, looking doubtfully at the lumpy gravy.

"I haven't figured out how to keep the lumps out." Lark shrugged.

"That's all right—I love lumps in my gravy," Larado declared and poured some on his lumpy mashed potatoes.

"I ought to put the lumps on your head."

"Now, sweetie—"

"I'm not your sweetie."

"Don't I know it." He gave her his most charming smile. "That's all right, I didn't marry you for your cookin'."

"If you think that's gonna get you a little dessert with your nap, don't hold your breath."

He sighed. "I don't reckon there's any real dessert?"

She shook her head. "You really are trying to be a hero, aren't you? After my hard biscuits and lumpy gravy, would you really be willing to chance one of my pies?"

"Reckon I'm not that brave, but maybe someday you'll learn to cook." He got up from the table, pulled out his pocket watch and checked the time. "Well, if that's all I'm gonna get, I'll go out and wait for Ben to deliver the horse and buggy. You want to see it?"

She shook her head.

"After that, reckon I'll ride out and look over that ranch I'd like to buy."

"She going to meet you out there?" She felt a twinge again of that unfamiliar emotion.

"Now why would you think that? She's probably under that fat man right now, payin' for those jewels she was wearing this mornin'."

In her mind, she saw the whore spread out with the fat man naked on top of her. The thought made her shudder. "Too high a price, if you ask me. You do whatever you want—I'll clean up the kitchen."

"I thought you weren't in the least domestic?" He leaned against the doorjamb.

"Somebody's got to do it—we're running out of dishes." She wondered then if she could learn to make pies and cakes. She suddenly wanted to best Dixie at something, and she didn't think she could do it in bed.

"After the buggy gets here, you wanta go look at the view with me? There's only a shack, but there's a hill that would be a good place for a fine ranch house later."

"I've seen that place, remember?" She shook her head.

"I don't see any point in going again. You know as soon as I have enough money, I'm leaving."

"Maybe I'll leave first," he said.

"That'd be okay, too."

Larado went out, and Lark watched through the window as the new surrey and horse were delivered and he took them into the little barn out back. Later, when Lark heard a horse leaving she ran to the window and looked out, watching him ride away on Chico. What a mess. She couldn't imagine that they would be able to keep this masquerade going much longer—and yet, she was coming to love this little town. If things had been different, she might have been happy to stay in Rusty Spur, running her small shop and blissfully married to the local sheriff. Except he didn't care anything about her.

Lark returned to the kitchen, thinking about home. No doubt Aunt Cimarron would be having the usual big Fourth of July celebration for all the people on the ranch. She wondered how her twin was doing. Probably married by now to that Homer What's-his-name. Lark had thought him a bit dull, but he was Lacey's type. Lark felt a wave of homesickness and wished she could be at the ranch for the holiday, but of course she was too proud to go home now that she'd made such a mess of her life.

As she finished the dishes she heard the sound of a buggy's creaking wheels and ran to the window. There was a buggy passing, but it didn't stop. She frowned when she recognized the livery stable's rented rig. Driving it was Dixie, and she was all alone. Now just where did that slut think she was headed?

Larado rode out to the ranch with a heavy heart. Things were going from bad to worse. First he hadn't cared about Lark, he'd only wanted to ensure she kept her mouth shut. Then he'd taken her virginity in a wonderful night of passion, and he couldn't stop thinking about that. Just when he'd thought she was softening toward him and they might have a chance at happiness, Dixie and the banker had showed up—and Lark wouldn't believe he was innocent this time. Well, that cinched things. He didn't know what Dixie's game was, but he figured it was only a matter of time before—if he didn't clear out of town—he'd be exposed. That would bring trouble to Lark. He didn't want to hurt her. Worse than that, sooner or later his worse secret might be revealed, and then he'd be in real danger. He'd been lucky so far.

He rode out to the land he wanted to buy and didn't have a chance of ever getting. Tying his horse to a tree, he sat out on the rise and watched the valley below. Here was where he would build that big, fine ranch house if he had plenty of money. The original house was not much more than a shotgun shack in the area of the oil seeps. Larado reveled in the view and wished Lark were there to enjoy it with him.

He heard a horse whinny and whirled around. In the distance, he saw a buggy coming toward him. Lark? His heart skipped a beat. No, it was a bay horse pulling it. He squinted as it came closer and he recognized the driver. It pulled up and the driver stepped down. "Dixie, what the hell you doin' out here?"

"Now, honey," she crooned as she came to him, "that ain't a nice way to greet me after I went to so much trouble to get to Rusty Spur—just 'cause I heard you might be here."

"I ain't glad to see you." He turned away. "What happened to Snake? You tell him about the fake money?"

"I really never got the chance. And anyway, I heard he murdered a marshal tryin' to hold up another bank a few days later. They say he's in Huntsville, waitin' to be hanged."

"He got me in enough trouble." Larado shook his head.

"What I want to know is how you ended up as a lawman?" She laughed.

"It's no joke with me, Dixie." He frowned at her. "Oh, I took it to begin with just because I was desperate and lookin' for a place to hide out awhile. But I like protectin' folks and the respect I get."

"Respect?" she scoffed. "Are you *loco*? There's no money in bein' a lawman."

"Sometimes there's more important things than money," Larado said.

"No, there ain't," Dixie said. "Why do you think I ended up with the banker? I do my duty in his bed, and he buys me stuff. I like that."

"You always were a whore at heart."

"You sound pretty high and mighty," she said with disdain, "considerin' you're married to a saloon girl from the Last Chance."

"Be careful what you say about her, Dixie—she's different than you."

"Oh, so that's the way it is, is it?"

"Naw." He shook his head and sighed. "She don't care no more about me than a penny with a hole in it."

"So you two are just hiding out here, pretendin' to be law-abiding citizens?"

He glared down at her. "We *are* law-abidin' citizens, Dixie. That thing back in Buck Shot was just a big mistake."

"You think the good citizens here would be understandin'?"

Larado shrugged. "I never understood exactly what happened. One minute, I was blowin' my nose, the next thing, Snake's got his Colt out, then everyone's yellin' that we're robbin' the bank."

Dixie studied her nails and laughed. "You're as innocent as a baby about some things, Larado."

"I don't reckon I understand." He took off his Stetson and ran his hand through his shock of black hair.

"It turns out Snake didn't get nothin' much but silver in his bank bag, either."

"Then who got all that money the newspapers said was took?" He blinked at her.

"You figure it out. You see which man I ended up with, don't you?"

He shook his head. "It don't make no sense. Are you tellin' me Barclay robbed his own bank?"

"Yes."

Larado swore under his breath. "Well, I'll be damned."

"We'll probably all be. The banker got away with the money, but you two got the blame."

He glared at her. "You little bitch. You could have gone to the sheriff and explained, and you didn't?"

She didn't look at him. "I—I'm sorry about that, Larado. I was mad at you over that Lark and besides, the law might not have believed me nohow. Anyway, I reckon it don't matter now since you're safe and Snake's in prison, waitin' to hang."

"I ain't really safe as long as I'm tied to that bank robbery." He exhaled in an angry rush.

"I said I was sorry."

"Well, I reckon Snake deserves what he's gettin'. Huntsville's a tough prison. I sent a railroader named Otto there a few weeks ago."

"How come you married Lark? You care about her?"

"Naw," he lied, shaking his head. He didn't want Dixie to think he was soft. "I'm just tryin' to keep her mouth shut, that's all."

"That's good to hear." She put her hand on his arm, running her fingers up and down the sleeve of his shirt. "You know, Larado, Barclay might plan to pull this whole trick again."

"What do you mean?"

"I mean, sooner or later, some outlaw will hear about this fat bank and try to rob it. I reckon Barclay will slip him the fake money bag and hide the real money for himself. The townsfolk will never know the difference."

"Suppose I tell everyone about Buck Shot?"

She laughed and ran her fingers up and down his arm. "You can't do that without your part coming out and putting you and your lady at risk. Barclay's a respectable banker. You think anyone would believe you, especially when they hear you're wanted for robbin' that bank?"

He didn't answer, understanding the truth of her words.

"I got a plan, Larado. Suppose you and me clean that bank out—some night after everyone's asleep—and take off? I ain't got the combination to the new safe yet, but I'll bet I will finally get it if I keep sleepin' with that fat pig. You and me could have a good time down below the border on that money."

"But you're married to the banker," he protested.

"No, I ain't." She smiled and examined her fingernails. "We're just living in sin, as the proper ladies would say. He'd probably like to get rid of me if he got the chance, since I know enough to put him in prison."

"Then you're playin' a dangerous game, Dixie."

"I like danger, Larado. That's why I always liked you." She leaned forward and slipped her arms around his neck.

"Don't, Dixie."

"Don't what?" She kissed him then. For just a moment he stiffened. Then his man's hunger took over, and with his eyes closed, he could almost imagine it was Lark in his arms, kissing him with hot abandon. The kiss deepened and lasted a long time. *Lark*, he thought, *oh, Lark. . . .*

"Well, excuse me!"

He opened his eyes to see the other buggy with the gray horse just pulling up, and he jerked away from the blond whore. "Lark, sweetie, it's not what you think—"

"Oh, I'll just bet it is!" Her dark eyes were full of hurt and fury. "You lied to me when you said you two hadn't made plans. I was almost stupid enough to believe you. Well, I won't make that mistake again."

He ran over, grabbing the bridle. "Listen, Lark, you've got to hear me out."

"Let go of my bridle, you rotten sonovabitch!" She lashed out at him with her little buggy whip, striking him across the face. He shied away from the sting of the lash, losing his hat in the process. Then he tangled his fingers in the whip and jerked hard enough to pull her off the seat. She lost her balance and fell toward him, and he caught her.

"Damn it, Lark, listen to me. It's you I care about." He kissed her then, kissed her the way he'd dreamed of kissing her all these lonely, empty nights. Her mouth was hot. For a split second, she surrendered, letting him pull her hard against him while he ravaged her mouth. Then she seemed to remember and clawed at his face, fighting until he let go of her. She fell in a heap of petticoats and light green fabric. She scrambled to her feet and grabbed up her whip.

"I hope you both go to hell," she spat at them as she got back up in her buggy. She snapped the whip at her gray horse, and the buggy took off in a clatter.

He stood looking after her in frustration, wiping at the bloody scratches on his face. "Don't say anything, Dixie. You've caused me more damn trouble than I want now."

"You only married her to keep her quiet?" Dixie laughed without mirth. "You weren't kissin' her like you cared nothing about her."

"Shut up, Dixie." He leaned over and picked up his Stetson off the ground.

"I ain't afraid—you ain't the kind to hit a woman." She started for her buggy. "I'll tell you another secret you're too stupid to realize. That woman cares about you."

"Now I know you're *loco*." He wiped at the bloody scratches on his face again. "She'd like to kill me, that's what. One thing for sure, what happened just now has made things a lot worse."

"You got that right." She stepped up in her buggy. "You ain't gonna end up in her bed, so you might as well have the money and me." She winked at him. "I really know how to give a man a good time, as you surely remember. You wouldn't regret it, Larado."

He sighed. "I'm regrettin' it already. Now head back to town before Barclay comes lookin' for you."

"You think about what I said, handsome. Mexico, a woman who knows how to make a man happy, and plenty of money. That sure beats being a poor sheriff with a cold wife—and maybe dying in the street, shot by some drunk."

"I'll think about it. Now get the hell out of here."

He waited awhile after Dixie left before riding back into town. It was nearly dark when he unsaddled Chico. He gave Chico a rubdown, feeding him, the little donkey, and the gray buggy horse. "You three better save me room," he said. "I may be sleepin' out here with you tonight."

He went inside. Lark sat in the parlor, sewing on something—but she didn't look like she had her mind on it. He hesitated in the doorway. "I don't reckon it would do any good to say I didn't plan to meet up with her out there."

She looked up and blinked rapidly as if to clear her vision. "I don't believe that any more than I believe she came to town just because our sheriff was so law abiding."

"Well, you are right about that one thing," he admitted with a nod. "But she did tell me Barclay's a crook, and she thinks he'll try to rob his own bank again."

"What do you mean *again?*"

"I told you I didn't get any money in that holdup. Well, Snake didn't either, but he thinks I did. The banker slipped me a bag of paper and took the money."

She shook her head, her eyes swollen. "Don't lie to me. He's a respectable citizen. Are you telling me he killed his own teller?"

"It don't make sense, do it? You just have to trust me on that."

She laughed, but it sounded as if she was about to cry.

Larado sighed. "I don't know why I bother. I reckon I just thought you might care a little about me—at least enough to believe I wouldn't shoot a man in the back. Anyway, I don't shoot well enough to—"

"What?"

"Never mind. It don't matter."

"What does matter is I show up and find my husband kissing another woman like he's about to take her down in the grass and tear her clothes off."

"She was offerin'—and I'm not gettin' any at home."

"You rotten—!" She stood up and swung at him. He caught her hand and jerked her to him. Lark struggled, but he wasn't about to stop. He kissed her, kissed her like he'd been wanting to do for weeks now. He kissed her with a hunger that would not be denied as he pulled her against him so tightly she could not breathe. And when she gasped and her lips opened, he plunged his tongue inside, ravaging her mouth as his free hand went to cover her breast.

For a moment she struggled, and then she could not keep herself from surrendering to her own needs. She returned the kiss, not caring what had happened that day, not caring about anything but uniting with this virile male in heated passion. "Oh, Larado," she gasped, "Oh, Larado, please. . . ."

"That's just what I wanted to hear." His voice was as cold as his heart. He let go of her so suddenly that she fell against the settee. "Well, no thanks, lady, I ain't interested. How does it feel to beg? If anyone needs me, I'll be down at the Cross-eyed Bull getting stinkin' drunk. And Miss High-and-Mighty, you can go to hell!"

He slammed the door so hard as he left, the house rattled.

Chapter Fifteen

Lark went to bed, but she could not sleep. She hated herself, but especially him—for the need he had aroused in her. He probably aroused the same emotion in Dixie and every woman he met. She lay awake worrying about him since it wasn't like him to drink much. It must have been halfway through the night when she heard him stumble up on the porch, struggle with the door, and come in the house. He banged around the parlor, cursing when he bumped into objects in the dark. Would he attempt to come into her bedroom? Did she want him to? *Are you loco, Lark? Of course not.*

She heard him sit down heavily on the creaking settee. She got out of bed, moved the chair, and peeked around the door. He didn't look up as he attempted to take off his boots, finally mumbling "To hell with it." Falling over on the settee, he began to snore.

Lark breathed a sigh of relief. At least he'd made it home safely. Now, why should she care? She'd be better off if some outlaw shot him in the back. They'd have to shoot him in the back, because Larado was too famous with his gun skills to face in a shootout. She put the chair under her door again and went to bed, but she couldn't sleep. Things had gotten so bad between them that they were both nearly to the breaking point. Dixie and the banker showing up in town made things much worse. Talk about a Mexican standoff!

Light was streaming in the window when she awoke and went to check on Larado. He still lay on the settee, snoring and reeking of whiskey. Now she noticed the lip rouge all over his face. Damn him anyway, he'd probably spent part of the night in some whore's bed. She didn't want to think about that.

It was a hot morning as she walked to her shop. Tomorrow was July Fourth, and on every post and bulletin board were notices of the town's shooting contest. It was the town's best marksmen's chance to show off their shooting and win a prize. She was tempted to enter, certain she was as good a shot as any of the men. Her uncle Trace had taught her well. However, if she won it might end up in the Austin and Dallas newspapers, and she didn't need the publicity. Larado would probably throw a fit anyway, certain she would make a fool of herself.

About noon, Larado lurched into her shop. His face was a pale shade of green. She peered at him. "Are you all right?" Not that she cared, of course.

"Now why wouldn't I be?" He seemed to be having trouble focusing his eyes.

"Because you look like you've been dragged through a knothole backward."

"You!" he growled. "My life was pretty good until you entered my life. You've been the fly in my buttermilk, the pebble in my boot, since the first time we crossed paths."

"So now you're blaming the way you feel on me?" she asked primly. "Wipe your face. Some whore's lip paint is all over you."

He pulled out a bandana and dabbed at it. "I couldn't get any kisses anywhere else," he grumbled.

"Oh, don't give me that!" she snapped. "Dixie was licking your face like a hound dog eating bacon grease."

"Well, I didn't encourage her." He groaned aloud.

"Don't give me that. You think I'm blind?"

He sighed, took off his Stetson, and rubbed his head as if it ached. "I don't reckon you'd have a cup of coffee?"

"I might." Her heart softened a little at his evident misery. She got him a cup and motioned to a chair. "Sit down before you fall down."

He sipped the brew. "I think I'm gonna throw up."

"Don't you dare! Not in my shop."

He tried to focus his eyes. "You don't care about me. You only care about your damned shop."

Dealing with a drunk or a barely sober cowboy was a lot like dealing with a small child. "Look," she said patiently, "why don't you go home and sleep it off? Paco can handle your duties for a few hours."

He shook his head and groaned again, gulping the coffee.

"You owe me an explanation, mister," Lark confronted him.

"About what?"

"About what?" Her voice rose. "About me finding my husband in the arms of a notorious whore like Dixie. Just what was she doing out there?"

"She says she followed me—wanted to talk."

Lark snorted. "That didn't look like talking to me."

"Spoken like a jealous wife." He managed a weak grin.

"I am not jealous, and must I remind you, I don't even think we're legally married."

"Neither is Dixie."

"What?"

He shook his head. "She's blackmailin' that fat old banker."

"Why?"

"He robbed his own bank—gave us fake money. He shot his own teller too."

"You have reached a new high—or maybe I should say low—as a liar." Lark glared at him. "Why would he want to do that? It doesn't make any sense."

He took off his hat and ran his hand through his hair, flinching. "I told you I didn't get any money, and now I know Snake didn't either. Barclay got the money, and we got the blame."

Lark shook her head. "It doesn't make any sense that he would kill his own teller."

"It would if the teller saw him switching the money. Lark, he was killed with a shotgun. Neither Snake nor I had a shotgun."

She recalled the details of that April morning. Larado was right. "Oh my God. Larado, you need to tell the U.S. Marshal."

He leaned back in the chair and put the coffee cup on the counter. "Oh sure. Do you think anyone would believe me?"

She digested that fact. "Maybe you're not lying this time."

"Thanks a whole heap." He buried his face in his hands and moaned.

"So Dixie is blackmailing him because she knows. That's a pretty dangerous game. Has he figured out who we are?"

"Who knows?" Larado took another sip of coffee. "In the meantime, they are part of society here in Rusty Spur, and we're all in a Mexican standoff."

She shook her head and walked up and down the shop. "I can't live under that kind of stress."

"You could always just fold your hand and get out of this poker game."

She whirled on him. "You'd like that, wouldn't you? Then I wouldn't be a threat to you."

He grinned at her. "Or you could just stay here and tease me every night, make my life miserable."

She drew herself up with dignity. "I do not tease you."

"Oh, hell, no, you don't. You're in my house, in there in my bed every night, and I'm on that hard settee, thinkin' about you just beyond that door."

"Well, stop thinking about me and take your business elsewhere, like you did last night."

He shook his head. "I tried, but somehow, I couldn't get beyond a few kisses. It ain't the same for me anymore."

"I don't believe a word of it."

He shrugged. "That don't make me no never mind, Miss High-and-Mighty."

Lark glanced up at the clock on the wall. "My, it's almost lunchtime. If you'll get your lanky carcass off my chair and out the door, I think I'll go over to the hotel dining room for a bite."

He took out his gold pocket watch and held it so close to his face, he was almost cross-eyed. He must be having a difficult time focusing. "Can I go with you?"

"May," she corrected without thinking. Land's sake, she was getting more like her prim sister every day.

"Thanks," he said. He stood up, still a little wobbly on his feet.

"You look too green to eat a bite," she snapped. "You'd probably throw up on Mrs. Bottoms's nice carpet."

"Your concern for my welfare is overwhelmin'."

"I wasn't the one who poured all that rotgut down you."

He seemed a little wobbly still as he went to the door, waiting for her to close it and follow him out onto the wooden sidewalk. Magnolia came around the side of the building and fell in behind them as they walked.

"I don't know whether you've noticed or not, but I think we're bein' followed," he said.

"What?" She whirled and looked at the little animal. "Oh my, not again."

Larado laughed. "She'll attract some more strays, and then she'll have a foal. Next thing you know, you'll have half a dozen—and nobody much wants them."

"Well, that isn't today's problem. Must you eat dinner with me?"

"Now what would folks say if I didn't accompany my wife to lunch?"

"Oh, shut up." She went into the hotel dining room.

Mrs. Bottoms rushed up to them. "Come in. I've got a table right by the window where you can watch Main Street."

Not that there was much happening outside. The hot July wind blew a tumbleweed down the street. Two horses and a buggy were tied up along the row of businesses, and Magnolia was munching the daisies in a window box.

As they went to their table, the room full of diners nodded and spoke to them.

"Hey, Sheriff."

"Hello, Mrs. Witherspoon."

"Hey, Sheriff, you gonna shoot in the big match tomorrow?"

Larado shook his head. "Now, as good a shot as I am, it wouldn't be fair, would it?"

"That's right," the blacksmith agreed. "Our sheriff is a dead shot, but a good sportsman."

They sat down at the table.

Under her breath, Lark said, "Is it against the rules for the sheriff's wife to enter? I'm a better-than-average shot with a rifle."

He favored her with a condescending grin. "Now, sweetie, women won't be shootin' in the contest."

"Well, I don't know why not. I'll wager I can outshoot most of the men in town."

"Think about it this way." He leaned across the table and smiled. "You show up these Texans by outshootin' them, how many do you think will come into your shop to buy play-pretties for their wives and sisters?"

Lark thought about it. "It shouldn't be that way, you know. They shouldn't care if the winner is a man or a woman."

He grinned. "Easy to say, but you know Texans."

"I know Texans, all right," she griped. "You can always tell a Texan, but you can't tell 'em much."

He winked at her. "Ain't it the truth!"

Larado took a deep breath and shook his head. Lark ordered stew.

Mrs. Bottoms was talking a mile a minute as she served them. "You want biscuits or cornbread?"

"Tortillas," Paco said as he sauntered up, grinning.

"Pull up a chair," Larado said.

Paco took off his Stetson. "Mrs. Witherspoon?"

"Yes, pull up a chair, Paco." She was glad she wouldn't have to talk to Larado the rest of the meal. The stew was savory, hot, and delicious, but Larado looked a little queasy when he looked at it.

"I—I'm not hungry," he said.

Paco raised his eyebrows.

"Whiskey," Lark said by way of explanation.

"Oh, *si.*" The young man nodded knowingly. "That ain't like you, boss."

Larado sighed. "Things ain't so good at home."

"Oh?" Paco asked.

She felt the blood rush to her face. "Paco, are you—are you going to take part in the shooting match?"

He nodded, but he kept glancing from one to the other. "I tried to get the sheriff here to enter, but he says it wouldn't be sporting since he's such a crack shot."

"Yep, everyone knows that," Larado said.

About that time, Banker Barclay and Dixie entered the dining room. Mrs. Bottoms ushered them to a prime table, everyone speaking and nodding to this newest addition to Rusty Spur's society. The pair nodded to Larado and Lark as they passed.

Lark nodded to the gentleman and favored Dixie with a chilling stare. The banker appeared puzzled as he stared at them, then shrugged and went to his table.

The delicious stew suddenly seemed to lose its flavor. She looked at Larado, and he turned a bit more green.

Paco wiped up the bottom of his bowl with a tortilla. "Boss, I been thinkin'. We work so well together, you reckon if you ever managed to buy that ranch you want, I could work for you there?"

Larado shook his head. "Paco, I'll never be able to get the down payment. But yeah, if we're gonna dream, we might as well dream big. You can be my ranch foreman."

Paco grinned. "We'll raise cattle and some fine quarter horses."

Little Jimmy came to the table and poured more iced tea all around. "Maybe you'd have room for a kid?"

Lark smiled at him. "Now, Jimmy, what would Mrs. Bottoms do without you?"

"I'd rather live with you two," he said. "When I grow up, I want to work for the railroad."

"And maybe you will," Lark said kindly. With the mess she and Larado were in, they couldn't drag an innocent child into it.

Larado sighed and put his hand to his head as if it ached. "In the meantime, the town needs protectin'. We'd better get to it. Sweetie, you pay the bill, all right?"

"Certainly." Her voice was sarcastic, but neither man seemed to notice as they left the dining room.

The next day drew a big crowd to the little town for the festivities. The mayor made a speech about freedom— only mentioning Sam Houston twice and the Alamo three times, which made the real Texans question his patriotism.

There was a little parade of the Odd Fellows band, some of the town notables in red, white, and blue draped buggies, lots of horses, and small children carrying Texas flags. Indeed, many of them thought they were celebrating the day the Union had been lucky enough to join the Lone Star State. Lark made Magnolia a new white hat with red, white, and blue ribbons. The pair marched in the parade with the burro wearing an advertising sign for the French Chapeau.

Two subversive groups from the big city of Dallas came to town to march, the temperance ladies and the suffragettes who were hoping to get the vote for women. Since most of the men were well oiled by the time of the parade, they treated the two groups with benign courtesy and refrained from pelting them with rotten fruit. Besides, what could one expect from those liberals in Dallas?

Later in the day, the local ladies set up tables under the shade of some cottonwood trees at the edge of town and served a wonderful lunch, complete with huge piles of fried chicken and barbecue, ice-cold lemonade, and plenty of watermelon. As usual, when they were finished the little boys threw rinds at each other and put hunks of cold melon down the backs of the little girls, who immediately tattled on them. Magnolia ate a whole melon by herself.

Now it was time for the shooting match. Targets had been set up at the end of the street, and all the cowboys lined up for this contest, as well as some of the local saddle tramps from the saloon. It was a sweltering-hot day with little breeze, perfect for the contest. Women holding small babies gathered in front of the stores to gossip. Local men watched and laid side bets on the outcome. Small children ran in and out of the crowds, and the enterprising Abner Snootley had set up a small stand selling candy and sarsaparilla.

The mayor got up on the little platform and spoke again. Someone must have questioned his loyalty because this time he mentioned Travis, Bowie, Crockett, Sam Houston, and the Alamo again. He also introduced the town council and the new banker, who made himself very popular by declining to speak but saying he would host drinks at the hotel dining room that evening. That brought forth cheers from the thirsty Texas males, although most of them preferred the Cross-eyed Bull. Lone Star men preferred liquor to speeches every time.

Again the Odd Fellows band played "For He's a Jolly

Good Fellow." Truth was, Lark thought, they didn't know too many songs besides that one, "The Eyes of Texas," and "The Yellow Rose of Texas." However, for all the Texans, those three songs were enough of a repertoire for any band.

Abner Snootley, who seemed to have a snoot full, decided that he, as a member of the town council, should speak, too.

"Good citizens of Rusty Spur," he began, "when Texas was its own nation, it was founded by people of rare courage and foresight—"

"Oh Lord," one of the men groaned, "I hope he ain't gonna get wound up."

People began to applaud and whistle until he could barely be heard.

"I ain't done yet," he complained.

"Yes, you are, Abner." His wife stood up beside him. "Now just hush. Folks didn't come here to listen to you talk for two hours."

More cheers.

"All right, all right." The homely, balding man made a calming gesture. "I was just gonna talk about how the town is growin' because of the new railroad—and we got a new bank and everything—and to remind everyone that Snootley's General Store is always a good place to shop."

More whistles and catcalls came from the crowd. "Get on with the shootin' match!" some wag yelled.

The sheriff stood up and made a calming motion. Lark noted that everyone fell silent. She wondered if it was because they feared him or because he was that respected in the town.

"All right, fellas," Larado shouted. "Here's the rules. You get three shots, and if you don't hit the center of the target, you're eliminated. We'll shoot in rounds, and the last one standin' gets a nice basket of goodies, courtesy of Snootley's General Store."

Mr. Snootley and Bertha stood up and bowed. When

Abner acted as if he were about to make another speech, his stout wife yanked him back down.

"Don't forget about the saloon," someone in the crowd yelled.

The crowd roared its approval.

The sheriff nodded. "Yes, the saloon is selling beer half price all afternoon."

More cheers from the crowd, but from the temperance ladies there were cries of "Shame! Shame!"

"Hey," some farmer in the crowd complained. "That target's pretty small—I ain't sure anyone can hit it."

"Aw, the sheriff could," Paco said. "Hey, Sheriff, won't you give us an exhibit of your shootin' skill?"

The sheriff hesitated, licking his lips as he stood at the podium. "Naw, I—I wouldn't want to show nobody up. After all, this is a day for amateur shooters, not professionals."

Mrs. Bottoms smiled and nodded. "That Sheriff Witherspoon, he's as modest as he is brave. Three cheers for our great sheriff."

"Hip hip hooray! Hip hip hooray! Hip hip hooray!"

"That's enough, folks." The sheriff nodded with a modest smile. "I'm much obliged for your confidence, but now let's get on with the program."

The crowd cheered as Larado stepped down off the platform and came over to stand by Lark.

"Land's sake," she scolded. "You could have indulged them a little and let them see you shoot."

"Now don't you start in, sweetie. I wouldn't want to make these fellas feel bad."

The first men were lining up to shoot their rifles. The noise of the gunfire set a baby to crying, and two horses reared and whinnied, pulling away from their ties at the hitching post and running away. Lark watched, itching to compete. She was better than most of the male contestants, she realized as she watched the contest. She had a terrible urge to push forward and say, "Here, let me show you how it's done," but she managed to control herself. Texans liked their women feisty, but they didn't want to be shown up by them.

In the end, it was Paco who won the shooting match. He accepted the basket he'd won with cheers from the crowd, although Lark heard Mr. Snootley grumble, "I didn't know I'd be giving a basket of stuff to a Mexican."

"What?" Lark whirled on him.

"Never mind," he said. "Some of us ain't as democratic as you and the sheriff are. I wouldn't have given him a job in the first place."

"He's a good deputy," Lark reminded the man with a steely gaze.

Paco strode up just then, his dark face lit by a big smile. "Did you see me shoot, *señora*?"

"I certainly did. Congratulations."

It was almost dark now. The crowd was scattering, some to the saloon, and some to the hotel, and some were standing around waiting for the fireworks.

The sheriff boosted little Jimmy up on his shoulders for a better view when the sky rockets began to explode in the black, hot night. Lark stood next to them and thought about what it would be like to be a real family. *Stop it, Lark,* she scolded herself, *this can't work out and you know it. As soon as you get enough money, you're going to do what you always do, flee.*

However, she was going to have to stay in this sham marriage for at least a few more weeks. She felt like she was sitting on a keg of blasting powder to have the banker and Dixie in town—but worse yet, to have to share a house with Larado and lie in bed at night, knowing there was only a weak door between them if he ever decided not to take no for an answer.

At last the festivities were over. Larado went on home to feed the livestock, and Lark stayed to help Mrs. Bottoms and the other ladies clean up the mess and put away the food. It was dark as the inside of a cow as she walked home. The town was quiet in spite of the big day.

She stepped in a mud puddle without seeing it and paused at the front door, swearing under her breath. Well, she didn't want to track mud into the parlor. Quietly, she went around back, wiped her feet, and entered through the back door.

Larado sat at the kitchen table reading the local paper. He did not look up, so she knew he had not heard her enter. Then she took a better look and gasped in surprise. Larado was wearing his mother's gold-rimmed spectacles. When she gasped, he looked up suddenly, his expression one of panic. He ripped off the eyeglasses, threw them down, and jumped up from the table.

"What—?" she asked.

"You tell anyone, I swear, I'll—" he came at her, grabbing her arm.

She shook his hand off. "Larado, why are you wearing your mother's glasses?"

He sighed, looked around as if trapped. For once, he wasn't breezy or lighthearted. "Why don't you just pretend you didn't see that, and we'll forget it."

"But I don't understand."

"Don't you get it?" He roared at her, "I can't see! My eyesight is no damn good. I'm a four eyes! I can barely find my way around town without my spectacles."

"Oh, Larado—"

"Don't you feel sorry for me," he shouted at her. "Don't you dare feel sorry for me!"

"But you're such a good shot. How—?"

He paced up and down. "Everyone *thinks* I'm a good shot. Have you ever seen me shoot? I couldn't hit a barn with a scattergun at ten paces. I'm a fake, Lark, a failure."

Her heart went out to him. "For a failure, you're doing a pretty good job as a sheriff."

He shook his head, his rugged face a show of misery. "My old man called me a 'Nancy boy'—a weakling, because I couldn't see well, so he dumped us both. My ma worked like a dog as a bunkhouse cook to buy me spectacles, and the kids at school ganged up on me and broke them."

"Oh, Larado, I'm so sorry, I had no idea."

"Forget it!" he snapped and paced some more. "We had no money for new ones, so I had to wear the broken ones wired together. It got so bad, I quit school."

"And became a cowboy."

"A saddle bum," he corrected. "Now I've got respect, and people like me. Nobody knows my secret—nobody but you."

She shook her head, her voice gentle. "I wouldn't tell anyone, Larado. Besides, this town wouldn't care—they'd like you anyway."

"Ha! Whoever heard of a half-blind sheriff, wearin' spectacles? Why, if that got around, they'd all laugh, and half the outlaws in the state would come to take a shot at me."

"But as it is, you're taking a chance that someone you don't see will kill you."

"At least I'd go down respected," he muttered. "And the whole town would come to my funeral and talk about what a good sheriff I was."

She walked over and put her hand on his arm. "Larado, that's *loco* thinking. Just start wearing the spectacles—no one would care."

He shook her hand off. "And get me laughed at again? Can you imagine Wyatt Earp wearing glasses? It don't fit the lawman image."

"Men!" she snorted. "You're more vain than most women."

"If you'd been through what I've been through . . ." He hesitated. In his dark eyes she saw the misery he was remembering—a poor, scrawny child beset by school-house bullies. "I finally got big enough and good enough with my fists to defend myself," he said. "The rest, I bluff my way through."

"But it made me think you couldn't read."

"I don't very well, but I'd rather be thought stupid then blind. I'm a loser, that's all. My old man was right."

She had never felt as sorry, as sympathetic, as she did at this moment. She moved closer. "Look, Larado, you have my word that I won't tell anyone."

He looked uncertain. "You sure?"

She nodded. "Cross my heart and hope to die." She made the appropriate gesture.

"I wouldn't blame you for telling everyone in town, Lark, holding me up to ridicule—not after what I've put you through."

"That wouldn't be fair." She shook her head. "Like shooting a man in the back. This will be our little secret."

He looked at her a long moment, as if wondering if he could trust her. Finally he said, "Thanks. I'm much obliged." His manner was gentle, not smart-alecky as in times past.

"There's only one thing I'm worried about now," she said.

"What?"

"If you don't wear your glasses and you have to face down a real gunfighter, he'll kill you."

He shrugged. "The rumor got started that I'm an ex–Texas Ranger, so most *hombres* think twice about challengin' me. They think I'm a dead shot, but even with my spectacles on, I'm not that good."

"Then you're taking a big chance being a sheriff, aren't you?"

"What can I say?" He looked at her, earnest now. "I've got respect, a place in this town. I'm tired of bein' a saddle tramp. I don't wanta run anymore."

"Someone said it's better to be a live dog than a dead lion."

He shook his head. "I don't believe that no more. Sometimes a man has to stand for something if he's goin' to keep lookin' himself in the mirror."

"Well, thank God I'm not a man, then," she sneered.

"Running is what I've always done when I came up against something I couldn't deal with."

"Runnin' is for cowards."

"Okay, so you'd be called a coward," she conceded with a nod. "But you'd be a *live* coward."

"Lark, you're a Texan and you know the code. A man's gotta do what a man's gotta do."

"That's *loco*. Sooner or later, some gunfighter or robber will shoot you down in the street, and you'll be a dead hero."

He shrugged. "I reckon. Now you know what my weakness is, you could get me killed real fast by spreadin' the word."

"Damn it, I don't want to get you killed, I just want to keep you out of my bed, you rascal."

"Do you really?" He came toward her and stopped close enough that she could have reached out and touched him. For a long moment, she felt the electricity pass between them, knowing that all she had to do was look at him or open her arms, and he would sweep her up and kiss her the way he had in all her troubled dreams. Maybe he didn't even have to wait for a signal— maybe if he just lifted her and kissed her, carried her into the bed, they would both be swept away in a dizzying, heated passion that had nothing to do with love or marriage.

She took a deep breath to quiet her screaming nerves and turned away from him. "I don't want to be married to a lawman, Larado."

"You mean a half-blind saddle bum, don't you?"

"That's not it, and you know it."

"I don't know it. You've got a family, Lark. You could go home, and you'd be welcome there."

"I'm too proud." She began to weep. "I'm more proud and maybe more foolish than you are, Larado. I ran because I was weary of competing with my sister. I ran because I did poorly at school. I've run from every difficult thing that I couldn't handle, instead of standing my ground."

"Well," he said, "if you decide to pack up and go home, I won't follow you or try to get you in trouble. Folks will finally forget about what happened in Buck Shot. You can go home and make a fresh start."

She shook her head and wiped away her tears. "I'm not going home until I can go home proud."

"And bein' married to a failure—a saddle bum wanted by the law—is not good enough, is it?"

She shook her head. "I—I've got to sort things out."

"I reckon I have my answer, then. Let's eat a bite, and I'll go sleep on the settee."

"Or maybe with one of the girls at the saloon?" She was angry with him, remembering.

"I never cared about anyone but you, Lark, and I took you any way I could get you—and I'd do it again. It's rotten of me, I know, but I'm a rascal—you've always said so. That one night in your arms was worth everything you've put me through since, teasin' and tantalizin' me until I was half *loco* for need of you. I've lied, and I've cheated, and I'd do it again for that one night I spent in your arms."

She was crying now. "I fear you're lying again, saying whatever it takes. You and Dixie are probably planning to rob the bank yourself and run off with the money."

He swore softly. "I don't know whether you're a fool or just stubborn, Lark, but I've tried to be honest."

She whirled on him, eyes blazing. "Honest! Why, you saddle tramp, you don't know the meaning of the word!"

"I reckon I know where I stand with you—I kept hopin' for something better. Okay, I'll move to the hotel."

She watched in horror as he began to gather up his things. "The hotel? What will everyone say?"

"I really don't give a damn, my dear Lark. You can tell about the robbery, or about me being half blind, or how I begged for your love while you laughed at me. It's bad enough to have to go sleep on that damned settee every night—knowing you're just past that door—without having to live with your insults too." He strode into the bedroom and began to jerk clothes out of the bureau. "I've been teased enough!"

"You can't leave!"

He threw some things into a valise and pushed past her to the front door. "I can't leave? Just watch me, sweetie!"

And with that, he was gone. Lark stared after him and began to sob. She wasn't certain whether she was weeping with relief or with sorrow.

Chapter Sixteen

The next morning Lark was late opening her shop. In a small town, bad news traveled faster than gossip at a church social, so she wasn't surprised that local citizens passing by peered in curiously or stopped in little groups out on the street to talk. Two ladies came in to ask if there was anything they could do to help.

Bertha Snootley came into her shop for the first time since she and Lark had had their differences. Very sanctimoniously, she told Lark she had heard about the marital troubles. "I'm so sorry you and your husband don't get along as Abner and I do. Why, we have a marriage made in heaven."

Lark knew that wasn't true, but she only said, "I'd prefer not to discuss my marriage."

The plump lady sniffed, evidently displeased at not picking up any juicy details. "Well! Very well, then. I'm leaving to go to Abilene. There's just nothing worth having in the shops here." And Bertha Snootley sailed out of the shop.

Lark sighed and leaned on the counter. She wasn't surprised that it was already around town that Larado had moved into the hotel. Damn him anyhow. Why couldn't he have slept on the settee and saved her from all this embarrassment? Because he was a thoughtless clod who wanted to humiliate her, she decided. It occurred to her that she could go to the sheriff's office and ask Larado to move back into the house.

"Beg that scoundrel to move back in? Ha! I wouldn't give him the satisfaction. Besides, he might figure it would come with bedroom privileges, and I certainly don't intend to offer those."

Banker Wilbur Barclay twirled his cane as he walked toward the millinery shop. He'd figured out now where he knew the sheriff and his pretty wife from. He'd also decided why Dixie had been so insistent that they move here.

"Damn the slut," he muttered under his breath. "She's got the hots for that sheriff and thinks I don't know what's going on." He smiled to himself as he sauntered down the wooden sidewalk. He was sick of Dixie and wanted to be rid of her, but then she'd tell what she knew. She expected to be well cared for in exchange for keeping her mouth shut about what had happened in Buck Shot. "I'll take care of her, all right, first chance I get that won't incriminate me."

What had taken his eye was the pretty black-haired girl who had married the sheriff. Now he walked into the millinery shop and bowed low. "Ah, Mrs. Witherspoon, good day to you."

For a split second, the tall brunette looked disconcerted, then she nodded and tried to smile. "Good day, sir. Hot enough for you?"

A lady had entered the shop behind him, and now he hesitated. "Of course it's always hot in Texas." He turned to the other woman and smiled. "Oh, do wait on this lovely lady first, then we'll talk about a special hat for my wife."

The customer smiled. "So sweet and thoughtful. I'm so glad I've put my money in your new bank, Mr. Barclay."

He bowed low. "I don't have many depositors as lovely as you. You can certainly trust the Barclay bank with your money, dear lady."

The woman was all smiles and blushes. She looked around a bit, didn't seem to see anything she liked, and left, still atwitter at the banker's compliments.

He waited, twirling his fine cane.

"Well," Lark said, "now what may I show you for your wife?"

"Let's cut the nonsense, honey." He leered at her.

"I beg your pardon?" Lark blinked and took a step backward, staring at the fat, balding man.

"Oh, don't play innocent with me, sister," he hissed. "It took me a little while to figure out where I knew you from, but now I recognize both you and your so-called lawman husband."

She did her best to appear calm. "Surely you must be mistaken—"

"Ha!" He twirled his cane and leered at her. "Don't give me that. There was a teller killed in that robbery, did you know that? There's a warrant out for that cowboy, and it seems there was a pretty dark-haired girl holding the horses and being the lookout for that pair."

She felt her face go ashen. "Ob—obviously a case of mistaken identity. Why, we're both sterling members of the community."

"In that case, if I wire the authorities to investigate, you wouldn't be concerned, would you?"

"Not—not at all," she lied, trying to appear calm. Oh Lord, she'd thought she had problems before—they were a lot worse now.

She took a deep breath. She had played a lot of poker with the boys at the ranch bunkhouse, and now she decided to bluff. "Speaking of investigating, I wonder what the locals would think about putting their money in your bank if they knew Dixie used to be a whore working at the Last Chance Saloon?"

He grinned and twirled his cane. "I'd simply plead that I hadn't realized who she was—that I was an innocent man who'd been taken advantage of by a loose woman. Anyway, I'd say murder and robbery are a little more serious than taking up with a whore."

He had her there. "This whole thing is a big mistake."

He guffawed. "I don't think so, sister."

Lark licked her lips that suddenly went dry. "What—what is it you want?"

He leered at her. "You—I want you, honey."

"What? What about Dixie?" She moved behind the counter to put it between the two of them, wishing a customer would come in, but they were alone.

He stepped forward and leaned on the counter. "That blond slut? I never married her, and I don't intend to. You and I could have a little thing going on the side for a while. Then I wouldn't be tempted to tell what I know."

"That's blackmail."

He twirled his cane. "I know."

"My husband will turn you inside out—"

"But you're not going to tell him, honey. Besides, I hear he's moved into the hotel."

Lark glared at the banker. "How long do you think it would be before he found out?"

The fat man shrugged. "By then, we'd be gone. Honey, you deserve a lot more than this hick town and this pitiful little shop can give you."

Lark was indignant. "You called it a promising, up-and-coming town in your speech when the mayor welcomed you."

He pointed at her with his cane. "You should have seen through that. I'm here because there's a lot of ranching money under mattresses in the area, and soon, most of it will be in my bank. Sooner or later, some idiot will attempt to rob my bank, and I've got it all planned out."

Lark blinked. "What are you talking about?"

"Didn't your stupid cowboy tell you? I simply slipped

the robbers some change and a bag full of chopped paper, and I put the real money bag out the back door until later. They got the blame and I got the cash. It was very profitable for me."

So Larado had been telling her the truth. "Why are you telling me all this?"

He winked at her. "Because when I leave next time, honey, I'd like to take you with me."

"You mean dump Larado and Dixie?"

He shrugged. "They deserve each other."

"I'll tell everyone."

He laughed. "And who would you tell without explaining how you and your stupid cowboy were involved?"

"Mr. Barclay, you are an evil man."

"But a rich one." He ran his tongue suggestively along his thin lips and came around the counter. "Think of what I could buy you—jewels, furs, the best St. Louie or Kansas City has to offer. I want you in my bed, my dear."

Lark slapped him then, slapped him hard.

His florid face turned even redder as he rubbed at the mark her hand had left. "You bitch, you'd better think about this. If you're smart, you'll go along with me."

"I'll tell Dixie what you're up to—I'll tell my husband."

"What can they do without exposing themselves? I think Texans call this a Mexican standoff."

"Get out of my shop, you coyote, and don't come back."

"Think it over, honey." He leered at her as he turned to leave. "I could buy you a lot of nice things."

"I can't be bought," she snapped.

"Then you'd be the first woman who couldn't." He winked at her and sauntered out of the shop, twirling his cane.

Lark leaned against the counter, shaking. Oh my. How in the hell had she got into this mess, and how would she get out? She put a "Gone To Lunch" sign on the door and left. She'd better go warn Larado that they might be exposed.

Land's sake, what did she care if he ended up in jail?

She could pack up and leave suddenly without a trace.
Certainly the banker couldn't track her to expose her,
nor could Larado. She'd paid back everyone who had in-
vested in her shop, except Larado, so she could clear out
with a clean conscience. Yes, she'd keep a bag packed. If
things came to a boil, she'd empty her cash register and
run, rather than facing up to the consequences. It had
been her pattern all her life.

Dixie peeked out of the second-story window of her
hotel room. She saw Wilbur Barclay leaving the millinery
shop, smiling to himself and twirling his cane. "Now
what the hell is he up to?" She considered that he might
actually be buying a new hat for her, then shook her
head. "Naw, that rat hates me and would get rid of me if
he could."

She had no doubt that it was only a matter of time
before the banker tired of her blackmail and figured out
how to dump her . . . or worse. Could the rat be in cahoots with that Lark?

Dixie waited until she saw Barclay go inside the bank
so he wouldn't see her, then she put on an elegant pale
green silk dress and matching hat, got her purse, and
headed for the sheriff's office. She looked around carefully to make sure she wasn't seen before she entered.
Larado sat behind his desk, talking to that Mexican
deputy. Both paused, startled, then they pulled off their
hats. The sheriff stood up awkwardly. "Why, hello, Mrs.
Barclay, what brings you out today?"

"Can we talk?"

"Sure." Larado gestured toward a chair.

"I mean *alone*," she said pointedly, glaring at the
deputy.

"Uh, Paco"—Larado gestured—"you go put up those
new wanted posters down at the post office, okay?"

"*Sí*, boss." The man nodded toward her and left.

"Well," she said, "he didn't make no bones about not likin' me. He made me feel about as welcome as a skunk at a garden party."

Larado shrugged. "He suspects you ain't on the up-and-up, and he thinks my wife hung the moon."

Dixie snorted. "She ain't so hot."

He started to say something, seemed to think better of it. "I'd rather not discuss my wife."

"Don't give me that. The fact that you've moved out traveled faster than gossip at a sewin' circle."

He flushed, looking angry. "That's hardly your business."

"Ain't it?" She leaned back in the chair and smiled at him. "Maybe she's already lookin' for something better. I just saw Barclay leavin' her hat shop."

"Oh?" He shrugged. "So what?"

"Well, what do you think he was doin' in there?"

"How the hell should I know? Maybe he was buyin' you a new hat."

"Ha! That fat old banker would steal the milk out of a sick baby's bottle, or the pennies out of a blind man's cup."

"I reckon you'd know more about that than I would."

She studied her nails, and her diamond rings sparkled in the light. "I figure he's lookin' her over because she's pretty, and maybe his money attracts her."

He shook his head. "Lark can't be had for money."

"You don't know much about women, sport. Any woman can be had when a man starts offerin' jewels, furs, and easy livin'."

"Not Lark."

"You gotta lot of faith in her for a man who's moved out."

He made a gesture of dismissal. "I don't want to talk about her. Now what is it you want, Dixie?"

She put her elbows on his desk and leaned forward so that he got a good view of her full breasts in the low-cut green silk dress. "I want you, Larado, you know that."

He leaned back in his chair. "We've already had this conversation."

"Yeah, but that was before your lady threw you out."

"She didn't throw me out, I moved out on my own."

"We could be good together, Larado. I know how to please a man."

"I reckon you do, you've laid enough of them."

Rather than be offended, she laughed. "Gettin' moral on me? You, who are wanted for murder and bank robbin'?"

"You know I didn't do that."

She nodded. "I know, but the rest of the world don't. You got the name, you might as well have the game."

He reached in his pocket for a sack of makin's and began to roll a cigarette. "I reckon there's a point to all this? If not, get out, Dixie. I got work to do."

"I told you how Barclay switched bank bags back in Buck Shot? I figure he's plannin' on doin' it again as soon as his bank gets full of the ranchers' money."

He rolled the smoke and stuck it in his mouth. "As sheriff, I can't do anything about that until he breaks the law here."

"Why don't we do it first? I'll get the combination to the safe. We could clean it out some night and clear out, just the two of us."

"Dixie, we've had this conversation already. You never change, do you?"

She laughed. "Leopards don't change their spots, cowboy, and neither do saloon girls and saddle bums. You got nothin' to hold you here—that uppity girl don't care anything about you."

He sighed. "I reckon you're right about that." He struck a match against the sole of his boot and lit the cigarette. "But I've got a job, Dixie, and respectability. I kinda like that."

She snorted in derision. "You think this town wouldn't turn on you if they knew your past? And even if you keep the job, you'll die broke on the piddly pay or get shot down in the street by some gunfighter, and for what?"

He smoked and stared into the distance. "Reckon what you say makes sense."

"Then you'll consider it?"

He shook his head. "If I take that path, I'll end up dead or in prison. That ain't better than what I got here."

She ground her teeth in rage. "You're a damned fool, Larado. You'd better thank your lucky stars that they're gonna hang Snake. Otherwise, he's find you sooner or later, and he's a damned good shot." She stood up and started to walk away, but Larado jumped to his feet so fast that his chair fell backward with a clatter.

"What's that supposed to mean?" He grabbed her arm.

"Let go, you're hurtin' me."

"Dixie, you just hinted at something, and I reckon I need to know what it is."

She didn't look at him. "Nothin'."

"I don't believe you."

"Well, okay. It was when you two robbed that bank."

"I'm listenin'."

"I—I never told Snake your bag was full of chopped paper."

His grip tightened and there was a stunned silence. "What—?"

"You heard me. I told you he had come and gone when he hadn't. After you left, I burned the bank bag and told him you never showed up."

He let go of her with a disgusted sigh. "So he thinks I betrayed him and ran off with a bag full of money?"

She shrugged. "I reckon that's about the size of it."

"And being the kind of woman you are, with a nose for gold, you hunted up the man who really had the gold and took up with him."

"Well, why not? Life is tough, Larado, and I'm not gettin' any younger. We could do the same thing—clear outta this hick town with enough to last us the rest of our days. I could make your nights worth it."

"Dixie, get the hell out of my office and don't come back. I ain't interested."

She smiled archly at him. "Don't say no just yet, sport. I don't reckon that uppity straitlaced wife of yours is puttin' out any or you wouldn't have moved to the hotel."

"That's hardly any of your business."

"Just think about it." She gave him a coy, inviting look and slowly ran her tongue across her lips in invitation. Then she left, waggling her bustle invitingly.

Larado stared after her. His groin tightened just thinking about how good Dixie was in bed. Why shouldn't he help himself to that, even if he didn't rob the bank? Old Barclay need never know Larado was dipping his pen in the banker's ink.

"Damn it!" He tossed his cigarette into the spittoon and returned to his desk. He'd hardly sat down before the door opened again, and Lark entered.

"Well, I see Dixie was just here. I can smell that strong perfume she wears."

He didn't answer.

"Are you denying it?"

He stood up, standing so close, he could have touched her. He could feel the heat of her, see the swell of her breasts as he looked down. She was tall for a woman, but he was taller. He had an insane desire to grab her small waist in both hands and pull her to him in a torrid kiss. But he knew she would probably slap him. When he looked at that full, moist mouth, he thought it might be worth it.

"Have you nothing to say?"

"Lark, you just here to tease me some more, or to invite me to move back in?"

"Neither."

"Then why don't you get the hell out of here before I throw you across my desk, rip that pretty yellow dress down the front, and take you like I'm thinkin' about right now?"

She took a step backward and gasped. "How dare you?"

"Oh, don't give me that." He turned away to keep from grabbing and kissing her. "I know who just left your shop."

"He—he was there to buy Dixie a hat."

"Is that right?" He turned and glared down at her. "Or pick out a sweet little something for himself?"

Her eyes widened and her cheeks flushed. He thought she had never looked as beautiful as she did at that moment. "That's not fair. I'd never cheat on you, which I suspect is more than I can say for you."

He shook his head ruefully. "I hate to admit it, sweetie, but I just turned down the ripest, most skilled slut in the business. She wants me to run off with her, and she promised I'd never regret it."

"And you turned her down?"

"Maybe. I said I'd think about it."

Tears came to her eyes, and she blinked rapidly. "You've got the whole town laughing at me."

"You're the one who threw me out. I figure this marriage is over."

She seemed to be biting her lip. "I—I think it never really had a chance. It's probably not legal anyway."

"I took your virginity, that makes it at least a common-law marriage in Texas."

"Will you stop reminding me of that?" She almost screamed it at him. "The banker wants to run off with me. Maybe I ought to take him up on it. I'd be far away and safe, and I'd have lots of pretty things."

"Lark," he murmured, "the only place you'll ever be safe is in my arms, and you know it!"

Her tears overflowed now and she looked up at him, eyes streaming. "I hate you! You brought me nothing but trouble! As soon as I can, I'm clearing out of here—and I hope to God I never see you again!" She turned and ran out the door, bumping into Paco, who was just entering.

Paco looked after her, turned, and looked at Larado.

"Don't even ask," Larado snapped.

"*Sí,* boss." He leaned against the door jamb. "Two beautiful women. Most *hombres* would be pleased to have *one.*"

"You don't know the half of it," Larado muttered, reaching for his Stetson. "The one I could have, I don't want—and the one I want, I can't have. It's about as bad as Apache torture."

Paco looked puzzled. "If you say so, boss."

About that time, old Bill, the telegraph operator, came running, waving a paper and spitting through his gapped front teeth. "Hey, Sheriff!"

"What is it, Bill?" Larado was in a foul mood, not in a mood to visit with anyone.

"Just came in over the wire." He waved the paper.

"What?"

"There's been a big breakout over at Huntsville. The prison's tryin' to alert all the lawmen in Texas."

"They wantin' us to get up posses?"

The other man nodded. "Yep, they think the whole bunch is headed for either the Gulf or the border, but they'd like to intercept them afore they get too far."

Larado paused. "I reckon I can deputize a bunch of men, but the Texas Rangers will probably get them quick."

"You gotta feel sorry for the towns and ranches between Huntsville and the Gulf," Paco said. "The convicts will try to make it down to Galveston and board tramp steamers."

"Not all of them." Bill shook his head. "They found prison clothes abandoned in the rail yard where some freights head west, and some lady near there reported clothes stolen off her clothesline."

"Hmm," Larado mused. "That means some of them may be tryin' to head west and then south—get to Mexico."

Bill hesitated. "Sheriff, I might as well tell you one of them missing jailbirds is Otto."

Larado took a deep breath. "He wouldn't be *loco* enough to come back to Rusty Spur."

"Maybe not, but there's worse killers in that bunch."

"Oh?" Paco asked.

"Yep. Matter of fact, one was due to hang next week, and now he's loose," Bill said and spat through the gap in his teeth.

Larado began to get a funny feeling deep in his gut. "Who's the condemned man?"

"A rough galoot who killed a lawman a couple of months ago. An *hombre* named Snake Hudson."

Chapter Seventeen

Somewhere in southwest Texas . . .

Snake Hudson took a deep breath and paused, looking around at the rugged landscape of prickly pear and sagebrush. "Damn, these clothes I stole off that line is too tight."

Otto snorted. "At least you got men's clothes. How come I got stuck with the dress?"

"'Cause I'm meaner than you are." Snake grinned, surveying the other man in the pink flowered dress and bonnet. "You look right purty, except you need a shave, lady."

Otto scowled. "That ain't funny. Wonder how far the law is behind us?"

Snake sat down on a rock and examined the soles of his worn-out prison shoes. "They don't know we caught that freight and headed west. Anyhow, what the hell difference does it make?"

"You'll know if them Texas Rangers get us. We should have made a beeline for the Gulf like the others did, caught a tramp steamer out."

Snake rubbed the red scar on his forehead. "Listen, you yellow railroad bum, we got a better chance losin' ourselves in west Texas, and then headin' for the Mexican border."

The big, dirty Otto took off his bonnet and rubbed his ragged beard. "We ain't but about fifty miles from it, if we turn south now."

"Good." Snake grinned with satisfaction, thinking. "We'll steal some more clothes and horses, maybe some guns. I was hopin' to kill a few lawmen before we cross into Mexico."

Otto frowned and scratched himself. "I know one lawman I'd like to kill, but I don't reckon I'll get the chance. He's the one who put me in Huntsville."

Snake shrugged and rolled a cigarette. "I killed me a lawman. That's why I was due to hang next week. I never asked you what you did."

"Gimme a smoke," Otto demanded, and Snake shared his cigarette. "I was drunk and stabbed an *hombre* with a railroad spike, then tried to top a pretty black-haired girl. Tall, she was, with a face like Lillian Russell—plumb beautiful. The sheriff 'bout beat me to a pulp. Left-handed gun, he was. Reckon he would have killed me if she hadn't stopped him."

"Don't find many left-handed guns," Snake grunted and took the cigarette back. Otto resisted, but Snake cuffed him and reclaimed his smoke. "Wonder if I ever ran across him?"

"Donno. I was buildin' the railroad there in Rusty Spur and got a little drunk. I heard her call him Lawrence or something like that."

Instantly Snake perked up. "A left-handed gun? Are you sure about that name? Maybe it could have been Larado?"

"I—I'm not sure. I was drunk as a boiled owl."

Snake mused a moment and shook his head. "Naw, it couldn't be the same one. The one I knew was just a dumb saddle tramp. The gal worth it?"

Otto shook his shaggy head. "Donno that either. He

came after me like she belonged to him. I think I heard him call her name, maybe it started with an *L*."

"Hmm." Snake thought a long moment, remembering how he'd been duped and double-crossed by Larado. He recalled the tall, pretty brunette who worked at the Last Chance. What was the possibility it was the same pair? Still . . . maybe Larado and the pretty Lark were enjoying the bank funds Snake had counted on. "Reckon they laughed about what a sucker I was," he grumbled. The more he thought about it, the madder he got.

"We'd better get a move on," Otto said. "I don't want to run across a posse. Rangers might have bloodhounds out."

"Maybe." Snake stood up too, tossing away his smoke. He was getting madder by the minute, thinking of Larado laughing at him while he spent that bank gold. "Where'd you say you saw that galoot?"

Otto scratched his beard. "You mean the lawman? Rusty Spur. Listen, Snake, I got a bigger beef with him than you do—but he's supposed to be a fast gun and he's tough as a longhorn steak. Revenge would cost too much."

"Speak for yourself, you yellow-bellied coward. You think I'd enjoy starvin' in Mexico, knowin' that double-crosser might be in Rusty Spur, enjoyin' that money I stole and laughin' at me?" Snake scowled and ground his teeth.

"It ain't worth it, Snake," Otto argued. "You might get killed."

"It'd be worth it to me to risk gettin' killed."

"Let's just head for the border like we planned."

"Shut your damn face afore I shut it for you. I reckon he's got all that bank money hid, waitin' for things to cool off so's he can spend it."

"What money?"

"None of your damned business. You can go on to Mexico, but I'm goin' to Rusty Spur. It's near Abilene, ain't it?"

Otto nodded. "You're *loco*. You'll run right into a posse, and they'll string you up *pronto*."

Snake grinned. "I know this country, reckon I can avoid them. See you in Mexico, maybe. I got to see a man about a bank job."

"He'll kill you," Otto cautioned, hiking up his dress and scratching his rump.

"Maybe not." Snake ground his teeth with rage. "I survived tanglin' with an *hombre* with a bull whip; I reckon I can deal with a lawman. I'm a pretty damned good shot."

Otto shrugged. "Don't say I didn't warn you."

"I owe him," Snake snarled. "And besides, it might be interestin' to see who's the fastest gun. Now tell me how I get to this hick town."

Otto squatted, picked up a stick, and drew in the dirt. "If you can get to this point here, you could catch the new train into town. It arrives at high noon on Saturdays."

Snake grinned. "Sounds good. *Adios*, Otto, drink a few bottles of tequila for me when you get to Mexico."

"*If* I get to Mexico," Otto said. He started walking south through the brush and prickly pear.

Snake watched him go, a ridiculous figure in a pink flowered dress and bonnet. Otto would draw too much attention if he got near any ranch and get shot. Snake didn't want to be anywhere near that moving target. Somewhere up ahead, there was bound to be a ranch where Snake could steal fresh supplies. He started walking through the brush.

Sure enough, only a couple of miles north, Snake found a ranch with nobody home. He got food, good clothes, new boots, a couple of guns, and a really good horse from the barn. If anyone tried to stop him along the trail, he'd pass himself off as a local rancher. And if they got too suspicious, he'd kill them. He didn't intend to be stopped 'til he'd gotten his revenge on that double-crossing Larado.

* * *

Meanwhile, back in the Rusty Spur sheriff's office, Larado paused, squinting at the new wire the telegraph operator had just run inside to hand him. "Bill, I—I got dust in my eyes," he lied, blinking. "Read it to me."

"My hands shake so bad, it'll be a problem—but I'll try," the old man said. "'Texas Rangers have caught most of the breakout gang near Galvestion. Stop. Condemned killer Snake Hudson and another man, Otto Swartz, thought to be headed west or south to Mexico. Stop. Texas Rangers requesting every able-bodied man to join a posse. Stop. Must catch them before they make the border. Stop.'"

Larado took a deep breath. *Snake Hudson and Otto.* Otto didn't worry him. He reckoned the cowardly railroader would head straight for the border, but Snake was something else. Larado would never feel safe until the *hombre* was cold as a dead armadillo. Worse than that, Snake would be merciless to anyone who got in his way. No doubt there'd be some dead men along whatever path he took.

Paco walked up just then and shook his head. "You know this Snake Hudson?"

Larado nodded. "Yep, and he's mean as a rattlesnake. See how many men you can round up for a posse. Tell them there's probably a reward for most of them escaped convicts."

"*Sí*, Boss. I'll get my rifle and meet you back here."

"About thirty minutes," Larado called after him. "Tell them to bring blankets and grub. We'll be out a long time."

"I'll get my horse." Bill turned and limped away.

Larado watched the two go. Maybe he'd better tell Lark what was happening. He strode down to the millinery shop.

There were two ladies in the shop trying on hats.

"Mornin' ladies." He tipped his hat and waited patiently for them to finish and leave the shop.

Now Lark confronted him. "What are you doing here? I thought we had finished whatever business we had together."

"We got a problem, Lark." He was so serious, she paused and looked long at him.

"What is it?" She was suddenly afraid because he appeared so grim.

"Snake Hudson was on death row at Huntsville, but he and a bunch of others have escaped, including Otto."

"Oh my." She thought a minute, then shrugged. "They'll head for Galveston or the Mexican border." She began to rearrange a hat display.

"Maybe not." Larado shook his head. "Although that would be the smart thing to do. Rangers have wired all the law enforcement to mount up posses and give them a hand."

She took a deep breath. "You aren't going? No better than you shoot?"

"I got to, Lark. What would people think if I don't?"

"Land's sake, someone's got to protect the town."

"From what? Magnolia? A couple of hound dogs and old Miss Wiggly?" He gestured and she turned to look out the window. Besides Magnolia chomping on the hotel flower box contents, the only visible living things were two brown dogs asleep in the middle of Main Street and the old lady mincing along the sidewalk on her weekly trip to the general store.

"Well, if it's peaceful, you made it that way," she said. "You and your legend of being an ex–Texas Ranger."

"Yeah, and to keep that legend alive, I'll have to go on this posse. Paco's organizin' the men now."

She was afraid for him, but she didn't dare admit it. "You think every man will go?"

"Most will because it'll be fun to get away from their wives. They'll camp out, tell tall tales, drink whiskey, and maybe never get within fifty miles of the escaped convicts."

"Men!" she snorted in derision. "All right, go on. See if I care whether you get shot or not."

He turned and looked at her. "Would you care?"

"Hell no, but Dixie might."

"I thought you might give me a kiss for good luck." He grinned at her.

"You know better than that."

"Well, see you when I get back."

"Maybe not. I might pack up and leave town."

He paused in the doorway. "Sweetie, I'd hate that." Before she could answer, he turned and went out, taking long strides down the wooden sidewalk. Even with his poor vision, he could see a big crowd of mounted men gathered in front of the sheriff's office. Good, it looked like most every man in town was going.

"Come on!" Paco yelled. "I got your horse saddled."

Larado nodded and quickened his step, watching the posse rather than the wooden sidewalk ahead. That's when he made a misstep and hung his spur on a loose board. He tried to catch himself as he went down, but he was too late. He cried out at the sharp pain as he fell.

The wooden sidewalk came up to meet him, and he hit hard, knocking the breath from his lungs. He lay there a long moment, only aware of the pain ripping through his right leg. Paco dismounted and yelled for the doctor. Behind him, he heard Lark running out of her shop, asking what had happened. He closed his eyes and winced in pain, feeling a wet kiss across his face. "Lark?"

He opened his eyes to stare up into Magnolia's big brown ones as her wet mouth nuzzled his face. "Damned donkey."

Now there was a crowd of men gathering around.

Lark knelt beside him. "Are you hurt?"

Hurt? What a stupid question. Of course he was hurt. His right leg felt as if it were on fire. From somewhere, he heard the gruff voice of old Doc ordering, "Let me through, let me through, please."

Larado tried to get to his feet and almost made it, but when he put pressure on that right leg, it folded under him. Paco and Doc caught him, lowering him to the sidewalk again.

"Damn it, I'll be just fine," he said. "Let me up."

He looked up into Lark's worried face. She took out a dainty hankie and wiped cold sweat from his face.

The elderly doctor was feeling his leg, pulling on it. "Does that hurt?"

"Ow! Damn it, yes, it hurts. Quit yankin' on it. Put a bandage on it, and let's get movin'."

Doc shook his head. "Hate to tell you this, Sheriff, but you can't sit a horse with that leg."

"What? I've got to lead a posse."

Doc chewed the end of his white mustache and shook his head. "Somebody else is gonna have to do that, Sheriff. Maybe you can stand if I can get a splint on it."

"Naw." Larado shook his head and tried to get to his feet again. "It ain't bad, just put a bandage on it."

"He's a little stubborn," Lark said to the doctor.

"A little?" Doc snorted. "Why, he's worse than Magnolia here."

The donkey promptly brayed at his insult, and the horses nickered and stamped nervously at the ungodly noise.

Doc turned to Paco. "Some of you men carry him up to my office, and I'll see if I can splint it. He ought to be good as new in a few weeks."

"A few weeks?" Larado roared. "I can't be down a few weeks. We've got a posse."

"I'll lead it," Paco said. "I'm a good shot—maybe not as good as you, boss, but I'll do the best I can."

"I won't be left behind," Larado insisted.

"Oh, yes, you will." Doc turned and looked toward Lark. She nodded. "Do what you can with the stubborn coot, Doc, and have the boys carry him to the house. I can close the shop for the day."

With Larado still protesting, four men carried him down to Doc's office where the old sawbones ripped his pants, splinted the leg, and had the men take Larado to the house. Later, he watched glumly from the settee as the posse rode past the window. "If this ain't a sorry state of affairs."

"Oh, shut up, and I'll fix you some chicken soup."

"I don't want chicken soup. I want a big bowl of chili, hot peppers, and a cold beer."

"Knowing the way I cook, you'd eat my chili?"

"Why not?" he snapped. "Nothing worse could happen to me today, so I reckon your cookin' won't kill me."

"Thanks a lot. You're lucky, you know that? At least the posse won't find out you're half blind and can't shoot well enough to hit a bull in the ass with a bass fiddle."

"I'm the sheriff. I'm supposed to be leadin' the posse."

She looked at him a long moment. "You know, I think you're beginning to take this sheriff thing seriously."

He scowled at her. "I reckon I am. For a minute I almost forgot I'm nothin' but a saddle tramp."

She started to say something, shrugged, and went into the kitchen.

"Hey, sweetie," he called, "since we're back together—"

"We aren't back together," she snapped, looking around the door at him. "I was the only one available to look after you. What I'd like to do is what folks usually do to a horse with a broken leg—shoot you."

"Yeah, and you'd enjoy doin' it, too, wouldn't you?"

She grinned. "Don't tempt me, cowboy."

Snake Hudson rode northwest on his stolen horse. He camped overnight, then started out again toward the town of Rusty Spur. "Just you wait, Larado," he promised as he rode. "I want to see you sweat and beg before I shoot you down, you double-crossin' sonovabitch."

Suppose the sheriff of Rusty Spur turned out not to be Larado? Snake grinned. Then he'd kill the lawman just for the fun of it.

After a couple of days, his stolen horse went lame. Now he was afoot, and there was nothing a cowpoke hated as much as being afoot. Snake began to walk, swearing at every step in the July heat. Somewhere up ahead he heard a noise that sounded like a cross between a man moaning and a cat being tortured. *Injuns?* He didn't give a damn about who was being tortured, but maybe he could steal a horse. Cautiously he dismounted and sneaked closer. Three white men sat around a camp fire.

One of them plunked on a guitar and they all sang: ". . . Oh, come sit by my side ere you leave me, do not hasten to bid me adieu, just remember the Red River Valley and the one who loved you so trueeee . . . ."

Snake winced at the sound. It reminded him of coyotes howling. He ought to shoot them *hombres* to stop their damned noise. Except he hated to waste the bullets.

At that point one of the three attempted to yodel, and it was so bad that even their ugly horses laid their ears back and whinnied in disgust.

Again he was tempted to kill the singers and put them out of their misery. No, maybe he'd wait. He could use some rest. Later, he'd kill the men and steal their supplies. He put his hand to his mouth and yelled, "Hallo the camp!"

"Hallo yourself!" yelled a man with a strange accent. It was definitely not a Texas drawl.

Snake was cautious as he peeked through the sagebrush. "Can I come in and set a spell?"

"You can come in and visit, if that's what you mean," said another man with the same strange accent.

Snake strode close enough to take a good look and grinned. There were three of them, and they looked as out of place as a pimple on Lillian Russell's beautiful face. "I'm lost and hungry," he yelled. "You got any coffee?"

"We got tea." One stood up. He was short and round, with the same features as the other two.

"Tea? Cowboys don't drink tea." Snake snorted as he walked into camp.

"They don't? Couldn't prove it by us."

Snake looked over the three greenhorns and relaxed. "You all Yankees?"

"Yeah. Why does everyone in this part of the country talk slow and say y'all?"

"'Cause this is Texas," Snake said. "God's country."

"Oh," said the short, fat one. "We're the Bloggett brothers from New Jersey. Welcome, stranger, you can have a bite with us. We're Clem, Lem, and Slim."

"Let me guess," Snake said, "you must be Slim."

He nodded. "Would you like a bagel?"

"What in the hell is that?"

"Something we eat back East."

Snake snorted in disgust. "Ain't you got no real he-man cowboy food like chili and tortillas?"

The three looked at each other with their big, bushy eyebrows raised, then shook their heads.

"It gives Lem gas," the fat one explained.

He ought to kill all three of them just because they annoyed him, Snake thought. But on the other hand, they were amusing, and he was tired. He squatted by the fire, rubbing his hands together. "What the hell are three greenhorns from New Jersey doing down here in Texas?"

"I'm Clem, pleased to meet you." The thin one stood up and offered his hand, which Snake ignored. "We owned a broom factory in Newark, but we've been reading Ned Buntline's books about the Old West."

Slim nodded. "We want to be rootin', tootin' cowpokes."

"Well, you look like damn fools." Snake looked them over. They wore Stetsons too large for them, brand-new denims, fancy boots, and the furry chaps of the high plains country. He reached to pour himself a cup from the big pot. He shuddered when he tasted the tea. "If you're gonna learn to be Texans, you got to learn to drink strong coffee and good whiskey."

Lem said, "We don't much care for either."

Snake laughed. "You'll never make it as cowboys."

"We got pistols." Slim stood up and showed off the new six-gun in his fancy holster.

"Can you shoot it?"

They all looked embarrassed and shook their heads.

"Fine cowboys you are." Snake spat to one side. "Texas babies cut their teeth on a gun barrel."

"Maybe you could teach us?" Clem's voice was hopeful.

"Reckon not. I'm in a hurry."

"Who are you and where you going, stranger?" Lem asked.

"The first thing you'd better learn if you're gonna stay alive in this state is not to ask questions," Snake snapped, tossing the rest of the tea into the fire. "I got to hunt down a fella."

All three men's eyes widened. "You a lawman?"

"Hell, no, I ain't no lawman, I'm a gunfighter."

All three sighed loudly. "Did you know Billy the Kid?"

Snake shook his head. "He wasn't so much anyways. He got shot."

They looked at each other and then at him. "We been looking for someone to teach us about being a gunfighter. See? We're wearing our guns tied low and practicing our quick draw."

"You got your holsters tied low enough to pull your pants down," Snake guffawed. "Real gunmen don't wear their pistols like that."

"Now how should we know? We ain't never met a real gunfighter before," Slim said. "Could we ride along with you? We keep getting lost."

"Hell, no. I'm on my way to kill me a sheriff, and I don't want to drag along no greenhorns. You got anything to eat? Maybe some beans?"

They shook their heads.

"Gives Lem gas," Slim said.

"You seen any posses?" Snake asked.

"Bunch of men passed us this morning, said they was looking for escaped convicts."

"Is that a fact?" Snake rolled a cigarette and lit it with a branch from the campfire.

"Said they was from the town of Rusty Spur. That's a funny name for a town, so I remembered it." Clem said.

"Sheriff with them? Tall, handsome, dark young *hombre*?"

Slim shook his head. "Said the sheriff was hurt, so they left him behind."

Snake grinned without mirth. "I'll just bet the bastard was. Too yellow to come lookin' for me and feared I'm gonna find him for double-crossin' me."

"You gonna shoot him?" Clem looked hopeful.

"'Course I'm gonna shoot him," Snake assured him. "I'm gonna shoot him down in the street like a dog if'n I get the chance."

"We'd like to be gunfighters," Lem said wishfully. "They all seem so romantic in the dime novels."

"Tell you what you can do," Snake grinned. "You can ride into Rusty Spur and tell him I'm comin' in for a showdown."

"What's a showdown?" asked the thin brother.

Snake sighed audibly. "We meet in the middle of the street and try to kill each other."

"Why?" Clem asked.

"Don't you remember from the dime novels?" Snake said. "'Cause a man's gotta do what a man's gotta do."

"You can't be no gunfighter," Lem, the one with gas, challenged. "'Cause you don't got cold, gray eyes. In the stories, gunfighters always got cold, gray eyes."

Snake frowned. "I'll show you who's got cold, gray eyes. How 'bout if I shoot yours out?"

The three looked at him, mouths open. "We—we ain't got cold, gray eyes."

"It don't matter none." Snake shrugged.

"If you're a gunfighter, have you got notches in your gun?" Slim asked.

Snake snorted in disgust. "Now why would anyone do a fool thing like that?"

"So you can keep up with how many men you've killed," Lem said.

"I can count," Snake said, "and I don't see no need to carve up a good Colt."

The three half-wits had a quick, whispered conference.

Clem asked, "If you're gonna shoot a sheriff, can we go along and be your sidekicks?"

"What in the hell is a sidekick?"

Slim pushed back the too-big Stetson, revealing a balding head. "You know, like your partners."

"If'n I was to want partners, it wouldn't be three little Yankee brothers who couldn't pour piss out of a boot with directions writ on the heel."

"What?"

"Never mind. I tell you what I'll do," Snake said. "I'll let you be my partners if you'll ride into Rusty Spur and tell the sheriff I'm comin'."

"That's better than the dime novels," the three agreed, nodding eagerly. "We'll do it." The three stood up, wearing their new Western clothes and wooly chaps.

"By the way, my horse gave out. You got any money?"

"You can have one of ours," Clem volunteered. "And we got a little money. We was going to buy train tickets back to Newark when we got tired of the wide-open spaces."

Snake looked over the tired old nags tied to the nearby bushes. "Some horse trader seen you galoots comin'. Them's the sorriest nags I ever did see. A self-respectin' hound wouldn't eat 'em, and I damned sure wouldn't be caught dead ridin' one of 'em. Now give me your money."

They hesitated, looking at each other.

"Damn it, I said give me your money."

"Then how we gonna get back to Newark?" Slim quavered.

"Maybe I'll let you help me rob the bank, shoot all the

men, and kiss all the purty women," Snake said. "You can share the loot."

"Is that the same as money?"

Snake sighed. If he didn't need them, he'd kill them. He took the crumpled dollars out of their soft, pink hands. "I might even take the train in." He laughed, thinking. "Just imagine him all sweaty and scared, knowin' I'm comin' in on the train for a showdown at high noon."

"What we don't understand," Lem said, "is why gunfights are always on Main Street. Don't they have no other streets in these Western towns?"

"Reckon not," Snake said, counting the money.

"And why is it always at high noon?" Clem asked.

"So everyone can watch the shootout durin' their dinner hour without missin' any of the action," Snake said.

The three looked at each other, awestruck. "Makes sense, don't it?"

"You three ask too damned many questions," Snake complained. "Get on into Rusty Spur and deliver my message. When I get there, I'll buy you three a drink."

"In a real Wild West saloon?"

"Yep, in a sure 'nuff Texas saloon. You can watch me shoot the sheriff, rob the bank, and kiss the pretty girls."

The three nodded. "He's a Texan, all right, that's how they do it in the dime novels."

They got up and began putting saddles on their horses. It took them a while.

"Fer Gawd's sake," Snake complained, "just go bareback."

"Hurts our butts," Clem said.

"I'll hurt your butts if you don't scat," Snake said. He watched in disgust as they attempted to mount their old nags. "Lord," he grumbled, "you'd never make it if you had to vamoose *pronto*."

"What?"

"Just go!" Snake snapped.

"We'll see you in town, partner," Lem said. "There's some bagels in the knapsack if you're hungry."

And they rode out singing, " . . . oh, bury me not on the lone prairieeee . . ."

Somewhere, a coyote howled in protest.

Snake watched them ride out at a dead walk. "I woulda shot them, but they were too amusin'," he said to himself. He grinned thinking how startled Larado would look when he got the message that Snake was coming for him. "That double-crossin' thief. Wonder what he did with all that bank money? Did he spend it on liquor, cards, and women, or did he just waste it? He couldn't have any left or he wouldn't be workin' as a sheriff."

Well, he might not get his share of the loot, but he'd get the pleasure of killing Larado. Then, like he'd told the Bloggett brothers, he'd rob the bank and kiss all the pretty women. If they were pretty enough, he'd do more than that. Later, just for fun, he'd shoot the Bloggett brothers. Snake dug in the knapsack for some grub, wondering what a bagel was. After he got a little shut-eye and some food, he'd steal another horse, ride to a railroad station, and catch a train.

High noon on Main Street. Yep, it was the code of the West.

Chapter Eighteen

As the evening progressed, Lark had to move Larado off the settee and into the bedroom to make him more comfortable. He put his arm around her shoulders and hopped along as she helped him. She helped him off with his shirt, but there was no way she could get his pants off because of the splints. He'd have to sleep in those. Now he lay grinning on the bed, looking up at her. "We've had some fun on this mattress," he said.

"Land's sake, don't men ever think of anything else, even with their legs broke?"

"Whiskey, and cards, and horses," he answered.

"I swear, I should have had them take you to the hotel," she snapped.

"What would everyone think?"

"They'd have thought I was a terrible wife," she complained, "but I reckon all those women who find you so charming would have been fighting each other for a chance to look after you—especially Dixie."

"I ain't interested in her. I'm interested in you."

"You're such a liar. I can't believe a word you say."

"I'm a Texan—what do you expect?"

She leaned over and fluffed his pillow. "Go to sleep, you arrogant rascal."

He caught her hand. "Ain't there no way I can make it up to you?"

"Be honest with me for a change." She tried to pull away from him, but he hung on to her hand.

"Lark, sweetie, since you think everything I say is a lie, you wouldn't believe me if I did tell you the truth."

"Stop it, Larado," she snapped. "You won't charm me this time."

He let go of her hand, looking depressed. "You're really gonna leave me, is that it?"

"I already have," she reminded him. "I've just let you move back in because of your bum leg. You aren't staying."

He sat up on the edge of the bed. "Then maybe I'd better go ahead and move over to the hotel." He stood up with great difficulty, tried to take a step and stumbled.

Without thinking, Lark slipped under his arm, steadying him. "Take it easy," she said. "You end up in the floor, there's hardly a man left in town to help get you up."

He had his arm around her shoulders, his face inches from hers. "Ain't you the softhearted one?"

"Don't you try to charm me, you rascal. I know you could talk a cow out of her calf, but you aren't changing my mind."

He sighed. "I know I'm a bad *hombre*, but you're the only woman who ever made me want to stay instead of just driftin' on."

Their faces were only inches apart. His dark eyes were so earnest, his mouth so downturned and vulnerable. She almost melted, then remembered and shook her head. "Get back in that bed before I take you up on your offer and let you limp all the way down to the hotel."

"You're a hard woman, sweetie."

"And don't you forget it. Here's a crutch Doc left for you. Go sit in the kitchen and I'll cook you some food."

He put the crutch under his arm and limped toward the kitchen. "That oughta finish off a sick man," he muttered.

"What did you say?"

"I said I'm really lookin' forward to dinner."

"If you'd wear your spectacles you wouldn't have tripped and fallen," she scolded. She followed him into the kitchen and sliced off some of the crusty bread Mrs. Bottoms had sent over. Then she got out the skillet to scramble some eggs.

He shook his head. "You know what would happen to my reputation in this town if anyone caught me wearin' specs like an old geezer? Everyone would laugh and laugh. I'd have to leave town."

"It seems to me," she said as she made coffee, "that shouldn't bother you. Haven't you been a saddle tramp all your life?"

"Yep, and I think I'm tired of it. Rolling stones gather no moss—and no respect, neither."

"Then why don't you stop running when the going gets tough and face up to life?"

He turned in his chair and looked at her. "Is that the pot callin' the kettle black?"

She flinched. "Reckon I deserved that."

"Lark, I'm sorry. I shouldn't have said that. I didn't mean to hurt you."

"We seem to be a bad fit, Larado."

"Maybe we're just too much alike—but that could be good."

"Don't kid yourself." She began to scramble eggs and slice bacon. "We're like fire and kerosene together."

"But, oh, we make a hot flame, don't we?" He grinned at her and she felt her face flush.

"Don't talk to me, you scoundrel."

He didn't say anything more while she concentrated on getting the food ready and putting it before him. She kept her voice cold. "With that broken leg, you'll be more comfortable in the bed tonight."

He looked up, eyes alit.

"I mean *alone,*" she said. "I'll sleep on the settee."

"I might need something in the middle of the night," he said. "Maybe if you'd sleep next to me—"

"If you need something, you can yell loud enough to reach that settee just about ten feet away, can't you?"

"I reckon." He began to gobble the food. "Honest, Lark, your cookin' is improvin'."

"Don't try to be nice to me, Larado. It'd take years for me to learn to cook an egg so a dog could eat it."

"Maybe I'm not as picky as a dog. I'd eat your cookin' anytime."

"Thanks a lot." She began to eat, thinking maybe he was right, it wasn't as bad as it had been in the past.

He pushed back his empty plate with a sigh and sipped his coffee. "I feel dirty as a pig in a puddle. I could use a bath."

"With me helping, no doubt?"

He grinned. "Thanks, I'd like that."

"You can just go dirty 'til Paco gets back in from the posse. How long you think they'll be gone?"

He shrugged. "I don't know, maybe a week or two. I don't know about the other convicts, but Snake'll leave a trail of dead all along the route to Mexico. I won't breathe easy 'til he's killed or captured."

"They'll get him," Lark assured him. "You can't help it you couldn't go, Larado. Right now, with that bad leg, you'd slow the posse down."

He took his crutch, hobbled to the window, and looked out. "This town is really dull with most of the men gone."

"They aren't all gone—Wilbur Barclay and Abner Snootley didn't go, plus old Doc and Bill down at the telegraph office."

"The banker and Snootley ought to be ashamed of themselves for not goin'. The other two are too old." He stared out the window.

"Knowing the first two, are you surprised? Besides, they'd probably say they stayed behind to protect the town in case some rowdies try to take advantage of most of the men being gone."

"I don't reckon there's much can happen in a few days," he said, staring out the window. "Nothin' that I can't handle."

"Not unless they find out you can't shoot."

He turned and looked at her. "It ain't that I can't shoot," he corrected her. "With my specs on, I'm not too bad."

"With any luck, you'll keep bluffing bad guys and never have to shoot anyone. By the way, just how did that start about being an ex–Texas Ranger?"

He looked at her innocently. "I'm sure I wouldn't have any idea."

"Uh-huh."

"Magnolia's out again," he said, staring out the window.

"So what else is new? She's sort of become the town mascot."

"I'll tell you one thing," Larado laughed, "she sure lets you know she's around. She brayed and caused a team to run away the other day."

"I'll take her around back and lock her up," Lark said, "but she'll be out again before morning."

He yawned. "Reckon we might as well think about goin' to bed again."

"You go right ahead on," Lark said. "After I put away Magnolia, I'll clean up the kitchen. Then tomorrow, I've got to open the shop. Will you be all right going back to work tomorrow?"

He nodded. "I'll use my crutch and hobble around town some. Most people will come to the office if they need anything. But if old Miss Wiggly's cat gets up in a tree, it'll just have to stay there until Paco returns. Help me back to bed?"

"All right." She slipped under his big arm and they limped back into the bedroom. He turned his head ever so slightly and kissed her cheek.

"Stop it, Larado."

"I was just thankin' you for helpin' me." His voice and

expression were so appealing, her heart almost melted. She wanted to return that kiss, and it would be so easy. All she had to do was turn her face ever so slightly and their lips would touch. Then she wouldn't be able to stop what would happen next. No, she wouldn't *want* to stop what would happen next.

"Here," she said, dumping him unceremoniously on the bed. "I'm going out and put up Magnolia. Then I'll make myself a place on the settee."

"You'll find out it's pretty hard."

She frowned at him. "Not as hard as my heart."

"Reckon you got that right."

"What?"

"Nothin', sweetie." He grinned at her.

"Don't call me 'sweetie'." She went out the back door and slammed it hard. She caught Magnolia and penned her up, feeding her, Chico, and the buggy horse. Lark came in and cleaned up the kitchen. Then she got herself a blanket and went to bed on the settee. From the bedroom, she could hear Larado's gentle breathing and wondered if he was asleep or only pretending to be. How she wanted to go to him—but she was certain he had never really cared about her, that he only wanted to amuse himself with her before he drifted on to the next town. The only way out of this mess was to pack up and leave town. Yes, that's what she was going to do. It was only a matter of time.

From her fine new apartment over the bank, Dixie could see the sheriff's house. She stood there at her window now as darkness came on, watching the lamp lights glowing from the small place and wishing she were the one in there fixing supper for Larado. Later, they would be warm and cozy in bed together. . . .

"You coming to bed?" yelled Wilbur Barclay.

"So you can climb all over me? No thanks!"

"I pay enough for the privilege," he complained.

She turned and looked at him. He was a fat, balding pig. "I hate being with you."

"Oh, shut up, you slut. You got clothes, jewels. What else could you want?"

"Love," she said, looking toward the sheriff's little house.

"You come to bed, you whore, and I'll give you plenty of love."

"That ain't what I mean, and you know it."

He smiled at her. "We ain't foolin' each other, Dixie. We each got something out of this deal."

She sighed and began slipping out of her dress and into an expensive purple nightgown. "I think maybe it cost too much."

He reached for her and seemed to ignore the fact that she was stiff and wooden in his arms. "If it weren't for me, you'd be working some cheap crib in a cowtown. Instead of just me, you'd have a dozen men every night. Now give me what I pay for."

"All right." She lay down on the bed without enthusiasm. He didn't seem to notice—or maybe he didn't care—as he jerked open her bodice. "Don't rip it," she complained as he nuzzled her full breasts. "It cost plenty."

"You think I don't know that? Hell, I paid for it."

He climbed on her and handled her roughly, kissing her mouth with wet lips. She let her mind go far away and imagined that it was Larado who embraced her.

After a moment, Barclay was finished with her. "You slut, you could have at least acted like you liked it."

"You know better than that." She wiped his kiss from her lips and turned over.

"Someday, Dixie, I'm gonna dump you."

"Need I remind you about the letter I gave my sister? If anything happens to me, my sister in Atlanta's gonna turn it over to the law. You'll go to jail for what happened in Buck Shot."

"You bitch. I'm not sure I believe there is a letter."

"It's the truth."

"Is it? I just had a private detective do some investigating. I just got a reply yesterday, and guess what?"

A sudden chill went up her back, and she didn't answer.

"It seems you don't have a sister."

"Well, she—she's not really my sister, she's a good friend."

"Uh-huh. And to think I've let you blackmail me all these months. You better keep me happy, you slut, or I may just decide I can live without you."

He'd kill her without a second thought, she realized. And that would protect him from any charges over Buck Shot. She rolled over toward him. "Now, honey," she crooned, "you know I was just in a bad mood. You want me again? Here, let me make you happy."

She began to kiss his bald head. After a moment, his fat, sweaty hand grabbed her breast and pulled her to him. She was going to have to do something soon because now that Barclay knew the truth, her life was in danger. *What to do?* There was no way she could escape with the bank's money—she knew now that Barclay would never give her the combination to the new safe. She wanted Larado, but that wasn't going to happen. Who else was available who had enough money to help her? As Barclay pawed her naked body again, she coolly went through a mental file of every available man in town.

In her mind, Dixie saw Mrs. Snootley. The woman often made trips to Abilene to buy the latest styles. That must mean the general store did pretty well. Old Abner Snootley had looked her over several times with that yearning, lusty look she knew so well. Tomorrow, she vowed, she would make a play for the old codger. Mrs. Snootley was out of town again. Maybe Dixie could seduce the old man into cleaning out his safe and running off with her. That would put her out of the banker's reach. Beyond that, she had no plan—but she'd always struggled to survive, this bastard daughter of a rebel whore and a Yankee soldier. Life was tough in postwar Atlanta, and she was on the streets by the time she was fifteen. Yes, tomorrow she would seduce old Snootley.

Lark awoke at dawn on Friday and sat up, almost groaning aloud. Larado was right, this settee was miserable. Well, she wasn't about to sleep in the bed with him. With his charm, he'd have her in his arms and on top of him to compensate for his splinted leg. She went in and shook Larado awake. "Are you all right?"

His dark eyes flickered open and he grinned. "Glory be. Are you an angel, or am I dreamin'?" He caught her hand and kissed her fingertips.

"Or maybe your worst nightmare," she snapped, pulling out of his grasp. "I'll fix you something to eat, and then I'm going to open the shop. You gonna be able to manage today?"

He sat up, gloriously bare chested, and stretched. His muscles flexed and rippled. She found herself staring at him. "I'll manage okay," he said. "There's nothin' much gonna happen with almost every man gone on the posse. I can hobble down to my office and maybe do a little paperwork."

"Remember to take your specs, then."

"All right. I don't reckon anyone will see me wearin' them."

"That wouldn't be the worst thing that could happen," she said, pausing in the bedroom doorway.

"Ha! For a tough Texas sheriff to be caught wearin' glasses? Are you kiddin'? I'd have to leave town."

"Sooner or later, Larado, we've both got to quit running when things get too tough."

He snorted. "Speak for yourself, sweetie."

"All right, I deserved that." She went into the kitchen and began making coffee.

"Hey," he yelled from the bedroom. "I could use some help gettin' dressed."

"I don't think so!" she yelled back. "I'm not stupid enough to get close to you with you rested and half naked."

"You're not at all trustin'."

"Let's just say I know you, you rascal. How do you want your eggs?"

"Sunny side up."

She did her best, but she broke the yolks as she tried awkwardly to get the eggs in the skillet. "You're getting them scrambled."

"Then why did you bother to ask?" He came into the kitchen, still bare chested and barefoot, his hair damp from washing. He hobbled up behind her and put one arm around her, beginning to kiss the back of her neck.

She felt the goose bumps start up her skin with the warmth of him and the hardness of his erection against her back. She resisted the urge to turn in his arms and kiss him the way she yearned to. "Stop it," she ordered. "One of us is going to get burnt."

"Okay," he sighed, hobbling over to take a chair at the kitchen table. "What kind of day is it going to be?"

She dished up the food and joined him at the table. "What's July always like in Texas? Hotter than hell with the lid off."

"My leg is itchy and sweaty under the splints," he complained as he sipped the coffee and shuddered.

"Oh, hush. Maybe there'll be some interesting new settlers on the train tomorrow." She glanced toward the front windows. "Oh my, I see the banker's wife is out early today."

He sipped his coffee. "Oh, she comin' here?"

"You want her to?"

"Honestly, Lark, sweetie, what kind of question is that? You sound like a jealous wife."

"Oh, shut up." She got up and went to the window. "No,

she's headed down toward the general store. Funny, I thought she had a maid who ran all the errands for her."

"What do we care?" Larado yawned and scratched that bare, magnificent body.

"I wish you'd put a shirt on."

He grinned. "Look your fill, lady."

"Oh shut up, you scoundrel. In a minute, I'll help you with your boots." She returned to watching Dixie walk down the wooden sidewalk, her bustle wiggling.

Mr. Abner Snootley looked up as the bell rang on the front door of his store. It was the banker's wife, what a beauty. He came out from behind the counter, nodding and smiling. "Morning, Mrs. Barclay, what can I do for you today? Awfully early for a lady to be out."

She smiled at him, and his insides churned. It had been a long time since a woman had looked at him that way. He searched his memory. No, even Bertha had never looked at him that way. Certainly, his cold wife hadn't slept with him or even kissed him in the last several years. He felt as nervous as a rattlesnake on a hot griddle as he popped a peppermint in his mouth.

"Well"—she smiled even bigger, her long eyelashes fluttering—"I don't know, I thought I'd just look around to see what you've got to offer."

She wore a pink dress with lots of lace, drawing attention to her big bosom as she took deep breaths. He took a couple of deep breaths himself, looking at her. She wore a musky, strong perfume and twirled a lace parasol.

His hands started shaking, and he almost choked on his peppermint. "You don't see what you want, I can order it—ship it in on the train." He could use a big order. Bertha's constant trips had put him in heavy debt. He didn't see how he was going to make it even one more month, unless a miracle happened.

The blonde came over to him, laid her small hand on

his arm, and gave it a slight squeeze. "You are so accommodating," she drawled.

"I do love your accent," he stammered. "You're a real Southern lady. We don't see women of your class in this town. I reckon your rich husband just spoils you rotten."

Tears came to her eyes. "Well, money doesn't buy everything, you know." She turned away and wiped her eyes.

He felt awkward, but he offered her his handkerchief. "You got that right. I thought when I married Bertha and her rich uncle funded this store, things would be great—but it hasn't turned out that way."

She walked up and down, looking at merchandise. "Bertha out of town again?"

"She's always out of town, always gone to Abilene buying stuff," he complained.

She whirled and looked up at him. "Reckon your store must do pretty well to allow her to do that."

He smiled. "I can't complain." His ego wouldn't allow him to tell her that no one controlled Bertha and that he was on the verge of bankruptcy if things didn't change soon.

"Dear Mr. Snootley—"

"Call me Abner, please." He lowered his voice, a little shaken, but pleased to be taken into such confidence by this beautiful wife of the richest man in town.

"Abner," she corrected herself with a smile, leaning toward him. "I just thought I might buy something amusing in your store for myself. You know, all my husband thinks of is work, work, work. I get so lonely."

He couldn't take his gaze off those full breasts as she leaned closer. He lowered his voice. "I get lonely myself sometimes. Of course everyone thinks all I think of is running this store, but sometimes I wish Bertha was as interested in me as she is in clothes."

She paused and looked up at him, running her pink tongue along her full lips. The gesture made his heart hammer. His hands shook as he popped another peppermint in his mouth.

"My husband just doesn't pay one bit of attention to me. I swear, sometimes I just want to get on that train when it comes through and leave town. 'Course it would take a very interestin' and intellectual man to make me leave my husband."

Did she think he was interesting and intellectual? She had him so stirred up, he couldn't think straight. "Mrs. Barclay, maybe I shouldn't say this, but I've been watchin' you since the day you came to town."

She smiled and leaned closer, and he smelled the scent of perfume wafting up between her full breasts. "And I've been watching you. Do you believe in fate, Abner?"

He was almost drunk with her closeness and the smell of her perfume. "I—I don't know. Maybe." Frankly, he had never given it a thought.

She put her hand on his arm and squeezed. "Maybe we were fated to meet," she whispered. "And maybe if we both got on that noon train tomorrow, we could find happiness such as we've never known."

He hesitated. There wasn't twenty dollars in the cash register, and his debts were mounting—but hell, this rich beauty was offering to run away with him. She wanted him, Abner Snootley, and she'd have tons of money from her rich husband's bank.

"The noon train tomorrow?" He licked his lips, trying to make a decision. Bertha might be coming in on that train. It would serve her right if she found him gone. And wouldn't the town gossip be delicious? He could already imagine the headlines in the *Rusty Spur Beacon:* PROMINENT CITIZEN RUNS OFF WITH BEAUTIFUL, RICH WOMAN. All the men at the cafe would look at each other and say, "Boy, I wish it had been me. Abner must have really known how to wow the lady and make her want to drop her drawers."

"The noon train tomorrow." She paused in the doorway and blew him a kiss. Then she walked out the door and down the street. He stared after her, all aroused, his hands shaking with excitement. Tomorrow night he might be in some fine hotel in Kansas City, paid for with the banker's money, making love to that beautiful blonde. Why, she was almost as pretty and desirable as the sheriff's wife—but of course, he knew that if he even looked twice at Sheriff Witherspoon's woman, the sheriff would beat him to a pulp.

Dixie hummed to herself as she walked along the sidewalk. The old fool had fallen for it. All she had to do was pack and keep Wilbur from finding out until she was safely on that train. Of course, she was going to have to put up with that clumsy old fool's wet peppermint kisses, but that was the story of her life. By the time she went through the store owner's money, some other man would come along, and she'd dump Snootley without a second thought. She was a survivor, and tomorrow was another day. As she passed Larado's office, she decided to drop in. If he'd only give her some hope, she'd stop all this nonsense and run away with him. She'd rather be poor and sleeping in Larado's arms than rich and sleeping in any other man's.

She stuck her head in his door. "Hi there. You doin' okay after that bad fall?"

He looked up from his desk, and she could see the boredom on his rugged features. "Oh, hello, Dixie. You're up awfully early."

"Ain't you gonna ask me to come in?"

"Sure, sure," he gestured. "Take a load off."

She sat down on the corner of his cluttered desk. "That ain't no way to talk to a lady."

"We both know you ain't no lady. What do you want?"

"I came to say good-bye. I think I might leave town."

"Oh? Okay."

Could he be any more disinterested? She wanted to slap

him, but of course she didn't. "I think I'm in danger from the banker."

He shrugged. "No wonder. Most folks don't take kindly to blackmail."

"I was protectin' you, Larado."

He grinned. "Don't make me laugh, kid. You're lookin' after yourself, just like always."

She gave him her most bewitching look. "I'd like to be leavin' with you."

He shook his head. "We've been over this before, Dixie. I hate to admit it, but Lark's the girl I care about."

"That don't seem to be goin' too well, does it?"

He shook his head ruefully. "But that don't change it."

"All right. I thought I'd just give you the chance to change your mind. Most of the men in town are gone. Maybe we could rob the bank and leave together."

"And leave this town without a sheriff?"

She made a dismissing gesture. "Who the hell cares about this town?"

"I've begun to, Dixie. I feel like this is my town now; I belong here."

"Don't be a fool. They ever find out about your past, they'd either fire you or lynch you."

He leaned back in his chair. "That's a chance I take."

She reached over and put her hand on his arm. "You're a damned stubborn fool, Larado. With what's in the bank, we could live the rest of our days in New York or Chicago, and you'd have me in your bed every night."

"Good-bye, Dixie," he said softly with a nod of dismissal. "I wish you well."

He looked past Dixie's shoulder, and she saw the sudden widening of his eyes. She whirled. Lark stood outside the window, staring in at them. Then she raised her head high and marched off down the street.

"Damn it," he said, struggling to his feet with the crutch. "Now you've done it."

"Aw, she ain't gonna believe you, whatever you tell

her," Dixie said. "Forget about her, and let's clear out of this hick town."

"Dixie, get the hell out of my office. You've just messed up any chance I had of changin' her mind."

"You're a fool, Larado—a lovesick, honorable fool!" Dixie flounced out of his office and back to her fine apartment. She was out of options. There was nothing to do but run off with that skinny old shop keeper and his money. There was no mistake, she'd seen that look on Lark's face. She was in love with Larado, whether she was willing to admit it or not, and he was certainly in love with her.

It was afternoon when three strange-looking dudes came into his office. "Can I help you, gents?"

The short, fat one nodded. "I'm Slim, and these are my brothers, Clem and Lem."

"I'm guessin' you ain't from around here." Larado smiled at the outfits they were wearing: shiny new boots, Stetsons too large for them, and woolly chaps that he had only seen in Montana and Wyoming.

"I don't know why everyone says that," said the taller brother. "We're here to represent our pard, Snake."

Larado's chair came down on all fours with a bang. "Snake? You seen him?"

"Seen him?" The middle one snorted. "Why, we helped break him out of jail."

Larado doubted that—the trio didn't look like they could open a can of beans alone. "He's heading to the border?"

The three threw back their heads and laughed. "No, he ain't. He's coming here."

"What?"

The fat one leaned on the desk. "You heard me. He's coming in, and he's coming in for you because he wants revenge. Get ready for a showdown!"

Chapter Nineteen

Larado stared at the trio. "You're bluffin'. How do I even know you know Snake Hudson?"

The fat one reached into this pocket for makin's and tried in vain to roll a smoke. The tobacco went everywhere, and he finally gave up in disgust and threw it over his shoulder. "Big guy, ugly as sin."

Larado shrugged. "That could describe half the men in Texas."

The skinny one gestured. "He's got an ugly scar on his forehead. Looks like it might have been made with a whip."

That described Snake, all right. Larado took a deep breath. "Snake comes here, the law'll be waitin' for him. And if you *hombres* are part of his gang, you'd better clear out now."

"We already checked around," the middle one said, hooking his thumbs in his gun belt. He was wearing it so low, it threatened to slide down his hips and hit the floor. He hoisted it back up. "You're the only law within forty miles. We reckon we'll stay around to watch our pard kill you."

Larado took a deep breath. Maybe that would happen, all right. "So when's Snake comin'?"

The trio shook their heads. "Don't know for sure. He said his horse was played out."

"Get outta here before I toss all three of you in jail."

"For what? We ain't done nothin'."

"Litterin'," Larado said, nodding toward the tobacco on the floor.

"Now, Slim, how could you do that?" the skinny one scolded. "What would Mama say?"

Slim immediately dropped to one knee, raked up the mess with his hands, and put in it the spittoon. "Let's go down to the bar and have a drink—and wait for Snake."

They turned to go.

"You reckon they got sarsaparilla?" Clem asked.

"Real men drink whiskey," Slim informed him.

"I can't drink whiskey, it gives me gas," Lem said as they left.

Larado watched them go and chewed his lip, thinking. *Yes, it would be just like Snake to show up here, fooling all the posses.* The town was almost deserted, and it was defenseless. After the outlaw killed Larado, he could rob the bank and rape all the women. Larado couldn't let that happen. He grabbed his crutch and hobbled toward the telegraph office. It was hot as a bear's breath—not a blade of grass stirring. He stuck his head in the door at the station. "Bill, get some telegrams out as fast as you can. Tell all the law enforcement that Snake Hudson is headed to Rusty Spur."

The old man's eyes widened, and he spat toward the spittoon through the gap in his front teeth. "How do you know that?"

"That trio of fools you've seen about town came in to tell me he's gunnin' for me."

The old man's hands shook badly. "I still got a pistol left over from the Civil War, Sheriff. I'll help you stand him off."

"Thanks, Bill, but there's no use you gettin' killed. Snake is a crack shot. He'll probably get me and then take this town apart. Get me some help as fast as you can."

Old Bill shook his head. "I'll do 'er, but it'll be a while before the posse can get back. They're maybe almost to the border by now. Reckon when Snake will get here?"

Larado shook his head. "No way to know except the trio of idiots said his horse had played out. That means he'll either steal one from a local ranch or take the train."

"The train? Surely he wouldn't be fool enough . . . ?"

Larado shrugged. "It's just the kind of grand play he would do, arrive at high noon tomorrow on the train. When you get the wire sent, warn everybody in town to lock their doors and stay inside 'til this is over."

"Don't you want I should try to round up some help?"

Larado laughed, but he did not feel humorous. "Now, Bill, you know every available man has left with the posse, except you and Doc, the cowards, and the bums at the saloon who wouldn't do nothin' to help a lawman."

Bill made ready to tap out the message with his shaking hands. "Maybe you should clear out, Sheriff, if he's comin' for you. With four of them, you ain't got much chance."

Larado leaned on his crutch. "Snake's the only one I'm worried about. Now get that message sent."

The telegraph keys were tapping fast as Larado hobbled out of the office. All these women, children, and old people were in danger with Snake in town and no one to stop him. Larado didn't want to panic anyone, but the public needed to be warned. He hobbled over to the hotel.

"Mrs. Bottoms, I want you to stay calm, but you've got to spread the word."

"What's wrong?" She peered at him over her spectacles.

"Snake Hudson's avoided the posse and headin' this way."

"Heavens. Well, maybe he won't come to Rusty Spur."

Larado frowned. "No, he's comin' here. He and I have old business and he wants a showdown."

Mrs. Bottoms smiled. "Well, that just shows what a fool

he is, takin' on a tough sheriff like you. I reckon after you kill him, we'll bury him in boot hill."

Larado shook his head. "It ain't that easy." He hesitated, not wanting to say her trust was misplaced. Now he considered running, leaving the town on its own and at Snake's mercy. "You just spread the word for the next couple of days to stay inside and keep the kids off the streets."

"I'll do it." She nodded.

He hobbled to the door.

"And, Sheriff, good luck."

He nodded, knowing he was going to need all the luck he could get, and so was the town.

He limped down to the bank. Dixie was acting as cashier behind the wire cage. "Hello, Sheriff, to what do I owe the pleasure of this visit?"

"This ain't a visitin' call, Dixie. Snake's comin'."

Her face turned ashen. "Here? He's comin' here? How do you know?"

"I ain't got time for all this." Larado cut off her questions with a gesture. "He's comin', maybe on the noon train tomorrow. You'd better warn your husband, because you know if he gets a chance, Snake will clean out the bank."

"Okay, but he's really coming for a showdown with you, ain't he?"

"Yeah, thanks to you, I reckon."

She didn't look him in the eye. "I was mad at you, Larado—I didn't mean to cause you no trouble."

He shrugged. "It doesn't matter now. You just make sure all your money is in the bank's safe."

"I ain't got the combination to the lock," she said. "Wilbur don't trust me with it."

"Now I wonder why?" Larado's voice was sarcastic. "You just warn him. He'll probably want to close the bank tomorrow."

"But tomorrow's Saturday," she protested. "That's our busiest day."

"I don't think there'll be many people on the street once word gets around," Larado said.

"You gonna make a run for it?"

"I don't know." He shook his head. "If I do, I leave this town completely defenseless. Bill's wired for help, but that posse can't possibly get back from the border in time."

Dixie smiled at him. "You and me could hold a gun on Barclay, clean out the safe, clear out before Snake arrives."

"You don't ever change, do you, Dixie? Always tryin' to beat the odds."

She scowled. "It's that prissy Lark, ain't it? Even if she's thrown you out, you ain't gonna leave her behind."

"Don't even let her name touch your dirty mouth," he threatened. "Now get the word out to as many people as possible. If your husband locks down his bank, maybe he can save the people's money from Snake."

"You're not gonna try to stop him, are you, Larado? Snake's one of the best shots in Texas."

He shook his head. "I ain't figured out what I'm gonna do yet."

"Better to be a live coward than a dead hero."

"That's what I'm thinkin'." He hobbled out of the bank and looked up and down the street. Word was spreading, all right. He could see people locking up shops and calling children in off the streets. About the only able-bodied men in town would be those in the saloon, and they'd relish seeing him shot down. No, there was no one able to help him. He had to warn Lark.

The hot wind came up and heated his face as he hobbled down the almost deserted street. He pulled his Stetson down to keep it from being blown away as he hobbled down to the millinery shop.

Lark looked up as he entered. "What is it you want?" she snapped. "I don't reckon you came in to buy a lady's hat?" The expression on his rugged face stopped her cold in her tracks. "What is it?"

"Snake's comin'."

"What?"

He told her what he knew.

"Oh my." She sighed and went to the window and looked out at the deserted street. "I saw that trio. They look like big dudes. You could toss them in jail."

Larado shrugged. "I'm not worried about them, it's Snake who's the danger."

"Land's sake, you could meet with him and try to settle your differences."

He laughed without mirth. "You don't understand, Lark. He wants revenge . . . and some of that pot of money he thinks I got from that robbery."

She whirled on him. "Then just explain to him that the banker fooled you both."

He threw back his head and laughed. "You think he'll just mosey in and we'll go sit in the hotel dining room for lemonade and sugar cookies while I explain it to him?"

"So he'll kill you." It wasn't a question, it was a statement.

"Unless I clear out of town."

She nodded. "That would be the smart thing to do since you're on a crutch and not a good shot besides."

He came toward her, then hesitated. "Lark, I want you to go with me. We'll make a fresh start somewhere else."

"I said the *smart* thing, not the *right* thing. You'll leave the town completely defenseless."

He shrugged. "Maybe that don't make me no never mind." He reached out and touched her face, tilted her chin up. "You, that's the only one I worry about."

He kissed her then, and she let him, melting into him and returning his kiss with all the pent-up ardor she had so long denied. She took a deep breath and pulled away. "What's the plan?"

"We'll clear out tonight. Nobody'll know we're gone."

She nodded. "That makes sense. We'll just turn tail and drift on to the next town until another outlaw like Snake puts us on the move again."

He shrugged and turned away. "It's a tough world. Everybody's got to look out for himself."

"That's right, isn't it? Somehow, I figured you'd changed, Larado."

"I reckon a skunk can't change his stripes. I'm just a saddle tramp, remember? Not a Texas Ranger."

"All right. I'll get the shop ready to close, empty the cash register. What about Magnolia?"

"What about her? We can take Chico, tied to the back of the surrey, but we can't be draggin' a little burro along. She'll slow us down."

"Can we wait and leave on the train tomorrow?"

He shook his head. "I reckon Snake might come in on the train. It's just the kind of grand gesture he'd like."

"All right. I'll see you at the house by dark."

"We'll leave before dawn when everyone else is asleep."

She nodded and watched him leave. She went to the window and watched him hobbling down the street, stray tumbleweeds blowing past his long legs. The town was mostly deserted with the men gone and the women and children disappearing inside and locking their doors. Lark had always fled when faced with difficult choices, but she was surprised at Larado. She'd begun to think of him as an ex–Texas Ranger, even though she knew it wasn't true. Of course no one could blame him for running, certainly not her. He was walking with a crutch and he wasn't a good shot, even wearing his spectacles. Snake would gun him down out there in the street, with Larado's blood making dark puddles in the dirt.

Larado hobbled down the deserted street. People were heeding the warning, all right. He sat in his office all afternoon, waiting for Bill to bring him a message from the Rangers, but none came. The town looked like a ghost town as sundown settled all red and gold across the plains. Finally, he locked up his office for the last time and started home.

As he walked, Jimmy ran out from the hotel, looking up at him. "Sheriff, is it true? Is that outlaw comin'?"

Larado looked down at the anxious, fearful child. "Don't worry about it, Jimmy. You'll be safe enough."

"Oh, I know that, Sheriff." The scrawny child grinned up at him. He reminded Larado of the child he had once been, thin and undersized in a world of bullies. "I told Mrs. Bottoms that with you here, he ain't gonna do anything but end up dead or in jail, right?"

"Sure, Jimmy, sure." He patted the boy's thin shoulder, but he didn't look into the dark eyes.

Mrs. Bottoms waddled out of the hotel. "Jimmy, come in here, now," she called. "Sheriff's got plans to make, don't need you worryin' him."

"He ain't worryin' me," Larado yelled back. "Now, Jimmy"—he lowered his voice—"you need to stay inside and look after Mrs. Bottoms and the maids, you hear?"

The boy nodded. "I'd rather be out here in the street with you, shootin' down the bad guys."

"I'll handle this," he assured the child. "Now you scoot and look after the ladies, okay?"

The boy nodded and ran back to join the old lady. The two of them went into the hotel. Larado stared after them a long moment. Jimmy would be awfully disappointed when he woke up tomorrow and found the sheriff had fled like a scalded yellow hound. Hell, no one in town could blame him, with Snake's deadly reputation. He hobbled to the house and went out back to check on the horses and feed them. Long before daylight, he and Lark would be safely on their way and out of Snake's reach. The town was on its own.

Lark came in soon enough. "Anything happening?"

He sat down on the settee and shook his head. "Nothin'. I checked the buckboard and oiled the wheels. You pack us a few things, and we'll be out of here before dawn."

"Okay." She nodded and went into the kitchen. "I must admit I feel bad about leaving the town undefended."

"I know." He rolled a cigarette, staring out the window. "But it's suicide to stay and face him down, you know that."

"I saw little Jimmy stop you on the street," she said, bustling about the kitchen. "What'd he want?"

Larado sighed and stuck the smoke in his mouth. He felt a deep, nagging shame. "He's certain I can handle the bad guys. He wants to help me."

"Well, he's only a child, he's too young to understand."

"Right." Larado smoked and stared out the window. "I kinda had my heart set on that ranch, settlin' down."

She paused, skillet in hand. "Now, Larado, you know that what we're doing makes sense, right? We can't stay here."

"I know, I know. Once a saddle tramp, always a saddle tramp, I reckon."

"Sometimes it only makes good sense to clear out. Who was it said 'discretion is the better part of valor'?"

"Whoever he was, he wasn't a Texan."

"You gonna give me 'Remember the Alamo'?" She began to fry a steak.

"I reckon not. I'm too big a coward to have fought at the Alamo. I'd have been that one *hombre* who went over the wall and ran."

"At least he ended up alive," she reminded him as she sliced potatoes.

"Yeah, and I'll bet he went around with his head down the rest of his miserable life."

"That's *loco* talk," she scolded. "We'll be alive, and we'll have each other. Doesn't that matter to you?"

"You matter to me." He crushed out his cigarette in the ash tray, took his crutch, and hobbled over to her. He put his arms around her and kissed the back of her neck.

She turned in his arms and put hers around him.

"Oh, Larado, I'm so scared." She kissed his cheek. "I know we're doing the right thing. Snake might not even come here, and after all, didn't you say Bill had wired for the Rangers? They'll be here in a day or two and the town will be all right."

"I wish I could be sure of that." He kissed the tip of her nose.

She looked up at him anxiously, fear in her dark eyes. "I hope you're not thinking of making some grand play. You aren't Travis, or Crockett, or Bowie, you know."

"I know what I am—I'm a yellow-bellied coward."

"Don't say that. You're sensible, that's all. What good would it do to get yourself killed? You haven't got a chance against Snake, and you know it."

He went back to the table and sat down heavily. "What is it the Rangers say, 'No one can stand up to a man who's in the right and keeps right on comin''?"

"Yes, and how many Rangers get killed doing that? Just think about us, Larado. We'll start a whole new life. I'll make you glad you chose me over playing the hero."

He sighed and pulled his watch out of his vest, checking the time. "I reckon you're right." He began to whistle "The Streets of Laredo."

"Stop that," she snapped. "Don't you know other songs?"

"Sorry, force of habit." He shrugged. "You empty your cash register?"

She nodded as she dished up the food. "Not much, but it'll get us a ways down the road. Then we'll figure out what to do next. I fed Magnolia and the horses. I'll leave Jimmy a note so he'll look after her. I hate that he never got his train ride. He'll be disappointed."

"He'll be more disappointed to find out I ran when the chips were down." He grabbed a fork and dug into the sizzling steak and potatoes. If he hadn't been so worried, it would have been delicious. Lark was learning to cook.

"You know," she mused, "we might just get on the train."

"What?" He paused and stared at her.

"Well, maybe we can sneak onto the last car as Snake gets off, if he's even on it. He needn't know since it's only in the station about ten minutes. We'll be gone while he's hunting around town for you."

"Runnin' like scared rabbits," he grumbled as he ate. Suddenly he had lost his appetite as he pictured the face of the small boy tomorrow afternoon. "You pack some stuff?"

She finished eating, gathered up the plates, and took them to the sink. "Yes, I'll pack us each one small bag. There's no point in trying to take more." She paused and looked around.

"What's the matter?"

"Oh, nothing." She shook her head. "I've just gotten used to this little house, this town. That ranch you loved, I'd begun to dream of living out there."

He laughed. "Saddle tramps can't have the luxury of dreams. I'd never be able to afford that place on my salary. I can't even come up with the down payment."

"That's okay," she soothed, "we'll start over. You're doing the right thing, Larado, and you'll have me."

He looked up at her, and the expression in his dark eyes told her everything she wanted to know. "If I've got you, Lark, that's all the world to me."

"I feel the same," she said. "Now come on into the bedroom. I'll pack and we'll get some sleep so we can be out of here before dawn."

He nodded and followed her into the bedroom. He sat on the bed and watched her as she hurried about, packing. "I know you're right," he muttered, "but I feel like a rat."

She could not allow him to weaken. She finished up her packing and went to him. "Larado, I love you," she whispered, "and I want you alive. Think of all the years we've got ahead of us."

She knelt before him, began to unbutton his shirt, her fingers trailing gently over his bare skin as she did so. She felt goose bumps rise on his flesh where her fingers touched. "I'm going to remind you why you want to stay alive," she whispered, and she kissed his bare chest. She let her warm breath caress his muscular body as her lips moved slowly across his flesh. Then very deliberately, she touched him with the tip of her tongue, leaving a row of kisses over every inch of his chest until her mouth touched his nipple.

He groaned aloud. "Oh, Lark, I'm powerless when you do that, you know that." He pulled her up to him and kissed her, his warm mouth caressing her lips, her neck.

She gasped at the sensation of his hands and mouth as his hands slipped inside her clothes. "Give me a chance to get undressed," she gasped.

"With my bum leg, you'll have to do most of the work." He didn't stop kissing and caressing her.

"I can do that," she said, "oh, yes, I can do that!"

She slid down to her knees and took off his boots, then shed her own clothes. She took them off very slowly, provocatively, knowing he was watching and savoring her every move. Now she stood naked in the golden glow of the lamp. She shook her hair loose and let it tumble down her shoulders and over her breasts.

He took a deep breath and his hand trembled as he reached over to blow out the lamp. "You haven't let me touch you since our wedding night."

"Just remember," she breathed as she leaned forward so that her lips brushed along her collar bone, "this is only the first of many, many nights like this, if only. . . ."

He pulled her to him, kissed her breasts, his desire mounting. He wanted her more than anything in the world and he could have her . . . if he was willing to turn his back on this town. Lark against the needs of Rusty Spur.

He lay back on the bed and let her amuse herself with him. Her wet tongue played across his nipples, and then she was sitting astride his hips and all he could think of was plunging into her. He looked up at her in the moonlight and he thought he had never seen such a beautiful woman, all naked and passionate. He reached up and caught her breasts, pulled her down to him. "You'll have to do all the work," he reminded her again.

She smiled and leaned over him, her long hair brushing across him like strands of silk. It set his body tingling and he put his hands on her hips and lifted her. She came down, all wet and velvety on his hard, throbbing manhood.

Lark came up on her knees, came down again on him deeply, thoroughly. This was a man; a stallion of a man. Even with a hurt leg, he could satisfy a woman better than most men and he was hers to enjoy. She began a slow rhythm of pleasure, rising up so that he was almost out of her and then coming down on him again so that he was in her to the hilt. She ground herself against him, pleasuring herself and him.

He gasped under her, controlling himself so that it would last and last until she began to reach her pinnacle of pleasure. Lark threw back her head, crying out and at that, Larado grasped her small waist in his two big hands and increased the rhythm, bringing her down on him again and again in an ever increasing, hard driving action.

Then as she gasped, "Larado! Now! Oh, yes, now!" he reached up and caught her breasts in his hands bringing her down so he could cover her face with kisses. As they locked in a hot, torrid embrace, they both reached ecstasy.

To Lark, the pleasure seemed to last through a black velvet eternity and when she came to, she was lying on his muscular chest, cradled in his strong arms with him still deep within her. "Oh, Larado, I love you!" she whispered against his neck and he reached up and pulled her closer, gently stroking her hair. "We've got the rest of our lives to make love, all we have to do is leave in the morning while there's still time."

"Sure, sweetie, sure," He held her close and listened to her steady breathing as she dropped off to sleep. But he did not sleep. He had never known such joy with any other woman and he loved this one as he could never love another. Lark versus this town. It was no contest.

Chapter Twenty

Lark awoke in the darkness and stretched, smiling. Larado had proved he was still all man, even with a splint on his leg. Maybe last night's love would result in a child. Larado would like to have a son—they'd even talked of adopting Jimmy. Reality came down on her like a stampeding herd as she remembered they were fleeing today. Well, of course the boy would be just as well off with Mrs. Bottoms as on the run with them.

She realized suddenly that Larado was not in bed. Quickly, she grabbed a robe and got up, peering at the clock. It was a little before five. It would be light soon.

She looked toward the kitchen. Larado sat at the table, smoking in silence. She could see his big silhouette and the tip of his glowing cigarette. The scent of tobacco floated on the hot summer air. He was already dressed. She lit a lamp and went into the kitchen. "Couldn't sleep?"

He shook his head and she turned up the lamp so that she could see him. He looked troubled.

"Don't worry," she assured him as she bustled about, making coffee and stoking up the fire in the kitchen stove. "If Snake should ride in today, we'll be long gone."

"I know," he said, but he didn't look at her.

"Last night was wonderful, wasn't it?" She turned from the stove, smiling at him.

"Best I ever had," he said, but he didn't smile.

"Just think of all the nights and months and years we'll have like that," Lark assured him and began to cook up bacon and make biscuits.

"Uh-huh." He was staring out the kitchen window, and there was something about him that made her nervous. She went ahead fixing breakfast. He did not move or speak.

He needed cheering up, she thought as she put two heaping plates of food and a pot of strong coffee on the table. "It's going to be fine," she said. "After breakfast, we'll just take the rig. You get the horse harnessed and I'll leave a note for Jimmy about Magnolia. In an hour, we'll be miles from here."

"And then what?" He ate without looking at her.

"Well, I don't know. We'll find jobs in another town or something."

"And always on the run because there will always be bastards like Snake Hudson if someone doesn't take a stand and stop them." He sipped his coffee.

"Land's sake, we'll just find a home some place else. Let someone else stop them." She finished her food and carried the dishes to the sink. "I've got a few more things to pack. You finish your coffee and go harness the horse."

He didn't answer, and she went into the bedroom to see if she'd forgotten anything. There was not much she could tuck in two bags. There were memories in this little house: the wedding gifts, the bed she and Larado had made love in, the dainty lace curtains she had made for the windows. Well, it couldn't be helped. She made up the bed, which seemed like a futile gesture, but she didn't want whoever moved in behind her to find things in a mess. She could see the first rays of light through the bedroom window.

She grabbed her two bags and went back toward the kitchen. "Larado," she called, "I may not have gotten everything you want to take. You better come tell me what—"

"No." He still sat at the breakfast table, staring out the window in the coming pale gray light.

"What do you mean, no? You'd better hurry if we're to be on our way before sunup."

He shook his head and looked at her. "Lark, I want you to go, catch the noon train."

Her nerveless fingers dropped the valises, but she barely heard them hit the floor. "Without you?"

He nodded. "Without me. I want you to be safe, but I can't desert this town."

"What kind of fool are you?" Her voice rose in her terror. "You know you haven't got a chance against Snake Hudson. It's stupid to stay and get shot down out there on the street."

"Well, I might get him first."

She began to cry in her frustration. "We both know better than that. You haven't got a change against a top gun like him. I love you, Larado, and I want you to live. Think about it! Think about last night. Don't you want more of that? What kind of man are you to tell me you'd go and then change your mind?"

"I'm a Texan, Lark." He turned and looked at her. "If I run like a scared rabbit—like a shiftless saddle tramp—I'm less than a man." He took his crutch, standing up with difficulty.

She was both furious and scared. She ran at him, beating him on the chest. "You're *loco*, that's what you are. You're gonna stay here and die when you could live. What good is that gonna do anyone? Suppose I'm expecting a child after last night? You gonna leave him orphaned?"

He tried to catch her hands and hold on to her, but she was twisting and broke away. "You clear out, Lark. I want you to be safe. If I don't make it, tell my son that I finally stopped running, like I've done all my life, and stood my ground like a man—like a Texan."

"Oh, you're a damned fool, Larado," she wept. "You've begun to believe that *loco* stuff about Texas heroes. I hate you for telling me you'd go and then changing your mind."

He swallowed hard. "You don't mean that, sweet. Oh, you might be glad if I went with you today, but after you thought about it you'd despise me for being yellow, for not protectin' this town."

"But you're hobbling on a bad leg, and you can't see—and even if you could, you're not a good shot."

"That's all true," he said, "but I'll do the best I can. That's all any man can do."

"Yes, remember the Alamo and all that crap!" she screamed, and then she slapped him hard. She turned and ran into the bedroom, slamming the door.

He sighed, staring after her. He had never loved a woman so much as he loved this one, and she could not, would not understand. He hobbled to the closed door. "Lark, I'm goin' down to the sheriff's office now to wait for Snake. You be on that noon train out of here."

There was no answer, only angry sobbing.

"I just want you to know, Lark, that if I don't make it, my last thought will be of you."

"You're *loco*. You know that? I hate you!"

He sighed and hobbled over to the table. He paused, and after a moment, picked up his gold-rimmed spectacles and dropped them in his pocket. Maybe while he was sitting in his office waiting, he might try to read the Bible that lay on the desk there.

He went outside. As the Cheyenne would say, it was a good day to die. It would be warm and windless with a clear sky the color of that dress Lark wore the first time he saw her. *Jimmy*. He must write some kind of note for Jimmy to find that would make the boy proud and teach him what courage meant. Not that Larado was any great role model.

The streets were deserted, but inside the bank already, he could see the banker moving about. That puzzled Larado. Hadn't Dixie warned him about not opening today? Maybe he was just moving the money out of his safe to hide in case Snake made it that far. There was no chance

the posse could get here before Snake did, so that meant
Larado would have to handle it. He smiled, thinking of the
trio from back East. This wasn't the way it was done in the
dime novels, a crippled-up, half-blind sheriff going to a
showdown against a tough outlaw. Well, he'd do the best
he could, but his mind was in turmoil, wondering if Lark
didn't make sense. He was a fool to be so noble.

He paused out on the wooden sidewalk and took a
long, deep breath. It was going to be a hot day, a Texas kind
of a day. He knew he would not be around to see the sun
set, but he was okay with that. Larado had only gone to school
a couple of years, but now an old poem that a teacher
had once read to the class came to mind: . . . *I could not love
thee dear so much, loved I not honor more.* . . . Lark. He only
wished she understood.

He went to his office, sat down at his cluttered desk, and
looked through some wanted posters. It was going to be a
long morning. He glanced up at the big clock that hung on
his office wall. It ticked loudly in the silence. Almost nine
o'clock. He pulled the pocket watch out of his vest and
checked to see if the big clock might be wrong. It wasn't.

If Snake came by horseback, he could be here earlier
or later than noon. It was also possible that he'd think
better of it and not come at all. After all, it made good
sense to get across the border, with a hangman's noose
waiting for him if he was recaptured. The trio of buf-
foons might not know what they were talking about.

He wrote a note to Jimmy, explaining about why he
had made this decision. If Larado never saw him again, he
wanted the boy to believe in Texas and her heroes. It meant
something to Larado to have the child and the town know
that he had died doing what he thought was right—just like
Bowie, Crockett, and Travis. Others might laugh about the
Alamo, but Texans lived by its legends. There was a reason
the Lone Star flag had a crimson stripe—it represented the
blood-soaked ground Texans had died defending.

About ten o'clock, a handful of the elderly men in the

town came into his office. There was Bill from the telegraph office, the two old Civil War veterans, and Doc. "Sheriff, we come to help."

He looked them over. Two of them had hands that shook so bad, they probably couldn't hit a barn door with a shotgun. Of the two old veterans, one only had one leg, and the other was blind in one eye. Doc was pretty frail, and he was the only doctor within a hundred miles. They couldn't risk losing him. Between them, they were carrying outdated weapons. One of them even carried a musket. "Thanks, men, you're true Texans, and I'm really obliged for your offer, but I think I can handle this."

"But we want to help," said Bill.

Snake would kill them all without blinking an eye, and Larado couldn't have that on his conscience. "Tell you what," he said, "if I don't come out of this showdown, you'll be the last line of defense against this *hombre* until the posse gets back."

Bill leaned closer. "What you want us to do, Sheriff?"

"I want you to hang on to your weapons and stay indoors. If he gets me, you four will have to go it alone."

They looked at each other, nodding. It made sense.

"All right," Bill said. "I wired the Rangers like you told me. They wired back that they'll try to get some men here in time."

"Everything will be fine, then," Larado assured them with a confidence he did not feel. "You know the old saying: one riot, one Ranger. I can handle this 'til they get here." He stood and herded the old codgers toward the door.

"We didn't want to desert our sheriff," one said as they stood in the doorway.

"And you're not," Larado assured them. "You just be in your homes and ready in case Snake Hudson gets me. You'll have to deal with him 'til the posse arrives."

They went out reluctantly. Larado stood in the doorway and watched them limp off down the street. From the saloon blared laughter and the strains of drunken singing: ". . . as I walked out on the streets of Laredo, as I walked out in Laredo one day. . . ."

Judging from the horses tied out front, there were a lot of *hombres* in that saloon, drinking to Saturday and no doubt, to Larado's death. The only men in town that could help him were the ones in the saloon, and he knew they wouldn't turn a hand to save a lawman. It was sort of ironic, him playing the hero when he was a wanted man himself. Well, maybe that would never come out. He didn't want this town, especially Jimmy or Paco, to think badly of him.

The clock ticked so loudly, he felt it could be heard all up and down the street, ticking away the hours and minutes of his life. He must not think of that, or he would be too afraid to do what—as a man—he knew he must do.

He returned to his desk, put on his spectacles, and opened his Bible. Any other time he'd have been worried that someone might see him in his eyeglasses, but there was no one on the streets. Everyone was behind locked doors, awaiting the arrival of Snake Hudson.

He had never been a religious man, but the feel of the worn black book comforted him somehow. He stared up at the loudly ticking clock. It was almost eleven o'clock. *My, don't time fly when you're havin' fun?* he thought ruefully.

Lark was probably packed by now. Had she taken the buggy, or was she waiting for the train? A thought crossed his mind—he had an hour to change his mind, just in case Snake came in on the train. One hour to make a choice between Lark and life, or being shot down in the dirt of a west Texas town. He wavered, remembering the taste of her lips, the ecstasy he had known only in her arms. Yep, it was tempting. He stared out into the hot summer day, thinking about his choices. He ought to write Lark a note explaining everything and telling her how much he loved her. He wrote a couple of lines, then ran out of words. Besides, what good would it do if she'd left town and never read them? He crumpled the paper and tossed it away.

He was wavering, thinking about dying. Life was sweet, and he didn't want it to end yet—he'd had so little of it. Right now he was not so afraid of dying, since that was a foregone conclusion. What worried him was dying badly, maybe shot in the back because at the last moment he tried to run and took the bullet like a coward.

He flipped through the worn pages, looking for a clue or something that would make him not so afraid. Even with his thick glasses, he squinted at the fine print. . . . *for if God be with me, who dares stand against me . . . ?*

He laughed and closed the Bible, taking off his spectacles and putting them in his shirt pocket. God wouldn't be with a saddle tramp who had never done a right thing in his whole life. Yes, he'd done one right thing: he'd loved a woman, really loved her, with no thought for anything but protecting her and cherishing her. And for doing the right thing, she was deserting him.

He leaned back in his chair with a sigh. Mesmerized, he watched the clock hands move forward.

Over at the bank, Dixie watched old Barclay sort through his money and close the safe. Damn, she'd hoped he might turn his back and give her a chance to load her purse up with greenbacks, but that wasn't to be.

He cleared his throat. "I don't understand it," he grumbled. "There's hardly anyone on the streets, and it's Saturday. I was expecting a lot of business today."

"Who knows?" She hadn't warned him. In fact, she'd be delighted if he got killed. She'd hoped she might figure a way to get some of that money before she caught that noon train, but he'd been too watchful for her. Oh well, Abner Snootley had plenty of money. They'd make do with his. She yawned. "I reckon I'll go back up to the apartment. What do you want for dinner?"

"Steak," he said. "And then I want you under me."

She sighed. "Let's not."

"You know better than that, you slut," he snapped. "That's what I keep you for, remember? That, and to keep your mouth shut."

"Sure." She went out, cursing silently. That bastard had put his clammy hands on her for the last time. She'd be gone on the noon train—her bags were already packed and waiting. That fat bank would be too good a lure for Snake to resist. She hoped Snake killed Barclay as he robbed it.

Dixie went upstairs and checked her valise. She had a few nice pieces of jewelry, but she had counted on cleaning out the bank safe, and now she wasn't going to be able to do it. Oh well, she'd meet Abner Snootley on the train, sleep with him a night or two until he was off guard, then she'd steal everything he'd taken from that thriving general store of his. *Larado.* She smiled, thinking of him. Hell, there was one last thing Dixie could do for him and his lady. Dixie had never done a good deed in her whole desperate life. Yet now she sat down with a pen and paper and wrote:

To the sheriff of Buck Shot, Oklahoma Territory.

Dear Bob:

I'm writing to tell you you've been chasing the wrong hombre. *Snake Hudson and Wilbur Barclay were the ones who actually robbed the bank. Larado and Lark had nothing to do with it. In fact, Barclay killed his own teller because the man saw Barclay switching the bank bags. Barclay's been paying me these last few months to keep my mouth shut, but Larado's too decent a guy, and I'm ashamed. I swear on the Confederate flag that this is true.*

Thanks for the good times,
Dixie.

She reread it with a smile. Yep, it felt good to do something decent for a change. Now she addressed an envelope and put a stamp on it. She'd drop it at the post office as she sneaked away to take the train.

The banker had stared after Dixie as she headed upstairs. He was damned tired of the slut, but she was still good in bed. She knew too much about him for him to do anything but kill her. He hadn't figured out how to do that yet without arousing suspicion—maybe he'd push her down the stairs tonight after he'd had his fill of her. Yes, that might work. She stepped on the hem of her lacy pink nightie, fell all the way down the stairs, and landed on the marble hallway. The woman he wanted next was that tall black-haired beauty who belonged to the sheriff. Well, money could buy anything, maybe even her.

At his home, Abner Snootley packed a few personal items in a carpetbag and walked down to the general store. The streets were deserted, except he could hear the drunken crowd at the saloon celebrating Saturday. He'd heard that an outlaw was coming into town for a showdown with the sheriff. Some of the old geezers were organizing to try to help the lawman, but of course, Abner wasn't interested. He didn't give a damn what happened to Lawrence Witherspoon or even this town. Thank God that banker's wife had plenty of money, because there wasn't more than ten dollars in the store cash register. He smiled, picturing Bertha's homely face when she came in and discovered he had fled and left her with a bankrupt store. Instead of shopping, his snooty wife would have to get out and get a job. Well, she deserved that. He glanced up at the clock. Eleven-thirty. In a few minutes he would mosey down to the station, going through the alley so he wouldn't arouse suspicion.

* * *

Lark had sat on her bed, sobbing until her eyes were swollen and red. She heard a noise and jumped up, running into the parlor. "Larado? I knew you'd change your mind . . . ."

She realized then that it was only the horses moving around out in the stable. Maybe if Lark went to his office and begged Larado, tried to reason with him, he might change his mind and go with her. It made no sense to get himself killed going up a deadly gunfighter. She shook her head. He had changed over the last few hours.

Well, she didn't have to stay here and witness it. Damn him, anyway. Lark had loved him like she had never known she could love a man, and this was how he repaid her. She looked at the clock. Past eleven-thirty. She went into the parlor and looked out. The hot street looked lonely and deserted. Everyone was inside, waiting for the inevitable duel.

"Damn you, Larado," she whispered through gritted teeth. "If you cared about me, you wouldn't stay here and die, making me run all alone. Well, I reckon there's nothing to do but get myself to the station."

She double-checked her two small bags to see if she'd forgotten anything. His still sat empty on the floor, his things still in the bureau drawers. The shirt he'd worn last night lay crumpled on the floor, and she leaned over and picked it up, holding it to her and hugging it as she wished she could embrace him. The shirt reminded her of him. It smelled of fragrant bay rum hair tonic, tobacco, and horses. He'd probably never wear it again. With a shuddering sigh, she hung it over a chair, smoothing the wrinkles from it. "Damn you, Larado," she said. "Damn you for being so noble. I reckon after all, you're a better person than I am, and a Texan to the core."

Somewhere in the distance, she thought she heard the faraway whistle of the train drifting with the wind across the prairie. It was time to go. He'd made his decision, and now it was time to make hers. She wiped her eyes and reached for her purse. If Snake Hudson was on that train, she didn't want to know it. When she climbed aboard, she'd never look back—and maybe she'd never know if her love had survived the gunfight or not. Well, it was his choice. She got her bags and looked around the small house one last time. She'd spent two nights of passion in this bed with Larado, and she might be carrying his child. What would she tell his son? Your father died a hero, or your father died a damned fool?

She heard the distant whistle of the train again. It would be here in less than ten minutes. She'd better go. She grabbed her luggage, stuck her chin out resolutely, went out the back door, and headed to the station.

Larado sat with his face in his hands, listening to the relentless ticking of the clock on the wall and the faraway whistle, now echoing through the hot July air. He'd pray, if he knew how. He hoped that Lark made it to the train okay, and that maybe later, she'd understand. It crossed his mind than he could still go out the back door, and by hobbling fast, make that train. If he came in from the far side, Snake might get off without knowing Larado was getting on.

The whistle sounded again. It couldn't be time yet, could it? Time moved so fast, yet so slow when a man knew he was going to die. He looked up at the clock, watching its hands move. Then he pulled the big watch out of his vest and checked. Yep, it was almost noon. He glanced toward the gun rack in the corner. There were rifles there, but he'd never been good with a rifle. Hell, as bad as his eyesight was, he wasn't much better with a six-gun. He decided he wasn't going to go down without a fight. He'd do what he could to protect this town—*his* town. After that, it was up to the little group of old geezers who hadn't done much shooting since the Civil War.

The whistle screamed again, sounding closer now. The train would be roaring into the station in less than five minutes. . . . *Yea, though I walk through the valley of the shadow of death, I will fear no evil, for Thou art with me, thy rod and thy staff comfort me* . . . .

He pulled out his Colt and whirled the chamber, making sure it was loaded. He might never get a shot off, knowing how fast a draw Snake was, but Larado wasn't going to sit in his office and be hunted down like a fearful deer. He'd at least go on his feet like a man. The train whistled, and whistled again. He could hear it chugging now as it came toward town. He put on his Stetson, put his Colt in his holster, and reached for his crutch. It was almost high noon and time for the showdown.

The Bloggett brothers staggered out of the saloon. "I think I hear the train," Clem burped.

They listened, all of them more than a little drunk. "Yep, it's the train. Let's go meet our partner down at the end of the street."

"Let's."

They staggered down the deserted street as they heard the train hissing and chugging toward town. One of them pulled out his watch. "Right on time."

"You think Snake will remember us?" Slim puffed.

"Course he will. We're gonna form a gang, rob the bank, and grab some pretty women."

"Eat some barbecue," Clem suggested.

"Can't," Lem belched. "Barbecue gives me gas."

"Let's go meet the train," Slim puffed.

"Yippee ti yi yo, get along little doggies," Clem said.

"Now what in the hell is that supposed to mean?"

"I don't know—I read it in a cowboy story."

"It don't make no sense. Why would cowboys be singing about dogs?"

"Well, they sing in the dime novels."

"Shut up and walk faster, the train'll be in before we get there."

Pulling their big Stetsons tighter against the wind, the trio walked in their painful heeled boots to the station. The train was just arriving.

Snake Hudson peered out the dirty window of the first coach as the train slowed.

The conductor came down the aisle. "Rusty Spur," he sang. "Everyone off for Rusty Spur!"

Snake grabbed his sleeve. "You know the sheriff here?"

"Heard of him." The old man nodded. "Sheriff Witherspoon, one tough Texan."

"What's he look like?" If he had the wrong man, Snake might stay on the train.

"Tall, dark, maybe some Injun blood. Ladies say he's real handsome. Best sheriff this town ever saw."

Snake grinned. That sounded like Larado, all right.

The conductor continued down the aisle as the train slowed. "Rusty Spur, coming into Rusty Spur! All off for Rusty Spur."

Snake looked out the window. Those three idiot brothers were standing on the platform. They all looked so drunk, they couldn't hit the ground with their hats in three tries. Now what was he gonna do with those coyotes? They were amusing, so he'd keep them for a while and maybe kill them later when they annoyed him. He stood up on the swaying lead coach and grinned. It was going to be a good day if he got to kill that double-crossing Larado. Maybe there was a saloon and a fat bank, too. No use wasting the opportunity.

The train slowed to a stop, and Snake slouched down the aisle. There didn't seem to be anyone getting off but him. He caught the old conductor by the sleeve. "What's goin' on here? I don't see a soul on the streets."

The conductor nodded. "Hear there's a manhunt, most of the men gone on a posse."

Wasn't that just great? Snake grinned even wider and rubbed the red scar on his forehead, then he stepped down off the train. "Hello, boys."

The brothers staggered toward him. "We brought the message like you said. You gonna have a showdown?"

"Shut up," he ordered. "Wait until the train gets out of the station before we start any trouble." He strode out onto the platform and looked around. Yes, a promising little town with surely a big fat bank. And all the men were gone—no doubt the posse was riding toward the border. He grinned at the irony. The lawmen were on a wild goose chase looking for him, and here he was in town. What a joke on them. He put his thumbs in his gun belt. "Sheriff in town?"

The fat brother nodded. "Think so."

Snake took a deep breath, pulled his pistol, and checked the cylinders to make sure it was fully loaded. He'd emptied it last when he killed that rancher and took the cash box for enough to buy his ticket and then some. Behind him, the train idled, steam drifting along the wooden platform in the hot noon air. "Let's go, boys."

He started off the platform, the trio trailing along uncertainly behind him. Snake didn't look back, but he could hear the conductor yelling, "Five minutes, we'll be here only five more minutes."

Snake walked slowly down the deserted main street. There might be someone on the train who would object to what he was about to do, or at least wire ahead for some Rangers. He'd give Larado ten more minutes of life so the train would be gone from the station. He hoped the saddle bum appreciated his generosity.

The wind blew dust down the deserted street, and he had a feeling there were people watching silently from behind lace curtains. He didn't care if women and old geezers saw him; he'd give them something to talk about. "You," he nodded toward the skinny brother, "go over there where no one can see you, shinny up that pole, and cut the telegraph wires."

"Me?"

"I said you, didn't I? If they didn't already take you serious and send for help, I don't want them doin' it now. I'm gonna tree this town. We'll kill the sheriff, rob the bank, and have some drinks. Then we'll drag the prettiest women out of their houses and enjoy them."

The three grinned. "Is that what real outlaws do?"

"Sure. Ain't you been readin' them Wild West stories?"

Behind him, he heard the conductor shouting, "All aboard! All aboard! Get on board, folks, we're leavin'."

He glanced back. Indeed, the train was puffing as the steam built up, and it whistled a warning.

"All aboard!" the conductor yelled. "Last call, all aboard!"

Snake grinned and looked up and down the road. No one was stepping out to challenge him. "In just a minute," he promised to the nervous trio behind him, "we're gonna kill us a sheriff."

He kept walking down the middle of the deserted street.

Chapter Twenty-One

Dixie hurried down the alley toward the train that was about to pull out of the station, pausing only to mail her letter. Barclay would find out too late that she was gone. Her only regret was that she hadn't managed to get the money out of the safe. Oh, hell, Abner Snootley had plenty of money. She was very careful to go to the far side of the train and hurry aboard the last coach. She went down the aisle, searching. There he was.

Snootley looked up, his one long lock of hair swirled and greased down to cover his bald spot. He greeted her, reeking of peppermint. "There you are. I was afraid you weren't coming."

"Naw, I was just bein' careful." Dixie took a deep breath and they both looked out the dirty window past the station and down Main Street beyond. There were four men starting down the street, and one of them looked familiar. "Oh my Gawd, I—I know that *hombre*."

It was Snake, there was no doubt of it. He had his back to her, but there was no mistaking him. Three ridiculous-looking fellows greeted him and they walked a moment, turning toward the bank. Snake hadn't seen her. She slid down in her seat with a sigh of relief. She was clearing out of town just in time.

"Oh, Lord," Abner Snootley groaned.

"What?"

He gestured, then slid down in his seat. "My wife, getting off the front coach. I didn't think she'd be back 'til next week. She was shopping and visiting her sister."

Dixie peered over the edge of the window at the broad back and massive purple hat with its plumes. It was Bertha Snootley, all right, no doubt about it. "Well, she ain't seen you. By the time she gets to the store and figures out what's happened, we'll be long gone."

He nodded and smiled, popped another peppermint between his yellow teeth, and crushed it. "That's right, isn't it? I didn't leave anything in the cash register but a good-bye note. She'll have to go to work as a maid or try to run the store herself, and she always hated working."

"Serves Mrs. Snooty right," Dixie grinned. "Oh my Gawd, I don't believe it. Look who else is comin' aboard."

Lark was out of breath as she boarded the last coach and hurried down the aisle. The train shuddered as if it was about to move. Tears blinded her, and her emotions were asunder over Larado. She put her valises on the overhead brass rack and collapsed onto a seat.

"Hey, what you doin' here?"

She opened her eyes at the familiar voice and saw Dixie across the aisle, sitting next to the shop owner. "I might ask you the same thing."

Dixie looked puzzled. "So we're all rats leavin' a sinkin' ship?"

"I—I don't know." Lark didn't want to talk to the woman or even wonder what she was doing on this train.

"You're leavin' Larado?" Dixie sounded astonished.

Lark nodded. "It was just no good between us, and he's such a fool. I tried to get him to go with me, but he was determined to stay and protect the town if Snake showed up."

"He showed up—look." Dixie pointed out the dirty window at the big ugly man now striding toward the bank.

"All aboard!" the conductor yelled. "All aboard!"

The train shuddered again and blew steam, whistling one last time in warning.

Lark felt tears begin to overflow and trickle down her face. "Larado's a fool. He can't stand up to Snake in a gunfight, and I'm not going to stay and see him get killed."

Dixie frowned at her. "You're a idiot, you know that?"

"How dare you—?"

"No, I mean it, honey." Her voice was as hard and cynical as her eyes. "You're leaving him to face danger on his own? What kind of woman are you?"

The train began to tremble and hiss, moving very slowly.

"I—I don't know what you mean."

"Yes, you do. Larado loves you—I've seen it in his eyes. Now you're gonna run like a scared rabbit and not do anything to help him? A real Texas gal wouldn't do that."

Lark stared out the window, letting the words sink in as the train began to pull out of the station. Dixie was right. All her life, Lark had fled when she was faced with tough decisions instead of standing her ground. Now she was deserting the man she loved just when he needed her most. Oh God, she was a coward—and Texans hated cowards.

The train was moving. In another minute they would be away from the town of Rusty Spur, and she wouldn't have to watch Larado die. In her mind, she saw him crumpling into the dirt and no one there to help him.

By God, not if there was anything she could do to stop it! She jumped up, grabbing her bags and running down the aisle.

"What the—?" Abner Snootley said, but Lark didn't answer. She ran to the end of the coach and threw her valises out, watching the ground crawling slowly past.

She was going to have to jump from a moving train. She almost wavered, then she saw Larado's rugged face in her mind. Whatever she could do to stop Snake, she had to do it. Taking a deep breath, she leaped. She hit the ground hard and fell, rolling over and over. She lay there a moment, decided nothing was broken, and struggled to her feet, dusting herself off. She turned and watched the train disappearing over the horizon.

Aboard the train, Dixie and Abner watched in disbelief. The man shook his head. "If that don't beat all!"

Dixie sighed, wishing she loved a man enough to take the chances Lark was about to take. If Larado had ever shown the slightest interest in Dixie . . . Well, money was all she could count on. She'd used good timing, since Snake might have killed her too. As it was, it appeared he was going to rob the bank—and if Barclay resisted, he might find himself dead. "I think that outlaw is gonna rob my husband's bank," she laughed. "Too bad I couldn't get it open before I left."

The train was rushing along now, picking up speed as they left Rusty Spur behind.

Abner's homely face went pale. "What—what do you mean? You haven't got any of the money from the bank?"

She shook her head. "Naw, but with what you got from your store, we can live pretty good, can't we?"

He began to laugh. He laughed and laughed in a way that scared Dixie. "What the hell you laughin' about? Tell me—tell me what's so damned funny?"

He wiped his eyes with the back of his hand. "It's just so ironic. We're both a pair of fools."

"What?"

He shook his head and kept laughing as the train raced along the tracks, picking up speed now as it left Rusty Spur far behind. "You've got no money—I've got no money. We're both a pair of damned fools!"

"We're—we're both broke?"

He was laughing too hard to do anything but nod.

Oh God. She had a sinking, desperate feeling. She'd always made wrong decisions, and now it had happened again.

Lark stumbled to her feet, bruised and sore, trying to decide what action to take. She'd seen Snake and his friends heading toward the bank. Maybe she still had time to help Larado—but what to do? Maybe she could at least warn him Snake was coming and he wasn't alone. The sheriff's office was farther down the street. She went through the alley to avoid being seen, heading toward Larado's office.

Snake walked into the bank. The fat man behind the cage was counting bills as he looked up with a greasy smile. "Welcome to First National Bank of Rusty Spur, what can I do for—"

"You can give me all your damned money," Snake growled and pulled his pistol.

"You! I recognize your voice!" The fat man's voice quavered. "You robbed my bank at Buck Shot."

Snake grinned. "I thought you looked familiar, fat man. Now hand over the money."

The other hesitated. "I—I'll have to open the safe."

"I got time—open 'er up."

The banker's pale hands shook as he fiddled with the dials on the big safe.

"Wait a minute," Slim said. "We could get in trouble for robbin' a bank."

"No." The other two set up a chorus. "We want to be buckaroos, but we don't want no trouble with the law. Why, you can go to jail for that."

"I'll show you trouble," Snake snapped, annoyed with

the banker because he was taking so long. As the safe door swung open, very deliberately, Snake shot the banker in the back.

"Oh my Gawd!" howled the trio. They turned and stampeded out the door.

Snake chuckled as he went around behind the teller's cage. They'd just saved him the trouble of killing all them later so he wouldn't have to split the loot. The banker was still breathing. Snake grabbed his limp arm and dragged him out of the way. "Snake Hudson," he laughed, "just makin' a withdrawal."

He reached into the open safe and grabbed two big bank bags. Abruptly he remembered what had happened before. He wasn't going to be tricked this time and get a bagful of coins. He checked them both. One of the bags held real money, the other chopped paper. Now just what the hell was the banker trying to pull? Well, it didn't matter. He had the money. Now all he wanted was to kill Larado for double-crossing him and clear out of town.

Larado had heard the train puff into the station. He took a deep breath and stood up, looking up at the clock. He wondered if Snake Hudson was on that train, then hoped against hope that he was not.

He checked his pistol again with nervous fingers, knowing it couldn't make much difference. He had no chance against a top gun like Snake. He pulled his hat down hard on his head, put his crutch under his arm, and opened the door. The warm summer air blew gently though the office. Somewhere in the distance, he heard the train whistling and chugging as it picked up speed.

Then he heard a single shot. "What the—?" He hobbled out onto the wooden sidewalk and looked down the street. All he saw was that idiot trio of greenhorns mounting up and attempting to get their old nags into a

gallop as they headed out of town across the tracks, disappearing into the landscape beyond. He forgot about
Snake, forgot about everything except that his only love
was probably on that train. Even now he wanted to run
after it and make her get off, but it was too late. He'd lost
her forever because of the choice he'd made.

He'd lost his love, but he'd found his honor. Up to
now, he hadn't had any. At least now he felt like a real
man. He had to protect this town. Where had that shot
come from? It sounded like it had come from the bank.
The street out front was deserted, the heat waves rising
up from the sun-baked ground. He started hobbling
toward the bank.

Lark ran down the alley behind the sheriff's office. If
she could reach Larado in time, she could warn him
Snake was in town. At least he wouldn't get surprised.
She ran past the pen behind her shop. Oh darn, Magnolia was out again—but that wasn't important now. She
was breathless when she burst through the back door of
the sheriff's office. Too late. The front door stood open,
the breeze blowing through. Had that shot she'd heard
been Snake killing Larado? She ran to the front door
and looked out. Larado had his back to her, hobbling
down the street toward the bank. Then she saw Snake
come out of the bank building. Oh dear Lord, what
should she do now?

She whirled and noted the gun rack in the sheriff's
office. There was a shotgun and a couple of rifles. The
shotgun would do more damage, but only at a short distance. She grabbed the Winchester rifle.

What to do now? Lark was a good shot, better than most
of the cowboys on her uncle's ranch. Her uncle Trace had
taught her well. She peeked out the front window. She didn't
have time to get behind Snake, but what else could she do
to help Larado? Then she saw the two-story hotel across the

way and got a desperate idea. She took the rifle, going out the back door and around the building. She waited a split second, then ran across the street and into the alley behind the hotel. There was a ladder on the back of the building leading to the roof. With her long yellow dress and the rifle in her hand, it was difficult to climb—but she knew she had to do it or watch Larado die. She'd give her life to save his, she knew that now. For whatever it was worth, she was through running.

Lark crawled across the flat roof of the second story of the hotel. Keeping her head low, she peered over the edge. Snake Hudson stood in front of the bank, facing Larado and grinning, his hand well away from his gun belt. "Hey, you! Let's throw in together! I've got the money. Let's ride out of town together and enjoy it!"

Larado took a deep breath. With his poor vision, the man at the end of the street was a fuzzy image. "Throw down the money and clear out of town, Snake, if you want to live!"

"All right, you double-crossin', yellow-bellied sonovabitch!" Snake shouted. "Don't say I didn't give you a chance! It's about time we had a showdown."

Larado leaned on his crutch, watching the dim image of the man at the end of the street. He'd have to get much closer to have any chance of hitting him. "You don't want to do this, Snake. You kill me, they'll hang you!"

Snake threw back his head and laughed. "Hell, I'm already scheduled to hang! They can't hang me twice! Are you all that's standin' between me, and all this money, and the pretty women in this town?"

"I am," Larado admitted.

"Then they're in a hell of a bad fix, you cripple!"

He could say that again. Larado hesitated, thinking of Lark. Maybe she'd been right. Life had been so sweet with her in his arms. The July breeze whipped a tumbleweed past his boots. In the hotel's front window, he could see a small, strained face looking out. *Jimmy*. It wasn't good for the boy to see a man shot down. All up and down the street, he sensed that people were watching from behind their curtains, afraid and knowing that Larado was all that stood between them and this killer. When Larado went down, the whole town would be at Snake's mercy. He hobbled a little closer, hesitating.

"Hey," Snake shouted, "you can still back off, Sheriff. Just go in your office and close the door. Let me do what I want for a couple of hours, and then I'll ride out of town."

Larado glanced toward his office. Oh, the offer was so tempting, but Jimmy and the whole town were watching.

"Well?" Snake challenged.

Larado took a deep breath and shook his head, remembering the code of all Texans: Nothing can stop a man who's in the right and keeps right on coming.

He had turned tail and run his whole life—drifting, not standing for anything. Today that ended, even if it meant his death. "Can't let you do that, Snake. Now throw down your gun and I'll see you get a fair trial."

Snake laughed again. "Why should I? Where's your backup, Sheriff? Where's your deputies?"

Somewhere in the distance, Larado thought he heard a train approaching the town. No, that couldn't be, the train had just left. Maybe he wanted Lark so badly, he imagined that the train was returning. No matter, by the time she arrived, he'd be dead.

What was that gray blur with the big ears? Oh no, that damned little burro was out of her pen and walking along behind Snake. The outlaw didn't seem to notice the ridiculous little animal in the street behind him. Well, that didn't matter now.

Very slowly, Larado reached into his shirt pocket, took out the gold-rimmed spectacles, and put them on.

"Hell," Snake shouted, "I didn't know you was a blind four-eyes."

Larado winced. Once again he was a scared, skinny

kid being picked on by school bullies. There were more important things in life than being taunted—there was honor. With his spectacles on, his vision improved, but he knew his shooting wouldn't. He flexed his fingers, making ready to draw. "I'm givin' you one last chance to surrender, Snake."

"I'm gonna kill you, you four-eyed coyote!"

On the roof of the two-story hotel, Lark aimed her rifle. If she missed, Larado would be dead. Worse than that, if she saved his life he would be so humiliated, he'd never speak to her again.

Was that a train whistle? She must be imagining it. The train had already left the station. Oh my God, there was Magnolia, wandering along the street right behind Snake, looking ridiculous in her big pink straw hat. Snake might kill the burro just for fun, but right now he didn't seem to notice her at all.

The two men were shouting at each other, and Lark saw Larado put on his spectacles. She sighed, knowing how much that was costing him in pride. He'd rather be dead than be laughed at. But he was all that stood between the killer running rampant through this defenseless settlement, and he knew it.

She took a deep breath, watching the two men flex their gun hands just above their holsters. She knew Snake was a gunfighter and that Larado was none too good with a pistol, but he was standing his ground, not running. She had to admire him for that.

There was a split second as both men slapped leather and she realized that Snake was going to beat Larado to the draw. And at that instant, little Magnolia let loose with an earsplitting braying: "ee haw, ee haw, eeee haww!"

Lark saw Snake start, his eyes widened with surprise as he hesitated. He pulled his Colt a split second before

Larado fired. She said a quick prayer, aimed, and pulled her trigger.

She flinched from the sudden thunder of noise and gunsmoke as Larado cried out, staggered, and fell. Oh my God, Snake had killed him.

Snake still stood, grinning for a split second more, and then very slowly he dropped his pistol, half turned, and tumbled to the dirt.

People ran out of buildings, shouting to each other. Magnolia wandered over and began to nibble the flowers from the decorative pots in front of the hotel. The train whistled again, and from the rooftop Lark could see a train roaring into town.

Nothing mattered but reaching Larado. She dropped the rifle and clambered down, hurrying around the building and into the street. Larado was lying where he fell, Jimmy by his side.

She ran to him. "Oh, Larado, how bad is it?"

"I—I think I'm dyin'," he groaned. "Remember to wrap me in white linen, sweetie, like the song says."

Little Jimmy looked up at her, tears in his dark eyes. "You missed the whole thing, Mrs. Witherspoon. There was a gunfight, and the sheriff won!"

Mrs. Bottoms nodded. "Heavens, I never saw such shootin'! Why, the sheriff got him right between the eyes!"

Lark knelt in the dirt of the street and took Larado in her embrace and began to examine him. "I don't see any blood."

"No blood?" he asked. "But I felt the slug hit me."

Old Doc came running with his medical bag and knelt in the dirt. "That was the bravest thing I ever saw, Sheriff—but then, we all knew you was a good shot!"

Lark attempted to hold back her tears, but they ran down her cheeks anyway. "He—he says he's hit, but I don't see any blood."

Doc began to examine him. "Where does it hurt?"

"Right here." Larado felt around in his vest and slowly brought out his pocket watch. It was a broken mess of springs and metal. "Well, if that don't beat all. That damned *hombre* broke my good gold watch."

Doc turned and yelled at the crowd. "He's all right, folks. His watch stopped the bullet! Sheriff, I never saw such good shooting."

Larado sat up, beaming at the admiring crowd. "Well, I reckon I'm better than I thought I was."

She could have smacked him for his arrogance if she hadn't been so relieved that he was alive. She walked over and looked down at Snake. His mean eyes looked straight up, and there was a bullet hole between them. Her rifle had aimed true. So where had Larado's shot gone?

Magnolia brayed again, and Lark ran to the donkey. There was a hole through her pink straw hat, right above the top of her head and between her long ears. Larado was indeed a bad shot, but no one need ever know that. She'd burn Magnolia's pink hat and get the burro a new one. The little animal deserved it, having startled the outlaw so that his shot didn't get Larado through the heart. "Hey!" she shouted. "Here's a bank bag in the outlaw's hand. I reckon someone had better check the bank."

The train pulled into the station and a bunch of men jumped off, all armed to the teeth.

"What's going on?" Larado asked.

Old Bill limped up. "Special train coming in, Sheriff, bringing the posse and some Rangers back to help. Sorry they didn't get here in time."

"It's okay," Larado said. "I handled it."

"Wow!" little Jimmy said. "Look, the sheriff wears glasses. I want a pair."

A bunch of children gathered around. "We want some of those, too. If a sheriff can wear them, I want a pair."

Larado grinned. "I wear 'em 'cause I don't see so good. It's okay to wear glasses."

Some of the posse went into the bank. They came out again, hurrying down the street, and surrounded Larado.

Paco asked, "Boss, are you hurt?"

"Bullet hit his watch," Lark assured him.

"I think a grateful town will buy him a new one," Paco said.

Lark asked, "What's up at the bank?"

Paco shook his head. "We found the banker. Before he died, he identified Snake Hudson as the man who robbed him over in Oklahoma Territory. I reckon the sheriff gets that $1000 reward the banker had put up."

Larado shook his head. "A lawman can't take no reward."

"Oh yes, he can," another citizen said, "since it was put up by a private citizen."

Lark sighed. It was ironic that the reward money would be going to Larado. Banker Barclay wouldn't have liked that at all. "Well," she said, "now I reckon you've got enough down payment for that ranch you wanted."

He looked up at her as she wiped the dust from his dear face. He stumbled to his feet and slipped the crutch under his arm. "Only if you love me enough to share it with me."

"Oh, you rascal! I came back, didn't I?" And she kissed him with all the ardor borne of the anguish she had felt when she thought he was going to die. "That was the bravest thing I ever saw."

"I'm not a saddle bum anymore," he whispered. "I'm a Texas lawman, and I'll protect my town."

"That's a fact," old Bill said. "This town is mighty beholden to you, Sheriff."

Little Jimmy sighed. "You know, I always wanted a daddy who was a lawman."

Larado looked toward Lark, and she nodded and smiled. "Well, Jimmy, how would you like to have us for parents?"

"You mean that?" His small face lit up with joy.

"Sure do," Larado said. "Now go catch Magnolia and put her back in her pen."

"You can't keep a burro penned up," Jimmy said. "Everybody knows that."

"Land's sake," Lark said, smiling. "Once we get that big ranch, she can roam all she wants, can't she?"

"And we'll get a couple more besides, sweetie." Larado grinned at her.

She thought about the secret she would keep all her life about Magnolia's hat. "You're a damned good sheriff," she said as she went into the embrace of his one good arm. He held her close and kissed her until she was breathless.

He whispered into her ear. "Mrs. Witherspoon, I think we'll have to confess all to the town council, and let the chips fall where they may."

She whispered back. "I reckon they'll forgive you, now that you've proved you're a real lawman and saved this town."

The crowd cheered. "Three cheers for the best and bravest sheriff in all Texas! Hip hip hooray! Hip hip hooray! Hip hip hooray!"

Magnolia joined in the noise, braying loudly enough that dogs started howling all over town.

Jimmy grabbed the donkey. "Come on, you, back to your pen . . . at least for now."

Lark stood on tiptoe to reach Larado's ear and whispered, "I've got to wire my aunt and uncle so I can mend fences there, and then I reckon they'll want to put on a big Texas-sized wedding under my *real* name."

He grinned down at her. "I can hardly wait to meet my new in-laws."

About that time, Bertha Snootley came running out on the general store, waving a paper and snarling, "He's gone! The rotten bastard's run off with the banker's wife!"

"Land's sake." Lark hugged Larado again. "Who said there's no justice?"

"I love you, sweetie. You don't mind me callin' you that now, do you?"

She kissed him again. "I'm beginning to like it just

fine. I love you, best and bravest sheriff, and I'll prove it tonight."

He hugged her one more time, grinning. "Oh, sweetie, I hope you don't mean you're gonna cook supper."

She stood with arms akimbo. "Shut up, you rascal, you'll learn to like my cooking."

"Well, if Snake couldn't kill me, I reckon your cookin' won't. You don't mind bein' married to a lawman?"

"I *love* being married to a lawman." Lark kissed Larado with the promise of being together forever, right here in Rusty Spur—children, donkeys, and all.

Epilogue

Dear Aunt Cimarron and Uncle Trace:

Well, Larado hit another gusher last week. Like your land, the pasture is so full of those stupid derricks, I can hardly enjoy the view anymore, even though we did build a big new house overlooking the valley. Our head maid, Bertha Snootley, says it's as big as a hotel, and complains that she keeps getting lost in it.

Speaking of hotels, maybe you remember meeting Mrs. Bottoms when you were here for a visit? She just opened another one—I think that makes twenty-five hotels she owns. Don't know where the old lady gets the energy.

Paco is still running Sweetie Oil Company for us and bought the ranch next door to our place for his family. Old Bill is pretty frail, but quite rich from his investments in telegraph and telephone company stock. He also bought a gold tooth to replace that missing front one. Oh, I forgot to tell you that when Jimmy graduated from Baylor, Larado bought him a railroad company as a graduation gift. You know, Jimmy always did like trains.

Larry Jr. says he wants to go to Harvard next semester, but his daddy says no son of his is going to attend some prissy back East damned-Yankee college when the University of Texas ought to be good enough for God himself. I reckon young Larry will end up being president of that big Dallas bank we bought last year.

Our twins are still planning to take part in Cousin Lynnie's protest march at the state capitol, even if they all get thrown in jail for trying to get women the vote. Their doting daddy says the governor had better not throw his daughters in the hoosegow or he'll repossess all those cows the governor bought from us. That said, Larado isn't dealing too well with women's liberation. He says if they get the vote, next thing you know, they'll be wanting to join the army or law enforcement, as if that could ever happen.

Anyway, say hello to Ace and Lacey's bunch, and of course Raven and all the rest of the family. Since you came to our house last Christmas, we'll drive over for the big family celebration at your ranch. Yes, I said drive. We bought an automobile. Never thought Larado would give up his buckboard for one of those. Now he wants to talk to Uncle Trace and Uncle Maverick about buying up some automobile dealerships, just in case there's a future for those machines. I reckon they can talk about that over the turkey and pumpkin pie. Or, knowing Texas men, cigars and bourbon.

Much Love,
Lark

P.S. Magnolia's still spry for her age, and we gave her a new red straw hat for Christmas—which, of course, she promptly ate. Her granddaughters and great-granddaughters had more babies this year. Would anyone like a little burro, or maybe two or three?

To My Readers,

Although both Buck Shot and Rusty Spur are imaginary towns, the wild and lawless "whiskey towns" of the Oklahoma Territory were a reality. Even most Oklahomans whose families have been here for generations do not know about this obscure bit of history.

Oklahoma was split into Oklahoma Territory and Indian Territory after the Land Runs. Oklahoma Territory sold liquor, but whiskey sales were illegal in Indian Territory. Not willing to pass up a chance to make illicit money, at least seventeen "whiskey towns," selling liquor to Indians and outlaws, sprang up along the border between the two territories. When Oklahoma became a state, combining the two territories, the whole state went dry and the whiskey towns dried up. Most became ghost towns, victims of that law and the civilization that was turning the uncivilized places into peaceful settlements. I'm a member of the Oklahoma State Historical Society and found this intriguing bit of history in the *Chronicles of Oklahoma*, issue 74:2, (Summer, 1996).

Since I have identical twin grandsons, the subject of twins interests me. Mine are not "mirror" twins, but approximately one-quarter of all identical twins are. We know that mirror twins will always be of the same sex and that much about them will be opposites, as if looking in a mirror. Thus if one is left-handed, the other will be right-handed. If one has a dimple in the left cheek, the other will also have a dimple, but in the right cheek, etc. Scientists are still studying this interesting phenomenon.

For more information, check out the Internet. I found what little I know at twinstuff.com/mirrors.htm.

So what gave me the idea to write about a lawman with poor eyesight? A small item I discovered about the famous Wild Bill Hickok, who, as most of you know, was shot and killed by Jack McCall in a Deadwood saloon while holding the famous "dead man's hand" of aces and eights. Wild Bill was known for his steely gaze, which might have been the result of poor eyesight. At the time of his death, Wild Bill was going blind, possibly because of either venereal disease or trachoma, an eye disease that was quite common then. I found this item in a book called *What They Didn't Teach You about the Wild West* by Mike Wright, published in 2000 by Presidio Press, Novato, CA.

Now I'm going to tell you something you probably don't know about the old western song, "The Streets of Laredo." Actually, it's not Western at all, but has its roots in an ancient Irish song dating back into the 1790s. The original, titled "The Unfortunate Rake," concerns a young British soldier who is dying of venereal disease given to him by his sweetheart. Somehow, the song migrated to the West, had a change in words, and became a favorite of cowboys. My source for this is *Songs of the Great American West* by Irwin Silber and Earl Robinson, published by Macmillan & Co., 1967.

If you are interested in Texas, your public library should have a copy of an entertaining book that I highly recommend: *Lone Star, A History of Texas and the Texans* by T.R. Fehrenbach, publisher Macmillian & Co.

I have spent a lot of time in Texas; two of my three children were born there. If you get a chance to go to the Lone Star State, there are at least two places I feel everyone should visit. One is the Alamo in San Antonio. Remember that this originally was a church and is now the state's most revered shrine. I can guarantee that you will be touched and impressed at this place where outnumbered brave men made their last stand. If you're interested in the famed Texas Rangers, they have a good museum in the city of Waco.

I want to talk about burros. Indeed, when leaving the West, many prospectors did turn the little animals loose to roam and mingle with the wild horse herds. Today, the government has a rescue and adoption agency for both. For more information, here's a phone number: 1-866-4 mustangs, and an Internet address: www.wild horseandburro.blm.gov.

I also have two other Internet Web sites you can visit, one in the United Kingdom, the other in Tehachapi, California. Both are always in need of donations to rescue mistreated and abandoned donkeys. The Peaceful Valley Donkey Rescue in California also places donkeys for adoption if you can meet their strict requirements. By the way, the English group told me many of their donkeys live into their late twenties, but at present, their oldest resident donkey is fifty-six years old. If you would like to help: donkeysanctuary (British). The California group is donkeyrescue.org.

I know some of you are going to write and ask about Lark's twin sister, Lacey. I've already told Lacey's story in *To Tempt a Texan* (February 2005). As most of my regular readers know, all my books connect in one long, long saga called the Panorama of the Old West. I am telling some of the most interesting events of the Old West that occurred roughly between 1850 and 1900. The story you just finished is #25 in the series, and there have been two short stories that also connect. In fact, this latest novella is in an anthology on sale now titled *My Heroes Have Always Been Cowboys* (Kensington, March 2006). It is a funny story based on historical fact about "The Great Cowboy Race."

If you'd like an autographed bookmark that explains how all the stories fit together, send me a stamped, self-addressed envelope at: Georgina Gentry, Box 162,

Edmond, OK, 73083. Foreign readers please send a postal voucher that you can buy at your post office and I can exchange for American postage, as I am not allowed to use foreign stamps. Or check my Web site for the latest news at: www.nettrends.com/georginagentry.

Adios until next time,
Georgina Gentry

For a rollicking good time, don't miss Georgina Gentry's fun and sexy novella in the brand-new anthology, *My Heroes Have Always Been Cowboys* . . .

Those deep-brimmed Stetsons. Those faded jeans. And that's just the beginning. Cowboys are everything a fantasy man should be—tall, tough, and oh-so-handsome. In this wonderful new collection of original stories, meet the wild boys of the even wilder West who know more than a thing or two about roping a girl's heart. . . . Saddle up, ladies.

The Great Cowboy Race
Georgina Gentry

Whispering Moonlight
Teresa Bodwell

The Reluctant Hero
Lorraine Heath

My Heroes Have Always Been Cowboys

On sale now from Kensington Books.

Complete Your Collection Today
Janelle Taylor

Experience the Romance of
Rosanne Bittner

__Shameless	0-8217-4056-3	$6.99US/$7.99CAN
__Unforgettable	0-8217-5830-6	$5.99US/$7.50CAN
__Texas Passions	0-8217-6166-8	$5.99US/$7.50CAN
__River of Love	0-8217-5344-4	$5.99US/$6.99CAN
__Sweet Prairie Passion	0-8217-5818-7	$5.99US/$7.50CAN

Available Wherever Books Are Sold!

Visit our website at **www.kensingtonbooks.com**.

BOOK YOUR PLACE ON OUR WEBSITE AND MAKE THE READING CONNECTION!

We've created a customized website just for our very special readers, where you can get the inside scoop on everything that's going on with Zebra, Pinnacle and Kensington books.

When you come online, you'll have the exciting opportunity to:

- View covers of upcoming books
- Read sample chapters
- Learn about our future publishing schedule (listed by publication month *and author*)
- Find out when your favorite authors will be visiting a city near you
- Search for and order backlist books from our online catalog
- Check out author bios and background information
- Send e-mail to your favorite authors
- Meet the Kensington staff online
- Join us in weekly chats with authors, readers and other guests
- Get writing guidelines
- AND MUCH MORE!

**Visit our website at
http://www.kensingtonbooks.com**